Between Soul and Stone

Between Soul and Stone

MARGO BERDESHEVSKY

THE SHEEP MEADOW PRESS
RHINEBECK, NEW YORK

All inquiries and permission requests should be addressed to:

The Sheep Meadow Press
P.O. Box 1345
Riverdale-on-Hudson, NY 10471

Designed and typeset by The Sheep Meadow Press.
Distributed by The University Press of New England.

Library of Congress Cataloging-in-Publication Data

Berdeshevsky, Margo.
Between soul and stone / Margo Berdeshevsky.
p. cm.
ISBN 978-1-931357-86-9
I. Title.

PS3602.E7514B88 2011
811'.6--dc22

—I have halted my horse by the dove-moaning tree—

—St.-John Perse

Contents

– I –

Between the Wind and Hill

My Long Drum

But I stopped the prayer.

When the stair broke under the weight of wanting You.
Closed the now-I-lay-me-eyes. Fists in them like guns.

While temple candles spit light at You who made it.
Light. (Not a plastic red lamp above an ark.)

Light. While You who made it,   was that
You, crying? Begging for water in the dark, You, God?

In birch trees, You knew me   knelt while I   held me   while
Bone after bone after bone. Bent. Unblinking, listened. Unhearing,
Hear o Lord the Lord our—is one.   Deaf stones in Your ears.

But knew the reach of my paw, its red flesh.
Hear o Lord the Lord our,   I'm starting. I'm standing from fallen
Wish. Branch. Mud of Your making. Standing ash. Standing woman.
Of my making. Starting.   Adding,   please,   Dear.

Between beg and mouth, black praise, going silver. Yours. Or mine.
Between Hear o Lord my—may the words of my mouth, say—Hear,
The words of this mouth. Say leaves turning silk. Say dove.
Your hand, how it strokes my   bended.   How You love.
Closed, now, my now-I-lay-me, and hear: Lord, let me.   A river. Let my
Skin. Let the mud. Let the praise. Let spilled word   un-know. The knife
—Withdraw. Let me be woman. Let each eye un-shroud. Let God   be holy
In my mouth. One morning.

My long drum,
My long drum,
My long drum,

where You have
halted Your horse.

Once

Once upon a time at the window, a cat's head, her teeth dripping a tiny finch's blood.
Once upon a time at the window, my father's hand blessing me, over and over and

over. Once upon, we wakened to every beak's trill, improvised our thanks for
dawn, the white iris, horizon's sentinel, (witch, opening the hill,) its skins.

Once upon as one, my friend and I, our open palms each on each side of a train
window, our heartbreaks parting, wheels hurling us to move us into two until
tracks polished sparks and our women-of-the-world sobs.

Once in an oak, an onyx song, a crow's vowels like my French and German grand-
mother's, whose hair reached her knees and I brushed it—Amelia—her name in her
own mouth keening like a battered war blossom.

Once the window held me still as slate in fog banks—and in Bluebeard's bedroom when
he wasn't there—a lover might visit—might kiss me in the other man's bed, might pick
figs with me when spiral galaxies fell down chalcedonic skies in the west

—the lover didn't visit. Stubborn hills. Wildflower yellows for company, lambs
crying for more life, their skins *x'd* with marks for early kills. Their sudden quiet.

In the old man's bed, I too could stop crying. Enough peace to die in, once, to go
on. Once upon a time, I was beloved. Once upon a time, the cat stopped before
her teeth stopped the minute finch's breath.

Once upon a time, naked, no curtain, no grave, the lover I deserved
filled my windows.
No winding-sheet-perfume of *fleurs de lis*—all that night.

An Empty Place

On the island that gathered
bones for stars, *Eat stones*

sang its gone queen, in her grief's prison,
and she meant how land fills

an empty place, a belly.
I have home in a raptor's nest, rooftops'

pewter air, window-nets of woven spiders,
they want to be poems. This is home,

I have been learning its walls all my life.
In the coming autumn flame I'll step

out of the sky,   will   mount a roan animal
who'll tell me my name, tear it to pieces, running.

The nest will fall to cement, but I'll find it—
Who will mother a bird when she loses her balance

in the nest? None, I'm told. I'll carry it aloft—
Neither of us can hold an address, not bird

or I,   I had an island home and gave it away like
Dinesen's Africa, I have a home in window-lace woven

of country centipedes, they want to be words,
or devil-birds. Cormorant or crow

can open wide, un-flying, un-perching in trees,
more like strong bones bleaching in sun-spermed

mornings, then resting where there are stars.
The birds are waiting for gods,   are they?

The gods are waiting for them to die,   are they?
For days I haven't thought of war. I've watched sheep

who will be slaughtered for rosemary sauces, watched
them transfixed, until I'm finally tired of watching sheep.

I stop at every pasture, try to know their language
: a clarinet piping of infants, the bassoon-bellow-bleats

their blue-eyed mothers make. None know their future.
I watch. I watch kindergarten-lambs chase each others'

fleece across gold,   oak-forests near as my breath,
all hissing owl secrets   about to be exposed.

If it's the Last Full Moon,

—it loves sand, and lingerie, both. The silence of vines. A drying lizard. The forest's thrum, decaying—its budding stones sprout ferns from their vaginas. They nestle under pillow-mosses loomed by crones to clothe their sleep. While I wear the blue silk and tinted lace under my walking gear, drizzle's seed on my tongue. Oak-stands are stern ancestral guardians—hold me like see-through hands. Are you lonely, other women want to ask. Age, like this—I'd say no—is kind enough to endure. If it's the last full moon, I'll hold it. A land of stones old as dead minstrels' vibrato, and not moving. Wet grass, where the new moon is un-doing. Crossed rocks for cattle pens, un-walling. Falling. Deserted chimneys, un-building. Crows come to blacken all boulders. How they wait to be touched, like my breasts. Swifts are eating the sky, and barefoot in damp sprouts where weeds go yellow—I stand quieter and quieter. The sheep are near the moon. Home is far from here and darker. Home, and land, and nation, and human, and hill, and rain, and holy—so many words I keep trying. If it's the last, how long can I stand, while the walnuts harden? Once upon a time.

On Giving Away the Stone

In new rocks new insects are sitting
With the lights off —*from "Whenever I Go There"* —*W. S. Merwin*

i
I had a stone. The book of common armor slams, it is no
speaker-stone, it is no protector, *shhhh, ptuiii,*
I gave away my open mouth to my elder

so he'd love it for me—love me for it—here,
godfather, put him in your garden. Older one, see how he is stone and
living? See how his natural beak is wide for saying? Let him

whisper new speeches as your fierce hands age—here is what the ibis
sounds like wading in white morning, her down-curved beak
shut. Here is my suitcase full of old Eden, its contents of spilled milk.

I wanted to give him one gift. Solemnly, I'd wrapped it
in a moist leaf so it would never be thirsty, and
gladly, I gave the stone.

ii
When I lifted the barn owl's wing, the distant stone's
gift, it stroked the faith I'd lost. Small rain massing
between grasses. The lamb's miniature knees were

buckling, her effort to stand as her species.
When I lifted the silken thing of brown feathers,
fingering it, smelling the blood-body of it—

I stroked my own face with it.
Breeze that had been bath-warm all summer chilled the *maronnier*
catching flame, and the old man whose house I was sleeping

in,   goldilocks, godchild-woman,   would return next
week and I wouldn't be there, would he die there   or on our

island   when the minute came   don't die, don't die. His owl
—or mine: shifted feet on its twig.

Twice the Darkness

Call her Mazie. She's the child in me, my nipples hot with mid-life,
night-lit. The dark of a pulsar shimmers like a baby turning. Dawn's dim
forest I left, all slopes, seas. No more twice-broken as though a soul

were a breadfruit, a plum, so full, so ripe, so ready to be injured by falling. Say
I find faith. No. Say a volcano's silver sword stabs my sleep. Say no. Say guardian
of a crater, its charred descent, its white split-tailed birds, diving.   Say

goddess of ash. Say ash of kiss. Say ebbing courage, even when prayer
and what is that?   has a star's clack of visible radiation.
So many other days can flay an eye. Please   say I'm a good girl.

Say a spider's sticky gray threads are all strings inside my skin and that child
I am wants to say thank you to someone,   still.   Infested heart   go away,
go home.   Fall.   Get out of my heart.

A golden ring on my left thumb, worn—I lie with the only lover left: sky.
Dry-land beast, double humped, led by its tiny rope across the sudden black
ecliptic,   and a golden ring on my left thumb, now,   I've married my self,

now. Dressed me like a weighty queen in my skimpy-dress. Cleaned
inside my bones with steel brushes. Hid from dogs in the bed
while my own eclipse is a solarized star, crossed out by moon, dropped

down between a camel's sway and burden.   There,
my hermit's candle, and nipples flamed.
Like all surfaces, I can fracture.

No rainforest ferns outside the kitchen step, uncoiling like a baby's sex.
No pulsar, heard now. No ricocheting in church between pillars and space
and space. No neutron-fast-percussions, imitating guardians of time.

No.   Summer's first clean white nights—twice the darkness, heard.
Once for an hour, I helped a father buy a tiny carousel for his faraway girl.
It hummed *La Vie en Rose, La Vie en Rose,* I hope she thanked, I hope she

loved. (I never heard her name.) The only child I name is Mazie, child in
me, who roasts her small snail meal on a charred long stick—she's a girl carved
on an iron fire screen. Mazie. My star. The child I am wants to say: thank you,

to someone, someone, please,
say I am a good child.

A Step She Knew

Poetry: language of the soul. My nemesis. My grace.
Racing horse. Cave of blankets. Cave of scorpions.
Cave of milk. More than I deserve. Less than wind
between breasts. Pebbles. Stones. A little more than
grief.   Ecstasy's infant.   Good for me.   Secret.

Egotistical. Dawn's ghost, under nakedness. Slow
stations of an unspoken cross. A religion, if I let it. A kiss
on my forehead (as I sleep.) A thing with fingers asking
the next question.   Asking if it is love.   Susceptible
to cross-genre.   Susceptible to morning.

Did the Tools Make Noise When he Carved the Heart?

The pigeon has found a crippled
moon who will not stand again for days. Has
found water's silence,
and the winter wren trusts me.

A seed pearl rain. Slopes greener this year than
seasons when in axe-hard quiet, they were barren.
The hill-women say so. Draped,
a first wing, a second, close-mouthed.

The silence of sun insists through mists stacked like slaughtered ewes.
A heroine's refuge.   I am no heroine.
A lost tawny owl.   Its shoulder feather, dropped.
Silence, my great friend derelict, you don't howl.

I've howled. I am no heroine.
On the edge of things dark, acacia's thick honey,
no-sound-sweet, where the wren lands.

Outside—on his granite seat—a single heart is carved
into its spine, who carved it, did the tools make noise?

Like a Garden

What word could be mouthed in the fog?
Woven-white and almost not there so fixedly
it's always there. Quiet as thanks down on her knees.

What word is mist and shape-changer. Oak.
Such a slow dancer, it aches to be held.

What word is well—she is well,
single in a couple's house of pale
doors, one upper double
window full of the tall walnut's ripening.
Ripening.

What word finds her soul–shout again,
grazing on warm figs, road-vine blackberries
bruising her tongue. Un-owned, a land of

lime, of olive and nephrite and onyx—of brass, midnight-
shadow-green, sun-spent,   citron, lichen, spider-sac, mould,
and bamboo-shoot glass-green—and ours.

Ours. What word can love itself
after re-birthing all the earth as kind—
—trying out every chair, every bed,
while opening pages at every table
slowly, barefoot in a wide room?

Glass, lifting the mourner's cloth that covered it.
Her ritual days have lasted years. There, a stippled
mirror shadowed into cloud, mouthed into fog
mute as a garden—and there, its small blue door to forests.

Of Men's Kitchens

Echo and echo of the sheep's sloe eye
blue like a fragility of bat flights torn out of barns,
gray lace, at last possible light.

I had begged his gardener not to mow,
don't shatter the spells. Begged the candle
on my neighbor's kitchen round wood to pray.

His framed quilt on the left says over and over
Remember me, a sampler, red stitches faded still
say *The fear of the Lord is the beginning of our*

love and *Teach me o Lord the way of Thy statutes* and
I shall keep it unto the end. His modern clock above it
ticks at the new sky, no wrens sing yet, it's dawn.

His valley, dreamt in mists—white mists into white
there, there a first, a second start, there digits of branches
pointing bones at their sky where once the old man

once a black haired boy watercolor-sketched
himself cape-flying past a cloud to reach the castle towers,
clouds as above, below.

That miniature on his French farmhouse wall is dated
long before he wrote of white hair and vixens and witch fires.

I remember after Prague's Vaclav Havel had served his
last hours, he said he'd always wanted to be the boy storming
a castle to save his people, now he knew he couldn't save,

who saves?   He was glad at last to leave the tower that had been home of his government, its velvet revolutionary gloves. He wanted to return to a kitchen, to his writing, to stir white mists of words to warm milk.

Blooding the Body in the Southwest

Night-beaks match cicada solos. All night: night before its silver heat, its final moon in full
eclipse—will there be others, or any more summers as we knew them, or any more

weathers our bodies sleep well in? Soundless, careens of lightening lurch long ahead of dawn,
a hundred fire-birds repeating, there.

Your rocker drawn at the open upper latch—there, blazed wings widen where fallen larks
live and live no more; there, a wheel, no chariot, there, silent as black roses in their private

darkness, nut-branches invent the arabesque. A Gabriel, an Uriel—thin as lifelines in a hand.
A plum, heavy with midnight juice, no interruption but an apple's fall. The black lamb has

just invented being born. Learn "mothering"—a woman told me—her chair opposite my tin
winter shawl. No nests I could think of, then, no winter swallows. Learn to mother

the self, then. But I knew no lullaby. Mothering my own soul is what I'm doing in the old
man's valley. Bells of Saint Jean-Baptiste toll the mizzle. Downhill, a dun Giselle sweeps petals.

A loft of nested bones, to cradle in, while new lambs are learning night; while I hold my
breath, who had no son or daughter, who gave my breast, once, to my girlfriend's freckled son

—kissed my drunken mother in the dawn before she died. Older than she was then, now
—blooding the body of time, I have time.

Alone in the Old One's House

A hay round bulging in the *compline*-
light, swallow-cries' medieval memory—
your pale blue doors and shutters unlatch
my hand,   all children push at all secret
gardens, touching everything: a cream rose
open as a woman's thighs, after. A salamander,
changing colors. A plain wooden headboard
passion must have strained at, love must
have polished—hand after hand
I'm touching everything you've made here,
careful not to leave jam-prints, only joy
bulging naked-soled, following the bee
to her fig, the smell of wet pebbles
to their mossed cistern. Verdigris
in the shade, jade velvets in sunset's
death—below, valleyed in seven
greens, I'm counting—a hamlet's umber
roofs any piper could lead children up
to, any troubadour—lute for, a raven
woman waiting at her needles—what
other plain wood headboard waiting for thrusts,
and the polish of marriage no church needs to
sanctify? In Upper *Quercy* hills, late
air is an angel's windstorm, a coming rain
sanctifies the too many plums, the apples
bursting—hay, packed like a fat woman
impregnated with the country.
Autumn lambs are birthing in dark purple blood,
a season for a middle-aged woman falling in love
with ghosts on the landscape,   troubadours luting
her greened prayer into its starved mouth.

– 2 –

A Land Where—

Her Detail—Paris Cherry Trees

The distant woman remembers—Paris but not what trees were blooming
then, when she hung under their fallen nail parings in a June, or what blooms

in April, do cherry trees bloom in April, yes, I'll tell her, but these times do we
know what is about to open, the hand, the cannon, the heart, I send her mad

Van Gogh's *marronniers* instead, did he even then mistake their fists for stars—
I'll hope this is for a page, I'll tell her, not for a science experiment on deaths

of birds who have forgotten when to sing, is it in winter or in autumn when
Tuileries garden grandmother crows counsel how easy it is to lose a voice

that bloomed in hope—   Someday you'll visit Jerusalem, a visiting woman
speaks to me over buttered salmon, I've been visiting churches, she says—their

martyr-song no different than our wailing wall, I see it—   she is touching
the knife, now— all one, all one— nodding over the pink dead fish we feed on.

If I can give you one question from Paris, dear visitor, dear distant woman
unsure what tree, dear self, and I hope it is not for science of failing

blossoms or the death of gods, with and without my dying faith, could it be
this, what faith does a soul need, to flower? any? winter or in spring, in

bright or in black, even when it loses its skin, a healthy snake has
a heart that is in danger of peace—shedding, let us make

peace this season, even if it kills us there is nothing more to die for.
We bow to one another at the corner of a boulevard I once walked with my mother,

her twentieth century sobs turned to gin, l'Hotel Lutetia housed German generals
when cherry blossoms bloomed, even then—every

year, every year, all falling, all flesh, all unsure of what day it is
hope—loses and wins the dawn, its white petal . . .

Not a Land Where Oranges

I don't have a land where oranges open their mouths to nightfall.
I don't have a man in my teeth when the light is over.
My hot voice wakens me. A trumpet. A cupboard of laundered sheets.
I waken God: I want to belong to a pinion. A hill. A skin. He
should know why.

Hands like featherless sparrows that haven't woken to April,
April has come with all its sun again and dogwood,
its bouquets of pale flesh, sun and white tulips, sun and sleep
rising.

Lovers that don't belong to me. Windows that let in claxons.
I wear a dark color. Spring doesn't belong to me, I don't know why.

How can anyone die today, it's spring. Spring. A thousand have.
The flowering of guns. The shorn branch of fruit trees.
One old friend. Many words are better than mine: swans
on the flooding Marne—opening their breasts to one another.
Pinion me like a small gear-wheel, God.

Scene Two

In another garden, a poet's brother had called the lark a fist
of blood and feathers; she couldn't tell me that.
A shaman, failed, o my poor brother, she whispered for me to hear.

Low light had sprawled on feathers at the base of some soldier's bronze,
abandoned, chewed wing, had fallen on some newly planted blood-
brights and one ivory chip the gardener added to the bed, its Easter tulip.

On the heath, scene two : drop by drop-cloth, no magicians, no Lears
no fools, no daughters, more morning light and landscape hangings' murmur
after dark—Gainsboroughs' costumed static. Or grief.

I borrowed a second poet. He led me to his favorite Lady Briscoe
for her silver high-coiffed tragic—her beauty's tag, a powdered chalk
that painted her naked throat. She's a stopped animal. Satin-fold-sky. Bone.

She's pale in the fashion that would kill her three weeks after that
portrait's last stroke, it was the lead, buried in her chalk. Borrowed
hand, my poet leads with whispers for the sun—and April comes.

Blooming *magnolia stellata,* or *lacei* speaks for warmed stars, first
snow's falling lace of perfumes, like coconut milk from islands I'm
missing. I'd make love with these branches hung for a ripening woman to bury
in, laugh in, twirl in. In front of my eager God and everyone, my lips hurt every flower.

Here, a man made the night bird's happiness immortal, and lyric raised its children.
Here, London. Here, heath and magnolia : an ancient genus
evolved before bees appeared, loved by starving beetles, all crawling for its center.

I'm a woman of a certain age, deciding she'll live. April at the poet's razor.
This middle. This vast. *"What thou among the leaves hast never known..."*

Empty, a Sky Opens

—incomparable, white and round. A halo of such a size, for such a gathering of quiet screams. It holds the white moon to love us. Shimmering, to love us—wet and vertical and human and not touching, washing all we must not carry to the morning.

Stars scream, *Come closer.*

This unbreakable umbilicus.

Stars scream, *Come closer.*

A one-eyed net   watches us,   so tenderly.

Naked, a night-ocean waits. Naked, we drink her broth.

Touch forgiveness, like a fish.

Violet Dialogue, After All it is

A man beside his hill,
bird blessings from him
under her folded wing.

She returns them to his
mouth—breath to mouth.
Her word unsure what color.

She's so found and so lost, at the same pure water.
All it is.

—My hand is an oar to plow our brazen light,
—My last dark flight again, here is my gift. A man, and his hill. Or water.

Violet
deep as dusk's exhale,

Violet, he says
passionate, he says

Dawn's sheet, too hot for sleep

So often how she holds
a word, all that it is,

How she mouths shadow,

That shade, that
bloom in its bruise and beauty.

Its dress
that always needs to be

Unbuttoned.

Deep as dusk's exhale,

Prayer, a pocket gathering
rain, its bruise, and beauty.

Dawn, too hot for
sleep, or darlings.

Unfastened as two wings,
one of instinct, one of dark blue.

Air. Violet, he says
passionate, he says

So often,
how she holds a word

All it is, for the color.
Violet. Violence. Bruise. Or, beauty.

Pale—she waters her burgeoning
hydrangea, instead.

Hydra-headed. An unfinished garden.
Isn't it a star half written

but in skies across two oceans here we

You and I were born on two sides

suns, my 29 plus 29 minute turns of a hand
after high noon.

an oar to plow our brazen light.

Its dress
that always needs to be

Unbuttoned.

Prayer, a pocket gathering
rain. All it is.

Unfastened as two wings,
One of instinct, one of flight.

how we dropped tears
to water seeds not ever planted there,

plant, and here we plant
night, as if it were made of threads.

of day, your moments after midnight

My hand is a line drawn point to point,
spare with flight.

So found and so lost
at the same pure water.

Sans Eyes,

There are 6,000 species of the true butterfly.
Under-wings of some: dead leaves.

Colors of a compassionate deity, on top,
for the sun.

I've thrown my mourning cloak to ground.
Nude. Aged.

Soul bows made in a darkened-from-the-heat
room. Silken.

Cocoon. *Love/beloved,* you say, I say
man-wings on my shoulder, landing,

were you stream who dreamed me
where the rainforest last listened to my

cry? The claret cyclamen opens night
here, its blare against vines trying to climb

summer, the city of light.   You—
remembering whales, the stir of stones, time

undressed.
Eyeless, I say: *believe.*

Brothers / Thirst

Send a strengthen-her-faith prayer my way on a red
wind—friend, who knows my empty tins,
my hard heartbeat.
The emerald crowned mallard comes to our shore not
because we ask it but because it does, and dusk shuts it
in. The pre-frost noons fill with woodbine, black pearl,
last circles of yellows hung like tracing-paper thins
in all space where shade was, sun was,
they were see-through, they shone like yearning,
yearning   must be love.

Remind me. Remember for me.

Thirsty, I am touched by the bending nearer me
hem,   down from the lowering October star.

Once, mourners, we saw our younger brother—
how he asked for a holy space to cast his mother's ashes
into the wind, and how we found him a cliff, found
him a cantor, and a woven basket,
watched his hand dip in and dip in it, hungry,
watched him raise his handfuls of her he'd
loved, raise her name he wanted to remind with a cantor's caw,
her son was writing her dust across the long cloud, saying soul,
quietly. Her stick-to-his-fingers ash
he spelled across a mottled parting cumulus.
Her child of hunger. Her child who spun and spun
and twirled, for applause. Her small-boned man,
now, jagged-dancing down to a bending, nearing sea.
That was love, wasn't it?
How touch comes near not

because we ask but because it does,
but only the hem, and of what garment?
(In secret, o my brother, o I twirl,
I twirl too—to be held.)

Needle-rains of color came that afternoon,
touch, shapes, the olive's skeletal twig held over our heads
in a dun pigeon's beak, speaking how a day keeps
coming to broken shore, nearing—
remind me, is that love,
—or its question?

Blackouts

Out of a sense of purity: blackout.
No other voice of any other
(God.)

No other voice
comes to her tiny garden.

No rain
but stinging nettles,

and no other soul but hers, parched.

On the footpath, a blue cypress, unhurt.
Tall as a July sun, reaching.

Its own opal halo flung wide on the landscape.

Wild and bruised.

Blackout.

~

Bruises on the damp nature.
Far from the sound of the lure.

What was it she promised when she was an imaginative child
whispering hard at her own low window, mouth to that low

opening—was it to love? to be better than any sword?
curled at her air-slit in between the house-stones

no higher than her two hands—window no larger than
her face, burning?

There— her sky— there— her sky— its feral, cobalt voice,
and sun that tasted of young honey.

A girl called Joan who would ask a thousand times—
"To shut me out from the light of the sky?"

Who thought a nation
could be ordained.

Cypress. Crepuscule. Lamb. Blackout.

No other voice, a thousand times.
Like bees.

(for Joan of Lorraine, her sky.)

Bad Child

Dawn in the valley cradle is a color of broken pearls, is a roiling milk
lake, is a blinding curve sky—cypress heads or castle turrets, sudden
owls' flat hammer heads like nails. Mists of rust. Mists of gold.
I'm a good child. This, from the upper window, waking. *I'm a good
child.*

This below: the orchid showing her tongue, her clitoris.
Some are used dead angels, burned, withered in among the healthy.
While banks of royal vesture purples fold : old woman church-lace
lavenders. Spotted-orchid, there, a hungry winged thing one could feed
souls to. *Feed it.*

Don't pick it. *I won't pick it.* Leave the shed snakeskin self with dry
blooms, let it disappear in sun, when it comes.
There's no sun, not now, next season, when I'm older.
Then, let the ants come drag it to their unlit homes.

When I'm older. *I'm older.* Let me be older. Let me move in
black forest mud and murmur with what grows, all that grows,
court solitude like a long night's body, its blue bones,
stroke its head,   darling,   next to mine.

Dear, listen to the three different voices of wings,
can you name them? Step out to the chill grass,
its bite,   whose song is it, whose child, whose cry?

I climbed the mist barefoot, losing my skin.
Prayed for the singers,   worms,   ants,
screech owls,   my own heart,   and the victims of a distant
quake—their lost tongues, their dried cry,
their bellies churned to knotted stones. It was there,   it wasn't
here, it didn't kill this valley,   it was there,   it wasn't here.
It's in the heart of God,   pray for God's heart,   let Him stop
being so enraged, solitary, breaking His own toys.

– 3 –

Love's Famine in Me

Cassandra on Moving Day

The cartons' rough tongues loll for my contents, say
throw it away, I say precious packed blankets, keep me
warm, they say where is your dead mother? I want her
now, don't you have a color photograph?

She comes to me in summer dream in the covering-me
palm-strokes of the most beautiful woman in New York
who knew her, who knows no body, now, who died last week,
who changed her hips so she could be a ballerina,

still—it didn't work. She adds a cotton wrap to my midnight
chill and covers me, Cassandra, I murmur, you're not mama, no,
she won't be coming, she messenger-mutters—she vanished last
night, the heavens don't know where, I'm not so

beautiful any more, I'm a dead actress, and you are her girl. Get
packing, your paper animals are hungry, your beauty will splinter
like mine, but not yet, darling—you have skeletal
stars to polish, still.

Of the Owl: Stripped Of

Of the owl: stripped of its feathers, the naked
bird would weigh less than
its feathers, owls are all wings, are all feathers,
weigh nearly nothing,

this is an owl feather,

already important to her. She has it wrapped in
a bit of cloth in her purse. She believes in bird
magic, watching her,   her tired coal-rimmed
eyes, black suns leveled in them, watch back.

In this, there may be no

bodies but the land. How the mountain spills his
seed to a sea. How a blue heron
perches at its wet circumference of dawn.
How a field only wants to be
bedded, the demon owl to circle it
and circle it because dusk is
its dinner hour, moonlight its house.

In this, we are not

skin and we have no story. If we devour
one another, it is as the elements
feed on us, outlast us. In this, there is
fire and water, air and earth, and no fear.
Is love necessary, in this?

At the horizon

where mushroom and orange fungus and
bark and moist and twitter
hush, and are one—on the river, dragonflies,
born. One garden that was never planted.
Cells that were never used or captured. Cells,
metastasizing like music when music has
never been. How the mountain lifts, and
spills his seed. How the sea is the sea
and a cannibal feeds upon herself,
before growing old.

Body – 1

(after George Herbert)

Body, the lover's table, seraph's ledge,
        Love's famine in me—scraping the heart's womb.
        Its breath in skin—my woman's sacrilege.
Pendulum casting lines for birth, or fulcrum,

Machine of promises, hunger's hard tooth,
        Quiet sky's volt, ascetic's undone vow,
        A calendar torn at our time's thin root,
Invented cadence endured, endowed

With desire. What's blessed or what's cursed, illusion.
        Love, exalted. Peace, in danger.
        Or snake or angel in the selfsame cage.
The rib un-woman made. Tongues stained. Bloods fused.

        Rivers beyond night rising have bent to our
        Ripened mantra: make us one, once, this only holy hour.

The Wound That Comes Closest to the Sun

The eye. The breath. The whisper of both.

Leaning like a woman in a high belted April green kimono, a tall walnut tree
had bent at the second storey window of the old writer's house. He'd loved

it since he planted the palm-of-his-hand-sized sapling into soft summer dirt—
beside three irregular walls and a chaotic stone-pile on a quarter acre

he'd spent his dead father's unimportant bequest to buy. He was only twenty
then, author of insignificance he imagined a house made from what was

before him. What had been a house was older than anyone he knew, he restored
it one word at a time. Lover of rocks, stone after stone, he spoke to them, urged

them into place, hired men with rougher hands to help him, then sent them away
—so he could be alone.

By the day he was eighty-five, his tree had thickened wider than an embrace,
leaned into a high perch where he spent afternoons in a bentwood chair facing

west, and wrote miniatures that were occasionally admired. He wrote one
on a hushed red November afternoon,

a love note to the tree as though it could be the woman he had never sought
or found.

When he was ninety-six he took a stone axe and cut it down, it had broken
his windows in last night's winter storm, thrashing furiously against them,

had pelted his roof with its yield of hard shells, like bullets. But the storm was
to blame. No, the tree. The tree or the house, he'd held his axe all morning

before weeping—voice of a strangling boy—chilling, barefoot in an ongoing
rain, one howl, and then he executed his tree.

He'd written one good page in his life. Killed a tree. Never married. Never
stroked a child. He went to his knees and kissed the felled trunk, stroked its bark

with smooth hands of an aged man who had not labored. Entered his house
that he'd lived in since he was just past twenty, waited for it to thank him.

It didn't. There was no sound. He closed its windows and shutters and doors,
silenced in the rest of his days. He arranged his papers.

He'd written one—that he could admire. A love note to the tree he'd killed.
He burned it in the last fire he built with the last of his wood.

It was the coldest night he remembered, ever. And the house turned very warm.
A quilt of indigo smoke wrapped the old man who had become forgetful, forgotten

to open the chimney, stared fixedly into flames he'd made to warm his house, his
house, to thank his house, his house, and his murdered tree for keeping him warm.

America Poem

i

This middle. This vast. This trim of the last
first snow in ditches. This hard-lined
space for fattened sows and lone-tribed

starlings seeding the sky, chanting falcons
sure of this one thing: below is the traveler.
But they have a home, and a mystery.

Leaves beyond cut corn crumble the only
willow, the only hawk beyond desolate pink. Your sky
is a soft drum-beater, calling if I have a home, a history.

I remove the tarantula's furred sound. Balance its thrum
with the quiet layers of a second snow as it hardens.
On one side they lie, shades, winter-shadow tombs

and a train going somewhere every hour. All
day it snows. All night: the season's
eyes. Every hour the Rock Island Line quakes walls,

hoots its music—a train is always
going from where it wheels, I hear its warning.
I seek the sleek still of I-beam tracks bearing

Lacawanna's tundra crossing seamless white and sisterhood.
I need to have a thousand feet to pace a thousand shores,
a thousand eyes to feed on each fat sparrow—may I?

ii

Isolate, undulated plain. Am—sun's round burn
settling her night-haunch behind the tilted barn,
am tilled dirt, am ready, am cold.

Night thumb rolls—in his corner of my sky.
Whose quilt am I
mending? Whose hand may I
loosely finger under a sheet, come midnight?

The porch-man? Stout
overalls all soiled with all day dying a little?
Slow, in place, some wife inside cooking soup?

I am Blavatsky, surrounded. Am an Arab son
high on his camel's moonlit mount, bearing.
Am an indulgent lover wiping sex-sweat

with her pillow sham, cream white hip
swept with light.   I am.   I require.   Single silo.

Single sun, descending   You
may clean old wars.   I am in the no
where, where the crows who scan for
footprints in a calm, have no boundary.

Almost winter. Almost naked. Almost
ragged lingerie hung dry and brown from branches.
Pilgrims, calling it home.

iii

Your Iowa farm is faced with sky, corn, space,
oak, pig, snow,   —soon, arid,
Your space is daubed with gnarled arms, dry-willow
tears, long-johns on a line at the end of colors, clinging
to brittle, and all the gleaming, all
the porches where what goes on? Sperm?

iv

My sister wants to pray a circle, death to a man
who devoured the digits of her heart, her children.
Not sex, nor a new son in her womb assuaged that
bad man's hunger. Death to a devil, she hopes; hangs
a thought not done, a tea brewed, never sweetened.
Not a monster, I, but her sister.

I, with the pale hair, I with the wide hips,
I who have—not a hundred hands, not a single
eye, am no daughter of Titans, no monster I,
but her sister. Known to beggars, falcons.

Her baby slathers crackers with his cream;
throws fits like a millionaire
enraged his shoes have not been shined.
While the street-man, voice crimped as used
gum chants: *Yes!*
Jesus love never found me, yes! Jesus love
never found me, yes! Jesus love never
found me, yet this I know, He loves me so.
And he's no seed of Titan either, but my brother.

I need a thousand eyes to pace. To feed on each
still 'scape.   Old geezer on his farm porch
—bandaged toe in one blue slipper—
I think I hear America screaming.
This bandaged land. This middle. This vast.

– 4 –

Light Unrepentant

… almost the quality of disappearance/ In its cage of visibility. —*Hayden Carruth*

When Are You Not

When are you not a poet and just a woman
the lover asks, manna on his false tongue,
jackhammer to a swollen earth of your breasts.
Never, you want to scream, never
not a linguist of the soul daring word
to prayer, and rage, and please, peace. *Never*
not a maker of the small, to serve.
(But not your kind of a mother.)
Never not a chisel to the morning leaf
or the sorrow of the storm. Never not
a gatherer of cries in these hands
that have lost thumbs, but have prayers.
When are you a normal person gathering overripe
fruit for juice, not for the mystery of the tree?
Never not watching the larvae, the hungry
white fly, its kiss. Never the thigh not jiggling
at tedium—so eager to leap stones at a stream—
imagine the gazelle.
Never when the sperm is pulsed at the womb, no music,
no colored cry, no muted sax playing an Almighty's baritone.
Ask the lover, when was Christ not a carpenter? When
He hung on wood to die? Or building chairs for thieves,
to His future right, and to His future left? Ask the lover
when are you not a man, and just a woman, love, there
in line at the new Eagle Brand Hardware store, waiting
for its morning doors to open, so you two may buy nails,
a ladder, gladioli   newly born.

Lilith as a Babe

A gashed boat, on a fierce rock ice-slope.
The night-birds, strangled. The light, unrepentant.

I'm not sorry.   I'm not sorry.   I'm not sorry.

~

Night's hand hot mad-gladdens your
sleeping. For a good time call Lily.

Scavenge-sweeting. Insect   —her. Howling.
Tongue-fiddler.   Teaser.   Dearest.

~

You lookin' good fo' yo' age,
the street women approve of me.

Naked as a shaman's cape. Hungry.
Being   a babe.   I'm not sorry. I'm not sorry.

For all old love.   For all old men.
You were my howling-space.   Wing and freefall.

What prayer was of use,
making me of skin?

For a Festival of Women

(After Louise Bourgeois' "Seven in a Bed")

Louise has seven in a bed.   Her lonely pink litter of pups.
Dear women: I'm so unsure of a body,   as a life.

My four—
Are unknowns in my own   bed, in the dawn-dream,

Are in a man's skin, in a woman's skin,   flesh, are
Trance-dim are hemmed in the sheets' flat heat, faceless

Flesh. Are my wants, are my skins, are two and two, are
Me, are all me,   in the—

—That third body-boy is   too—
Young for me, is   just a baby tow-head boy   is

Me in my middle years midriff softened by kisses, cream,
He, a body I could want, see.   —Is he looking at aging, at mine?

While my red vines climb. While they wiggle like
Hearts in flames. Humming.   Bodies and bodies. Mine.

Well, we are four. We are thousands. Of flesh.
Louise's are two headed and kissing. Are sculpted and seven in a bed,

Are cotton stitched limbs, twisted pink. One
Is singing soprano—*Put your head on my shoulder.* Thousands,

I can hear it,   their lives looped into lives like the vines. Louise's
Are the color of a dying old lady bathtub pink I ripped out for a better

Boudoir, late in summer. Seven, for Louise. Lives.
Mine—all ready for an orgy that hasn't begun. Hers

Have exorcist-neck-twists, hers are joined in being joined, hers are
Stitch and stuffing. Are more human than mine. Entwining.

Flesh, they pretend. Flesh is lonely, I say. Not so pretty,
I say. You know, I say, Dear women, I'm so un-

Sure of a body, as a life. Are you? Her clinging pink litter of pups.
Her coition. Her softened by crying, her by woman-stitches. Her by

Flesh stretched, by neck twist—entering. In my
Dream of an un-begun orgy—we're ready.

We're waiting soil, and fallow. We are not moving.
My four in a bed. And she has seven.

My not-mine tow-head boy—eyes my pale—shakes his
No, Not touching it, says No, not your softened

—I can hear it. Humming-humbled, am
Too old.   Soft, am too

Not. In Louise's bed they're wrapped around and blind as worms.
Crying, maybe. A family, maybe, A full litter of

Pups in dying old lady pink embrace. Are loved.
Are disturbingly loved, and living like that. Joined.

In my house—it's yes autumn nearly, the ivy's fire-draping, now,
Virginia-creeper flaming, now, mounting walls like bats,
All passion-color brights, and—

I know so many women, aging, waiting, we—
All unsure of a body. Now, and later.

Oh my dear festival of women.
Gazelle again and young again. Yes. Tossing my yes, mirrored,
Yes,

About to be wooed and
Climbed yes, naked newly

Yes, or dead newly—to live newly,
Metal-spider-slowly.

How the fallow field is patient. One in a bed. Dear
Woman. I'm so unsure of a body as my life. Entwined. I.

Wind

The woman goes to parties, parties are important to her, events
in situ for worthy conversations, cells
of life, in her body, in her left breast, something is growing, her
new lover has noticed it, she's postponed
a probe, a day, a week, a month. *Life,* she says often. *Life.* A favorite
catchall word for her delicate antennae's thrill
to irony, to grace, to passion, to misery, subjects all too rich for
dinner's sauce, still her plate is full,
and she eats, like a hungry sparrow, sips *champagne*, her other
favorite word, sees breeze through every glass, and toasts *to life.*

How like a Grecian warrior boy with battle scars nipple to navel—
standing in a window of any season, any
bravery—that other woman with no breasts, now, but slice marks
healing on her field of stitched skin
cut, now, her second one severed—she stares down fate. They're
poets—eye to eye. Cut the marble to free its
interred wings—the sculptor Michelangelo knew, still not knowing
what winds can do to beautiful women.

I saw an angel in the stone and carved to set it free.

Again, the Cradle

i.

Again, the cradle. The bough breaks, the cradle,
quiet while lions wear their war weeds, bury silence,
quiet while a child in stains screams—*everything,*

everything here smells like the gas!
her propeller hands like trapped rabbits, twitching,

my hair,   *my mouth,*   *my breasts*   *—look!*
her tiny fingers try

cracking   the bough,   collapsing   the cradle—
look! my grandmother's bracelets all buried—

Look, no face!   Look, it's morning.
Look, it's God.   In Gaza.

Bandwagons line for each abject word—
where wheels don't stop exploded infants' fists,

or mother-skulls, lost,   lost mornings—

Brave holy land war.
Bright. Sun-split.

Where the bough has killed its cradle.

Bright, sun-lit ash,
its inexcusable shroud, rocking.

ii

They swept the dead like loosened crumbs from their fingertips, claws, curled. Brushed the dust, swallowed handfuls, hungry. Invented noise—in all that silence.

iii

An egg in her tiny right hand, blinded, seraph-child, she—was what was left of what had finished. Small-winged cataract, not much more. Killed

cradles, and skins, and old men, and kissing—stopped. Egg, in her sweaty small right hand, that hatchling meant for morning. Morning meant for saving. Or yet another prophet.

Prove it.

iv

She stole an egg
from the beast's bed—reeking, heaving nest builder.
Stepped blind, like vengeance. A cinder, empty eyed.
Hovered like a cloud of summer wasps.
Shifted, a gaunt lighthouse onto
promise, across all slaughter.
Reached.   —Held it.

What emerged bit her. What cracked its shell
licked her. What emerged, wanted her.

To do it all again.

v.

It didn't happen that way. She held the egg she'd stolen from God's nest and He whispered to her: Good riddance to it and to you. See if you can do any better with this one.

I tried and I'm tired of making eggs. Believe you stole it if that makes you feel brave or dangerous. Blessings. He showed his teeth.

It never—mattered, which came first, the father, or the mother, or the egg. Go ahead, my good thief. Go ahead, my bad angel. Bless. Happy morning.   She held the warm oval.

Held the breaking, mottled, hot ellipse. Couldn't remember—   why.   —Breathed it. Waited to feel a nervous thin-skinned thrum. One heartbeat.

She held it for such a long winter.

Hyacinths were blooming in January. Snows froze them, washed them. Still, she held it.

Her eye like the promise she finally remembered—   but from whom?—on a sparrow.

for Gaza. 1/2009

The Tent

Grain after grain, after grain,
on my dead and woven.

Here, let
the desert rain.

Here, in me.
Here, between my folds, my
new-with-flesh lips, too—opened.

Here, the man who was child, and lamb, and lost
—has crawled.

Here, this hour. Here, where
over my drapes, over my head,
suns
lowed like satisfied cattle.

Here, after the hour of the wolf has passed.
After the son who crawled here to drain his mother's milk,

has ended his howling
with a word into the mouth of his bride.
Here, after lament, I heard him laugh.

Here, after the mother faded like a last
filament, the new womb
lay open,

and star after star drank the couple's fire,
and the son whose father would have drawn

blood, by Yahweh's whisper—
spoke poems into the mouth of his doe from another land.

The hour of unkindness, past—
—my cloth held them.
Here,   and here,   and here,   they invented love.

Here, a home, now. Come unto me. Now, and again.
See how I am shining,   with your desert rain.

[After Genesis 24—Sarah's tent—may speak—

Light above Sarah's tent is said to have gone out, then shone again, when her Isaac wed Rebecca and he brought her inside.]

(OR… IF SHE WERE HEARD… AFTER DEATH…)

Humming Sarah…
Humming Sarah…
: *Why have all the   birds   now disappeared?*

Humming, drumming, Sarah behind Hebron's stone
: her black bell.

Eclipse, red moon. Stop weeping. Close me.
Who've known too much, in my century

plus twenty-seven desert *Yom Kippurs.* Atone.
I, in the womb my beloved honey-husband bought, cash
down. Obedient Jew, he. Call it a cave. Call it a tomb.

Say, for all stones over sand, and all mourners
: my beloved   would-have been   murderer,   he

: I, in the womb of—
: I, within the mother of—
: I—with my mothering mouth   eclipse
my beloved.   Eclipse   my own burial.

Down in the—   There, where
my heart would have chewed his knife to smithers. I say it,
Yahweh, are you listening, Maker?

Safe, they'll say.   Sorry.
Sarah, my name,   after,   after, and after.

My stone cries call to that broken throated
ram who lay last on my tall boy's would-have-been red sheet.
I'll lie quietly, now.   Good woman, I.

(Why have all the birds now disappeared?)

Let coins that bought my pillow, lie—let coins that wove my
blanket fall —husband of my longest dreams, my white yelp.

Let my life of seeds—and let my waiting. And at the mouth of my
cave, all my darlings, sing: for yourselves.

Know, that in such silence as mine, I am praying to my own
womb. For me. For you.
Eclipse, blood moon. I am watching.

[Of a man who thought his Elohim said: Sacrifice your tall son—son who lay for his father's blade, seed-obedient. Of a knife, mid-arc halted. Compassion's sharp fanged angel, was it? Was it his mother's bone scream, un-bonding? the ram's horn, hooting? Did she die of ache? Close her lips. Quietly.]

Of the Song Bird

Legend tells of the community of birds who had wings but no song as yet
: of a contest offered them by the god : of the prize of song—offered to that
bird who could fly the highest : of the tiny dun white-spotted-thrush who
knew she had no powers to fly high enough to win and wanted to—

Who crept, instead, who hid her small self in a white eagle's feathered crown
to fly far higher than all others : who dozed there, dreamed there, concealed in
her carrier's flight, and longing—and when her eagle tired, she who knew, and
bounded out and upward farther still—

Of the coveted prize of song she heard and learned there, in the heights
: of the thrush who returned with the song of spheres in her thirsty
small throat, who knew she had won by cheating : who saw the gathering of
birds below—a community, receiving, each, their entitled songs—

Legend of the thrush who went away then, hid in the deepest of forests out of
shame—but who could not help her song from rising, even in those stands of
webbing vine and shadow—of a quest for beauty, of goodness as we barely
know it but beg to receive it—that it brings us to longing, only—

Frailty, that rarely, like the thrush, the gorgeous song in us climbs, a bird
ashamed of its arriving at a possession of beauty by unsanctified means, a
slouching off to such a dim-lit place where the song erupts in spite, its
open-winged remembering, seining from the quiet—

Philomel

She wasn't thinking of she-wolves and old legends. Not of wolves, and not of children, and not of their suckling. She was thinking of a man who had been between her legs two nights before. Eager as a poem. Now a snow had covered his last cry and only she could feel it, ramming her. Now the beautiful. Or the blade attached to it. She knew that she would not see him again, and that there was no one to hurt in return. No one to mourn with either.

She permitted herself to accompany his last circle. His walk. His breath, graying under variable stars, dimming. Her eyes on the snow. An exercise, with her breath. To keep it from stuttering. She knelt to the spot and she began gathering fists of the snow into an uncertain, undefined shape at first. She didn't know how to make a golem

and she lay down into its scraped bed.

Still singing. A nightingale with its heart like a cut tongue. Her legs open, pleading.

Then,

tongues,   cut,
mouth their promises and we are lousy lip readers,
or will be swallowed still   by the ravenous,
the hell with prayer.

What last word wove our mourning-coat,
what expedition shattered continents to seed?
We will have no tears,
and will be swallowed.

When I shudder, call it mortal,   tears nailed to my eyes.
I have forgotten all the words for green; they are dried
children; they are peace abandoned.
Because we remember, because we forget, I write this
down: a laundry list for the personal dead.
I must buy soap. I must devise lye.
But there was never a lack of love. Even
then.

– 5 –

If it's the Last

One day I will be a bird / and will snatch my being / out of nothingness —Mahmoud Darwish

Taste of Vanilla

Somewhere on a bed, a woman, tasting rain.
Somewhere on the Seine, a motorboat, three
monks in gray cassocks and life-vests reach.
Their little launch idles where they clamor
out and up a jetty wall to buy ice cream cones at
Berthillon, re-board, and river-borne, lick prayers
as potent as vanilla, to bells—the most surreal
tourists in sight of Notre Dame, her steel eye.

Small pleasures beckon.
They will remember the taste
of *marron glacé* and *vanille* and the water spray
of a filthy river, mixed, for all their lives. It will
taste like sacrament, like sex.

Summer torpor makes us want to weep all
week, weep, for choking oil-slicked beaks,
weep for independence fallen, in our country,
weep for altars of an old light.

Cooled enough to cross again, sky
is metallic with albumin, gilded with vanished sun,
stains left behind like some slaughtered goat
carted off in pieces, magnificence of its kill-
color, smeared where it last cried.

Quieted, kinder, sky guards its monks on
a platinum Seine.
There is a Russian story: three
hermit monks on a desert islet, so old they
have forgotten how to pray. Their bishop's

voyaging ship stops, he lowers in a tiny boat,
and lands it at their shore to bless them.

We've forgotten, they confess, teach us, please,
again. And he does. And leaves them to their lonely
holiness. No sooner gone, than the old men forget
their prayer, bereft, one runs and chases after:
running on waves to cry oh Father,
Father we've forgotten, tell us again.

"... I Am the Weight Of This Incorruptible..."

Who weighs the hawk? The yellowing rushes
doubled in jade water? How heavy with
chalk is a sunrise-chorus, a young crow crying her freight
to heaven? A hidden owl is the weight of her feathers,
no more for her light heart, her perfected eye.

Love, said a man I learned with bruises to stop
loving: love is like holding water in your arms,
and then he made a war.

A full wide river of France holds
every kind of sheen the eye of skies suggested.
Which knows it's loved more? Morning's
one swan, cream explorer, borne mirrored
on a yearning current—or a gathered harvest
moon left to doze, while her birth fattens?

I vow to remain empty of everything but clouds,
bruised by only rain reflections holding me—
my thousands of new and soft-edged lovers.
There will be no war. There will be no war.

"I am the weight of this incorruptible, unpitying
air of these coasts and islands." Ulysses to Hector,
in "Tiger at the Gates," and then he made a war.
Who should Helen hold?

**["Tiger at the Gates," by Jean Giraudoux, was first produced in Paris, in 1935. WWII would follow.]*

Even With No Hand to Hold it

(After Picasso's "Caballo Corneado")

The horse holds frozen, her neck-stretched
gullet,   her head back-thrust as if to yowl
no sound she or we could bear,

we bear   a word
gyred to that wail for
warring so that God's our dirty word.   Bear

the horse, her knees wide-splayed to a blade-point
at her breast bone, the un-owned knife, like child-blood,
readying.

Bear the horse and the blade and no hand holding it,
no rider,   it's the horse, her utter quiet arc,   her
neck-stretched throat thrown backward as if to croon

no word that she or we can bear,   we bear that blade-
point keening up from soil that hosts it,   blade below
her lowered half-eviscerated roiled content of the living

body,   her forelegs' folded bones, her stiffened pose
of silence of   —crying higher and a higher
quiet,   it's the soundless point : up-thrust from no hate or
hand that she or we see.

Done,   its martyred
now—   has done.   Her breast so
near it will fall for it. Will give it what it wants.
Will fall for wolves   in the Mighty's clothing.

On Some Small History Of Epiphanies

On a sixth of Janus' two-faced winter-
gaze days, not called January, not then,

didn't soul-followers trace
a shining star from not yet Tehran, then,
not yet helmeted, not green, not yet blood
colored sand of miniatures, mosaics, measures,
verses, and arches under winter-cumulus—

Didn't they follow to Bethlehem's sunset
cradle—didn't they kneel to that
miniature they wanted so
to believe in—infant-fisted then, as now,
and didn't they say thanks, didn't they
gift,

didn't a later James call epiphany "the sudden
revelation of the whatness of a thing," moment when
"the soul of the commonest object … seems to us
radiant,"

and wasn't not-so-distant Lebanon's Kahlil
born on such a winter morning also, to whisper
of his prophet one day, but not then,
—how two mighty trees grow, each, not in
each other's shadow, each, reaching—

(when I fall, and when I fell,)

wasn't there a sharp-toothed rock in the road
that might turn to a star to follow—when
something has not happened yet
can we know, all winter, the meaning of epiphany,
how to bear cold that might fall from the nearest sun?

What Has Not Fallen

Kissing what gods? I do not know.

Not my language, flood, or palace, or Allah,
the violence of   —mourning, mourning, that
kind of mourning; memory, recoiling
when they speak the names of their beloved dead,

what language can draw a spectre,
its white desire? Ask me, ask me what is
an "I" at the unraveling of a world, was this

the end at the end of our time? Those who never had
enough except of luminescence and
                    too much broken,
                    too much dead,

—that flower had too much purple, too much gold,
too much red, and three petals, once,

—did you have time to kiss, any of you?
In every language, any, my only useful prayer.

"The sea has not fallen. The sea has not fallen.
(off stage whisper) The sea has not fallen."

Rupture

Pass a candle, sowing words in war time.
Angels have entered with their thousand eyes and shears.

Hold words in battle in my right,   water in the other hand,
and how it passes through the digits.

What is dangerous is the walk we walk on broken glass;
sand, and who is buried there,   dangerous words—
waiting for clean water; love, on a road of rifles.

I pass a candle in war time. The girl in the head scarf
holds it the longest.

A distance is required to view chaos. A way to cut. A rupture of the divine.

A bamboo porch and on it—a branched hand, and a baby with one brother
left. His torn yellow eye.

A dove, early purple in the crude dawn.
A slab and on it   as many needles as doves.
Their throats—that will not argue with words.

Wind and a Hill

Let me remember,   when I am born.
The poets are dying, darlings. It frightens me,
I try forgetting. With no memory, would I
Cry I want to be remembered—when

I am born? I've tried no history, tried to fathom
No homeland, no window. Said   any
Window will do. Said please   have no medals for
Wars, no gravestone thorns, no vines, no mama's name,
Mother, what's your maiden name? Child, who's your father?

Could that be better—when I am born? Give
Me wind and an invisible hill, no country,
Remember my hand on your sex or your breast,
That I was a woman in a window, when I die, and when I

Am born. Or serpentine birds, their twisting raw flesh under-belly
Necks, balletic in contortions—or a girl in socks, her crook-necked
Staff, her hand-of-Christ turn to Him sermon—burning.

Born, the new blood of late leaves, rarity
Of London sun loud as bells through turning yews.
While greens dry into old blood in a day or three,
Like the poets we bend our breaking branches to. Born,

I heard once, of a tribe of people painted blue,
Fallen from winter Pleiades, they said—and that they cannibalized
Their own, after. After death, they said, all the day it took to cook,
Consume, to brew and sip the body's broth, to chew its bones with

Love, they wept, and they loved. Born with breath, they blessed,
With breath, crooned. Remembered a birthmark, and a baby's step.
A greatness, a kiss, a scar. Every apology, born, and every battle.

The goodness. The crimes, and then it was done.
When all in their tribe had eaten well, and mourned
Well, and laughed. When they had spoken of—and remembered,
—Born, they quieted, and taboo said that born, the name of one
Dead—would never then be spoken.

In silence, one—would become—them. Swallowed. Born.
Un-born.
But the friends are dying, darlings. We are so afraid.
I try forgetting. My body. My words, my tribe.
With no tribe—I want wind, the unseen hill. In no country.
Let me remember that. Please. When I am born.

Beachfront

(Aceh was the epicenter—in 2005)

It's too hot not to swim. But in their dissolved cry?
Or is it only the insects? Or it begins again because
the world only ends in one place, and not in another.

When it begins again, one guitar in the shadows whose
darling died in December water. A cat, blind in one eye.
An inchworm, bursting.

A funereal tea with green sweet-cakes where only women
in *jilbabs* come, knees to the left. A man we could not save
with the laying on of hands.

High blood pressure, leg sores, the heartbeats like
hummingbirds,   the deep-voiced equator reciting
Allahhhhhhhh, Allahhhhhhh,   her twelve toes, curling.

A fever and a yellow cur, hunting. Crazy-woman who is
not crazy anymore, praying   and praying,   and praying.

~

The reel of bulldozers moving shore-washed and its bloated
broken—garbage and ghost and ghastly in loops, repeating.
In verses of the truth   down   in a monsoon dawn.

When it begins again, an old heat, white, imploding.
There were rebels, but not in the open green. Was horror under
a head-scarved sky.   Laughter, under the roofs before they

ruined,   breakfasting.   Horror is not made by any
hands that can be seen, here. Nor by silver monkeys, staring.

There are children who were hung in trees in a mother's
sarong, to be safe. Motherless, safe and staring. Old
women, softened with cotton yearning. A wise-man of
a village with so few to be wise for, any longer.

Pickaxes, ready for their ditches. Who knows these feet?
Incantation, for the stagnant, the breeding. The waters, and who
stands beside them. Sediment. Mercy, not really in sight.

For tomorrow, the heat and a free moon. Golden. Exaggerating.
For tomorrow, the tired, left, for the strong. A star, one star, falling.
All that loves, loving.   Even then.

For Ghosts, Only

Hot as a wiggled haunch, singing at the last bridge, a boat I ride
prays for me, I listen to its hands. There's all I know of prayer.

Did I say an egg shatters open on its branch? Or say in the red
room of nerves—when a cocoon un-spirals, one silken skein

reversing: You had long hands, didn't you, open knees, open
fingers, your eyes sewn closed to the sun. And, you are a ghost.

~

When the new black iris insists it can love humbly as dooryard
lilacs, let me kneel in a torn garden, cushioned only

by leaf-fall. You are in foothills,
crying all night, all noon, I've been listening—

—larks in the long rain's shattered pearls,
a train going north, an arbor of roots, wind of quince,

a fallen voice, and last night's hill of harps—

there was a room of them. Only harps.

~

One half-angel's thumbs, perched on strings. Only
her hands. Only rust light hovering down on

its own leaves behind us, darkening them as folded birds at our backs,
and two last swallows hurrying not to be locked out of love.

Down from the mountain-washed cloud-line, a knife-crescent moon
and a room of six coupled harps, two lutes, one violin lain like a short

femme on the mantle, two candles, and a woman only half-angelic, some-
one's dowager stout aunt, her thighs open, her harp leaning tall inside them.

Alone in the room, she could play only one harp of six.
Ghosts, at all the others.

Stopped at our notice, she quit her strings, quit whispers with what
lover she had—in flame, departed—while the others, harps with no hands,
stayed tall in their window—and said nothing.

In wolf-light, we entered number 33 where another wife steamed
meat. A heath behind us fed on fallen dark. A room with un-played
harps fed un-played music to its unlit candles. Only.

October Renaissance

Centaurs are a class of icy planetoids
named after mythic horsemen.

Ceres is a dwarf planet, and an asteroid.
Space-rocks orbit our hard star between

Jupiter and Neptune, we—orbit three rivers,
crossing Verdun, Chalon, Beaune,

to dine on *volaille aux morilles,*
our branches—licked with change.

Riverine and moist, the path-lights of early
first blood-spots on the turning trees,
like proof of a virgin's first nights—.

Crows crying their wares to the river
who speaks in floods to herself—the heron's
mirrored solitaire in liquid celadon, lone

as the ash-grove in another country's ballads.
This one's eye, silver-etched on rain, knows
sky and air as mine knew an island. Our boat

is an island, risen on the risen river.
If the globe sank today—we didn't know it.

~

Each oak has gone naked, stark mistletoe-nests of flesh
in its twigs. In a river: the living, the dying, the born.

The crow cries her hunger and another nation's choir
hums Babylon—*where we sat down, and there we wept,*

when we remembered Zion—No, we will not weep, here,
not tonight, here—but when another nation falls, lacking peace.

We are in peace. No virgin rape here. It was a boat-trip
on the Saône. Was a flood and an an *auto-da-fé* of seasons.

Was the peace of gods, dressed as swans, was a heron
in her mile of solitude, no mate until May—her eye on space.

~

Other centaurs may also be comets; other gods, in other flames.
In October when the river speaks to herself in mists, we're adrift

with a tint of washed violets, we call it wine. When the stranger
who finger-tipped my shoulder on a train—has come no nearer;

when the crazed—envy my glass calm; when stray cats in Verdun and
a rage-eyed woman in purple at her empty gate want soothing, only,

only want notice, only want love—that harvest moon that was full
last Wednesday is eaten—unseen insects in its sky-bed, unseen

dwarves and horsemen in its quilts. We, it, and I, need renaissance,
will reinvent an autumn soul, thin heron in her singleness—

the long-necked flights of swallow and shadow   in flooded chorus
for the waters   —orbits, rising.

Among the Trumpets

I dined with the dust, its strangers,
refused the offered oysters,
belly-danced to older women's

eyes, wriggling,
when the midnights bellowed.

Spun as blackbirds high on ferment's fallen
fruit. Relearning alphabets. Relearning fire.
Long, among the trumpets.

Or I dined in other rooms, with women.
Alone, a woman knows women.

The exile's dress, the color of her mouth.
The wounded rain inside the flesh.
The small loss of faith, like a tilted crèche.

~

Wanting His sound in my mouth,
sorry, skinless, quiet, He said He didn't
know how to pray.

While oceans buried babies,
their beaches lined with quiet dead.

While red giants they thought dragons, fed
among the high notes, backwards, walking,
toward the bloating sun, the troubled sand.

While deserts invented midnight-ways
to pull the wings from birds, but called it
the peace, and the war,

oh, who is left to envy?
Idols, with no information.
I send you red love,   more stars.

I bow to
light that has no shoes.
I cannot

cry. I cannot cry. I cannot cry.

~

One light-year is a vacuum
of the distance light walks in a year,
its trillion miles, its naked feet.

A star or stars in throes of death are
little ghosts, and little spiders.
Light-years-lonely.
One, the size of our sun, in its grasp.

A star will burgeon. Will become
what's called red giant. Will cry.
I send you red love. And stars.

~

I don't want to re-read an apocalypse, this night.
I send you supernova angels,
the finale of just another, one more star.

Among the trumpets, there will be no trumpets.
And I'll be relearning alphabets. Relearning fire.

Among the trumpets, it is not music, it is only light.
I will be looking for God's love   and hoof,   and star.

… My Long Drum

Am

between soul and stone.

Am

between

the wind and the hill.

My long drum.

In my mouth. One morning.

My long drum.
My long drum.
My long drum.

Where you have halted your horse.

… I know the stones gillstained, the swarms of silence in the hives of light …

—St.-John Perse

~

NOTES

• Epigraph—"*I have halted my horse by the dove-moaning tree,*" is from a line in *Song,* by St.-John Perse (translated from the French by TS Eliot).

• The cryptic queen who is mentioned in *An Empty Place,* is a deposed monarch, *Lili'uokalani,* of the wide spaces of once emptier Hawaiian islands; the empty place is also a land of pastures that haunted me in the southwestern valleys of France. Both regions deeply loved by W.S. Merwin, I've been privileged to find my own wide days in these two places.

• *The Wound That Comes Closest to the Sun,* title of a poem in section 3, comes from a line by René Char, *"The wound that comes closest to the sun is lucidity."*

• *"What thou among the leaves hast never known…"* is from Keats' *Ode to a Nightingale.*

• Epigraph to section 4 *"… almost the quality of disappearance/ In its cage of visibility"* is from *The Impossible Indispensability of the Ars Poetica* by Hayden Carruth.

• Lilith, that feminine shape invoked in so many Semitic renderings, in the Hebrew versions, is demonized as Adam's first wife who would not surrender. In Arabic telling, her name based on the same Semitic root, "Lail," means "night," beloved of a man who goes mad when her family refuses him; he writes her poems and more poems of love.

• *"I saw an angel in the stone and carved to set it free"* is from the notebooks of Michelangelo.

• Philomel: L Philomela, fr. Gk Philomele, an Athenian princess who was raped by her brother-in-law King Tereus, en route to her own marriage, and, after having had her tongue cut out by him, later was avenged and transformed into a nightingale. The nightingale in pastoral verse—symbolic of romantic love.

• *Beachfront* is a poem relating to a monstrous wave called the tsunami; it was written during my journey to Sumatra to work in a survivors' clinic there, at the epicenter in Aceh.

• *"The sea has not fallen"* is excerpted from a line by Andrew Zawacki

• *Again the Cradle*: in January 2009 … there was so little hope.

• The Biblical Sarah is said to have died at the age of a hundred and twenty seven, immediately after her husband's sacrifice of their son Isaac was halted, in the middle—of that obedient act.

• Epigraph to section 5 *"One day I will be a bird / and will snatch my being / out of nothingness"* is from *Mural* by Mahmoud Darwish.

• *Wind and a Hill* is dedicated to the autumn poets.

• Envoi: *". . . I know the stones gillstained, the swarms of silence in the hives of light,"* is excerpted from a line in section vii of *Anabasis* by St.-John Perse (translated by Eliot).

~

My ongoing and deep gratitude to poets whose words have marked me, inspired me, whose care for my own words sustains me in my darks—Stanley Moss, William Merwin, Jerome Rothenberg, Marilyn Hacker, Marie Ponsot, Cyrus Cassells, Ellen Hinsey, Jeffrey Greene, Robin Lim, Alice Notley. And how still, and still, each poet, each breaking—newly teaches me the word.

Acknowledgements

My gratitude to the editors of these publications in which poems from this book first appeared (some in earlier versions and/or with earlier titles): *Kenyon Review*, "Scene Two, "*Kenyon Review*, "of the songbird," *Poetry Daily*, "of the songbird," *Runes*, "of the owl: stripped," *Tupelo–Poetry Project*, "Beachfront," *Another Chicago Magazine*, "Beachfront," *Meena*, "What Has Not Fallen," *Nimrod International*, "America Poem," *The Southern Review*, "Among the Trumpets," *Beauty/Truth: A Journal of Ekphrastic Poetry*, "Even with No Hand to Hold It," *A Cadence of Horses, Anthology*, "Even with No Hand to Hold It," *Studio*, "Taste of Vanilla," "When Are You Not," *Poetry Review* (UK,) "Not A Land Where Oranges," and "Wind," *Crab Creek Review*, "An Empty Place," *Poetry International*, "Philomel," "On Giving Away the Stone," "Alone in the Old One's House," "Of Men's Kitchens," "For a Festival Of Women," *Cimarron Review*, "October Renaissance," *Pleiades*, "Wind and a Hill," *Persimmon Tree*, "Her Detail—Paris Cherry Trees," "Taste of Vanilla," *The Mom Egg*, "Again a Cradle." "Philomel" also appears in a different prose version in my story book, *Beautiful Soon Enough* (FC2/University of Alabama Press, 2009.)

Margo Berdeshevsky Writes:

I was born in NYC and currently live in Paris. A graduate of the High School of Performing Arts, I attended Northwestern and New York Universities, and quit for a role in my first Off Broadway play. I was trained as an actress by Lee Strasberg, performed in David Hare's "Slag," Harold Pinter's "Tea Party" and the world premiere of his"The Basement," worked in the companies of Lincoln Center and Joseph Papp's Public Theatre, and toured the USA as Ophelia. Nominated for a television Emmy award, I loved poetry more than Hollywood.

But a Passage in Wilderness was published by Sheep Meadow Press in 2007. *Beautiful Soon Enough* (University of Alabama Press, 2009), a collection of illustrated and poetic short stories, won the Fiction Collective Two's American Book Review/Ronald Sukenick Innovative Fiction Award. Other honors include the Robert H. Winner Award from the Poetry Society of America (selected by Marie Ponsot); seven Pushcart nominations and two Pushcart "special mention citations" for works in leading literary journals including *Agni, The Kenyon Review, Poetry International, New Letters, Pleiades, The Southern Review, Chelsea, Runes, Poetry Review* (UK), *Wolf Magazine* (UK), *Siècle 21, Confluences Poétiques;* the Chelsea Award for poetry; the Sue Saniel Elkind Award; and honorable mentions in the Pablo Neruda Award and the Ann Stanford Award (selected by Yusef Komunyakaa). Recent exhibitions of my "visual poems" have been seen in Hawaii and Paris. My documentary photographs and poems followed a journey to Sumatra in spring 2005, to work in a survivors' clinic in Aceh. They became my *Tsunami Notebook.* A cross-genre novel, *Vagrant,* is forthcoming.

92991494R00191

Made in the USA
Middletown, DE
11 October 2018

Had They But Known Her

J. A. Clapperton

ISBN 978-1-7752958-0-8

This is a work of historic fiction. While many of the characters lived and historic records exist in the public domain, the material in this book which reflects their character and actions is entirely the product of the author's imagination.

Cover photo of Olive Wilmot taken by
Burr McIntosh Studio
20 W 33 St. NY

This story is dedicated to Olive Wilmot's great-niece, Diana Grandfield, who passed away Sept. 14, 2016 in her 95th year.

I enjoyed many hours in Diana's company, hearing stories about the Wilmot family and specific anecdotes about Olive. The stories Diana had heard as a child led to much of my fruitful research.

Diana was a local historian and published author herself. Even in her 90's, she spent countless hours in her home office, surrounded by the history she was so fond of. When I last saw her in 2015, she was hard at work documenting her father's family history.

This grand lady introduced me to the past days of glory and I am forever grateful. I will always remember our times together.

Introduction

After moving to the village of Newcastle in southern Ontario in 2006, I was introduced to the rumours of the death of a local woman in 1903. Talk in the village, even 100+ years after her death, alleged that her lover had murdered her. I was intrigued.

But, while the myth of her murder might have caught my interest, historic research would unmask a life far more fascinating to me than her death. Following this trail of research kept me eager for more.

Olive Wilmot and most of the others in this story lived. Newspapers and historic records provided factual details but said little about character or context. My mind and the anecdotal family stories told to me by Olive's great-niece, Diana Grandfield, filled in the rest.

The background Diana provided fuelled my imagination and allowed me to take historic records to interesting places.

This book is my interpretation of Olive's life and the major characters who featured in it.

Summary of Characters

Samuel Wilmot m. Matilde (***Tillie***) Clark

Their Children:	Helen Thorne Charles Wilmot John (Jack) Wilmot Mary (***Minnie***) Galbraith** **Olive Winans Burchard Sanford*** George Wilmot Seymour Wilmot
Minnie Galbraith**	- Older and favourite sister of Olive; - Wife of Duncan - Mother of Marjorie and Vivian
Olive Wilmot*	m. Henry Romaine Winans (1881) m. Thomas Herring Burchard (1893) m. Henry Sanford (1898)
Henry Romaine Winans (***Harry***)	- Parents: Ted and Phoebe - Grandmother: Rachel Wells - Brothers: Theodore; Edward (Ed); Chauncey; Frederick
Thomas Herring Burchard	- Brothers: Lewis; Roswell - Uncle: Lewis Sayre (m. Eliza) - Sons: Leeds; Stewart
Henry Sanford	- Son: Samuel Simons Sanford (*Simon*) - Grandchildren: Kitty; Henry Jr.
Henry Sayre Van Duzer (***Sayre)***	- Cousin of Thomas Burchard - Olive's lawyer and best friend

<u>Lesser Characters</u>

Amy Lindsell	- ladies maid to Olive from 1893 until Olive's death in 1903
Mrs. Thomson	- housekeeper at Chestayne (Olive's summer home in Newcastle)

June 1903
Newcastle, Ontario

Chapter 1

Sayre fell to his knees at Olive's side, a low moan escaping his mouth. He dropped the fire poker in his hands and grabbed her shoulders with more force than he intended, saying "Olive, Olive"; praying she had simply fainted.

But the pallor and stiffness of her face denied this. His moan became a steady chant, gaining in volume and clarity until the servants heard his yell; "Call the doctor. Please, please … for the love of GOD, SOMEONE CALL THE DOCTOR. Olive has collapsed!"

The housekeeper, Mrs. Thomson, was the first in the room, with a chamber maid quick on her heels. They found Sayre, moaning quietly, holding a prostrate Olive in his arms. Mrs. Thomson took quick action, telling the young maid to call in the driver and telephone the local doctor to say he was needed immediately at Chestayne.

Mrs. Thomson gently removed Olive from Sayre's arms and placed a pillow under her head. This seemed all that she could do for the poor woman. Her eyes fell on the fire poker at Sayre's feet. It was out of place.

They had all heard the raised voices prior to Sayre's cries for help. It was hard not to jump to conclusions with such a guilty-looking object before her but it was not up to her to say what had happened in that room. It was clear, though, looking at Sayre crumpled at Olive's side, that it would be up to her to manage this situation.

The woman was more than capable of managing any situation. A stalwart Scot, she took no nonsense from staff or trades people. Nothing escaped Mrs. Thomson's eye but no words ever escaped her lips about what she might see or hear. As far as Olive was concerned, 'Discretion' was Mrs. Thomson's first name.

Mrs. Thomson had been hired by Henry and Olive Sanford five years previously on the advice of Olive's sister, Minnie. Olive needed someone she could trust; someone who had no interest in her past or the talk that circulated about her in the village of Newcastle.

Olive Wilmot Winans Burchard Sanford purchased a summer home in Newcastle in 1899, after an absence of many years. Still an outstanding beauty at 35, she and her 76 year old husband provided much to talk about in the village and areas around. The talk was not because of her outstanding beauty and presence; or the philanthropic work she did in Newcastle and New York City; or because she had been a Wilmot.

No, the gossip that traveled from door to door concerned her many marriages.

After a secret wedding in 1881 at just 17, Olive was not seen for two years. The only thing that saved her reputation from complete ruin after the hasty wedding was the fact that Reverend Brent performed the ceremony at her own church, St. George's Anglican. But even the good Reverend was unable to stem the speculation that went around the village once word got out.

There must be a baby involved. Who was this mystery man? Why was Minnie the only Wilmot at the wedding?

It didn't help that no one in the Wilmot family would discuss Olive or her marriage and that she wasn't seen again until 1883.

Her reappearance that year, with her father but without her husband, sent many village matrons into a tizzy.

Where was the child? Why isn't she in black mourning clothing if she is without her husband? Where has she been these two years past?

Theories abounded but none came close to the mark in accuracy.

Once again at Belmont, her childhood home, Olive stayed in the village for five years, living quietly and close to home with her sister, Minnie. Her presence at church every Sunday was enough to cause whispers behind raised hands. No explanation had ever been offered for her reappearance or lack of a husband (or child) so what else were they to do but imagine the worst?

When she left again in 1889, the family let it be known that she had gone to live with her Uncle John in New York City. Without her presence, the talk settled down.

But, in 1893, word got back to Newcastle that Olive had married a New York doctor.

How is this possible? What happened to her first husband? She never wore mourning so he must still be alive. How does she marry again?

In time, the village learned that Olive had divorced her first husband. Everyone agreed on the scandal of this and the talk continued. The fact that Olive and her new husband never visited Newcastle failed to quiet the talk this time.

The death of the doctor in 1896 brought a smidgeon of pity for Olive. Had she returned and lived quietly at that point, villagers might have allowed her to live a respectable life.

Instead, shock waves traveled the village once again: Olive had married Henry Sanford; a 75 year old multi-millionaire. Since she was just 34, any pity for the widow vanished.

Well, we can all see why she married him. I always saw her as an opportunist. What does her father think of his son-in-law being his age? I suppose money makes anything tolerable.

The talk took flight as never before, fuelled by her return to Newcastle with her elderly husband each summer. His luxurious private rail car and the frequent visits of a younger, single man established the type of life she was living.

Olive turned a deaf ear to it all. She was not naïve, however, and managed her life so that few details escaped to feed the hungry villagers. They were left to chew on just what was observed of Olive and her entourage each summer.

It was to this household that Mrs. Thomson willingly dedicated her summers. She acted as the barrier between Olive's house, Chestayne, and the villagers.

The arrangement worked well for her, a widow who lived with her son's family during the months she didn't live in for Olive. The housekeeper moved into Chestayne each May and capably hired the day staff needed to prepare and run the home for the Sanford's each summer.

The Sanford's lifestyle and the many New York friends they hosted each summer required kitchen and chamber maids and a laundry woman as well as a driver who managed the gardens as well. Henry's valet and Olive's lady's maid travelled with them to Newcastle each summer and their accommodations needed to be prepared as well as rooms for guests and their servants. Henry sent his cook one week ahead of their arrival to place the necessary orders and get the kitchen in shape. The cook had been with Henry for many

years; travelling between their New York City residence, the home in Bridgeport, Connecticut and Newcastle.

Mrs. Thomson expected closed mouths from all staff. She emphasized when hiring that what was seen in the house was not to become fodder for gossip outside of it. She ran a disciplined household; staff discovered whispering in corners were soon shown the door, ensuring the ones who remained or replaced them understood her expectations. Of course, she couldn't control their talk once they left the house each night but she kept her ear to the ground in the village. If she heard details that only someone working in the home might be aware of, it never took her long to locate and deal with the source.

Even so, she understood the nature of people and knew she was going to have a time of things when word of Olive's collapse got out. She'd worked for the woman long enough to understand the curiosity she was in this village and the jealousy that came from others observing her lavish lifestyle. Mrs. Thomson knew she would need to prepare the household staff for the busy body questions that would arise in the village.

The driver came running into the room. On the housekeeper's instructions, and with Sayre following, he lifted Olive gently and carried her from the morning room up the private staircase that led directly into her bedroom. Olive's lady's maid, Lindsell, had been at the back of the house when Sayre screamed and was unaware of what had taken place. She looked up from tidying Olive's vanity as they entered. With alarm in her eyes, she pulled the bedding down for the man to lay Olive on the bed.

"The doctor is on his way" said the maid breathlessly, rushing into the room. She looked to the housekeeper with questioning eyes. This was more excitement than the young girl had known in a year.

"Not a word, either of you" said the housekeeper, looking at the chamber maid and driver sternly. "Not even to other staff for now. Understood? Both of you?" she stressed, looking from one to the other. "Yes, Ma'am" they replied and left the room for the servant's staircase at the back of the house. She had no need to take the same promise from Lindsell. The woman had been with Olive through a divorce from one husband, the death of a second and marriage to a third very rich, very elderly man. The maid cared deeply for Olive and took pride in sheltering her from the worst of the intense gossip which

surrounded her. Mrs. Thomson knew Lindsell would rather die than hurt her employer.

The housekeeper turned to Sayre, clutching Olive's unresponsive hand, and said gently "there's nothing to be done for her until the doctor sees her, Mr. Van Duzer. Lindsell and I will try to make her as comfortable as possible but your place is not here. I suggest you send a messenger to Belmont for Mrs. Galbraith. She will want to be here for her sister."

"Yes, of course" replied the grief-stricken man. He was grateful there was at least something he could do. He would leave it to Minnie, when she arrived, to tell Olive's husband, Henry Sanford, lying ill in his room down the hall.

Sayre's hands shook as he wrote the few sentences needed for Minnie to drop everything and rush to Chestayne. He took it downstairs to the driver, urging him to deliver it to Belmont immediately.

Back in Olive's room, Mrs. Thomson said to Lindsell, "I'll go find Mr. Sanford's nurse. I would feel better having some medical attention for Mrs. Sanford while we wait for the doctor."

Twenty minutes later, the driver pulled Henry Sanford's car, with Minnie inside, up to the front of the house just as the doctor climbed slowly down from his old horse and buggy. With most residents of the village still in horse and wagon, Henry's newest model automobile garnered much attention and the driver was immensely proud to be the one at the wheel.

The tall, stoop shouldered elderly doctor nodded at Minnie. He was a fixture in Newcastle. Some would say his methods were better suited to the past century and his eyesight questionable but he had been the family's doctor for more years than even Minnie could remember.

She fell into step beside him and the pair walked in the front door together. No words passed between them; just a mutual sense of urgency to get to Olive. Minnie wondered briefly whether the sounds she heard as they climbed the stairs were the treads or the doctor's old knees.

As the pair entered Olive's pink bedroom, the nurse stepped aside from the bed. Minnie and Lindsell stood quietly during the doctor's examination. He might be old and provincial but the doctor had seen

much in his long career and Minnie trusted his judgements. When the doctor closed his case, she followed him out to the top of the main staircase and waited for him to speak.

"It's not good, Minnie" said the doctor. "She suffered a major stroke. Her high blood pressure has always been a concern but it's hard to say what might have brought on a stroke of this magnitude. All that any of us can do is wait and pray. If by some miracle, and I stress miracle, she does recover consciousness, I can't say that her abilities will ever be the same again. So tragic at her young age" he mumbled as he descended the stairs slowly.

Minnie looked up at a noise down the hall to see Olive's husband, Henry, in his robe and leaning on a cane. "What was the doctor doing here, Minnie? Has something happened?"

Walking slowly, Minnie guided him back to his bedroom and settled him in a chair before speaking. "I have dreadful news, Henry" she said with a catch in her throat. "Olive has had a stroke and is unconscious." The tears she hadn't allowed herself fell readily now as she grabbed Henry's hand and brought it to her cheek. "If a miracle happens and she regains consciousness, Henry, the doctor doesn't think she's ever going to be herself again."

Henry was ill with a recurrence of pneumonia. It had been his physician's suggestion that they remove him from the noise and pollution of New York City. Current medical belief was that fresh air aided the lungs so they had arrived in Newcastle the previous week, a full month earlier than usual.

Hearing Minnie saying unthinkable things, he questioned his own mind. In disbelief he whispered "stroke?" That very morning, his beautiful, vibrant girl had been worrying over him in his sick bed. She had talked of plans she had for nursing Henry back to his usual robust, healthy self.

He rose slowly, saying aloud "I must go to her" but Minnie held his arms firmly to prevent him from standing. "There is no point right now, Henry. Lindsell will see to her. Olive doesn't know any of us are here and it would just upset you."

Belying the weakened state he was in, before Minnie's eyes, he drew himself up, suggesting the powerful man she knew; in control, making decisions, giving orders and getting action.

"Have a telegram sent to Dr. Brown in NYC, Minnie. Tell him of the grave situation and ask him to contact the best doctor in Toronto personally to come immediately for a second opinion. My nurse should stay with her; you'll see to that? Where is Sayre? Tell him I want to see him. Olive said he had arrived; oh, my poor Olive." As quickly as he had gathered the strength needed to take action, he now visibly deflated, sinking back into his chair.

By God he loved her. She was the most beautiful woman he had ever laid eyes on; and he hadn't lived a sheltered life by a long stretch. He hadn't realized he had spoken aloud until Minnie straightened a blanket over his knees and settled him back in his chair. She did her best to quiet her elderly brother-in-law who meant so much to her; soothing him with the words that she would take care of everything; he wasn't to upset himself. Everything that could be done for Olive would be done.

Minnie knew that Sayre had arrived the day before from New York City. Henry Sayre Van Duzer was never apart from Olive for long, visiting Chestayne frequently during their summer stays. Family and close friends knew Sayre was Olive's personal lawyer but, more importantly, her closest friend. It was Sayre's frequent visits that kept tongues wagging in Newcastle; that a married woman would spend as much time as she did with a handsome, single man and right under her husband's nose. Although a friendship between a 'confirmed bachelor' and a woman was not uncommon in New York City, the less seasoned villagers of Newcastle called it for what they saw and talked endlessly about the pair.

Leaving Henry's room, Minnie decided she needed to meet with Mrs. Thomson before seeing Sayre. She needed answers. Her sister was a beautiful, healthy thirty-nine-year-old: far too young to have a massive stroke. But she had. Now Minnie wanted to retrace Olive's steps; to know what she had been doing when it happened.

Minnie was well aware of Olive's high blood pressure and knew that celebrated New York doctors who had examined her had never told Olive of the possibility of a stroke. She needed to know what had brought it on.

She went back in to take a look at her beautiful sister. Lindsell had removed her day dress and put a brilliantly coloured silk kimono on Olive. The maid brushed her hair gently, laying each tendril softly on

the pillow. She spoke quietly to Olive as she did. It was almost hard to believe that her sister was unconscious and not just resting. Minnie left the grieving woman to her care giving and went down the private staircase in the corner of Olive's bedroom. A morning room, also for Olive's exclusive use, was at the bottom.

Minnie sat at Olive's desk and remembered Olive's joy at finding the piece. The furniture and décor in the house had all been chosen by Olive but she had taken particular care in this room and the bedroom above to suit herself alone. Her choices were never based on current style. Instead each piece was selected for its beauty and how it made her feel.

The collective look, complemented in restful shades of green, with hints of butter yellow and cream, created a tranquil atmosphere. The silk draperies, floral wallpaper and Turkish carpets wrapped visitors in elegant comfort.

Indiscreet contractors working on the house during its renovations took home stories of the morning room and Olive's bedroom, with its luxurious linens and crystal accents. The details they shared about the décor, including Olive's choice to paint the room delicate shades of pink, fuelled countless hours of talk amongst wives and mothers of the village. They returned to the plain white washed walls, serviceable quilts and dowdy homemade rag rugs in their own homes shaking their heads at what they'd heard.

'If anyone deserves such beauty in their surroundings, Olive, it's you', thought Minnie, as she pulled a sheet of her sister's fine, palest pink stationery toward her and opened her fountain pen. The message she wrote to Dr. Brown was clear in what they needed.

She was folding the paper when Mrs. Thomson came into the room, responding to the button wired into the desk that Minnie had pressed just moments before.

She turned to face the housekeeper, saying "This should go to the telegram office, Mrs. Thomson. I will wait until that's done and then I want to hear everything you heard and saw today."

The housekeeper respected Minnie Galbraith greatly; together, the two women coordinated the upkeep of Olive's summer home, Chestayne. Minnie was Olive's trusted agent in Newcastle - happily so - and gave the home the attention needed until Olive and Henry arrived each July.

Minnie's mind drifted to thoughts of the fun she had known each summer since Olive's return to the village. She remembered well the many jokes her sister played on them. Oh, how Olive loved to laugh! It seemed to Minnie they all laughed a great deal more when Olive was in residence.

Would she ever laugh again, she wondered, as the housekeeper returned to the morning room. Turning in her chair, she said, "Alright, Mrs. Thomson; I want to hear everything you know to be true. Leave nothing out, regardless of how insignificant it may seem. My sister is fighting for her life up there and I want to know what happened."

The housekeeper said, "We all heard loud voices, Mrs. Galbraith. I was worried that their angry tones would bring Mr. Sanford down the stairs but, since the morning room is at the other end of the house from his bedroom, he must not have heard. I kept everyone on tasks in the kitchen and laundry to give Mrs. Sanford and Mr. Van Duzer privacy but, even so, their voices were hard to ignore."

"It's not gossip for me to tell you what I overheard" said Mrs. Thomson, hesitantly. She spent so much time counselling staff not to repeat things, it felt odd to be doing that very thing herself. But Minnie was family and Mrs. Thomson needed to unburden herself of the episode she had come upon.

"I heard Mr. Van Duzer telling Mrs. Sanford to be practical – something about Mr. Sanford and that it was time to make plans for herself. I could tell Mrs. Sanford was crying but, from what I heard, she gave back as good as she got from him. Her voice was raised also."

The housekeeper averted her eyes as she continued. "When I heard Mr. Van Duzer's screams, I ran into the room and found her collapsed by the fireplace. I knew by her colour that something was terribly wrong and sent for the driver to help lift her upstairs and the maid to call the doctor."

"While I was trying to make her comfortable I noticed the fire poker lying on the marble fireplace surround at Mr. Van Duzer's feet. It seemed very out of place to me but I determined to wait to hear what the doctor said before jumping to conclusions."

"Wise of you, Mrs. Thomson; the poker had nothing to do with Olive's collapse. It appears she has had a massive stroke. It may very well have been brought on by her heightened emotions" said Minnie.

"First things first" she continued. "We know that there will be talk in the village so let's agree on how much information will be shared to minimize the gossip.

Please make sure the maid and driver understand that Mrs. Sanford's stroke had nothing to do with her argument with Mr. Van Duzer. You can plant the seed in their minds that she had been unwell for some months and perhaps this will deflect any talk from Mr. Van Duzer's involvement in this."

"Now, you and I will deal with the household while Mrs. Sanford is unable to. The telegram I sent was to Mr. Sanford's doctor in New York. He will be recommending a Toronto doctor to come for a consultation. I will stay while Olive is unwell. When my valise arrives, please put it in the room beside Olive's."

When the housekeeper left, Minnie picked up the correspondence Mrs. Thomson had left on the desk for Olive to look over. There were merchant bills to pay which Minnie would take care of with Olive's household account. She tucked the personal letters for Olive to one side. She would leave them unopened but knew, at some point, she would have to respond to each.

She felt an overwhelming need to speak with her husband. Minnie would have loved to feel his arms around her but settled for a phone call asking that he send some clothing and personal items to her. Knowing that the operator heard every word of the call, Minnie said simply that Olive was unwell and would like her to stay.

Chapter 2

With the phone call over, Minnie began to shake. Mrs. Thomson returned with a tray with tea and a light meal for her. Thanking her, Minnie told the woman to ask Mr. Van Duzer to join her in the morning room and to bring something for him as well. Concentrating on pouring her tea steadied her as she waited for Sayre.

"Oh, Minnie, what will we do?" cried Sayre as he entered the room. Minnie stood to hold the man who loved her sister above all others, understanding his pain. Sayre was a cousin of Olive's second husband, Thomas. Only those closest to Olive understood the unique relationship she and Sayre shared.

Finally, Minnie broke from his embrace and settled on the chair across from him. He looked disinterestedly at the tray Mrs. Thomson brought to the table beside him.

"We will carry on as she would want us to, Sayre. The doctor said she has had a massive stroke." Each time Minnie said the words, it felt as though a knife pierced her heart. "I know this is difficult but I need to know what she was so worked up about before her collapse. Please tell me what you two were arguing about; you know she and I have no secrets from each other."

The poor man looked at Minnie with such pain that she almost regretted asking him but she simply must know what had so inflamed Olive. "I was telling her it was time to consider her affairs, Minnie; that we must prepare for when Henry is no longer with us."

"It was my saying it that caused her to get so upset. Initially, I was poking the fire and not looking at her so I didn't see how upset she was. She just kept denying that anything would happen to Henry as I insisted she listen to reason. She knows his will leaves no bequest for her; that's why he settled the sum on her when they wed, and there are investments and assets that need to be reviewed to make sure she will be cared for when he's gone."

"It was as her lawyer that I spoke; not as her friend, but she just would not hear anything about Henry passing."

"The level of her anger took me by surprise" Sayre continued. "I didn't think I was saying anything she mustn't have considered herself; he is eighty, after all. I know she loves him, despite the manner in which the marriage was entered into, but I had thought it

more like the love one feels for a parent. Her utter distress at the very idea of losing him made me see just how much she cares for Henry. She loves him deeply, Minnie" said Sayre, looking at Minnie with such sad eyes that Minnie's heart softened.

"I know she does, Sayre. I've known for some time that her marriage wasn't the arrangement everyone believed" replied Minnie.

Sayre continued as though speaking to himself. "She got angrier as I spoke and then collapsed beside me. I thought I was speaking with her best interests at heart but now am heartsick that I may have brought this about. Oh, God help me" he said, shaking. "Why is she the one lying upstairs at death's door?"

"Quiet yourself, Sayre" said Minnie, feeling compassion for the man but needing to take charge. "Henry wants to see you and I do not want him to be upset by any knowledge of what led to the stroke. All he knows is that she has had one. Please, do whatever you have to but enter his room as their lawyer and not a grief stricken friend."

Sayre rose to the sideboard and poured himself a Scotch. He emptied the glass in one gulp, pulling strength from the amber liquid.

As he approached Henry's room, he drew a purposeful breath and stood straight, looking every bit the capable lawyer he was.

Henry answered his knock and Sayre entered, shocked the man had aged even more with the events of that morning. The once vigorous man now seemed swallowed by the chair he sat in.

"Ah, Sayre" said Henry with great sadness. "I understand your grief to be as great as my own. I have requested my New York doctor to send someone from Toronto for a second opinion. I haven't given up hope but there are matters that need attention. I never thought I would be asking this but, is Olive's estate in order?"

"It is, Henry" Sayre replied. "Although her will is in my office in New York, I am fully aware of her wishes."

"Good, good" said Henry distractedly. With more emphasis, he continued "Spare no expense on the funeral arrangements, Sayre. Olive should leave this world with as much beauty and grace as she gave it. Don't hesitate over anything you think worthy of her; go to Toronto for whatever is unavailable locally. I won't question whatever expenses you incur."

"Understood Henry" replied Sayre gravely.

He left the old man and returned to his room to put preliminary plans together although his heart was down the hall with his dearest friend. He felt disloyal making such plans with Olive still alive but he was a practical man. He doubted a second doctor would bring any different diagnosis despite how hopeful they all were.

After Sayre left her, Minnie returned to Olive's bedside. She looked on her sister's prostrate body, unbelieving that this woman who had carried such a strong aura throughout her life should now be so still.

"You got attention just by walking into a room, Olive. But once people spoke with you, they didn't want to leave your side. I have yet to meet the person immune to your presence. But you never made yourself the centre of attention; your appeal came from your sincere interest in their lives. People fascinate you and they felt it."

"But those of us close to you treasure the storyteller you are. Your true self surfaces when you are amongst intimates. This has been a joy to all who have loved you, Olive."

Of course, Minnie knew all of the gossip about Olive. It bore no relation to the woman in front of her. As gossip always did, it came from the appearance of things rather than reality.

'Had they but known her' she thought, looking sadly on Olive's passive face. *'Her life had so much more substance than they could ever have imagined.'*

Her own relationship with Olive had been forged from the moment her father announced she had a baby sister. With just a teenage sister and older brothers to play with, at five years of age, she was overjoyed to learn that she now had a baby sister and took possession of the infant. The governess humoured her and, indeed, the entire family began to call her 'Little Mama', watching as she pushed Olive's pram around the property.

For Olive's first seven years, Minnie had been the central character in her life. The two girls had been inseparable. With no preamble from her thoughts to her words, Minnie asked "do you remember the day in the schoolroom that it had all changed, Olive"?

August 1871 olive 7 yrs old

Newcastle, Ontario

Chapter 3

The Wilmot boys; Charles, John, and George, stretched out lazily on the lawn after a rousing game of baseball with the children of the farm's hired hands. John jumped up to open the door for their sisters, Mary (Minnie to the family) and Olive, carrying trays of lemonade and biscuits. They all turned at the sound of a carriage coming up the drive.

"It's her" said Minnie, bitterly, setting her tray down. The return of Miss Campion, the governess, had been expected as August came to an end but Minnie was not happy about it. She envied Charles and John who would return to Trinity College School in Port Hope within days. She felt herself too old for the schoolroom and had argued fervently with her father, Samuel, over it.

At 12, Minnie didn't quite fit the Wilmot mould. They were an exceedingly handsome lot but Minnie's childhood had been consumed by the awareness that she stood out in her family for her unattractiveness. Although her siblings never remarked on her plain looks, she had once overheard her mother spell out to a friend that 'our Minnie is U-G-L-Y'. This had left an indelible imprint on Minnie's image of herself. It didn't help that her father sometimes affectionately referred to her as their 'ugly duckling'. In his mind, this meant he saw the beauty to come but hearing it just reinforced her mother's words in Minnie's mind.

No one could quite say why but, as a rule, the Wilmot children supported one another in an 'us against the world' manner. When discipline was to be handed down by their mother or father, they often all claimed responsibility, which ultimately meant that they all shared in the punishment. Strangely, this made them a tighter group.

So, although Minnie knew she looked different from her handsome siblings, she never felt separate from them. The long face she saw in the mirror each day might make her unhappy (she would eventually grow into it) and the severe overbite and crooked teeth cause her to be

self conscious in her smile but she was 'a Wilmot'. Who wouldn't be proud to be one of that group!

Perhaps to compensate for what she saw as a lack of looks, Minnie had been gifted with a keen intelligence and used this to her advantage. She was the peacemaker in the family; easing the boys back into the fold after they received harsh discipline for one of their many pranks. The boys created their fair share of mayhem both at home and at school. Minnie watched with admiration as, time after time, the boys' escapades caused anxiety to their mother and father. It's not that Minnie welcomed the wrath of their parents; she just admired her brothers' fearlessness. Well aware that girls were mostly valued for their looks, Minnie accepted that she would have to make her mark on the world in other ways. She did so by proving her strength and bravery, even though she was just a girl.

Minnie's argument with her father about the governess favoured the three younger siblings venturing to the local school in Newcastle, just as their cousins had done. She could imagine adventures on the mile-long walk to and from school and on the stormy nights that students had to sleep over.

"I'm well able to watch over Olive and George, Papa" she'd stated with confidence during their most recent discussion on the subject. "Our cousins did just fine at the school and I don't understand why we must stay in the house for our schooling."

"Well, my Dear" replied her father, "You must just trust that your mother and I have your best interests in mind when we make decisions. We think the private education you receive in our own schoolroom to be superior to lessons in the school."

Samuel was not angered by his daughter's persistence. He encouraged his children to have opinions and welcomed their thoughts on most topics. In this instance, though, he didn't really believe his own words. He had no sound reason for keeping the governess other than that his wife insisted and Minnie's defence of the local school wasn't strong enough to make him wish to disagree with her mother. Indeed, he enjoyed the younger children around the house.

Tillie had made it clear she couldn't be happier about the start of this school term and the return of this governess. With George now old enough to join the schoolroom on the third floor, this would be the first year that all of Samuel and Tillie's children would be in the

charge of teachers. Tillie looked forward to pursuing her own interests with all of them under the care of the governess. And her spirits lifted just by the thought of Belmont returning to a quiet and orderly home once the rowdy, older boys returned to school.

Her year ahead would be busy with the planning of her eldest daughter's wedding, set for the coming spring, and she was counting on Miss Campion this year to manage the younger children. She, herself, would be making trips into the city for Helen's trousseau; engagement teas and social visits and hosting Helen's fiancé's family when they visited from Toronto. This was to be their first wedding and Tillie was determined to make it the social event of the year.

Although Samuel and Tillie Wilmot had not known great success with governesses in the past, she had no reason to consider that Miss Campion wouldn't last throughout this year as she had the last.

It was true that until John's entry into the Port Hope academy the previous year, keeping a governess had proved challenging. Charles and John were too fond of pranks and even their father's stern discipline didn't curtail their behaviour. That Miss Campion was the first governess to return for a second year was encouraging to Tillie.

The children watched as their father helped Miss Campion down from the carriage and directed her into the house. As the door closed on their father and the governess, Minnie said impulsively "I can have this governess gone before the ice is on the creek". The sun shining down on them as she spoke was so hot that ice, other than in the blocks wrapped in straw in the ice house, seemed unimaginable.

Charles and John began to talk eagerly of Minnie's challenge. They contributed ideas of their own as to how the plan might be carried out. Young George and Olive listened wide-eyed as the three elder siblings so casually discussed the fate of this newest Governess.

The older boys were just a bit disappointed to be returning to their boarding school and missing out on the mischief to come. They recognized a plan of tomfoolery and regretted that their education was in the hands of the humourless headmasters of Trinity.

At five, George hadn't yet been exposed to the schoolroom and really had no idea what a governess was. But, like his older teenage brothers, he was a natural prankster and looked forward to having a fine bit of fun when he heard Minnie's plan. Besides, when his mother had explained that he would now be spending the day in the

schoolroom to begin learning, he wasn't overly smitten with her news. After a summer of catching frogs in the nearby creek; playing stickball, and following his older brothers around, the idea of spending hours inside left him pouty.

Olive was the only one to be concerned about the plan. She was a child of outstanding beauty with a gentle soul. To cause someone to lose their post was too much for her to consider and she said so.

"Oh, Olive; I've watched governesses come and go" said Minnie. "I can tell you that Miss Campion would simply move on to some other children in a neighbouring town, as so many others have before her."

Chapter 4

Young Olive worked on her sums on the slate before her when a commotion disturbed her concentration. Minnie had just loudly dropped her boot and Miss Campion appeared angry.

"Mary Wilmot. Put your boot back on and do not, for one moment, think that I will forget you do not know your sums" said the governess. "You may be able to distract your father with your little ploys but not I."

"But, Miss Campion" replied Minnie, "the boot fell off!"

'*Nice try, Minnie,*' thought Olive. But even Olive, at just 7, realized that a lace-up boot doesn't just fall off one's foot.

"Mary, do not lie. It is an unattractive trait in a young lady and shows a lack of morals. Tell the truth. You loosened your boot ..." prompted Miss Campion, through pursed lips. While Minnie and Olive loved to imitate that all too familiar face, Olive knew that, on this day, the look meant that things had gotten out of hand.

True to her word, as their days in the schoolroom began, Minnie wore Miss Campion down in subtle ways. The disruptions she created were never quite punishable offences but, rather, the type of annoyance that distracted the governess in her lessons. As the days went on under Miss Campion's tutelage, George rebelled against his confinement in the classroom and he soon joined in the fun, creating his own diversions.

This year, Miss Campion seemed no match for the inventive Wilmot children. Some nights, as she knelt by her bedside, she prayed with gratitude for young Olive's sweet demeanour and with fervent hope that she would have the patience needed to deal with the other two on the morrow.

She was unsure what had taken place from one year to the next but something had changed these children over the summer and she felt herself losing control. She regretted her return.

"I swear I'm telling the truth, Miss Campion" said Minnie. "The boot just fell off." Although unplanned, she was feeling herself lucky that the button of her boot had broken at the exact moment she gave her leg a good swing, taking her boot across the room.

"On your feet, Miss Mary." said Miss Campion. "It's time you and I had a chat with your father."

Minnie slowly laced her boot, minus the missing button; winked cheekily at Olive and George and followed the Governess as she flounced down the stairs to Samuel's study. Olive bent her head studiously, picked up her chalk and set to the sums Miss Campion had left on the board. George sat with a smirk on his face.

On Miss Campion's knock, Samuel bid them enter. He was dwelling on a thorny issue brought about by his position in the local government and was not upset by the disturbance.

"To what do I owe the pleasure of this midday visit, Miss Campion?" he asked kindly.

"Not a matter of pleasure at all, Mr. Wilmot" replied the Governess. "Your girl has disrupted our classroom for the last time. As I was attempting to teach George and Olive their arithmetic problems, Mary threw her boot at me."

"Is this true, Minnie?" Samuel asked, looking sceptically at his daughter. His doubts about Minnie's behaviour were second only to his thoughts of why the Governess would trouble him with one of those issues which should be under her control. Wasn't discipline in the schoolroom her domain?

"Oh, no, Papa." said Minnie. "The button on my boot broke off and my boot flew off when I was swinging my leg. It was an accident."

"My girl, you know that is not the truth." said a flabbergasted Miss Campion loudly. "You deliberately swung your foot to have your boot create a disturbance. It is no good to grow up with lies falling off your tongue. Tell your father the truth."

Unfortunately for Miss Campion, she did not understand the esteem in which Samuel held his children. Although he demanded respect and acceptable behaviour, Samuel believed his children to be exemplary citizens in every way. He was well aware that they were capable of hi-jinks but behaviour as reprehensible as lying? Never! In fact, he believed they all shared the same morals and values that he himself displayed; was he not their primary role model, after all? And, above all things, Samuel was a man of his word.

"Are you calling my daughter a liar, Miss Campion?" asked Samuel, his eyes narrowing as he looked at her.

Poor Miss Campion was so caught up in her belief of what was right that she failed to see the redness in Samuel's face. "Indeed I am,

Sir. And it's about time that this young girl was brought to task for the persistent disturbances she creates in the school room."

"Miss Campion, Wilmots do not lie" thundered Samuel. "Obviously, your influence around my children has not been beneficial to their development. Your time in this household is at an end. You may look for another post because you are no longer welcome at Belmont".

With that, he turned into his study, leaving a dumbstruck Miss Campion staring at his back.

Minnie fairly skipped up the stairs back to the schoolroom to share the news with her siblings. Despite her prediction, she couldn't quite believe that her little prank had really been the undoing of their governess. They no longer had to contend with the prim Miss Campion and her dull, dull, dull multiplication tables!

"Gee, I can't believe Papa took my side. He didn't march her out but she'll be gone tomorrow" she told Olive and George. Minnie was bursting with the sense that something remarkable had taken place. She had orchestrated life to get what she wanted. Now they would all go to the local school.

Minnie suddenly felt the weight of what had just occurred. With a touch of remorse, she said, "Miss Campion was no match, of course, knowing Papa as I do."

A lesson had been learned in the schoolroom of Belmont that day, although not an academic one. Minnie had shown that it is possible to direct the events of your own life.

Chapter 5

But Minnie was wrong. They would not be going to the town school.

By 1871, when the 'boot' incident took place, Samuel and Matilde (Tillie) Wilmot's marriage was on tenuous ground. What Minnie couldn't be aware of in her scheming was the strain losing yet another governess would put on her Mother.

Tillie had fulfilled the role of motherhood satisfactorily, giving birth to six children, but she was anything but maternal. Her expectations in marrying into the Wilmot family had been high; and her particular hope for life with Samuel Wilmot was to be the Grande Dame of Clarke township society.

Tillie's family was respectable enough; her brother, George, was a successful judge and close friend of John A. MacDonald.

The growth Cobourg experienced during her youth brought many industrialists and merchants and it was becoming the biggest city outside of Toronto and Kingston.

After 'coming out' at 16, she had been introduced to many sons of these titans of industry but none expressed interest in seeing her beyond the first meeting. Living with her brother, the Judge, without the guidance of a mother (who had died when she was still young), led Tillie to become an outspoken and opinionated young woman; one who followed politics and matters of the law rather than the latest fashions and hair styles.

Few men in the 1840s were accustomed to such behaviour in a woman. Since girls were generally not aware of much beyond the gossip of their communities, they learned at a young age to parrot the comments made by their male companions back to them, making the young men think the girl very agreeable. Hearing their thoughts repeated by someone else made their ideas seem even more interesting and many a young man's chest puffed up based on nothing more.

Tillie was different. She had an opinion on every topic and voiced it loudly, discomfiting the young lads she was introduced to. Many lacked confidence in the ways of courtship and were ill-equipped to respond to original thoughts from a mere girl. They preferred girls to hang on their every word; not dispute them, or worse, speak more original ones.

Although she told herself she had little interest in becoming part of a family of 'new money', as she thought of the young Cobourg men, by the time Tillie had reached 18 she was actually puzzled that no suitors had come forward. She believed herself to be attractive and intelligent but the young men she met didn't seem to appreciate this.

'More fools, them' she thought. 'I'll just wait for a mature man. No doubt an older man will appreciate my ideas and conversation.

Samuel Wilmot knew Tillie's brother well; their paths crossed often in the interests of local politics. It was during one visit to Judge Clarke's grand home, Strathmore, that Samuel was introduced to Tillie.

At 30 years of age, Samuel was more than ready to settle down with the right woman if he could just find her. He was driven in his various enterprises and wanted a wife who would support his ambition and interests; one who would talk to him on matters of substance.

Samuel was intrigued by the 18-year-old girl who behaved very differently from any young woman he knew. Tillie's confidence in herself and her opinions made her stand out. He enjoyed her intelligence and outspokenness and the wit she displayed in discussions with men much older than herself. In 1852, after a period of several months and many more visits to Cobourg, Samuel proposed marriage.

Love only rarely entered into the business of marriage in the 1800s and Tillie was certainly not some love-struck school girl. Despite Samuel's handsome looks and confident bearing, she had not found herself physically attracted to him.

She had hoped that when the right man came along he would cater to her, indulging her with thoughtful gifts and letting her know he recognized the beauty that she was. Samuel did none of these things.

But she knew that by accepting his proposal she would become a lady of position in the smaller community of Newcastle. His family's stature of long standing in the area and his father's position as Surveyor General and prominent land owner ensured her place in this society and beyond.

More to the point, she didn't see any other young men lining up at the door for the honour of her hand!

She was quick to accept Samuel's proposal, having no doubt that, with her help, Samuel would achieve even greater success than his father had.

Chapter 6

Samuel did indeed come from a substantial family.

The Wilmot clan had settled in New Haven, Connecticut after leaving their homeland in England in 1640. Their successes in the New World were many and they were well established by the time of the American Revolution, thanks in no small part to their loyalty to King George.

Unfortunately, this loyalty was their downfall when the colonies succeeded in their fight for independence. The Wilmots were treated as traitors; their property and businesses confiscated and their very lives threatened.

Known as United Empire Loyalists, all who had supported the crown, regardless of how long they had called the Colonies home, were soon forced to emigrate in search of a new home; one where their allegiances wouldn't brand them as traitors.

The Wilmots chose to begin life afresh in New Brunswick where the King and crown were still respected. As in Connecticut, they quickly achieved great success, establishing themselves in commerce, business and politics. The family's stately home, Belmont, reflected this status.

In 1796, their son Samuel Street (S.S.) decided to try his hand in another part of the Dominion, moving to Upper Canada. He trained as a surveyor and was successful under the watchful eye of the Surveyor General of the time, John Stegman. S.S. and Stegman's daughter, Marie, married in 1798.

It was while surveying Highway 2 in Newcastle that S.S. first laid eyes on the land which would eventually become his family's home. A stream, visibly filled with fish, ran through the scenic property and he could imagine a home on the rise affording a view for miles around. Knowing the land was on what would become the major highway between York and Kingston made it an especially advantageous location.

He purchased 400 acres around the spot he had discovered and in 1816 he and Marie moved their young family to Clarke Township.

In just a few years, S.S. built Belmont, modeled and named after the stately family home he left behind in New Brunswick. This large,

gracious home in Newcastle was known throughout the surrounding counties and as far away as York, Cobourg and Kingston.

S.S. continued surveying, often leaving his family for months at a time. Even with his intense surveying schedule, S.S. managed to build a substantial landholding and to hold local political office, thanks in no small part to his relationships with the government of the day. Although not part of the Family Compact; the group of men from influential families who controlled the government, S.S. recognized their influence and power. Just as his family's support of the King in Connecticut had ensured their prosperity (to a point), S.S. benefited in many ways by his arms length relationship with the Compact.

Over time, his land holdings grew to 2100 acres and housed many families who worked the land in exchange for their homes and a share in the crops and other farm bounty.

As S.S. and Marie advanced in years, they relied heavily on the only son remaining in their home; Samuel. It was he who eventually managed the farm operations, along with his retail ventures in the village of Newcastle and the political positions he held. Like his father before him, Samuel believed in loyalty; to his family; his employees; his village; and his country. He worked hard in doing what he thought was right.

It was to Belmont in 1852 that Samuel brought his new wife, Tillie. Since few couples spent time alone together before marriage, it was uncommon to know each other well. Samuel and Tillie did not and discovered the difference in their ages created a gap in common interests.

This was by no means the only divide between them. Samuel's initial attraction to Tillie's outspokenness soured soon after her arrival in his home as he discovered her opinions to be mostly self-serving rather than based on intellectual curiosity.

They lived at Belmont with Samuel's parents and Samuel had hopes that Tillie might be influenced by the love S.S. and Marie shared. He had witnessed this love throughout his childhood and was a thoughtful and caring man as a result. S.S. had relied heavily on Marie to manage the homestead during his many travels and his respect for her was evident to their children. Samuel's expectations for marriage were predicated on the example his parents had set; a union with respect, collaboration, and affection.

It didn't take Samuel long to realize his marriage would never embody these.

He was further taken aback when he realized Tillie had little respect for his parents; the two people he most esteemed. While he initially put her behaviour and attitude down to her youth, he soon recognized the selfish undertone in all of her relationships.

In truth, Tillie had no idea how normal relationships worked. Her brother, already a busy man when she was a little girl, had done little to foster friendships with other girls for her. While girls her age were giggling together and sharing intimacies, Tillie was alone with the collection of dolls and toys her brother showered on her, until reaching an age when she could respectfully take her place at his table.

She had been variously ignored and indulged by her brother (as it suited him); cared for by servants and had grown up knowing little of courtesy and respect. The lack of feminine influence in her life meant the finer notes of interaction with others had not been introduced to her. The only things Tillie understood were her own needs and whether they were or were not being met.

From the outset, Tillie was dissatisfied; with Samuel; his high principles; their life. He wondered why she had agreed to marry him but marry they had. As time went on, he began to see that it wasn't he himself who was the cause of her dissatisfaction; Tillie's nature was of the sort that tended toward unhappiness and she let everyone around her know it.

She assumed life would revolve around *her* wants and needs. Raising a large family made this nearly impossible, as much as Tillie tried to control things. Children were unpredictable and, in Samuel's mind, came first before their own needs. This broad difference in philosophy created further division between them.

On the death of his father in 1856, Samuel took over complete control of Belmont. These were busy years for him. Although he let his retail ventures go, he took on many roles in local government within Newcastle and beyond.

Who can know the truth within an intimate relationship other than the two individuals themselves? All that might be discerned is gained through their actions toward each other. Samuel accepted Tillie and their union as it was and gave her the respect due as the mother of their increasing family while giving her little thought as a

partner in life. With his attention and energies instead directed toward his children; his community and the farm, his success and reputation grew.

Just as Tillie had predicted, her presence in Samuel's life in time brought even greater success than his father before him had known.

June 1903

Newcastle, Ontario

Chapter 7

For those brief moments while caught up in memories, Minnie had almost forgotten her critically ill sister lying in the bed beside her. But awareness returned abruptly when Mrs. Thomson came to tell her the doctor from Toronto would be on the afternoon train and that her husband had arrived with her valise.

Minnie rose unsteadily from her chair, feeling vaguely adrift. She moved downstairs and into Duncan's arms as he stood looking uncertainly around him.

"What is it, Minnie?" he asked in a caring voice. "What has happened?"

"Oh, Duncan; Olive has had a massive stroke. The doctor said that if she wakes from it, she'll never be herself again. Henry has sent for another doctor from Toronto but I'm afraid."

Duncan shared his wife's alarm. Wrapping her in his arms, he said gently "I won't stay, Minnie. You are needed and there's precious little I can do to help. The girls and I will be home when you need us."

Seeing Duncan out the door but not really sure of what she should do, Minnie climbed the stairs to be with Olive again. Lindsell sat sewing quietly when Minnie entered.

"Any change, Lindsell?" Minnie asked.

The maid shook her head sadly. "While you were gone, I put rose water on her temples and rubbed her arms and legs with Ponds Extract. My mind tells me there is nothing to be done, but I want to believe I'm making her comfortable and perhaps easing some inflammation."

"I'm sure she is aware of your ministrations on some level, Lindsell. Why don't you go down to the kitchen for something to eat and then perhaps take a walk? It's important that we keep our strength up and minds clear to do our best for Olive."

With a nod, Lindsell left the bedroom, heading for the servant's staircase. Minnie pulled the comfortable chair closer to Olive's bed and took her sister's hand in her own.

"Goodness, Olive" she said, looking lovingly at her sister's face. "You have us all scared. But you've survived dreadful things in your life and I don't doubt this will just be another that we'll talk of in years to come. You rest now but I'm counting on your strength here to come back to us. Henry is beside himself, and Sayre. We all need you to come back to us."

Minnie stroked Olive's hand lightly as she looked around the room. Her eyes settled on the bookshelf and Olive's journals. They had developed the habit of journal writing at a young age and chronicled their lives to this day. Olive had gone to the expense of imprinting the year on the spine of each leather-bound notebook.

Picking up the oldest volume, Minnie opened to the first page and began to read. This wasn't an intrusion: Olive would never think Minnie's interest an intrusion. She and her sister had no secrets from each other. Indeed, they often seemed like two halves of a whole.

'You've sent me to this book for a reason, God' she thought, realizing the book she had in her hand was begun the year she had left home at 12, mirroring the very memories she had been reliving earlier.

Minnie's curiosity about the coincidence was soon forgotten as Olive's words and young handwriting grabbed her heart.

April 1872

Newcastle, Ontario

Chapter 8

Dearest Diary,

Today is my 8th birthday. This journal was Papa's gift.

I should be happy but am not. Mama and Papa argue a lot. Minnie says it's because our Governess has gone.

I overheard Mama talking to her friend about sending Minnie to school. Please, God, don't let that happen! I couldn't bear it if she is sent away.

I promise I will be extra good so Mama might not be so cross.

Yours, Olive

The loss of Miss Campion meant the three youngest children were underfoot and in their mother's care. This situation was a turning point in Tillie & Samuel's marriage. With the governess' departure, the arguments between them escalated to a level that even the children became concerned about.

One argument in particular rose above all: if they hoped to keep another governess, Tillie decided it was time for Minnie to go to boarding school. She was just too clever for her own good (or Tillie's). As angry as Samuel had been with the latest governess, his heart told him that Minnie had played a role in undermining Miss Campion and he regretfully agreed.

After consulting others within the family and her circle of friends for advice on an appropriate school for Minnie, it was decided that she would be sent to school in Quebec. Tillie justified her decision with the argument that adapting to a bilingual education would challenge the girl in ways a home education hadn't been able to and might actually settle her unruly behaviour.

Minnie was devastated when she heard their plan. It had never occurred to her that her mischief might result in this. Instead of going to the local school, her parents were sending her away alone. This banishment was a disaster!

The sisters were heartsick to be separated. As well as the bedroom they shared, they had an uncommon bond for sisters five years apart in age. Since her first steps, Olive had followed Minnie everywhere, her shadow in everything.

They were rarely seen apart from morning til night. They had followed the same routine since Olive was out of her crib. Saying goodnight to their parents, the pair climbed the staircase to the room they shared. Minnie helped Olive into her nightgown and brushed her sister's long hair the required 100 strokes. Before the two climbed into the bed they shared, they knelt beside it to say their prayers. Once comfortably settled in bed, Minnie read a story but Olive was rarely awake to hear Minnie say 'The End'.

Their parent's acrimony made Minnie instinctively protective toward her young sister. Olive, however, had no need of a protector. A strong will hid behind her gentle exterior. With a bored and disinterested mother, Olive learned as a toddler how to get her needs met and she could, when needed, be quietly and methodically tenacious in getting what she wanted.

But, other than her mother's attention, things came to Olive with little effort. Indeed, the common adage about attracting more flies with honey than vinegar could have been written for her.

Her gentle, sweet nature was very different from her rambunctious siblings. While they might get the attention so craved from their mother by temper tantrums and arguments, Olive went overlooked by Tillie. This indifference toward their soft-hearted young sister bothered the other Wilmot children greatly. It might be unspoken but they all wanted to make sure Olive's needs were taken care of.

No one in the family, from the gregarious older boys to lively young George, would ever do anything deliberately to hurt Olive. And, while their father would never say he had a favourite child, he doted on Olive in a way that told everyone she was his.

Only their mother seemed immune but Samuel's love was enough for Olive. He adored this beautiful girl. His affection for her was so strong that she had never felt neglected by the absence of her mother's love; her father and siblings more than made up for the lack.

To Tillie, Olive was just another in the brood she had to deal with. Children were not meant to take priority. They were simply produced and allowed to get on with life, hopefully disrupting her own

as little as possible. But, although she wouldn't admit it even to herself, Tillie was jealous of the attention Samuel gave Olive; attention *she* deserved as his wife. It was this jealousy that Minnie had witnessed and which, even at her young age, had placed her in the role of Olive's little mother.

Chapter 9

Olive missed her sister dreadfully but life at Belmont settled into relative calm following Minnie's departure. Another governess had been hired and, with just Olive and George in the schoolroom, there were no serious incidents.

With the house under control again, Tillie sought amusing diversions outside of their home. She and Samuel maintained civility but, for the most part, pursued their own interests. For Tillie, an ever-widening social circle meant visits to people, often in surrounding towns; sometimes taking her as far as Toronto for visits lasting a week at a time. Samuel was relieved whenever she travelled, finding the atmosphere of the household much more to his liking. Besides, his thoughts were increasingly on an exciting new venture.

An inventive man who cared much for the environment, Samuel had witnessed a decline in the fish population in the rivers and creeks around his home. Belmont's foundation was built over a natural spring and he decided to use this to propagate fish eggs in the basement.

After some missteps he was successful. The Dominion of Canada took notice of his project, sponsoring a greater investment which led to the harvesting of greater numbers of fish. This work led to responsible roles in the government for Samuel.

Just as he enjoyed the house when Tillie was away, she looked forward to the more frequent and lengthier trips to Ottawa that this new venture brought. She found his absences convenient because she had become involved in an affair.

The reasons married partners begin affairs are many but some justify their actions by whatever is lacking in their marriage. Tillie felt she lacked attention and affection from Samuel and was flattered by the first man who gave her both.

Her affair began innocently, as they usually do. She enjoyed the attention he paid to her. Closer in age to her than Samuel, she found they had much in common. Opportunity meant that attention was soon joined by affection.

Tillie gave no thought to Samuel or the children. The excitement of the affair filled her every waking moment, leaving no time for remorse. Tillie, as a rule, rarely felt guilt over her behaviour anyway.

They saw each other sporadically, around Samuel's visits to Ottawa, but the year 1873 brought new opportunity for the lovers.

The Government was sending Samuel to Paris to coordinate the Dominion's participation in a fisheries exhibition. Organizing the exhibition meant extended time in Ottawa for meetings with politicians and bureaucrats beforehand as well. Samuel was exhilarated by his new enterprise.

While Samuel flourished, Tillie relieved the boredom of her life with her lover. Samuel's lengthy absence gave them unrestricted time together. With no one to answer to, she became more emboldened, even visiting his home, although taking many precautions not to be seen.

But spending so much time with her lover soon led Tillie to be bored by him. Frequent access took away the thrill of the relationship. By the time Samuel was on the return ship from Paris, she had ended the affair, although not without consequences.

Tillie was taken aback by the warmth in Samuel's attitude when he returned. Whether from his prolonged absence or the success and accolades he had experienced at the exhibition, he felt tenderness toward his wife again.

The evening following his return, Samuel surprised Tillie by joining her in the parlour after dinner. While they shared a family and home together, they were not a couple who made a habit of seeking out each other's exclusive company, he preferring his study most evenings. But he knew how excited she was by news of the larger world and he wanted to share his memories of the people he had met in Paris and his experiences at the Exhibition.

When Samuel paused in his discourse, Tillie glanced up from her needlework and said quietly, "Samuel, I have news as well. While you were away, I realized I am with child again."

Seymour

Samuel's heart skipped a beat. He felt joy at the news of another child. He went to Tillie's side, taking her hand tenderly in his own. "I would never have imagined such news at my ripe old age, my Dear. When shall we expect our newest offspring?"

But Tillie's answer left Samuel feeling anything but tender.

Many men might be naïve about women's bodies and creation itself but Samuel well knew the gestation period for babies. He also knew his schedule prior to leaving for France and when he and Tillie

had last been intimate. Even if she was off slightly with her calculations the timing of this birth could only mean one thing; he was not the father of this child!

Samuel had been suspicious about a possible affair for some time but had chosen to think better of Tillie. This news made that denial impossible. He felt no relief that his suspicions were confirmed.

A slow anger rose in his chest just as a dawning understanding came over him; he had no reason to maintain the façade that had been their marriage almost from the beginning.

His wife no longer held any control over him. He had lived as a gentleman throughout their marriage, behaving as he believed all husbands should. Her selfishness had irritated him but he had never treated her with anything other than the respect he felt a wife was owed. At worst, he had become a disinterested spouse but always remembered that they were married in the eyes of God and she deserved his esteem if only for that reason.

In an instant, his mind made a decision; he would keep up the pretence of their marriage until the birth but confront her as soon as she delivered.

These thoughts gelled as he continued to hold Tillie's hand; the only clue to his inner emotion a slight pressure he exerted on it.

Samuel managed to collect himself before leaving Tillie's side. Being careful not to look at her, he said "I will move into another bedroom, Tillie. This will help you to be more comfortable". In truth, he could no longer bear to be physically close to her.

Tillie almost purred with satisfaction. She felt reassured and emboldened by his calm reaction. '*Like most men*,' she thought; '*he hasn't put things together.*'

Since discovering her news, Tillie's world had been dark at the thought of telling Samuel. She felt no guilt at deceiving him – it was, after all, what all women did on finding themselves in this situation.

No, Tillie just had a healthy fear of being found out; the timing of the conception was questionable if Samuel took the time to think about it.

But, clearly, he had not! She had done it! She was free and clear. Nothing would change in her life. Tillie congratulated herself and felt invincible. The affair had ended, after all, and the father would make

no demands even had he been aware of the pregnancy. This infant would be another of Samuel's children.

The heaviness she had felt over the prospect of giving him the news was gone and she was quickly focusing once again on her own needs and the impact this pregnancy was having on her.

His absence in their bed bothered her not at all. It wasn't as though she looked for comfort from him when they did sleep together. She had endured his physical needs throughout their years together but now had several months ahead without that bother.

If Tillie noticed an emotional distance in Samuel during the ensuing months before the baby's birth, she didn't mention it. Her complaints were all about what this child was doing to her body and health.

Nonetheless, the birth went surprisingly easy. Within a day of her first labour pain, Tillie sat upright in bed in a fresh nightgown, newborn Seymour sleeping quietly in a cot in the nursery alcove of their bedroom.

After discreetly knocking, Samuel entered the bedroom and congratulated Tillie on the birth but offered no interest in the child or affection toward his wife.

The surprise she felt by his coolness was swiftly replaced by shock as she listened to Samuel's next words.

"I am under no illusion that this child is mine, Tillie" he said. "In the interests of my reputation, I will honour his place in this family and support him as I have our own children but his birth has forever changed your situation in this family. From this day forward, you and I are no longer married in my eyes."

"The boy will need you for his early years but once he turns three," continued Samuel, "I expect you to spend more time out of this house than in; returning only when I need you to fulfill your role as my wife or during my absences in Ottawa when the children need you."

"Whatever living arrangement you choose" said Samuel grimly, "I expect will keep our reputations intact. I will, of course, maintain an allowance for you in your new situation on the condition that you fulfill your duties when needed. I will leave the details of where you go up to you, other than to say, if you ever make any attempt to openly meet or live with the father, any funding I provide you will stop immediately."

"You have made a cuckold out of me in my own eyes, Tillie" said Samuel, shaking his head. "I'll be damned if I let you do so in front of the community."

Tillie sat in stunned silence as Samuel continued with his stipulations. "Seymour will remain in this house, growing as a Wilmot with his half siblings and will never be aware of his illegitimate status. This is an absolute, Tillie. Word of his parentage will never escape your lips."

The detail Samuel laid out to Tillie over what was to become their new arrangement was necessary; while divorce may have provided a more permanent result, it was not an option. Formal public separation and divorces were rare and complicated but, even had they been accepted, Samuel would not allow Tillie's actions to tarnish his reputation or that of his children. His strong faith would never allow one anyway. He was married for life.

Over the next three years, other than when Samuel was in Ottawa, Tillie spent an increasing amount of time visiting away from home. When their paths did cross at home, Tillie felt an outsider; aware that Samuel had stronger relationships with his children than he had ever had with her.

With his mother so often absent, Seymour relied on his nursemaid for all of his needs. It mattered little to him when, on his third birthday, Tillie announced that she would be moving in with her elderly uncle, on the pretence of caring for her relative. As specified, she was invited back to Belmont only when needed by Samuel for appearances or when he was away in Ottawa.

Olive and George were aware that something had shifted in the household after Seymour's birth; they certainly knew their mother was around less, especially when their father was home. But, in reality, Tillie's attitude toward her children hadn't changed so, although her lengthy absences were noticed, they were rarely remarked on. As ever, the children relied on their father, the servants and each other for both affection and structure.

In fact, the children preferred the atmosphere this development brought. Without Tillie's constant census, they were free to be children, with all of the noise and confusion that brings to a household.

As the last daughter at home, Olive should have been under stricter rules but, even during times when Tillie was present in the house, she had little to do with the children. Guiding her young daughter as she developed into a young woman held no interest to Tillie.

In point of fact, Tillie had no idea how to be such a role model, having lost her own mother at a young age. Her eldest daughter, Helen, had grown into adulthood with no advice or concern from her mother and Minnie was away at school during the years she most needed a mother's guiding hand. Now, with Olive's 12th birthday approaching, Samuel was concerned for her.

June 1903

Newcastle, Ontario

Chapter 10

The journal fell from Minnie's hands as her head nodded with sleep. Hearing the book land on the carpet woke her and, for a brief moment, she was unsure where she was.

The sound of Olive's faint breaths brought her quickly to reality.

'If I could, I would breathe life into you' thought Minnie with tears in her eyes. She looked up as Lindsell returned. Minnie returned the journal to the shelf and took the next volume out.

"The doctor's train is just getting in, Lindsell. Let's hope he has some alternative views on her condition. My valise is here so I'll take this time to go sort myself out. If you need me, I'll just be next door."

Hanging her dresses in the wardrobe and putting her toiletries on the dresser felt strange. As often as Minnie visited Chestayne, she had never stayed the night. Belmont was a short mile ride away and the sisters ventured back and forth throughout Olive's stays each summer. They also both saw a great deal of their eldest sister, Helen, who preferred her home around the corner from Chestayne to her family home in Toronto.

It was just as well that Helen was at her home in Toronto this month, thought Minnie. She might be the eldest in the family, but her addiction to laudanum, introduced at the time of the birth of her youngest daughter, had left her unequal to many tasks. Her dependence had become so strong that she rarely left Newcastle, where a local doctor kept her supplied with the drug. No, Helen would be of no help in this situation.

But it had been a much younger Helen who encouraged Samuel to send Olive to school in the city when she turned 12, reassuring her father that she would have eyes on Olive from her home in Toronto and all would be well.

1876

Newcastle, Ontario

Chapter 11

Dear Diary,

Papa says I must be strong. Twelve is almost grown up and Papa tells me it requires 'Maturity of Thought and Emotion' but just the idea of going away to school makes me want to cry. And just as Minnie is returning home permanently! It's so unfair! I tremble to think of life away from here.

It will fall to Minnie to see to George and Seymour but I will miss their mischief more than I can say. I'm also going to miss all of my duties around the house.

I never thought I would be sent away as Minnie was. I remember Miss Campion well and understood that Minnie brought her banishment on herself but what have I done? I can think of no reason for Papa to want to send me away, too.

God, keep me humble and accepting of this new change in my life.

Your loving Olive

Samuel was appointed Superintendent of Fish Culture in 1876 and his increasing responsibilities meant that more of his time would be spent in Ottawa than Newcastle. Even with the governess and household staff, he believed his absence was not a good thing for Olive. As her 12th birthday approached, he was forced to consider that boarding school was the only option, just as it had been for Minnie five years previously.

In truth, Samuel was concerned about Olive's fate with the lack of female supervision. His servants were wonderful and considered part of the family but it wasn't their role to guide Olive in the ways of women.

If Olive were to develop into an accomplished young woman she would need the counsel of wise, older women in her life and the experiences school would give her. As sad as it made him to see her go, he knew Olive would be the better for it.

The one criteria Samuel had for a school for Olive was that it be closer to home than Minnie's. Away in Quebec, Minnie had been home

for Christmas and summer breaks only. Tillie had made the decision of Minnie's school but he wouldn't make the same mistake with Olive. He would ensure she would remain as close as possible.

He selected Bishop Strachan; a Toronto academy for young girls, opened in Toronto in 1867 by the Anglican Church. Samuel's status within the church community was prominent; he had been instrumental in the building of St. George's Anglican Church in Newcastle in 1857 and the land that St. George's Cemetery sat on had been donated by his father.

The teachers at Bishop Strachan educated girls to be leaders. The female administration believed, extraordinarily, that women were valuable citizens. This was a school of order and regime, while at the same time led by enlightened women.

As Olive entered school in September 1876, a new Lady Principal was taking control; one who took a broad outlook over women's activities; rightful aims and highest life. The influence of such women, at a time when education and the battle for the rights of women in general was in its infancy, can well be imagined.

Helen, now a seasoned married woman of 23, reassured Samuel that she would watch over Olive while she boarded in the city. Her home was a reasonable walk from the school and Helen looked forward to seeing her young sister often.

Olive would be a short train trip away from home and, although she also returned home just for holidays and the summer, whenever he wasn't in Ottawa, Samuel knew he would make frequent trips into the city. He would be able to take Olive and her friends out for tea and to the theatre or an afternoon of horse racing enjoyed from his box at Woodbine Race Course.

Chapter 12

Olive enjoyed the rhythm of school life. She excelled in the intellectual atmosphere and was a ready player for any theatrics. She was popular with the other girls for her humour and comic mimicry of the instructors which made even the most homesick classmates laugh.

Still, as June arrived that year, Olive was overjoyed to return home. Her reunion with Minnie, now a sedate girl of 18, was joyous. The summer months flew by as the Wilmot children, and whoever might be visiting, enjoyed picnics at the lake, tea parties on the lawn and scavenger hunts. Even rainy days were welcome; favourite stories would be acted out for the enjoyment of one and all. Evenings were spent in parlour games and reading stories aloud to one another.

The girls shared their old room together. As Olive brushed Minnie's hair at night, she would replay funny situations with her school chums or teachers, mimicking them in character, and Minnie would laugh delightedly.

After a wondrous summer, Olive found the idea of returning to school more difficult with Minnie now a fixture at home.

She begged her father to let her remain home but he was resolute. Minnie was not equipped to give Olive the guidance she needed and the teachers at Bishop Strachan had much to offer her still.

In truth, he had enjoyed the summer as much as the children and was sad to see his girl go but he was needed back in Ottawa.

The years passed in the usual cycle for boarding students. By the age of 15, Olive was not easily overlooked. Her beauty stood out amongst other girls and the charm of her youth made her popular with all men. Because of the easy affection between Olive and Samuel and her brothers, she was comfortable around men; able to discuss current events of the day as well as issues of their livelihoods.

Like most girls her age, she adored lace and bows but, when home, could be seen as often in her sturdy muslin dresses, covered with a work apron. A large straw hat plunked on her head kept her long, thick strawberry blonde hair and complexion protected from the sun. In this way, she would wander to the barns to deliver messages to her father, staying to watch a birthing cow or the many piglets suckling on a fat sow. While Samuel liked a lady to be a lady, he did not see any

reason to protect his children from the natural ebb and flow of life and nature and Olive had never been a squeamish sort.

While men certainly enjoyed Olive's company and conversation, women were also drawn to her. She could be counted on to remember babies born; children's illnesses; the visits of relatives and friends and all of the minutiae of a woman's life. She did not, however, engage in the common gossip that women frequently shared about each other. Olive would excuse herself when conversation turned to gossip. She had wisdom for someone so young; understanding that what is said about a person is often not what is true about a person.

Olive's gift was that she actually listened during conversation, truly engaged in whatever the other was saying. In this way, she was able to remember the little details that people shared with her. Since there is nothing more flattering in life than to have another really listen to what we have to say, to find Olive next to you at the dinner table, even at her young age, was a pleasure.

Her ability to connect on any topic was due to her natural curiosity and the freedom in childhood to speak out. Unlike most parents of his time, Samuel endorsed free speech for his children and encouraged their involvement in adult discussions from an early age. This led to spirited discussions between he and the children. He believed they needed to be challenged intellectually and socially to become valued citizens in adulthood.

Unusually, the Wilmot children, once beyond their nursery years, ate with their parents in the dining room rather than the nursery. Samuel engaged the elder children in conversation, asking their thoughts on current or historical events. They had to be prepared to explain their opinions and back up what they said. To the younger children, he shared his own personal wisdom on topics, helping them think critically. They grew up understanding that their thoughts and ideas were of value.

Samuel still insisted on respect and traditional rules of decorum in these discussions; no shouting or interrupting was allowed. Surprisingly, since she herself had known similar freedom to speak in her brother's house, Tillie never condoned these dinner table debates. She felt it idiotic to solicit the opinions of children and, when in residence, kept much to herself over dinner.

But Tillie's likes or dislikes were no longer relevant. With family or neighbours, it was Minnie and Olive, when home, who shared the duties of hostess of Belmont. Minnie was a strong organizer and Olive created warmth and fun for every guest who entered. Together, they looked forward to the parties Samuel hosted. And there were many.

His many interests meant that Belmont hosted frequent guests from across Canada; usually to learn of his activities with the fish hatchery and the newly established fish museum on their property. His increasingly wide network in Ottawa brought politicians as well. They used Belmont as a stopping off point on their journey to or from Ottawa along the Kingston Road route.

For appearances sake with these visitors, Tillie was called home to act as hostess. She could be counted on to shine for important out of town guests who brought the outside world to Newcastle.

Despite Tillie's withdrawal from the duties of the home and family, Samuel continued to host the regular social events each season inspired. He loved nothing more than to share the gifts they all enjoyed from the land. The annual harvest ball for all of the families who earned a living on his farm was a particular favourite of Samuel's, although Tillie had always just tolerated the need to act as hostess to 'hired help'. With each passing year, the girls took on more of the responsibilities of organizing the end of summer event.

The full moon of winter solstice in 1880 brought one of Olive's favourite events of the year.

Friends and neighbours from far and wide came to Belmont for a light supper followed by indoor entertainment for the adults and moonlight sleigh rides for the young. While the parents enjoyed social time in the parlour, the young whisked their way around the countryside in the bright glow of the moon; stopping on a hilltop for hot cider and cake before returning to Belmont for charades and other parlour games.

Mothers played a critical role in the life of young girls in their courting years. It was a mother's task to ensure her daughter's reputation was impeccable. The young could be impulsive, not understanding the impact a moment's careless behaviour might have.

Donning their shawls and gloves to supervise the loading of each sleigh; a mother, sensing her girl's reputation may be cast in shadow by the seating arrangements, was quick to place a third in the sleigh.

Older cousins or unmarried spinsters would be called on to accompany the young people.

Reputations were highly guarded throughout a girl's teen years and early twenties but, once a certain age was reached and a woman remained unmarried, she was considered a 'safe' companion to younger girls.

Samuel had concerns for Olive, home from school for the Christmas break. She had blossomed since he had visited her last.

Samuel felt unequal to the responsibilities Tillie should have borne and was grateful that his older niece, Kate, was visiting from Cobourg.

"Kate, would you mind stepping outside to ensure nothing untoward is happening with Olive. I wouldn't want some young pup to take advantage of Tillie's absence."

Kate was more than happy to but decided a conversation with her uncle was needed to learn what plans he had for Olive as she turned 16. Kate was well aware that young men would be flocking to her like moths to a flame and she felt that someone should be taking control since, clearly, her Aunt Tillie was not.

Samuel was unconcerned about Minnie. Even though just 20, with no courtship on the horizon and still unattractively plain, she'd already been labelled a spinster. This point was driven home when a mother came in to call her out to take a seat in one of the carriages. Minnie was not happy.

Samuel was not naïve and admitted to Kate, when she approached him later on the subject, that he felt out of his element. Young as Olive was, Samuel knew that marriage was inevitable for his girl and he had better take control of things or be blindsided by some unsuitable courtship.

He and Kate decided they would make plans for the coming summer for Olive to have an unspoken 'coming out'. After the summer season in Newcastle, Olive would be invited to Cobourg where Kate would plan suitable social events with a watchful eye. In this way, they could control the men she was introduced to. Kate promised her uncle that, in the intervening months, she would think about who these men might be.

June 1903
Newcastle, Ontario

Chapter 13

Mrs. Thomson knocked on Minnie's door to say the Toronto doctor was with Olive. Minnie thanked the woman and hurried next door to Olive's room, surprised that she hadn't heard his arrival.

A man of middle years and average height stood over Olive moving a stethoscope around her chest. Minnie, watching as the man carried out his examination, took comfort from his appearance of competence. He brought other instruments from his bag and opened Olive's eyes to look deeply into them. Finally, he lifted each of Olive's limbs and noted as they dropped back onto the bed lifelessly.

The doctor turned toward Minnie. She introduced herself as Olive's sister.

"Is Mrs. Sanford's husband here?" he asked.

"Yes, he is ill and is in his room down the hall" she replied.

"I suggest we go there and speak with him" said the doctor kindly.

With dread in her heart, they left the nurse with Olive and moved down the hall to knock quietly on Henry's door.

"Come in" said Henry in a feeble voice.

"This is Dr. Andrews, Henry" said Minnie as they entered his room. "Dr. Andrews, Mr. Sanford, my sister's husband."

"I wish I could give you other news, Mr. Sanford" said the doctor. "Your wife has suffered an apoplectic episode; specifically a hemorrhagic stroke. This happens when an artery in the brain breaks open. My prognosis is that she will not recover; it surprises me that her death was not immediate but I do not imagine her lingering much longer. Blood is accumulating in her brain.

Henry said hopefully "I have heard of advances in surgical techniques for strokes, Dr. Andrews. Can she be moved to a hospital for surgery? Money is not a factor."

The doctor shook his head sombrely. "I'm afraid that, even were we to have a doctor capable of this surgery in Toronto and she were to survive the journey, surgery is out of the question. Her brain cells have been irreparably damaged at this point. You are not to be fooled

into thinking she will awaken from her unconscious state; life is no longer viable for her. I am sorry to be the one to bring you this news."

"I am, too, Dr." replied Henry. "I would ask that, as long as Olive remains alive, you come out to Newcastle each day to check on her."

"I can certainly do that, Mr. Sanford, although the train trip will be pointless since there is nothing I or anyone can do for her. The nurse you have here will monitor her and do what is necessary for her. There is really nothing to be done to even make her comfortable at this point. She is completely unaware. I want to emphasize that she will not regain consciousness. It is merely a matter of time before her organs shut down, if they haven't already."

"Regardless, Doctor" said Henry, "I understand you are the best in your field and I want Olive to be seen daily by the best doctor available. I realize the time this will take from your Toronto practice is inconvenient and will of course make it worth your while."

Minnie led the doctor out of Henry's room and back downstairs to the parlour where Mrs. Thomson had laid out tea. The evening train to Toronto was in an hour's time.

After directing the doctor to the powder room to refresh himself, Minnie poured tea and filled a plate with sandwiches and cake for the doctor. He looked with pleasure on the refreshments when he returned to the room. The trip to Newcastle meant he had missed his usual luncheon and dinner was still hours away.

Minnie busied herself pouring her own tea but did not touch the food she had put on her plate. She had been aware of the seriousness of Olive's condition but had still held out hope that she might awaken. The doctor's words had removed all hope.

Minnie was grateful when the doctor talked of arrangements for his planned daily return to Chestayne and she promised to take care of what she could at her end and to telephone him should anything happen in the meantime.

"Thank you, Dr. Andrews" she said as they walked to the front door. "We are all grateful that you have taken the time to come out and will continue to oversee Olive's care." She remained at the door, watching sadly as the car pulled away from the house.

Sitting in the handsome car, the doctor had no qualms about dedicating some time away from his practice for what he knew would be a lucrative payment. The Sanford house was modest by some

standards but Henry's wealth was evident in the staff they maintained and the fact that Henry had an automobile. The doctor had admired the 1903 Pierce Motorette when it picked him up at the train station.

'It won't be for many days, at any rate' thought the doctor as the car pulled up to the train station.

Minnie went in search of Mrs. Thomson to advise the woman of the doctor's daily visits and the need for the driver to meet his train each day.

"I'll take supper in my room Mrs. Thomson and I expect Mr. Van Duzer will do the same" she said, knowing that none in the house was up to small talk. She felt a need to be alone to absorb the finality of the doctor's words and feel her emotions in privacy.

Always the anchor in the family; the peacemaker and the connector, Minnie regretted her position now knowing it meant breaking the news to everyone. This included Sayre. She stepped into his room on his reply to her knock and saw a deeply pained man before her.

"Sayre, it's the worst news" she said, trying to keep her words even. "Olive has suffered a brain haemorrhage and will not recover. It's just a matter of time the doctor said."

An involuntary cry escaped Sayre's lips before he pulled himself together.

"I'll return to New York on the early train tomorrow. Henry has asked me to organize the funeral and I will need her will in my office safe. Of course, I will return immediately when something changes."

'W*hen she dies'* hung silently in the air between them.

Minnie made no protest. There really was nothing Sayre could do and he was just another body to be accounted for in the house.

Carrying on to Olive's room, she watched as the nurse pulled the blanket tightly over Olive's lifeless body, took her pulse and recorded it on a chart the doctor had left. The nurse excused herself to go see to Henry, leaving Minnie alone.

Tears streamed down Minnie's face as she looked lovingly at her sister. Lifting Olive's hand to her cheek, she murmured "I am so sorry, dearest. How can this be happening? I just cannot believe we will never speak together again. Oh, if only Dr. Andrews were wrong."

Her glance fell on another journal; this one from 1880.

"I haven't thought of that dark period of your life in so many years but those horrid memories will always be with me. I know I promised we would never speak of them again but I don't know what to do with the anger I'm feeling. When I think of his vileness, it makes me even angrier that you survived it only to end like this."

"I envied your strength to put those ugly years behind you. As much as I vowed to do the same, I continue to carry a seed of regret deep within me over the part I played in the whole sordid business."

"You were quick to tell me that you never assigned blame to me for my part in the marriage but I knew I should have done more to persuade you from it. God knows, my instincts were all screaming at me to do so. Instead I let your passion lead and offered only a feeble attempt to stop the marriage."

The years fell away as Minnie remembered Olive's first husband; his extraordinary handsome looks and charm that had caught Olive so tightly in his grasp. But Minnie knew it was not just Olive who had been blinded by the devil who had become her husband; she, too, had been naïve enough to see only the romance he presented. *'If only we had paid heed to Papa's warnings'* she thought.

1880

Toronto Ontario

Chapter 14

Dear Diary,

Can it really be my 16th birthday? I've waited so long to become the young lady Papa says I now am. I do hope he sends a little money with my birthday note so I can buy that charming hat I saw in Eaton's Department Store window. I can imagine all manner of outings when I will wear it so he couldn't say it would be a frivolous purchase.

Just two more months and I will be home again. Papa has promised he will be home for most of the summer this year and says we'll have loads of parties. I intend to press him to allow me to stay home now. What more could I learn by remaining here another year?

God, please keep my family well and bring me success with my exams. I promise to study so you needn't fear I am just looking for easy results.

Your loving Olive

Olive returned to school for the spring term in 1880, unaware that her fate was under consideration. Her 16th birthday in April was as any other with small, token gifts from her school friends and well wishes from her teachers. Congratulatory notes arrived from her mother and father (with the hoped for money) and siblings. Her concerns as she turned 16 were simple ones; not in the least about possible courtship.

The years at school in Toronto had given Olive the confidence to make decisions and to set her own path. The instructors had prepared the girls to take their places in the world; encouraging independent spirits and schooling them in the refinement well to do young women needed.

While decorum wouldn't allow Olive to set out alone on any excursion, she was the first to suggest adventures in the city, accompanied by appropriate chaperones. The city of Toronto was blossoming and she was eager to take advantage of every opportunity.

Her preoccupation with social life was not the only distraction from school work. Olive's dormitory room was scarcely a space

conducive to study, filled as it generally was with the chit chat of other girls. Discussions of philosophy or current events were a mainstay, with the girls enjoying the freedom to share their opinions with classmates. Like Samuel, their teachers encouraged this debate, recognizing that they were preparing a generation of young ladies to think for themselves instead of automatically adopting their husband's or father's ideas and beliefs, as their mothers before them had.

When Olive returned home, Samuel hosted several events to gauge her interest in the young men of the community. Although there were a few he considered suitable, by the end of July, he knew it wouldn't be a local boy who would capture her heart.

"Olive shows no interest in the lads around Newcastle," Samuel said to Kate during a visit that month. "Have you given thought to some of the successful young men in Cobourg she might be introduced to?" Kate was quick to respond. "My husband and I have discussed this and we have several in mind. As soon as I return home, I'll send the invitations out. I'll ask Olive to visit for the last two weeks of August, shall I?"

And so it was that on a warm August evening Olive was enjoying an interesting discussion at the home of her cousin. She was more than happy to spend time with one of her favourite cousins. Kate had acquired a degree of local fame when, as a new bride, she had danced with the young Prince of Wales at a ball held during his visit to Cobourg in 1860. Twenty years later, she was still viewed as a minor local celebrity.

Olive and Kate's other guests, had returned to the grand home for a late supper after enjoying an operatic production at Cobourg's Town Hall. Olive was chatting with a lawyer and his wife and a Cobourg businessman when her eyes chanced to fall on her cousin Kate across the room.

But it was the man at Kate's side who held her attention. The look of him quite literally took her breath away.

'*Oh, what a handsome man*' she thought, acknowledging just how inadequate the word was. She lowered her eyelids, not wanting her observation to be noticed, but strangely powerless to shift her gaze from him.

The man was statuesque, taller than many, and held himself in an elegant stance. His auburn hair was in the longish style of the time to

the level of his chin, falling from the centre part in soft waves that framed his face. *'I would so love to tuck that hair behind his ear'* she thought, surprised by the notion. The physical reaction she experienced was unfamiliar to her; a warmth spread through her body as her eyes travelled over his figure.

Unlike many young men of his time, his face was clean shaven save for the carefully shaped sideburns. The strong, square jaw line anchored his face. His thin, straight nose and prominent cheekbones reminded Olive of the statues she had seen in art history books at school. His eyebrows were thick and well defined and his eyes deep set. The overall effect was truly of a sculpted face.

The superbly tailored clothes he wore set him apart from the other men in the room. Olive could tell from a distance that the wool of his jacket was very fine. His trousers, cut in the newest, narrow fashion, outlined his long legs and well-developed thighs. Olive struggled to bring her attention back to her group.

The object of her observations, Harry Romaine Winans, was unaware of the young girl's attention and continued to discuss the opera they had just seen with his hostess.

It was Kate who drew his attention to Olive across the room. "What do you think of my young cousin, Mr. Winans?" Kate asked. "Isn't she the brightest thing in the room tonight?" Following Kate's nod, Harry turned and noticed Olive for the first time.

Kate had included young Winans in the evening on the advice of her husband. He had known Winan's father, Ted; a co-owner of a woollen mill in Cobourg some years prior and the pair remained in touch even though the family had since moved to Toronto. Kate's husband considered Ted Winans a fine fellow and had heard of the success of his sons with their own firm. He had received a letter from Ted Winans just recently which put Harry in his mind for Olive. Kate agreed and included him in the guest list.

Living with his parents and maternal grandmother in the old City Hall district of Toronto afforded Harry the freedom to come and go as he wished. His father had retired and Harry worked with his elder brother, Edward Culver (Ed), at E. C. Winans & Co., wool dealers and commission merchants on Front Street in the city.

Like his brothers, Harry had been educated at Trinity College School but his attention had always been directed toward the sporting

and gaming opportunities school provided rather than academics. In fact, he spent his youth taking part in every sport he could and was successful in most. He was feted for being a crackerjack athlete, rarely called on for anything resembling academic interest or responsibility in the family.

While the family had lived in Cobourg, Harry's elder brothers Theodore and Ed worked alongside their father in the family business concerns. Another brother, Stuart, had made a promising start in the business as a clerk.

Ted was more than pleased to have three of his sons apprenticing in his business interests and felt free to indulge Harry in his love of sport. There was plenty of time for him to develop in business.

But in 1870, when Harry was 16, the death of his brother, Stuart, of typhoid fever changed the course of the family business and the family dynamics. Harry's father was brought so low by the loss of his son that he sold his interests in the woollen mills in Cobourg and Newcastle and moved the family to Toronto, seemingly retiring from industry and life.

Theodore, married and with a family of his own, chose to remain in Cobourg and found a position with another employer. In Toronto, sponsored by his father, Ed opened his own business and carried on the family tradition in the wool industry using knowledge learned while working with his father.

As time marched on and Harry reached the age of majority, his father realized he was ill-prepared for any occupation. When Ted tried to discuss this with Harry, he was dismayed by the boy's lack of ambition. Oh, Harry searched about, without too much enthusiasm. But Ted knew his son had little head for business. There were few options other than to convince his son Ed to have his younger brother join him at E.C. Winans.

Harry's easy triumphs in sports had fuelled his unparalleled self-assurance. He had entered the workforce with every expectation that he would do well with little effort and he had, indeed, achieved a level of success in the business. To his brother's and father's surprise, Harry's gift of charm, coupled with his competitive spirit, meant contracts for new accounts seemed to come as easily to him as winning in sport had. His confidence reinforced; he never stopped to

analyse the real reason for most of the new accounts - the increasing market of a growing city.

Ever one to capitalize on his name, Harry parlayed his role of businessman and the son of a successful woollen industrialist into the younger Toronto society set, though not the established society his parents and brother would have wished.

His peers were primarily sons of the well to do, with little purpose in life other than to entertain themselves. Most had unlimited budgets for gambling and sport and Harry's skill at both made him a welcome addition to their crowd. Most weeks in Harry's life were filled with dinners, dances, the track, and women. At 26, he enjoyed the company of women so regularly that his attitude to yet another beauty was, at best, disinterested.

Although his response to Olive was indifferent, at Kate's prompt, he understood what was expected of him.

"Yes, I believe she is easily the most beautiful woman in this room," Harry replied, saying what he knew his hostess expected to hear. "How is it that I haven't met this vision before this evening, Mrs. Loscombe?"

"Oh, Olive lives during the school year at Bishop Strachan and at home in Newcastle in summers," explained Kate. "Her father, Samuel, my father's brother, has achieved some fame for his role in fish culture. Although I don't understand what it's all about, I know he's held the position of Superintendent of Fish Culture for the Dominion for some years now. It all sounds very important, anyway."

Harry let his gaze linger on Olive and took in the obvious features he could see from across the room.

Her height, at 5' 9", was near his own; her slim waist and small hips allowed her skirt to fall gracefully around her. The locks of hair that fell in curls framed her face in a youthful way, belying the mature look the chignon on top of her head was meant to achieve. Her face had pleasing contours but it was her smile and eyes that, even from across the room, Harry could see were the true source of her beauty. Her smile reached to her eyes and made those close to her feel as they did when the sun came out from behind a cloud. It was impossible to be near Olive and feel impartially toward her.

And, yet, Harry did. Oh, he could see she stood out in the room, as he had always known he did. His thoughts turned to the idea of how

they would look as a couple, dominating everyone with their height and combined good looks.

Chapter 15

Although Harry's world failed to turn upside down on seeing Olive, he admitted it was really something of a coincidence that he should meet her at this time. His father was on him again about the need to settle down.

His parents observed his lifestyle with concern. Ted and Phoebe realized that young men must sow wild oats, however, they were becoming increasingly disturbed by the crowd their son was running in. His evening social activities often extended into the small hours of the morning and, although Ted would never have told Phoebe, he was well aware of his son's gambling and drinking behaviours. As all mothers do, Phoebe just worried about her son burning the candle at both ends.

Harry recalled a conversation with his father just the day before.

"Your Mother and I feel it's time for you to consider a more stable life, Harry. This constant wining and dining will take a toll on you if you aren't careful. A wife would bring purpose to your life. Surely amongst all of the young ladies you escort around the city, there must be someone you've thought about settling down with. I believe the business is doing well enough to support two families."

Ted invested in the firm significantly to provide his elder son the necessary funds to start the business. If his father had ever felt the need to visit the business to check on his investment, he would likely have been shocked by just how little Harry did if and when he visited his office. The fact that he continued to bring in new contracts was due to fortuitous timing; as the city grew and new business interests opened, contracts to supply their textile needs came his way just because the business was convenient.

However, as time went on and Harry paid little heed to the needs of his customers, they eventually moved on to other wholesalers. Ed tried to hold his younger brother accountable but Harry saw little need to exert himself when customers were growing at such a rate. He felt this was obviously due to his skill at sales, reassuring himself that it was his gift that brought these customers to their door and it was up to others to keep them happy.

Of course, no salesman was worth his salt, he felt, if he didn't represent his own product. It was fortuitous that their products

allowed him to indulge his vanity for fashion. Harry's tailor created the most up to date trousers and coats for him in the finest fabrics E.C. Winans & Co. carried. Harry had no difficulty explaining to his father, when he quibbled about incoming bills, that the clothing was a reflection of the business he was in. It was imperative that Harry dress in the finest wools and linens from the textiles he was selling. Without a true understanding of Harry's actual performance on behalf of the company, Ted was not in a position to argue.

Harry also had enough ready cash to support the lifestyle he felt was his due as a businessman of the city and a young blade about town. The best of champagnes and restaurant meals were an expense to be expected in sales but cash was also needed to pay his way into the tables at the many gaming establishments around the city. Although he knew his father and brother didn't agree, Harry told himself this was a valuable pastime for the many contacts made.

His elder brother, however, approached business with a different view; preferring the refined atmosphere of evenings spent at the Toronto Club, which he had recently joined. He was finding his fellow members, businessmen like himself, quite open to discussing shared interests and the challenges of the marketplace.

On this night, as Harry stood watching Olive, his mind began to consider the benefits a woman like Olive might bring to his life.

"An arrangement with her is bound to stop Ed and Father's grumbling" he thought. *"If I establish an engagement, courtship would give me at least another year of life as it is. Really, though, even once married, very little would have to change. A young wife would give Mother and Father someone else to occupy their lives and leave me to carry on as now. And a young, naïve woman is just the ticket. She isn't likely to object to anything I do as long as she has the security of a home and husband. That's what all women are after."*

As Kate led Harry over to Olive's side for a proper introduction, he had already decided that this was the girl he would marry. It was a perfect scheme with all the advantages to suit Harry even while it had little regard for what might be best for Olive. And her beauty would, of course, complement Harry's image in the world. He never doubted she would consider him a catch.

Kate performed the introductions. "Olive, please allow me to introduce you to Mr. Winans. Mr. Winans, may I present my cousin,

Miss Wilmot. Mr. Winan's family is from Cobourg, although he now has business and lives in Toronto." Kate discreetly moved on to another group to allow the young people a chance to get to know one another.

"Have you come out just for the weekend, Mr. Winans?" asked Olive, shaking at his closeness.

"Yes. It's a bit of an expedition to get out here but I enjoy leaving the dust and grime of the city behind and returning to the country. I'll return tomorrow but have had a most enjoyable time" Harry lied. He was, in fact, beyond bored with the entertainment and his fellow guests and their rural conversations. He was anxious to get back to his city pursuits.

Harry had agreed to the invitation to Cobourg only on the direct command of his father who was not prepared to take any excuse Harry might have given. Ted thought the invitation from his old friend and his wife very timely. His father knew many of the people Harry would meet and believed them better than the unsavoury crowd he was fond of in the city.

Unaware of any underlying mission, Olive was overjoyed to discover she was seated beside Harry when the supper bell rang. Her food was nearly overlooked as they chatted about their respective families and lives in the city and country. Olive learned of Harry's love of sport, which she also was very fond of. In particular, they shared a love of horse racing (although Harry's interest leaned more toward the gambling opportunities it offered) and discovered they both attended the Queen's Plate at Woodbine Race Course annually. Harry said "I'll certainly keep my eyes open for you at Woodbine now that I know you attend."

As dessert was served, against all etiquette norms, Olive turned to Harry saying, "I'll be returning to school in two weeks time, Mr. Winans, but I would so love you to see Belmont before I do. If it's not too soon after your trip this weekend, you would be very welcome to visit us next weekend. The farm is always full of people and we have no end of fun things to keep ourselves busy. Belmont has some fine horses and countryside around us for riding and I know Father will insist you join him for an afternoon of sport fishing."

As soon as the words had escaped her mouth, Olive thought '*Now I've done it. He'll judge me by my impulsiveness and think me too young to be*

of further interest'. She knew she had broken all societal customs. Invitations were expected to be in writing at least one week prior to the event.

The voices of her school instructors rattled in her head, "*What sort of girl invites a man she has just met to her home?*" But, as the seconds passed in the silence waiting for his response, Olive felt no regret for her outburst. She could not imagine the evening coming to an end without knowing if or when she would see this handsome, engaging man again. She just knew that she had to take things into her own hands. She had plenty of time in the week ahead to worry about what her father might say.

Harry was not at all concerned by Olive's lack of propriety. His thoughts instead were considering just how dull spending time in the rural outpost of Newcastle would be but he was quick to realize this was an opportunity he should embrace. He was enthusiastic in his response, "I should enjoy that, Miss Wilmot. I'll plan on the morning train Saturday and can return after luncheon on Sunday, if that would be acceptable to your parents."

"Of course, it will be. My father is always happy to welcome new faces to the farm and we have plenty of extra bedrooms to accommodate you." Olive didn't dwell on what they would say in the meantime.

Chapter 16

Dear Diary,

I feel this man is tied to my destiny. I thought this past week would never end but, now that it has, I'm feeling a little breathless. My stomach is queasy just at the thought of seeing him again. It has taken all of my willpower not to seem too eager for the visit but I think Papa has seen through me. He was clearly surprised by my hasty invitation.

I do hope he likes Harry. I would never be able to consider a man that he didn't approve of.

How could anyone not approve of Harry? His gentleness; his conversation; his charming manners; he is truly an exceptional man, I think.

Be calm, my heart. It's a matter of hours before I will gaze on his face and hear his honeyed voice again.

The house that Harry stepped into that August morning was large and gracious; surrounded by rich farmland. The barns and outbuildings spoke of a sizeable and varied complement of livestock. Harry knew Olive's grandfather had built Belmont in the early years of the century. The size and quality of the home surprised him; he had been expecting a provincial farmstead – it was Newcastle, after all.

The bevelled glass in the grand front door caught the sunshine, creating prisms of colour as he knocked. The houseman opened the door and Harry entered a large foyer. He took in the grand staircase as the houseman led him across the parquet floor, through the grand salon which could easily accommodate 50 or more, and into a more intimate parlour at the rear of the home.

"Mr. Wilmot will be along shortly, Mr. Winans" said the houseman before leaving him alone to study his surroundings. The deep mouldings, wood paneling and upholstered seating created a comfortable room; one that the family clearly spent a good deal of time in. One wall was lined with books but Harry gave this little attention other than to hope they weren't the type of family who discussed literature at length. The subject bored him so.

Harry noticed a sideboard holding a tray with crystal decanters and finely cut glasses. *'Well, well. Apparently, the farmers in Newcastle enjoy the finer things in life, too'*, he thought patronizingly.

"Welcome to Belmont, Mr. Winans," said Samuel, entering the room, his hand outstretched. "I know you'll want to freshen up after

your dusty train ride but I wanted to welcome you and I thought a bit of refreshment might be in order after your journey." Harry was pleased to see Samuel turn to the sideboard and pour two glasses of what turned out to be quite a fine brandy. Harry's opinion of rural life was growing by the minute.

"Thank you, Mr. Wilmot, and thank you for your note confirming the visit. It's a pleasure to visit Belmont and to meet Miss Wilmot's family" offered Harry.

"Mrs. Wilmot and I were surprised by Olive's impulsive invitation. She's not a girl who acts hastily as a rule. We realized you had made an impression on her. We have always trusted Olive's instincts. She was born with an innate ability to judge character."

NOT

"But enough of that," Samuel continued. "I look forward to showing you around the farm and I know Olive and her brothers have many activities planned for the weekend. We can be quite a rowdy group, Mr. Winans, so I hope you have come prepared. I trust you'll find our rural ways as entertaining as the city pursuits you enjoy."

"Oh, I have no doubt of that, Mr. Wilmot," replied Harry, thinking *'the old man puts out a damn fine brandy at least'*. "I find my visits outside the city offer respite from the pace and noise of the city. From what I've seen of your home so far, I believe many in Toronto would be envious."

"Well, we do our best with what God has given us. Now, the houseman will show you to your room. We live a somewhat more relaxed life in the summer so luncheon will be in the sunroom in one hour. I believe the boys have some sport or other organized for after so dress casually."

Over the weekend, Harry believed he charmed the family; Samuel, by his (feigned) interest in fishing; Olive's brothers with his love of (and, he might be so bold to say, his success at) sports.

The Wilmot boys had organized a baseball game, joined by some of Samuel's hands who were often included in the family's amateur sports. Others from the household and farm cheered from the sides, creating an atmosphere of joyful competition. Recovering from her initial loss of composure when Harry removed his jacket, exposing his broad shoulders and narrow waist, Olive cheered along with the rest.

A croquet tournament followed. Harry recognized a competitive spark in each of the Wilmot's, as well as natural sporting abilities. Even Olive was a skilled croquet player.

Young people in the 1800s were never alone together before marriage. When he and Olive set off to ride through the surrounding countryside, they did so with others. The opportunities for conversation alone were limited but Harry was not overly dismayed by this since he was confident in the impression he had made on Olive. The weekend, in his mind, was intended to whet the appetite of the other Wilmots; to make them clamour for more of Harry, just as he was certain Olive did.

To his surprise, the weekend was more enjoyable than he had anticipated. His love of sport made him a strong addition to the games and the Wilmot stable held many fine horses. Harry was pleased to note that the table at Belmont was well laid and Samuel shared more of the fine brandy with Harry after dinner, using this time to query Harry on his business interests. He was even surprised on Sunday morning by the elegance of their small church; St. George's. It seemed the Wilmots did all things well, from what Harry could determine.

The Wilmot sons did clamour for more Harry. They thought him a great sport and good fun to be with. Minnie, still single at 21, had been entirely bewitched by Harry's good looks and charm. She thoroughly approved of him for Olive (Olive had confided her strong feelings toward him) and hoped he might become a successful suitor.

It couldn't be said, however, that Samuel was as smitten. While young people might be convinced by a person's outward behaviour and attractiveness, Samuel's life experience had taught him how fickle appearances could be. He couldn't quite put his finger on why he didn't warm to the boy except that he noticed Harry's smiles didn't extend to his eyes. Samuel thought an inner coldness lived within and he worried that the charming exterior was a façade. He determined to run some enquiries on the young man.

As Harry said his goodbyes on Sunday afternoon following luncheon, he felt assured that his courtship of Olive would be looked upon favourably. He invited Samuel and Mrs. Wilmot (who had been summoned home for Harry's visit) to meet his family in Toronto.

As Harry climbed into the carriage for the few short miles to the train station, Olive clasped her father's arm with pure joy. She had thought of little else since her visit to Kate's and this weekend with Harry had been even more pleasurable then she had anticipated. She looked up at her father affectionately with a questioning look in her eyes.

"We shall see" said Samuel, solemnly. Olive could not imagine any reason for her father not to approve and was happy. She returned to the house smiling broadly.

Chapter 17

Returning to school for her final year, Olive happily imagined the many visits she and Harry would have now that she was in the city. Her father followed his doubts and set to work to learn all he could about young Harry.

Samuel's first letter was to his old friend, Hart Massey. Despite his move from Newcastle some years previously, Samuel and Hart remained in touch and Samuel considered Hart one of his intimate friends. Samuel had been an early adopter of much of the farm machinery Hart had developed while his company, Massey Manufacturing, had been in Newcastle and the pair had strong respect for each other.

Amongst the many hats Hart had worn while in Newcastle, Samuel remembered he had been head of Newcastle Woollen Manufacturing Company. Samuel knew Harry's father, Ted Winans, had also been involved in this enterprise and expected that Hart would have maintained ties with Ted.

His letter to Hart was guarded; he avoided putting any bias into his enquiry but asked for the man's sincere impressions of the family and, specifically, of Harry, if he knew him on a personal level. The response Samuel received back was full of praise for the Winans family but Hart was unable to comment on Harry, a younger son unknown to Hart during the time he had worked with the father.

Samuel's further enquiries turned up nothing to justify the strong feelings he had experienced toward Harry. He decided the best he could do to protect her was share his feelings with Olive and insist that she wait for a year before beginning a courtship.

In late October, during a visit to the city, Samuel presented his decision to Olive.

"I understand you have strong feelings toward young Mr. Winans, Olive, but I have equally strong reservations about his character. I trust you will cede to my years of experience in what I am going to say."

"I insist that you not see the young man for now, at least until I have time to take a measure of the man. You are still young with years ahead of you to settle down and I would like you to enjoy this last year of school without the encumbrance of a courtship. If your feelings

remain the same next summer, I promise we will get to know Harry better and allow him to call at Belmont again. For now, let's consider the matter closed" said Samuel firmly.

Olive only just managed to stop the protest that rose in her, heartsick at his words. She respected her father above all men and had so hoped he would accept Harry and allow a courtship to proceed.

She had believed her father's endorsement of Harry to be crucial and guaranteed. Hearing his decision left her confused. She had no doubt about her feelings toward Harry. The pull he had on her was undeniable. Her life changed forever in that moment as she now realized her desire for him was far stronger than her need for her father's approval.

Unbeknownst to Samuel, Harry had wasted no time contacting Olive at school and had been seeing her weekly. She had so convinced herself of her father's pending approval that she readily agreed to go out with him or to have him to tea in the school's common room.

Olive was wise enough not to jeopardize her reputation and insisted their outings be in the company of others but that was the only common sense she demonstrated toward Harry. She was infatuated and this clouded her usually sound judgment. Harry brought out feelings and emotions she had never felt. He was like a drug that she had already begun to feel she couldn't live without it.

Her father's announcement unsettled her but she saw no reason to enlighten him. She only just managed to keep the inner turmoil she felt from her face as thoughts overcame her. In a brief instant, while her father accepted that she was absorbing his decision, she made the decision to continue seeing Harry. Convinced that her father would reverse his decision next summer removed the guilt she should have felt in going against his wishes.

'He would not feel that way if he just spent time with Harry, as I have' thought Olive. For the first time in her life, Olive was going to be wilfully dishonest. Samuel's obedient little girl suddenly knew the best way to approach her father about this deception.

"Of course, Papa" replied Olive, fingers of both hands crossed in her lap. "I know you have my best interests at heart."

As the winter months passed, her now clandestine encounters with Harry caused some feelings of guilt, mostly for having lied to her

father. But, the excitement of their secret meetings heightened her feelings, dwarfing any remorse.

On the rare occasion when she applied reason to her behaviour, she questioned how something as pure as love could be wrong. Besides, their hidden meetings would eventually be of no consequence once Harry had been welcomed by her family.

Samuel's continued perseverance with enquiries eventually paid off. He was, sadly, enlightened about the young man's lifestyle and propensity toward excesses in life. It brought him no joy to realize he would have to inform Olive when she returned from school that Harry would not be darkening their doorway again.

The only outlet Olive had for sharing her extreme emotions was writing letters to Minnie. Her older sister, still single and lonely at home, was swept away by the romance of it all. The secret nature of their relationship only magnified the romance in her mind. Unaware of her father's discoveries, she, too, felt it would all clear itself up once Harry was welcomed back to Belmont in the summer.

Olive never doubted her feelings for Harry to be anything but the deepest sort of love; she was too young to recognize that what she took for love was actually adulation. Every minute in Olive's company, Harry was charming and funny and her school friends who accompanied them on their outings were soon infatuated too. No one could get enough of the handsome young man.

As school drew to a close, Olive was ever more anxious to have her love be out in the open. Taking the train home, she was filled with anticipation for the summer ahead when their courtship could become public to her family; a decidedly short courtship if plans went as Harry had proposed.

At their last meeting, he suggested a marriage in the fall, giving her father suitable time to get to know him. They had agreed to be secretly engaged until all could be out in the open. It wasn't quite the romantic engagement Olive had pictured but made her feel grown up, nonetheless.

Samuel was out when Olive alighted from the carriage at Belmont's front door, looking at the house with new eyes. She was imagining a wedding breakfast on the sweeping lawns when Minnie threw open the front door.

"Oh, my darling, it's so good to have you back" Minnie cried. "Papa is at one of his political meetings until dinner. Let's get you unpacked and you can tell me everything!"

Minnie was beside herself on hearing Harry's casual proposal and, together, they began to make plans. Neither girl saw anything amiss in either Harry's hasty proposal or his lack of speaking first with Samuel. A lack of life experience, added to a love of romance novels, made the entire situation romantic instead of wrong in their eyes.

Olive walked down the staircase that evening in her most poised, grown up manner. She would do everything henceforth to make her father see how ready she was to wed. At 17, he still must give his permission for the wedding but, really, she saw no reason to doubt he would at this point. She knew he believed she had done as he had asked and now she waited eagerly to hear him say Harry was invited to Belmont again.

As dinner went on and Samuel did not broach the topic, Olive began to have concerns. Surely, inviting her future husband to their home should be a happy occasion and one which they would all enjoy sharing in but dessert was served with nary a word from her father.

"Please come to the study, Olive. I would like a word" said Samuel as they arose from the table. With a worried glance at Minnie, Olive followed.

"I will begin, Olive, by saying how happy we are to have you home again" said Samuel. "I'm looking forward to a summer with you and your brothers home."

"While you've been away, I have followed through on my enquiries into Harry's character and I'm afraid the results are not good. I realize you see the charm and personality he exhibits but I have discovered a darker side to the man that needs to be weighed before I would ever consent to an agreement between you. He is a regular at the gaming tables and he has a reputation as a heavy drinker. I won't tell you the other things I've discovered because they are not suitable for a young lady's ears. Suffice it to say, this is not a man I would want any of my daughters associated with."

"I think you see where this is leading, Olive," continued Samuel. "In light of the knowledge I now have, I am forced to forbid you from seeing Harry. I hope that the absence from him throughout this past

year will make this easier news for you to take and that you will consider how many other worthy young men are out there."

Never one to speak hastily, Olive was stunned into silence by her father's words. She had spent the school year counting the months until he would welcome Harry again. Olive's mind moved rapidly from one thought to another. *'He clearly was misled'* she thought. *'The man I know is intelligent and worldly. If he lived such a dissolute life, would he be capable of carrying on the informed discussions we've shared? No; Papa is wrong."*

Olive would never admit to herself that Harry's physicality was the biggest pull in her feelings. When he touched her, even just to take her arm as they walked, her body almost vibrated with a desire that she had yet to recognize and name.

Too young to separate these feelings from the words of her father, Olive was resolute in her determination to have Harry as her husband. She was, however, acutely aware of how difficult changing Samuel's mind, once made up, would be. She was in conflict, feeling that she knew Harry from their many visits but unable to tell this to her father since he had asked her not to see him. She needed time to think. *'I could not possibly give this man up. I'll need to consider other avenues to convince Papa. It may be easier now that I'm home.'*

With this resolve, Olive touched her father's arm, saying "I understand, Papa. Although I am sure there is more to this man than rumour has said, I will, of course, respect your wishes. I believe I will go to my room now. Goodnight."

'Well, that was easier than I anticipated,' thought Samuel, after she left. He had fully expected tears or histrionics of some sort but it was his Olive, after all. If there were one female less likely to make a scene, it was his girl. He was confident that summer events would bring other suitors forward to take Olive's mind from Harry and he gladly put further thought of the situation from his mind.

June 1903

Newcastle, Ontario

Chapter 18

Minnie remembered that summer well. She had felt caught in the middle between her sister; so in love, and her father; so steadfast in his decision.

At 22, Minnie had been labelled a spinster. She had long since resigned herself to the long face which somehow suited her. Observers thought her horsey-looking in trying to define her look. In fact, those who didn't wish to be harsh when speaking of her spoke of her stellar character – a true stab in the heart for any young woman.

"It was no surprise that I should get caught up in the romance of it, was it Olive" she asked her silent sister. "What life I had was completely without any male attention. That summer was all so exciting, although I thought the tension would kill me."

Standing to relieve her back, Minnie saw Lindsell napping in another chair. Minnie sat down again and took Olive's hand lovingly in her own.

"Dearest, can you hear me? I can't bear to see you lying so helpless but I'm going to presume you can hear me as long as you're with us."

"I'm reliving your life and my memories in these journals. Did you know how much I lived through your experiences as they were happening? The only excitement I ever knew was through you. Even after finding Duncan in my thirties and knowing love for the first time, the routine of our lives could never measure up to the drama of yours. Oh, I know you always said the joy of our two girls made my life exceptional but it could never compete with yours."

"Even though I know the story as well as you, as I sit reading your journals, my heart is beating quicker. Really, it was all too much for one lifetime and here you are, just 39. Is this why God is choosing to cut it short?"

"It is difficult to sit here, unable to help you in any way. I am praying, though. Can you hear my prayers? Although, as each hour passes and I understand more and more that you have left us, I'm no

longer sure of what I should be praying for. At least reading your journals brings you back in all of your beautiful spirit."

Minnie leaned over to kiss her sister's brow. She stopped for a brief word with Lindsell, now awake, before taking the next journal from the shelf and heading to her room. She doubted she would get any sleep that night but knew she must lie down for some time at least. As much as she hated to leave Olive's bedside for even a few hours, her body could not carry on without a rest. She knew Lindsell would wake her if there was any change.

1881

Newcastle, Ontario

Chapter 19

Dear Diary,

'Today, my life changes forever. My life as Mrs. Harry Winans and a new home in Toronto begins. I must have done something exceptional in my lifetime to bring this man to me.

Dearest Harry, I pledge to bring you nothing but happiness; to be an agreeable companion and tender lover. How sweet it is to picture the years ahead of us. I can imagine the children we will have; the boys looking like you and the girls, perhaps, like me. How many children, I wonder. Whatever number we are blessed with, each will know my love and the love I feel for their father.

The only blight on my happiness today is that I do this in secret. Please God, help Papa to one day accept this marriage and my husband.

Your loving Olive

Olive and Harry wed October 6, 1881. Although the marriage was entered into secretly, the ceremony took place at Olive's family church, St. George's, with Rev. Brent, a close family friend, officiating.

Sadly, the wedding was not a blessed family affair. The only member of the Wilmot family present was Minnie, co-conspirator to the young couple's affair.

After hearing her father's decision about Harry, Olive wrote to her beloved tearfully but with hope that she could change her father's mind. She said Harry should give her the summer to try to sway Samuel but suggested they continue writing secretly until then.

She instructed Harry to address letters to Minnie from a false return address. Her sister was ready with an imaginary friend if questions arose. The entire secret exchange aroused a mild sexual excitement in Minnie.

Harry, on reading Olive's words, understood that Samuel was not going to change his mind. After all, nothing he suspected the old man had discovered was untrue.

Harry continued running with the crowd which had marked him as unsuitable. He had no intention of curbing his activities even after he and Olive married. *'And marry we shall'* he thought. *'I've invested too much of my time over the past year to consider an alternate spouse. No, I'll just have to come up with another approach to go around the old man.'*

Olive took part in all of the summer activities but her thoughts and heart were in Toronto with Harry. She felt physical pain knowing she could not be with him without her father's permission for a wedding. They could wait four years for her to reach the age of consent but her youth saw that option as endless.

They kept a steady correspondence going through the summer; Harry's language becoming increasingly passionate. His letters frequently brought a blush to her cheeks and sometimes the language bordered on crude but Olive blamed their forced separation for his tone. She knew not to share these with Minnie who remained a great supporter of the prohibited romance. Plain Minnie never hoped to have such excitement in her own life and lived vicariously through Olive.

Harry had also been thinking of Olive through the weeks apart but only in terms of his search for a solution to her father's vehement objections. The plan he decided on stunned her. His letter said that, as he saw it, they had just one avenue open to them: an elopement.

As every young girl who read romance novels knew, such a step would bring only scandal. Olive would be ruined if she went off with a man without virtue of a family-recognized church wedding.

Her breath caught at his words; as much from dismay at the idea as the thrill that he wanted her at such cost. She ran to find Minnie to share this newest development.

Reading his letter, Minnie's opinion of the affair, and Harry, sank. She was simply aghast. How had she ever supported this man in his romance of her sister, she wondered?

"He can't really think this an option, Olive. He is taking away your family and your reputation in one step. You know that Papa would not let you back in the house were you to do this."

"After all these months of waiting, Minnie," replied Olive tearfully, "I just want to become Mrs. Harry Winans. I truly believed Papa would change his mind and allow a wedding but he is resolute. As Harry says, an elopement is the only option for us."

"Did Papa not raise us to be independent in thought and action? He will come around once he becomes accustomed to the idea. The more I think on it, the more determined I am. If elopement is the only way for me to be with Harry, so be it."

Minnie put her arms around her sister and begged, "Please let me think on this, Olive, before you reply to Harry. There must be some way round the scandal such a move will bring to you and our family."

Minnie spent days looking at the options open to Olive. She wanted so much to make her beloved sister happy and knew Olive thought this only possible if Harry were in her life.

A few days passed before she presented Olive with a scenario that might work. "The wedding must be at our church to remove any disgrace you would face if you just ran away with Harry. I will speak to Rev. Brent and impress upon him your determination in this. You will have to allow him to counsel you to change your mind, Olive. I can't imagine him performing the ceremony any other way."

"If you are still determined, I think he will see that agreeing to conduct the ceremony is the only way to save us from the shame, even though he will face Papa's anger. I could stand up as your witness from our family. I, too, will face Papa's anger but I will explain I did so to prevent scandal to the family."

Olive agreed and went off to write Harry that he should be ready for an October ceremony, assuming that Rev. Brent would be cooperative. Olive knew that Samuel would be back in Ottawa then, making it just a little easier to carry out their plans.

On the morning of the wedding, Olive and Minnie left the house pretending to have errands in the village. The evening before, they carried a trunk out to the carriage and covered it with a tarp. No need to set off any alarms with the staff. As the carriage wound down the drive, Olive looked wistfully back at her beloved childhood home.

"We have an appointment with Rev. Brent, Peter" said Minnie to the handyman, corralled to drive them to the village. The sisters held hands quietly during the short journey to St. George's church.

It pained Minnie to know Olive's new life was beginning in this manner. She felt mixed emotions toward Harry now and had no desire to meet his family and friends in a cordial manner or to spend an extended time with him. The irony that she was delivering her sister

to a life with this man was lost on her. "Please wait for us, Peter" she said as the two stepped down from the carriage.

As they waited for the ceremony to begin, Minnie folded Olive in her arms, saying "you still have time to change your mind, dearest. Think on the affect this will have on the remainder of your life. I will find whatever way possible to stay in touch but I know that, to Papa, you will be dead to the family. Is Harry worth this great loss?"

"Oh, he is Minnie" exclaimed Olive. "I am trembling just knowing I'm going to see him shortly after these months apart. This can't be anything but deep love. Truly, my heart is in charge at this point."

But Minnie saw conflict written on Olive's face.

"I've left a letter for Papa but please try to help him understand the depth of my feelings. He must know his responsibility in all of this. If he had given us any other course of action, I would not be doing this" said Olive, suddenly tearful.

The letter for her father had been the most difficult part of the deception. She wrote of her certainty of her love for Harry but also of her understanding for Samuel's part in wanting to protect her from unhappiness.

'You think me a young girl, unable to decide my own future' wrote Olive, *'but it was you who encouraged each of us to think and act for ourselves.'*

'I am old enough to recognize the reasons for your concern. It is to be expected, Papa, that you want to shield us from the pain you and Mother have experienced from an unhappy union. Harry has reassured me that his behaviour in the past was all part of sowing his wild oats (something I believe even my brothers do) and that he is a different man with age and pending marriage. Please rest easy that this is what I want. I hope that time will ease your anger at my deception and we might resume our relationship with the passing of both.'

Looking upon Harry as she said her vows, Olive's joy, as Rev. Brent pronounced them Husband and Wife, was infinite. *"I am going to be the best wife he could ever ask for,"* she thought, as Harry took her hand and they turned away from the altar.

Walking down the aisle, she caught the eyes of Harry's younger brothers, Chauncey and Frederick, and smiled shyly. These two young boys were her brothers now; with her 'I Do' said, she had become a Winans. Her life as a Wilmot was over.

Minnie left the church to take care of her last responsibility. She asked Peter to transfer Olive's trunk to the waiting carriage Harry had hired from the train station. She turned as the couple stepped out of the church and moved forward to wrap her arms around Olive. The sisters wept softly as they faced the moment to say goodbye for who knew how long.

Chapter 20

The train was crowded during the trip into Toronto. Chauncey and Frederick had taken the train east returning to Trinity School. She had been introduced to the three women Harry had invited as guests but was confused about their relationship to the family or why they had been included in his wedding party. Their talk was light; almost frivolous and directed exclusively to Harry.

But her thoughts were too pre-occupied to dwell on it and she soon forgot them as she and Harry said goodbye to the women who disembarked in Toronto. Harry and Olive changed trains for their honeymoon train to Niagara Falls. Harry explained to Olive that many famous people had travelled to the area for their honeymoons and they would spend three days doing the same.

'What a thoughtful gesture', thought Olive, as the train carried them south. *'We could just as easily have gone straight to his home. He understands my mixed feelings today and that I'm not ready to meet his parents.'*

She could not know that, as in all things, Harry was calculating. His motive in planning such a trip was simple; he was certain Samuel would immediately follow them and felt it best to make himself scarce for at least a few days. No need to encourage an unpleasant scene, after all. He also believed Samuel would try to insist on an annulment but, the longer he had with Olive, the stronger his control over her would become.

Taking a few days away was no hardship and he planned to send the bills for the trip to the company. He would tell his brother he had visited several manufacturers while there. Really, he had planned everything very well, he told himself smugly.

To Olive, their days in Niagara Falls were nearly idyllic. They wandered the village, stopping for tea or sherry, and were amazed by the falls. As they walked, she noticed how many gazes followed them and felt blessed that this man was her husband.

She refused to acknowledge that the nights were a disappointment. She had envisioned lovemaking to be an act of tenderness and affection. The reality was proving otherwise. Harry performed the act quickly, with no thought to Olive's pleasure or comfort. She ignored the pain, understanding that this was the lot for

all women and forgave his clumsy approach, putting it down to inexperience.

'He is as uncertain as I' she told herself. *'I'm sure all married couples begin this way. Time and experience will guide us.'*

Packing up on their last morning was bittersweet. She understood that they were now re-entering the real world and would face the drama of all that was to come. Harry reassured Olive that his parents were both looking forward to meeting her and having her in their home but Olive was not so naïve that she completely believed him. What parent would countenance a secret marriage, despite the presence of his brothers, she wondered.

Harry had been correct in saying his parents were pleased to meet her but had left key details out. It was their expressions of regret at missing the wedding that made Olive pause. She quickly realized Harry had neglected to tell them the nature of the wedding.

All that Phoebe and Ted knew of it was that Harry had made it clear to them that they would not be attending. Whatever his reasons were, they didn't know. They had long since stopped disputing Harry's decisions; it just wasn't worth the emotional turmoil that they knew would result if they did.

They had, together, decided not to hold their disappointment with Harry against his new bride and were indeed gracious in their welcome. This was, after all, what they had both been praying for and the manner in which it happened would soon be forgotten. This was not the first time Harry had overlooked them in his thoughts and actions. They assumed it was just they who had been left out of the ceremony, unaware that he had omitted Olive's parents (and their permission) as well.

Olive caught Harry's sharp look when his parents spoke about the difficulty she must have faced saying goodbye to her parents following the ceremony. Feeling his eyes still on her, she looked down and managed to mumble something without actually stating a lie, leaving Ted and Phoebe to understand it was a sensitive topic.

Olive didn't dwell on Harry's deception with his parents. Hadn't she deceived her own father? In the drawing room with Phoebe, Olive responded to the woman's gentle manner. Her pain at leaving Belmont was not easing, although she kept it to herself not wanting to

burden Harry. She took full responsibility for her choice and had no intention of letting it be a shadow on their happiness together.

Phoebe sensed nothing of Olive's internal emotions. She hadn't had much time to adjust to the idea of a young bride coming to live with them but whatever reservations she had felt were relieved on meeting her son's pretty new wife.

'Oh, she's lovely' thought Phoebe to herself, grateful for the presence of another female in their home. After a lifetime lived in an atmosphere of the noise that came with six sons, Phoebe welcomed sharing her daily routines with a woman other than her elderly mother who napped upstairs.

She was also hopeful that the sweet girl in front of her would return some cheer to their home. In recent months, with the younger boys away at school, the house had taken on an emotionally charged atmosphere. Harry was the only son at home now and his moods, when he was in the house, cast a cloud over his parents. Phoebe naively assumed a new bride was all that was needed to bring happiness to her irritable son.

A practical woman, Phoebe had been an attentive and caring mother to each of her sons but, if she were to be honest with herself, she would admit that her role in the family was most often viewed as decorative. It was Ted who ruled, although generally with a lighter hand than her own father had. Even though her husband was a caring man, Phoebe's experience with her father had indelibly marked her view of men. From him, she learned to stay silent, lest she set off his anger. The parallels she now saw in her own son's behaviour disturbed her.

Although Ted would say his wife had blessed him with six sons, he believed that a household with that amount of male energy required a firm hand at the head and sons should be raised in a manner that prepared them for the challenges of life. His own childhood had included authoritarian adults and corporal punishment and he believed his success in life to be a direct result of the discipline. 'Spare the rod; spoil the child' was, like most in his generation, his maxim for childrearing. Phoebe's softer approach to her boys was often overruled. If she might attempt to go in aid to her boys when they experienced injury, Ted would admonish her. "Don't mother the boy, Phoebe. He must learn to be a man and take what comes."

Ted was proud of his boys, believing that, through his strictness, he had raised admirable men. Harry, of all of his sons, had been the most challenging. Ted had never managed to 'tame' the boy, no matter the amount of necessary beatings he had inflicted. Unlike his brothers, Harry would take his punishment silently, never admitting guilt or expressing regret. In fact, his steely response to every beating sometimes enraged Ted, leading him to make the punishment more severe than it might otherwise have been. He would *beat* respect into the boy, if necessary. But Harry had no fear of Ted; as a young boy or as a man.

Ted's disappointment with Harry had been softened by age. As Harry reached his late teens, their relationship became one of mutual tolerance. Ted also loved sports and he was silently pleased and proud that Harry was a natural at many. Sport presented a topic of conversation that often bridged the silence between the two.

Phoebe's mother, Rachel, had lived with the family for some years and Harry believed she was the sole person in the world who understood him. In fact, she understood him too well; recognizing the brutality that lay within him; it mirrored the nature of his grandfather, her husband. She had no fear of this but let her faith guide her in her relationship with her grandson, as she had with her husband. Her gentleness came from her belief that he was inherently a good man and her God would eventually help him to put aside his angry ways. Rachel's increasing years had given her poor hearing and increasingly poor eyesight but took nothing away from the calming influence she exerted.

After Olive had been served tea by the family's long time maid, Mary, Phoebe rose and said, "Let me show you to the rooms you will share with Harry, Olive. I do hope you'll be comfortable with us. Perhaps you would like a short rest before dinner? Harry can have your trunk taken upstairs later."

"Oh, I feel fine, Mrs. Winans, but I think I would like to get unpacked and settled. There is nothing worse than living out of trunks and my gowns really should be hung as soon as possible" replied Olive.

"Well, let's get you settled, then, my dear. Harry," called Phoebe to her son, "the trunks can go right up."

Phoebe led Olive up the wide staircase. As they reached the second-floor landing, Phoebe pointed to the first door, saying this was her and Ted's room. "We keep the room beside us free for Chauncy and Frederick when they are home on school holidays. The next room belongs to my mother, Mrs. Wells. She naps each afternoon but is anxious to meet you" said Phoebe, as she rounded a corner.

"We've redone the schoolroom adjoining Harry's room and had a door put in between the rooms to give you a separate dressing and sitting room. There should be ample room for your clothing and treasures you've brought from home but there is also storage space available on the third floor."

"I'll leave you to your unpacking." With that, Phoebe opened the second to last door and Olive entered her new husband's bedroom.

Chapter 21

Dear Diary,

I will admit this is not the beginning I had hoped for in my new home but I have to presume that Harry knows what he is doing and is doing it for the two of us and the future we have together.

At least my new home is comfortable and my new family warm and welcoming. What more could I ask for; except maybe my husband in bed at my side on my first night in it.'

As had been her habit throughout her life, Olive wrote her thoughts before climbing into bed; alone. Earlier in the day, she had unpacked her clothes, surprised to find herself humming. The anticipation of meeting Harry's parents had hung heavily on her and she was relieved to have this behind her. Unfolding her wedding dress from the case, she touched the gown lovingly and tried to stroke the wrinkles from the skirt. She would have to ask Mary to press them out before she stored it away.

How she would have loved the visits to Toronto for a trousseau that other girls experienced before their wedding but she stood by her actions and the results they bore. There were so many things missed in their wedding; having her father walk her down the aisle not the least. This dress represented the strength she had shown in determining her own future and she would remember it always as such.

She tidied the dressing room after putting her things in the bureau and organizing her toiletries on the vanity table. Her glance fell on the bed and she shivered with the knowledge that this was where they would spend their future nights together; believing that tenderness would grow with experience.

Harry came in to change from his traveling clothes as she was finishing up. As he began to remove his tie and jacket, Olive found herself suddenly shy; very aware of his physical presence. "I'll just head downstairs, Harry, and have a few words with your grandmother before dinner" she said, leaving the room.

"Please don't rise, Mrs. Wells," Olive said to the elderly woman attempting to stand as Olive entered the drawing room. With the aid of her cane, Rachel Wells continued to rise in order to give Olive a

warm embrace. She was delighted to see the young girl as, she too, had been eager to see Harry settled.

"I've been looking forward to having you in our home, Olive. I think your presence will liven up this sad old place and the people in it" she said, taking Olive's hands in her own. "Come, sit with me and tell me all about the wedding and your trip." Olive wasn't sure what Rachel meant by her comment of the sad home but she was more than happy to relate the events of the past days with the elderly lady, albeit sharing more about Niagara Falls than their wedding ceremony.

At dinner, Olive thought the Winans subdued. Sitting at the table with her new family, she keenly felt the absence of her own. It seemed that she, Rachel and Phoebe carried on most of the conversation through dinner, with Ted and Harry contributing their thoughts only when asked directly. After the lively dinners in her own home, Olive found the atmosphere restrained. Although Harry appeared pre-occupied, she put it down to tiredness; after all, the days at Niagara Falls had been full with all of the various activities and there had been little opportunity for rest.

Olive was surprised, as they where finishing their dessert course, to hear Harry announce that he must go out that evening and would likely be late. A protest rose to her lips with her initial reaction; *'how inconsiderate to think of leaving me on my first night with his family'* she thought. *'He must know I am feeling awkward and homesick.'*

But it was Ted who spoke, saving Olive any embarrassment she might have felt by doing so herself in front of his family. "I would think that whatever business might take you out on Olive's first night with us, Harry, could wait until a more appropriate time" he said.

"I wish it could, Father, but this particular account has eluded me and I have the opportunity to catch up with the Principal of the firm tonight. I'm told he plays a hand of cards at the club when he is in town and he is here tonight. It's unfortunate that it has fallen on this night but I know Olive understands the importance of business demands" replied Harry smoothly.

Olive lowered her head and willed the tears to stay away. "Of course, I do" she offered in a quiet voice. "Harry must do what is best for the business. This night is just one of many and really is of no consequence. You go, Harry, and, if I'm awake on your return, you can tell me all about your success in landing the new account."

"I knew you were a sport, Olive," said Harry, rising from the table and coming around to give her a soft kiss on her cheek. With that, he headed to the front hall; collected his hat and coat and, with a final "Good night, all", was out the door.

Rachel was the first to speak, almost before the others had time to adjust, "Four is just what we need for a game of Whist. Are we all up for a game?" Olive wanted to hug the old woman for taking their attention away from Harry's hasty exit. "I would enjoy that very much, Mrs. Wells, if Mr. and Mrs. Winans are of the same mind." Cards were the last thing Ted and Phoebe felt like playing at that moment but they, too, were grateful to Rachel and graciously accepted the invitation.

Surprisingly, Olive enjoyed their game and was pleased to find the other three to be astute card players. As the final hand came to an end and Rachel rose to retire, Olive excused herself to Ted and Phoebe and offered her arm to Rachel to ascend the stairs together.

As they neared Rachel's door, the old woman looked up at Olive and said, "He has different ways than most young men, Olive. From the experience of my many years, I would have you know that time will forge the life the two of you will share. You have the ability to mould that life but it doesn't happen overnight. Be patient, my dear. It is the rare new bride who steps into a marriage fully formed."

Olive looked down into Rachel's kindly face; she had no doubt, despite the large difference in their years, that the two of them would become intimates. She couldn't help but wonder what her childhood might have been like if her mother had been a gentler woman like Rachel. "Thank you, Mrs. Wells. I appreciate your wisdom and do understand that relationships take time. You know this family so well and I would welcome your thoughts as I become one of its own."

"Goodnight, My Dear" said Rachel, as she entered her room.

Olive had only her thoughts for company as she undressed and prepared for bed. Rachel's words were a comfort and helped to put Harry's behaviour in perspective. '*I over-reacted*' she thought, climbing between the sheets. '*My husband has commitments other than me. I'm so lucky to have Mrs. Wells.*'

The sound of cursing woke her. For a moment, with the moonlight peeking through the draperies outlining a strange room, she was confused.

"Blast" said Harry, as he kicked his shin on the bedpost.

"Harry. Why don't you light a candle? I'm awake anyway" she said, coming to sit upright in the bed.

As the candle flame brightened the room, Olive was surprised at how dishevelled her usually carefully groomed husband appeared. His collar was askew and the rest of his clothing looked as though he had slept in them. But Harry's words and behaviour soon enlightened Olive about the cause. Rather than moving to the dressing room to remove his clothes, Harry tore off each item, dropping them on the floor as he did so.

"I'm glad you've warmed the bed, Olive," slurred Harry. "There's a damn chill in the air and I'm ready for some warmth between the sheets."

Olive put his coarse words down to alcohol. His breath on her face, as he climbed into bed, confirmed her suspicions. Harry had been drinking and quite a lot it seemed. Olive wondered if this was how business was often conducted.

Harry rolled over toward her. Lifting her nightgown to her waist, he said "Your thighs have been on my mind all evening. Made it damned difficult to concentrate at the tables, I'll tell you". Olive began to protest but Harry stopped it with a rough kiss.

"Now don't go all puritan on me. You're a hot-blooded girl or you wouldn't have run away with me. Now lie still while I enjoy what's mine" said Harry impatiently. He roughly spread her legs, lowered his body over her and began thrusting first his fingers and then himself into her.

Olive did as she was told, frightened by his brutality. While their couplings on the honeymoon had been less than tender, Harry's strength and crudeness this night was a shock. She didn't know this man who was so intently abusing her body.

She was wondering how long she must endure this assault on her body when the pain of his thrusts became too much. She cried out and, Harry, in his drunken state, imagined her to be crying out with pleasure at his performance. His thrusts gained in momentum until; at last, he collapsed over her. With his body pressing down onto her, Olive experienced a new feeling of claustrophobia. She realized with dismay that Harry was asleep on top of her. Tears ran down her

cheeks as she slid herself out from under him and gathered her nightgown back down around her legs.

Listening to the snores of the man beside her, Olive tried, without success, to make sense of Harry's behaviour. She was still in pain in heart and body when sleep eventually overcame her.

Chapter 22

Olive lay as still as she could when she woke, trying not to disturb Harry. It had been some time before she had fallen asleep; the cramping in her lower belly overshadowed by the pain in her heart. How could the man she worshipped have mistreated her so? Her thoughts before sleep were on the couples she knew. She knew enough of these couples to understand that the intimacy between them strengthened their loving marriages but what she had experienced was neither intimate nor loving.

The start of a new day brought with it fresh hope and the belief that Harry's hurtful love-making (although she was averse to naming it such) was from his drinking. She was certain that things would be different under normal, sober circumstances.

His warmth toward her at breakfast that morning reassured her. Olive rose before Harry, dressing quietly in the adjoining room so as not to wake him. Rachel, Phoebe and Ted were at the breakfast table when she entered the dining room.

"Were you comfortable enough, Olive?" asked Phoebe. "I hope the transition to your new home will be an easy one. You will let me know if there is anything you need, dear?"

"Of course, Mrs. Winans," replied Olive, walking gingerly to the table, still in pain but not wanting the others to be aware. "But, really, everything is just as I would have it at home (*'except for the strange man in my bed'*, she thought). Please don't worry about my needs. If there is something, I will certainly speak up."

As the four were finishing their meal and discussing their plans for the day, Harry entered the room and took the chair next to Olive's, leaning down to kiss her on the forehead before sitting. "Good morning, Dearest", he said, surprising Olive with his tenderness. "I'll just have tea and toast, please Mary," he said as the maid entered. "I really must get to the office and put together a contract for our new account."

"Congratulations, Harry," offered his father grudgingly. "It's good to hear that leaving us all on Olive's first night with us proved to be fruitful." Ted had been more disturbed by Harry's behaviour the previous night then he had let on.

"Oh, I was certain it would be, Father" replied Harry. "I allowed him to win a few hands. Few things will put a man in a mood more

conducive to doing business with you than beating you at cards." Ted, who had never played cards as a means of doing business, was sceptical but the proof apparently was in the new contract so he held his tongue.

"Don't be late today, Harry" said Phoebe. "Remember the dinner party at the Alexander's. They are looking forward to introducing Olive."

"I'll be home by 4:00; plenty of time to dress. I'm looking forward to showing Olive off tonight" said Harry, patting her on the shoulder as he left. '*Last night was clearly out of character*' thought Olive, feeling an inner glow from his attention. '*I will be patient, just as Mrs. Wells suggested.*'

She was dressed and sitting in the parlour when Harry arrived home that afternoon. He was later than planned and speed was necessary if they were to be on time so Olive didn't offer to help Harry, letting him go up alone to change into his dinner clothes. He joined the family just as the hired carriage pulled up to take them to the Alexanders.

Harry offered his arm to Olive, helping her step up into the carriage. A chill had set in that day and Olive was grateful for the warm wrap Harry tenderly laid on her lap. As the carriage made its way through the streets of Toronto, Olive and Phoebe chatted about the Alexanders and who Olive was likely to meet that evening.

The Winans' friends were warm in their welcome of Olive. Harry didn't leave her side throughout the evening other than through dinner when she was seated beside Mr. Alexander with Harry at the other end of the table. Every time she looked over at him, she found him watching her, making her feel extremely loved. She smiled frequently at him, letting him know with her eyes that she would have preferred to be at his side, although Mr. Alexander was an interesting host and Olive enjoyed their conversation.

As the gentlemen stood for the ladies to leave them to their after-dinner cigars and drinks, Harry came around the table, taking Olive's arm as she left the room. Olive thought the gesture touching and was effusive about married life when asked by the ladies gathered in the parlour. Each of them was reminded of their own start in married life and their talk naturally fell to their own expectations in their early

wedded days. Olive listened to the comments, basking in the attention of being a newlywed.

Saying goodnight to Phoebe and Ted at the end of the evening and entering their room, Olive felt a frisson of excitement, believing that Harry's attention throughout the evening meant that this might be the night she would experience tenderness. They had clearly enjoyed themselves and she believed their good humour would follow into their bed.

As he closed their door, Harry turned to her and said, "What did you find so engaging about Mr. Alexander, Olive?"

Still feeling the warmth of the group, Olive was unaware of the tension visible in the set of Harry's jaw. "Nothing of consequence, really" she replied. "We chatted about several topics. I always enjoy discussions with men of his age. They bring such a wealth of experience" said Olive, walking away from Harry toward the dressing room. Harry followed close on her heels.

"I hope you realize you will need to be more circumspect now that you are a married lady, Olive" said Harry. "Men will take a pretty face and encouraging smile in ways you don't intend, thinking you are being provocative."

Olive laughed softly, touched by Harry's concern. "Oh, Harry, he is a grandfather and committed churchman. And, besides, I have never said anything in my life that could remotely be misconstrued as provocative." Harry pulled Olive roughly into his arms, holding her arms pinned to her sides.

"Harry, you are hurting me" Olive said, her voice catching. Her fear of the night before returned instantly and she was surprised that the evening had so quickly turned from pleasant to frightening. Harry released her as he said "Just remember, Olive, you are my wife now and everything you say reflects on me."

Before leaving her side, he gently stroked his fingers under her chin in a way that left Olive feeling more threatened than caressed.

After undressing and tidying up their dressing room, Olive joined Harry in bed, wary of his changed mood. Rather than the tenderness she had believed would come that night, she was dismayed to discover a repeat of the previous night's performance by Harry and, this time, alcohol could not be blamed. Lying quietly afterward, she wondered who this man was and if this was to be her 'normal'. Despite her aching body, she eventually slept, silent tears drying on her cheeks.

The days and weeks moved forward as they do in every life. For some, time moves quickly. To Olive, time seemed to have stopped the day she moved into the Winans' home with the start of Harry's brutality. She felt isolated, cut off from her family but unwilling to mention anything to the only women in her intimate circle; Phoebe or Rachel. She certainly couldn't share her experience with Minnie in her weekly letter.

The months that followed were quiet in the Winans household and held few distractions for Olive. Compared with Belmont, where a guest or two seemed always in residence, she was surprised at how rarely Ted and Phoebe entertained.

Sunday was the one day they did, although on a small scale; just a couple or two from their social circle invited after church for luncheon. The first Sunday with guests was pleasant for Olive. She had met the couple previously at the Alexander's dinner.

After they had taken their leave, Olive excused herself and went upstairs for a quiet hour to write to Minnie. They had devised a manner in which letters from her would not arouse suspicion when arriving at Belmont and she clung to this only contact from her childhood home.

She was surprised when Harry joined her; she had expected him to spend the hours before dinner reading in the study. "Olive, I thought your comments today a tad personal" he said, as he casually stretched out in a chair beside the desk. "I would not have shared as much information about your family as you did."

Olive laid her pen on the desk, gaining time to think about how best to respond. Already, she had discovered that she needed to have her wits about her when speaking with Harry. He seemed able to twist her words and best her in every discussion.

In the few seconds available to her, she could think of no reason for his objection so decided to speak freely. "I welcomed the opportunity to speak of them, Harry. I have missed them greatly and sharing my stories of them made my happy" she replied.

"I understand, my Dear, but really would prefer that you keep your family anecdotes within our family. One never knows how others will react to the escapades of the Wilmot clan nor how I will be viewed by my association."

"Your father is connected and news of your estrangement from the family may be known. Some might view me negatively because of this. Please keep this in mind for the good of my good name. I think we should declare your family as a prohibited topic of conversation. I'll forgive today's indiscriminate speech but ask that you be more circumspect in the future." Harry rose and tenderly touched her shoulder before leaving her to her thoughts.

She found his tenderness, as always, confusing. She struggled trying to reconcile the man she had come to know in the night with this calm, persuasive one, even when his words didn't always sit right. It must be something she was doing that brought the aggressive side out in him. Olive determined to behave in ways that prompted the tender side of him.

'What could I possibly have shared that might be considered too intimate' wondered Olive. *'Of course, I can understand he is sensitive to public opinion about our marriage. I really must put more thought into my words before speaking. Harry is clearly far more discrete than I.'*

True-hearted to the core, Olive would never have guessed that Harry's reason for correcting her was his own jealousy. He resented the attention she received; attention that should be directed to him. His young bride had turned out to be a witty and entertaining storyteller but he would put a stop to that. It would just take time.

While she might be confused by these gentle but confusing corrections to her behaviour in the daytime, there was no doubt about his intentions at night. Harry took every opportunity to remind her that it was her role as his wife to satisfy him and produce an heir. No matter the time he arrived home, he would wake her to use her body. She could count on one hand the number of nights since their wedding that Harry had not demanded 'his due'. His sexual appetite was never exhausted and he became rougher and coarser with time.

Although Olive tried not to dwell on this side of her marriage, she couldn't help but remember her father's concerns about Harry. She now understood what Samuel had discovered about the life that Harry led and had learned more about him besides; Harry had a cruel streak. With his parents, it presented itself as bullying; with her, sexual abuse.

But cruelty is often perpetrated by cowards who prey on the weak and defenceless and gain strength in doing so. This knowledge changed nothing for Olive. She was helpless against Harry's

increasing strength. The isolation from her family and friends had created the perfect vulnerability in her for Harry's needs. Sadly, she understood she had no one to blame but herself.

His demands in bed were abhorrent to her but any protest she raised was quickly and, usually, violently quieted. She grew to hate what had once been one of her vanities; her long, thick strawberry blonde hair. It was too easy for Harry to grab a handful and yank roughly when he thought she might scream out. The inside of her thighs were covered in bites and bruises; another favourite way he had of silencing her. Still she tried to protest which only increased Harry's violent ways. Her protests came to a stop, though; the night Harry wrapped his fingers around her throat. Terror at what he might have done brought out her need for self preservation. From that night on, she acquiesced in silence, limply accepting whatever he did to her, bringing to mind one of her childhood rag dolls.

During the occasional hours they spent together in front of his family, Harry was gentle and attentive to her as he had been the first morning in his home. He gave every appearance of the model husband and Olive had no one to confide in that it was otherwise. She was no longer deceived by any pretence of tenderness on his part, recognizing it for the mockery it was.

Truly, this was not a subject of conversation with even her most intimate friend, had she seen them to spend time with. But she had found early in their marriage that Harry discouraged her from seeing any friends who sought her out.

He had worked hard to isolate Olive even ensuring that all mail arriving for her was given to him first. He instructed her to decline all invitations, citing their (imaginary) busy schedule, except those that he would be home for. School friends who were initially delighted to hear she was living in the city soon came to think she had become snobbish in marriage after receiving repeated polite regrets.

As for her family, the depth of Samuel's anger at Olive's marriage instilled fear in all of them. Her brothers and sisters could not remember a time when Samuel had been so enraged. On the rare occasions when Minnie and Helen managed to visit for tea during a trip into the city, Harry always made certain he was present, preventing intimate conversation between the sisters.

In his presence, Olive behaved as a happy newlywed, for fear of the consequences. The sisters saw nothing amiss, other than a slightly more subdued Olive. Minnie attributed her demure nature to a new maturity brought about by marriage.

In their early months together, when the family attended social events, Harry was as attentive to Olive as he had been during their courtship. Olive had begun to think of his public persona before their marriage as a trap and she the victim caught in it. Harry played the public role of husband so well that the Winans' social set admired the young couple. Olive was often struck by how horrified most would be if they but knew of his behaviour behind closed doors.

In fact, Harry's attentiveness when they were out in public stemmed from his need to know where Olive was and who she was speaking with at all times. Olive had learned quickly, in case Harry could overhear, to make her conversation so banal as to be dull.

Her old friends would not have believed it possible that those in the Winans' society wondered what Harry had seen in such an uninteresting girl. Her conversation seemed limited to the weather, the newest hat styles and the services at church.

"How absolutely flat, she is" said many. "Isn't it sad that charming, handsome young Harry didn't marry a more engaging companion? Clearly, he was taken by her unquestionable beauty, not realizing the rest of the package was so limited."

With their pattern in life established, Harry began to relax his vigilance. He knew he had the position of strength and was pleased with the timid woman he was creating. After some time, he no longer felt the need to be present at the boring social events so welcomed by his parent's friends. He returned to his past practice of evenings spent at the club; the races or late dinners with questionable companions.

Olive was relieved. He would come and go almost independently of the rest, spending time at home only when it suited him. The excuse of business demands had become unnecessary as Harry's confidence in his control in the household regained itself. All in the household knew he was spending time gambling and drinking but none had the power to curtail it.

Olive's daily life, when in Harry's presence, involved something akin to walking on egg shells. When anyone outside of the family was present, she remained generally quiet, always afraid that Harry would

later object to what she had said. When they were alone as a family, she remained wary around him; unable to determine what might set his mood off.

Just as she had said in her journal that she would work hard to be a perfect wife, her aim every day on rising was to be such. But her reason no longer came from a place of love. She was afraid of saying or doing anything that might bring his displeasure. It had taken little time for her to recognize the signs of tension that Harry displayed when something displeased him and she lived in fear of doing so.

She managed his wardrobe expertly, understanding that his clothing was an extension of himself. Each morning, after Harry had departed for his office, Olive went through his previous day's clothes carefully, looking for buttons that needed to be stitched on or fallen hems needing repair. She brought these, along with the soiled items, to Mary for laundering and mending. She returned each item to its rightful place so that Harry would always find his clothing exactly where it should be. Although he found nothing to complain about with such care, neither did he acknowledge it.

Mary managed the household so well that there was very little for Olive to do beyond clean the rooms she and Harry shared but she made certain these were always orderly and clean. She was a quick study; a hair brush out of place on his bureau had been thrown across the room at her only once; nothing was ever out of place again.

Chapter 23

Harry's confidence in his control of Olive and the family brought carelessness. His gambling debts were reaching a point that was out of his control to manage and his drunken behaviour had been noted by more than one society couple when their paths crossed his.

It didn't take long before this came to his brother, Ed's, attention.

While enjoying a quiet dinner at the Toronto Club one evening in February of 1882, Ed was pleased when a fellow member and customer of Winans asked to join his table. "Please do, John" he said. "Business kept me too late to join my family for dinner this evening so here I am. I had thought it would be a solitary dinner so your company is welcome".

The two shared general conversation for some time but it was clear that John had something specific he wished to speak of. Soon enough, he made this clear; he had something about Harry to share.

"I think you know that I am not one to gossip, Ed, but as my wife was with me at the time and Harry's actions were unconscionable, I feel compelled to tell you of a recent incident." Ed was certain he didn't want to hear what John had to say but had unwittingly ensured he was a captive audience by his invitation for the man to join him.

"Emily and I were getting into our carriage after a late dinner last week. It was a chilly night so I was taking some extra time to place the wraps around Emily before boarding. A raucous group was coming down the street and I was trying to get aboard before they reached us when I recognized Harry in the group. He recognized me also and stepped toward us with a woman at his side."

"He was quite clearly inebriated and commented on my wrapping Emily in the warm robes. I have to tell you I was disgusted when he said '*It's up to us to keep them warm, isn't it John? I'll be warming up this one's thighs very shortly.*' As you can imagine, I left immediately and refrained from commenting to Emily. Rest assured, Ed, the woman he spoke of was no lady."

Ed had made a practice of making concessions for his brother's lack of performance in the business. He felt a strong loyalty to his father that compelled him to continuously excuse Harry's arrogance and lack of performance. The loss of their brother, Stuart, while just beginning his career in the family business, had impacted the younger

Edward as much as it had his father. He became determined that the remaining sons would follow the example established by their father and keep the Winans name prominent in business. Ed had strong shoulders, he told his wife, and it was his responsibility, as the eldest brother, to guide the younger men in the family.

But this incident made it clear just how low Harry had sunk. Like his father, Ed had hoped that marriage would introduce stability to Harry but it had done the opposite; marriage had given Harry the cover he needed for an ever more reckless life.

Ed was humiliated that it was a customer who brought this to him. His concerns were many: for their business; their status within the community of Toronto; and his parents. Now his concern included Olive. What might Harry be exposing her to?

Returning home from the Club, Ed repeated the distasteful story to his wife. She was just as horrified as he to think Harry could behave in this manner and her thoughts immediately jumped to Olive.

"It's time I do something," said Ed. "I believe I have tried everything in my power to make Harry accountable for himself at work but I can no longer be quiet about his behaviour. This reflects poorly on all of us."

"You are right, Dear" replied his wife. "I suggest you have a word with your father and the two of you come up with an appropriate plan. I wouldn't want you to bear the blame alone for taking Harry to task when it is clearly a family issue."

Ed recognized the wisdom of this. If his father were not aware of the episode that had brought him to the end of his patience with Harry, he would forever question Ed's motives. He dropped by his parent's home the following day when he knew Harry was at an appointment. It brought him no comfort to share the story but he was relieved when his father took ownership of the solution.

"I see no other recourse, Ed, then for you to remove Harry from the partnership" said Ted. "It's no secret to me that he doesn't pull his weight in the business and your Mother and I have been very concerned about his lifestyle. I believe we are all responsible for the outcome to our actions and Harry is no different. If he is to amount to anything as a man, his feet must be held to the fire. You have my complete support in this action."

With sadness, Ed arrived at his office and made the necessary arrangements to meet with his lawyer to dissolve the partnership. He took no pleasure in telling Harry later in the day that the time had come for him to leave E.C.Winans. He admitted to his wife that evening that he had been surprised by the mildness of Harry's reaction.

"He expressed only a small amount of anger; certainly not the rage we usually expect. In fact, he was quite adamant that he is a desirable property to many businesses in the city and he looks forward to the opportunities waiting for him. I have to say, it was quite a relief."

Chapter 24

While the Winans family were concerned for her, Olive herself had become somewhat numb toward life. She wasn't certain when she began to lose herself but disassociating from the nightly assaults and daily recriminations left little of her true nature remaining.

Pity for herself never entered her thoughts; no one else was responsible for her life. Had she listened to her father, she would still be enjoying life at Belmont instead of the hell she now lived.

During Harry's nightly assaults, she would pray, giving all of her attention to God. During the nights when Harry was just relieving himself or was so drunk that he clearly didn't know it was Olive in his bed, she focused her thoughts on childhood experiences at Belmont, drawing on every detail in an attempt to engage her mind.

It was only this separation of her body from her mind that enabled her to cope during the days. She came to think of herself as two women; a powerless victim at night who, through willpower, could become the other woman at dawn; a normal young wife. While she thought the façade she created was convincing, Ted, Phoebe and Rachel noted a marked difference in her spirit as well as her physical appearance with the passing months.

The gentleness they presented each day acted as a salve on the wounds she experienced each night. With her father-in-law, she unconsciously sought the father she so missed and attached a false sense of security to him. He was, after all, as controlled by Harry as she.

Ted and Phoebe often spoke behind their bedroom door of the change in Olive. They worried that Harry's nightly absences were at fault although they were at a loss as to how they might change things. Although Ted tried to raise the subject with Harry on several occasions, his son ignored his concerns and Ted felt powerless. He suggested to Phoebe that they insist Harry look for a home of their own but Phoebe was quick to point out that this would not change Harry's behaviour or lifestyle and would not stop her worry for Olive.

Unaware of their concern for her, Olive carried on in the marriage she had come to accept as her life, disturbing as it was. Harry's grandmother, Rachel, brought the greatest comfort to Olive.

"I am so grateful to you, Olive, for becoming the hands I have lost use of" said Rachel one morning as Olive began to write a letter on her

behalf. The two had established a routine each morning, with Olive writing letters for Rachel, whose arthritis made handwriting difficult. Rachel had many friends and family with whom she corresponded and Olive found her style of narrative graceful and enjoyed penning her words to paper. "It gives me pleasure, Mrs. Wells," replied Olive. "You have no need to be grateful. I am just very happy to be useful while enjoying time with you."

Transcribing Rachel's words gave Olive opportunity to ask the older woman about her rich and long life. Listening closely to Rachel's words both said and held back, Olive realized that Harry was very much like his grandfather. While never complaining or criticizing, Rachel managed to give Olive the impression that her husband had been a charming man who controlled the household.

"Women had little power over their own lives when I was a young woman, Olive" she said. "We were considered the property of our fathers and then our husband. The lucky woman wed a kind and generous man but too many were surprised to find they had wed replicas of their dominating fathers; men who demanded compliant women in their households. I believe a special place awaits these women in Heaven for all of the trials they endured during their lives."

Olive thought this belief might be the source of Rachel's strength but found no comfort in it for herself when she was still so far from Heaven.

"Marriage might bring security and children to a woman, Olive, but it can also bring challenges that help to shape our character and give us strength" Rachel continued. While Olive wouldn't dream of confiding her fears and pain to Rachel, she took some consolation from the subtle support the older woman provided, understanding she was not the only woman to experience a marriage such as hers.

In spite of advanced arthritis, Rachel pushed herself to walk most days, saying it kept her limber. As time went on and Olive understood just how much pain Rachel was in, she admired the strength of character that refused to give in to weakness. Olive resolved to exhibit that same strength of character.

Never having known a grandmother, Olive embraced Rachel as her own. Beyond the wisdom that the older woman gave to the younger, Olive found Rachel's faith healing to her soul. After lunch and before Rachel's afternoon nap, Olive read bible passages to her

and found peace in doing so. At Belmont, Samuel had daily led the entire household (family and servants) in pre-breakfast bible readings and prayer and she found herself missing this faith-building practice.

Prayer and Rachel's presence were small antidotes to the darkness in her life.

His grandmother's presence also had a calming influence on Harry. She was the one person in his life who he respected and admired. When he wasn't in a foul mood, he could be teasingly affectionate with Rachel. Although Olive could never be jealous of the old woman, she longed to be the recipient of such playful affection.

The eldest and weakest member of the family was unaffected by his moods. Rachel was able to turn Harry's temper around and Olive learned to move nearer to her, seeking her intangible protection until he was calmer.

Olive pretended life was normal in her letters to Minnie. She wrote of her discussions with Ted; great details of the (few) social events they attended; chatter about the shopping excursions she and Phoebe occasionally made in the city; and of Rachel's wisdom and the hours they spent together. It wasn't lost on Minnie that the one thing she *didn't* write about was Harry.

Chapter 25

Samuel's position in Ottawa had become all-consuming and he made infrequent trips back to Belmont; instead corresponding with his Farm Manager to take care of most issues. The sorrow he felt over Olive's actions was immense and being away from home and able to focus on something larger than himself was a relief.

His passion for the science of fish culture consumed him; he believed this issue was paramount to Canada and the greater world. With fish one of the primary sources of food and wealth for the earth's inhabitants, his concern over the depleting stocks was strong. He believed God led him to Ottawa to have a voice in changing this.

Samuel had been awarded for his participation at the 1873 Paris Exhibition which featured the newest in technological and scientific breakthroughs and it was this recognition that now gave him the credibility needed to persuade Parliament toward his cause.

He found the close proximity to those in Parliament who wielded power intoxicating. If he were to affect any sort of change, it would be here, where the larger decisions affecting the nation were made. His days and evenings were filled with meetings and dinners, finishing most nights with brandy at his club alongside like-minded Parliamentarians. Although his position was an appointed one, Samuel had found many allies in elected officials who shared his concern and his vision.

While his mind was thus preoccupied, Samuel always enjoyed the letters he received from his family. They kept him abreast of their lives and, although he regretted the distance from them, allowed him to still feel involved in their days.

After reading a letter from Minnie one day, the sadness he felt from his severed connection with Olive weighed heavily on his heart. He couldn't stop wondering how her life was turning out and if marriage had brought her the happiness she deserved.

He had witnessed many young women wear their marriage like a heavy cloak; feeling the protection of their husband was worth the weight of new responsibilities and expectations. Women of his own generation became extensions of their husband in thought and manner following their vows but his views on women were far different. Indeed, he had been drawn to Tillie for her quickness of thought and

strong manner for the very reason that he wanted a wife to share her opinions and make her own decisions. He admitted only to himself what an error he had made.

Of his three daughters, Olive had responded to his challenges of thought and action the most. At home during her school years he encouraged her debating skills, enjoying her arguments. Her cleverness in formulating them made him proud. While Minnie showed strength in putting her own position forward, Olive had an uncanny ability to make others question their position, leading to thoughtful discussions.

He had hoped for so much more for Olive. He knew too well that her defiance of his wishes concerning Harry was not malicious on her part; simply innocence.

He knew, too, who bore culpability in Olive's decision. Wasn't it he who insisted his daughters had an understanding of their individual value and strength? His choice of Bishop Strachan School had been deliberate; he knew the students were encouraged in independent thought and his lessons would be reinforced.

Still, she had shocked him. He just hoped the strength she had demonstrated through her defiance would be there for what he suspected would be a difficult marriage.

He hoped with all his heart that Harry, at best, was living up to Olive's expectations. In his gloomier moments, he worried that Harry was proving to be a thoughtless and selfish husband. Never for a moment could he have imagined the actual man.

Putting his thoughts of Olive aside, he turned his mind to his responsibilities within the Dept. of Fisheries. His energies were increasingly on preparations for the International Fisheries Exhibition in London, planned for May to October of 1883. This scientific, cultural, and animal exhibition was yet another forum planned to showcase the wonders of the British Commonwealth and Canada had high hopes for its contributions to the Exhibition.

Samuel was to act as Chairman of the Canadian Commission overseeing the creation of the Canadian display. He planned to set up a mini hatchery, similar to the one created in Newcastle, and would be participating in the conference part of the Exhibition. He planned to express his concern about depleting fish populations to his peers from other countries.

Plans were underway for a move to London in November of 1882 to allow time for the preparations. He would remain until the following November after the conference's close. He had taken a lease on a home for one year and was busy preparing Belmont and his Ottawa staff for this extended leave.

The length of his absence prompted him to invite the children and their spouses to Belmont throughout the summer, allowing him time to spend with each; all except Olive.

Reading of this in Minnie's latest letter, Olive rested the papers in her lap to gaze out the window sadly. How she would have loved to spend the summer with everyone at Belmont. But even had she not been banished by her father, the likelihood of such a visit would have been slim. As Harry told her time and again, he was out pounding the pavement in search of a position to support her needs.

Her response to Minnie made no mention of Harry's new unemployment. She knew this latest development in her life would greatly worry her sister and so withheld it, even while living daily with her fear of the news reaching her family.

Chapter 26

Harry's response to Edward at the time of his dismissal may have been mild but he was infuriated when he saw the notice in The Canada Gazette at the end of March: "The partnership heretofore existing between E. C. Winans & H. R. Winans under the name Winans & Co. in the city of Toronto is this day dissolved by mutual consent and the business will be continued at same place and under same name of Winans & Co. by E.C. Winans."

"How does he think this makes me look" he asked loudly of his father, throwing the paper on the desk. "Could he not have waited until I had secured another position before publically calling attention to our split?"

"This is how business is done, Harry" replied Ted calmly. "Customers expect to be kept abreast of changes in the businesses they deal with. And be honest with yourself. How do you think Edward should have proceeded considering your behaviour is public knowledge? Really, Edward had no other option than to distance himself from you."

"Well, I can think of any number of stories he could have given when asked. This notice clearly reflects poorly on me and I have no doubt will affect my prospects in this city." Harry was just spouting air with this. He knew that his father was right. The story told to Edward at The Toronto Club had already circulated throughout the members, making it extremely unlikely that any would consider employing him.

It was really frustration that caused Harry's outburst that morning. He had done little in searching for a new position, having no idea how to go about such a task. Handed the position with his brother's firm with no effort on his part, he realized just how little he knew about job hunting. He understood that it was generally through connections with other businessmen that positions came about. But, with the gossip about him, this was clearly not an avenue available to him.

What was he to do? The advertisements in the Toronto newspapers were of no help for someone in his position. They were for clerks and other junior positions he was well beyond succumbing to. Any sales positions were generally in retail establishments.

He would just keep his ear to the ground and be receptive to business opportunities. Clearly, he would have to make it happen in some way. If the right proposition came along for him to start his own business, he was quite certain his father would back him, as he had Edward Jr. He just needed to make sure of all of his information before presenting such an opportunity to him.

In spite of unemployment, Harry's behaviour changed little during the weeks following his release from Winans & Co.; he still pursued the gaming tables; after all, one never knew who would join the tables on a given night. He had quickly used up the small allotment his brother had provided him as a separation allowance, considering this a wise investment.

Whoever had said 'you have to spend money to make money' had known what they were talking about. He would never find a position if he moped about the city looking every bit a job hunter. His approach was to remain larger than life, giving everyone an impression that he didn't need a position but would be a catch for some smart employer. At least, that's what he told himself.

By April, with no leads and the reality that he was now having to rely on a line of credit at the tables (his father's name and wealth still accounted for something in the city), he was still quite convinced of the soundness of his strategy.

It was purely by chance that Harry sat next to a rough looking character at a gaming table one night. This man talked grandly about the opportunities the north had to offer. The Canada Pacific Railway had just been completed to North Bay and this man had spent time in the north scouting out opportunities to make money. Harry was all ears.

Chapter 27

As Harry went out each night to conquer the world, the household continued in a state of normalcy but it was anything but for Olive. As April, and her 18th birthday, came and went and still Harry had not secured a new position, she began to feel uneasy about the likelihood that her family would eventually hear the news.

Olive admitted she was relieved when Harry's activities took him away from the house during the days. His attitude during these weeks was morose. Even his grandmother was unable to cheer him.

So, when he rose one day full of excitement for an opportunity he had learned of the evening before, Olive listened gratefully.

Her relief at his improved outlook was short-lived as the words he spoke sank in. "Think about it, Olive. The north is filled with trappers, miners and lumber men. Until now, they've had no avenue to spend the money they're making but, with a new train daily, the towns will grow and more people will come" Harry said, barely able to contain his excitement. "I think we're at a perfect time to establish a general merchandise store and develop it into a thriving retail establishment."

For the first time since knowing Harry, Olive sensed a boyish enthusiasm. She could almost picture what he must have been like and she might have been charmed. But her conditioned fear of him quickly surfaced. Was she, as a 'loving' wife expected to go along with this outrageous scheme?

Olive had long ago stopped expressing opinions with Harry; any time she had ventured an intelligent observation, he was quick to belittle her or fill with rage. While she might have been raised to think independently, Harry clearly believed women had no business thinking beyond their household. Olive dealt with this by pretending that all her cares were about him.

"I understand, Harry. My own father followed the same path in Newcastle before taking over the family farm. My concerns are about the expenses involved and, of course, about being so far from your family" replied Olive.

"The money is not an issue. Since my father backed Edward Jr., I don't see how he could possibly deny me this opportunity and, as I said, the trains will run daily so an occasional journey back to the city would not be difficult" reassured Harry.

His next words left Olive's head spinning. "This is our chance to make a success of our marriage, Olive. I know life hasn't been ideal for you here but I believe living under my parent's roof has adversely affected our relationship. Think of it: a new town, a new business enterprise, a new start for us."

Olive wasn't so far gone that she believed his positive spin; it wasn't living in this house that had damaged their relationship. But her exhausted emotions questioned if there might be at least some truth to this. She needed to believe him to understand how life had gone so wrong and to quell the slight fear that surfaced at the thought of living alone with him away from the oversight of his parents and grandmother.

"I'm sure you will research this enough for me to have faith, Harry" she said. "I'm your wife and my role is to support you in your dreams. North Bay it is."

"I couldn't be more relieved to hear you say that, Olive" replied Harry absentmindedly, his thoughts already on the next steps of his plan. Her agreement really was inconsequential to him; he just wanted her onside when he broached his father.

Thinking things through, Harry continued. "My plan is for us to head north at the beginning of June and take advantage of the summer trade. We can't afford to lose any time."

After a preliminary trip to North Bay, during which he secured a suitable building for the business and their accommodation, Harry returned home filled with stories of the beauty of the northern landscape.

The following month was filled by all manner of preparation. The short time frame left no time for Olive to worry. With Phoebe's help, she managed their personal needs while Harry sourced the supplies needed from various wholesalers around the city and arranged for delivery to North Bay. He telegraphed the Canada Pacific Railway Station Manager, requesting that the supplies he sent be appropriately stored at the station until such time as he arrived to transfer everything to the store. His industriousness surprised everyone.

While his father had been against the move in the start, Harry had managed to coerce him through guilt, accurately predicting that Ted would have difficulty denying him what he had willingly done for Edward Jr.

In private, Ted and Phoebe had to admit that this new Harry was someone quite unfamiliar to them. Ted theorized that it may not have been in Harry's best interest to be pigeon-holed into family business interests. Perhaps Harry's success would come when he had total control of his career. They prayed that this move was what was needed to finally bring out responsibility in Harry.

As arrangements came together, Olive's new ability to compartmentalize emotional pain allowed her to put aside the sad truth that she would now be living so much further from her family. Even though she was not welcome at Belmont, knowing they were a short train ride away had always been in her mind. She focused now on the best approach to tell Minnie about the pending move.

She wanted to fill in as many details as possible when she broke the news, feeling she would be less likely to despair if the plan seemed sound.

Minnie was quick to respond, *'As sad as I am that you will be so far from me, Olive, truly, I hope that Harry will make a great success of this opportunity and the two of you will become the mercantile barons of the north. I am certain that, with time, Papa's position will soften and I might be able to make a visit to North Bay. I will count on this.'*

Olive kept busy, allowing no time for fears or emotions. Her mind was filled with the details, shopping and packing; her body exhausted when she laid her head down at night.

The human mind is a curious thing; able to make truth out of lies and fact out of fiction when needed. With the start of each new day, Olive allowed herself to believe that this move would be the catalyst for a new relationship with Harry. Indeed, he was so wrapped up in his plans that his nightly outings had come to an end. Without the fuel of alcohol or his risky friends, his sexual appetite, while still not tender, became at least bearable.

Lying in bed as dawn arrived on the day of their departure; Olive actually felt a little excitement. Harry's comments throughout the planning made their move feel like an adventure rather than an ending. He had been clear that their living accommodation would, temporarily at least, be somewhat rustic. It would take some time for the business to take hold and give them the needed finances to build a home of their own.

This didn't disturb Olive. She remembered the stories of her own grandmother's pioneering experiences in Newcastle, which had been mostly forest at the time of their arrival from York. Although Belmont was soon built and the lives her grandparents had lived was anything but primitive, Olive reminded herself of the courage such a move had taken. She was determined to display the same courage. If her grandmother could embrace life as a pioneer, so could she. After all, that was how success was built.

Harry shipped all of their household goods ahead so their departure was a little easier with just the trunks of their personal clothing. Olive had determined, with Phoebe's agreement, to leave much of her clothing at their home. It was unlikely that she would require the gowns or dinner dresses for some time and these could be wrapped and shipped at a later date. Her day dress ensembles would suffice. She chose the simplest of her clothing; washable cotton for the summer and wool for added warmth in the winters.

Olive loved fashion and had looked longingly in the windows of Eatons at the new bustles with elaborate trains on display. They made a woman's shape very flattering but were highly impractical for northern Ontario. The streets may or may not have boardwalks and, without servants to care for their clothing, she had no desire to be spending her days cleaning mud from her skirts.

Waiting for the carriage to arrive to take them to the station, Phoebe and Olive sat together in the parlour. "I am going to miss your company greatly, Olive" said Phoebe. "Mr. Winans and I have so enjoyed your presence in our home. We pray that this opportunity will bring great success to Harry and happiness to you both."

"You and Mr. Winans have made me feel that this is my home, Mrs. Winans, and I will miss it as much as I have missed my own Belmont" replied Olive. "Once Harry has the business up and running and our situation in North Bay is stable, I certainly hope the two of you will visit us. I understand the colours of nature are quite spectacular in the fall so it might be a pleasant diversion for the two of you."

Rachel had been feeling unwell for some days and chose to remain upstairs as Olive and Harry made their goodbyes. They had separately visited her in her room to say their farewells. As eager as Harry was for this new start, he was well aware that he may not see his grandmother again, making their goodbye particularly difficult. For

her part, Olive wondered if she would ever know a woman so understanding and supportive in her life again.

The train trip was a subdued one; Harry obviously caught up in his plans and Olive feeling melancholic at a second separation from a home and family she had known and loved. Although she had trained her mind to think favourably on this move, she did not embrace it with the same anticipation she had felt at leaving Belmont to begin her new life as a married woman. How wrong she had been then.

As the miles passed, Olive was overwhelmed by the vastness of the countryside. She noticed with each stop the train made that the towns became smaller and more primitive. As they pulled into North Bay, she was reassured to see that at least its station was a substantial wooden building. Harry reached up to help her step down from the train and she had her first glimpse of her new town. Seeing the people on the platform waiting for passengers or freight, her enthusiasm dipped. She was the only woman present and was receiving considerable notice.

Harry supervised the removal of their luggage and arranged for a horse and cart to take them to the local inn. He had planned for them to spend the first nights there while sorting out their living accommodation.

To call the building an 'inn' was an overstatement, thought Olive, alighting from the cart. The wooden structure had just two small windows facing the street. The buildings around it were not much better and her doubts were building. What promise Harry could possibly have seen in such a place? The front room of the inn was a dining room of sorts and several patrons were eating and drinking. All eyes turned to Olive as she entered; once again, the only woman in the room.

A rather unkempt man stepped forward, recognizing Harry from his previous visit, to welcome them. As he came closer, Olive had the distinct impression that he hadn't bathed in some time. She was surprised to learn that he was the owner of the inn and several other local enterprises besides.

"It's a pleasure to have you in our midst, Mrs. Winans" said the man, who Harry had introduced as Mr. Johnson. "You may very well be the only woman for miles, other than those in the local Indian tribes. Most of the men who arrive here leave their families at home.

Speaks well of your hardiness that you would take on such an adventure."

It wouldn't be fair to say that Harry had deceived Olive in this; after all, he had shared little actual detail about the town or its inhabitants. He had merely withheld too much detail, understanding that convincing her to make this move would not have happened had she been aware.

Harry had never considered leaving her behind. In actual fact, he had given very little consideration to her, except in how she would be useful to him. His previous visit to North Bay had confirmed the value in having Olive with him. Although he understood that, for money, Indian women made themselves available to men here, he was not about to resort to that when he had a beautiful woman in his own home and bed available. Her usefulness went beyond his personal needs, though.

Harry thought himself to be an astute judge of the male character. He knew what was uppermost in all men's minds and that any woman would attract attention in this hinterland. A woman as beautiful as Olive would bring business to his doorstep.

As they settled in the room they were given, Olive found it impossible to keep silent. "I am mystified, Harry, as to why you would bring me to such a place knowing I would be the only woman" she said with great sadness. "Am I of so little value that you could expose me to this community of men with little thought to my feelings?"

"On the contrary, Olive" replied Harry, stroking her arm. "My feelings for you are so strong that I cannot imagine living anywhere without you. How could I be successful if I were so far from you? And, someone, at some point, must bring their wife if this town is to grow as we know it will," he continued persuasively. "Others are sure to follow suit once your presence is known. Does it not suit your spirit of adventure to be the first?"

Once again, Harry's words bewildered Olive. Had she been so wrong in judging him? "I imagine you are right, Harry, but it will not make my life any easier knowing I am to be the vanguard of change. I trust you will be patient with me in the coming months when I feel isolated and lonely without other women around."

"We will be too busy for you to feel isolated, lonely or anything else, Olive" said Harry. "I depend on your hands as much as your

company to get this business underway. Our work begins tomorrow with the unloading of all of the supplies for the shop. For now, let us consider the adventure underway and make our way back to the dining room for some dinner."

Olive put the clothing she had been unpacking aside and followed Harry. Their meal was plain but she gave it little thought as she listened to Harry's plans for them. He explained that their living accommodation would be the rooms behind the shop. He said they were small and needed considerable cleanup but all that they would need in the short term.

Chapter 28

Olive dressed in her most serviceable cotton skirt and blouse for their first work day. She pulled out the new apron purchased for the work she would now need to do around their household. Servants of any kind were out of the question but Olive felt more than prepared to do the hard work necessary.

Samuel was an egalitarian and his children had been expected to pull their weight around the household and farm as much as any of his employees were. Olive could make a batch of biscuits and loaves of bread as well as anyone and had spent many hours in her childhood making the weekly supply of candles from melted beef fat. Life in Toronto compared to what she had seen of North Bay was positively luxurious but, as she and Harry set out that morning, she felt more than capable of what was now expected.

They walked the short distance from the inn to the building Harry had taken for the shop. She agreed with Harry that these early months would be focused on the business and there would be time to look for a suitable house once the shop was successful. In the meantime, he explained, the rooms at the back of the shop, complete with a wood stove, she could set up as she liked for their own use.

Looking around the town as they walked, Olive wondered if such a thing as a suitable house existed in North Bay but she kept her thoughts to herself.

The first day was spent unpacking the few household items they had brought. Harry had arranged for their meagre furnishings to be delivered; a bed and dresser; table and chairs; and work table for the area dedicated to the kitchen.

Olive was surprised to find a large tub against the wall in the kitchen; clearly a thoughtful move on Harry's part to provide a means for bathing. The gesture was ill-considered, however, once she understood how many buckets of water she would have to carry from the well and heat on the stove to fill such a tub. She would make do with sponge baths for the most part, saving the tub experience for a rare treat.

With fresh linens on the bed and their belongings, such as they were, put away, Olive was done by mid afternoon. She went outside with a basket to pick wild flowers she had noticed growing in the

yard. She wanted to make their home, however primitive and small, as warm and welcoming as possible.

A farmer with vegetables passed on his way to the inn and Olive asked if she might purchase any excess vegetables he had. She was pleased when he filled her arms with early potatoes, asparagus, peas and baby carrots. They would have a feast that evening.

When Harry came through from the shop at the end of the day, he was clearly happy with all that she had accomplished. As they shared the meal she had prepared together, they discussed the future and all that it held. Olive found herself, uncharacteristically, relaxing in his company, relishing the pleasure of creating her own home for the first time in her life. '*This is what married life should be*', she thought.

The pleasure was short-lived. In bed that night, Harry was, if not the brute she had known in Toronto, certainly forceful and unconcerned about her. After he had fallen asleep, she cried quietly, for all that might have been.

She felt humiliated by her naivety in thinking their life would be different here just because Harry said it would. She thought of the hopes she had allowed herself as they had prepared for this move and realized that Harry's charm had once again deceived her.

One of those hopes had been that she might finally bring a child into a loving relationship. This thought had sustained her through her sadness at leaving the Winans and her own family but she now understood that theirs would never be the loving, tender marriage she dreamt of. She adored children and had always prayed for a large family when she married. With awareness of the future ahead of her Olive put this desire aside. If a child should come, she would, of course, think it a blessing but she would not grieve if they remained childless. The horror of imagining Harry as a parent helped her resolve in this.

Though still just 18, Olive gained wisdom that night. 'If nothing is to change in our relationship' she thought, 'success in the business will be the only thing that will bind us. I will focus my energies on it and put aside what might have been.'

The next day, and every day after, she spent in the shop helping Harry unpack; dusting and placing each item, leaving only to prepare a basic lunch and dinner. Each evening, Olive gratefully fell into bed, too exhausted to consider anything beyond the rest she needed.

As the cash register was placed on the counter at the end of the week, Harry turned to Olive, saying "That's it then, Olive. We are open for business."

Harry was pleased that Olive volunteered to join him in the store on their first day open. Seeing her behind the counter convinced him of the soundness of his plan. If anything was to bring men to the shop, the novelty of a beautiful woman would.

Although Olive felt out of her depth, she spent her days tidying shelves, sweeping the front boardwalk and washing down the outside window. She couldn't be much use to those few men who ventured in; she had no knowledge of tools or blankets or men's wool coats. She consoled herself that, once the women began to arrive, she could take a more active part in the selling of yard goods and dress and household accessories.

Initial traffic was mostly out of curiosity. Purchases in July and August were too few to cover their own needs, never mind recouping the expenses of setting up the shop. In speaking with other men in the town, Harry learned that the mines and lumber camps all maintained their own stores where employees purchased their immediate needs. It had not occurred to him that this form of income would not be overlooked by the large companies who had established themselves in the area. He now counted on the traffic the trappers would bring once snow fell.

In addition to the existing competition, the new train connection had not brought the influx of pioneers expected to flock to North Bay. As August came to a close, the romance of the adventure had been replaced by the reality and brought grave doubt about the potential for success. And, despite Harry's prediction, no other women arrived.

By September, the practicalities of their position lay heavily on Olive; how would they survive a winter without a garden or fruit trees to use for preserves?

In planning the move while still in Toronto, she had felt more than equipped to deal with the seasons but her experience had been of a bountiful supply from the gardens and orchards at Belmont and stores well stocked in Toronto. She and Harry had been enjoying a rich diet of game and fish thanks to the hunters who brought rabbits, pheasant and other small game and fish to barter at the shop. But she knew the supply of vegetables they had enjoyed through the summer was coming

to an end. No one with produce to sell had grown enough for preserving and they didn't have the funds to bring them in by train.

Her worries for their physical wellbeing were not the only dark thoughts she had. As the reality of their situation became clearer with each passing week, Harry blamed everyone but himself.

He was no different in his own business venture than he had been in everything in life to date; expecting instant success and giving no thought to any other scenario. He also hadn't considered that he now had no one to fall back on and the reality of his own responsibility was more than he could bear.

His attitude toward Olive darkened with each day.

The first time he struck her, Olive stood silent in disbelief. Could this really have happened? As afraid of Harry as she had felt over the past year, she had never considered him capable of this.

Harry immediately expressed remorse and cradled her in his arms. "Oh Olive, forgive me" he said. "You understand the strain the business is putting on me. I'm so sorry I lashed out at you. Let's put this behind us, shall we, as aberrant behaviour that won't happen again. Can you do that, my Darling? Tell you what, tomorrow's Sunday. Let's take a picnic to the lake and forget about all of our worries."

Olive could only nod in agreement; too afraid to let words escape her mouth.

It wasn't long before Harry's 'aberrant behaviour' became the norm, with him smacking or slapping her for any and every imagined fault and misdeed.

Olive soon realized that, without the presence of Rachel or Phoebe and Ted, there was no longer any reason for Harry to control himself and, seeing no remedy, despair of her situation took hold.

She spoke little for fear of causing a disruption. Her unhappiness took away any appetite and, never very large, she now became gaunt. This brought out increased brutality in Harry, as he complained about her skinny frame. Olive had become the source of all of Harry's disappointments.

Chapter 29

Samuel sat in his library at Belmont feeling very satisfied with preparations for his trip abroad. He had enjoyed the months at Belmont with his children and their spouses. His farm manager was an able man and the farm had done well while he had been in Ottawa and Samuel had no concerns over leaving the man in charge for the coming year as well. In fact, all details for his pending year abroad had been considered and looked after. All but one matter had been looked after: Olive.

With his departure approaching, Samuel felt it impossible to leave for England without having some indication of her wellbeing. During the course of the summer, Samuel had visited Toronto several times and heard disturbing things about Harry. Most, he put down to gossip but when the stories were confirmed by Hart Massey, whom he trusted implicitly, he began to take note. Hart was the one friend Samuel had been honest with about Olive's secret marriage.

Samuel had been invited to Hart's Jarvis Street home, Euclid, during one of his Toronto visits that summer. As staunch Methodists, no alcohol was served in a Massey home so it was over tea that Hart broached the subject of Harry.

"Samuel, you know that I am not a man to repeat idle chatter but I'm going to tell you disturbing news today that I am compelled to share because of my concern for Olive. When you first inquired about Harry Winans, I knew only of his father and elder brother but I am now in possession of new knowledge about young Harry."

"Edward Jr. and my son, Charles, are in the Toronto Club together and have become friends. Charles respects Edward greatly and I believe this to be mutual. I think because Edward recognizes Charles is not a man who spreads stories, he has confided in him."

"Edward and his parents suffered greatly, both financially and in reputation, because of Harry's behaviour and it was necessary to remove him from the business. They didn't take the step lightly but both Edward and his father felt they needed to take action. Harry was a constant at the gambling tables and a regular visitor at several brothels in the city. Edward and his father hoped to stop Harry's carousing behaviour by removing his regular income and making him stand on his own."

"I am sad to say that I know this was not the case. It's not unusual for Charles to be called to the factory during the night. Several times after Harry's dismissal, he witnessed Harry in compromising positions around the city."

"I feel regret now for not sharing this with you earlier but I believed that Edward's family was watching over Olive. When I learned of their move north, I hoped that this would be a watershed moment for Harry to change his ways but as I have prayed on this through the past weeks, I have experienced doubts."

"My experience is that men can change their character but it generally comes about after a cataclysmic experience in their lives. Harry's behaviour even after losing his employment suggested his character remained the same. Now I worry that Olive is living in a remote area with this man with no family around to support her."

Having unburdened himself, Hart looked sadly at Samuel.

Samuel said "My objection to this marriage was based on my knowledge of Harry's gambling but this is the first I have heard of the brothels. I cringe to think what he might have exposed her to."

"Although I had strong feelings about the man, I had no proof of his character. I forbade Olive to marry him based on my instincts but, sadly, she went against my command and wed anyway."

"You know that we have had no contact since her marriage" continued Samuel sadly, "but, with what you are now telling me, I see nothing for it but to take the train to North Bay and assess her situation firsthand. I do thank you, my friend, for your candour. You are the first to tell me the truth, although others have hinted at the gossip."

Returning to Newcastle, he made the necessary arrangements. This visit was to put his mind at rest; nothing more. God willing, he would confirm that all was well and be free to leave for London with a lighter heart.

Chapter 30

Samuel's first thought as he carried his carpetbag from the station in North Bay was of surprise that Harry could have thought such a primitive community had imminent potential. From its location and natural beauty, Samuel knew that, with time, the town was certain to become a metropolis of the north but he had enough life experience to realize that such development would take decades. He began to feel concern for what Olive had stepped into.

Truly, he hadn't slept well since Hart had confided in him about Harry's behaviour. Who knew what her life this past year had truly been like living with this man? He now regretted not stepping in before. His stubborn pride would be his downfall. He was still mad as hell at Harry (and disappointed by Olive) but he determined to pretend otherwise to get the true lay of the land between them.

Walking along the muddy path that was the main (and only) street, he came up to a shop with a sign above the door saying 'Winan's Mercantile'. The shop looked clean and well organized from the outside and Samuel opened the door, striding in with purpose.

A bell overhead rang as the door opened, bringing Harry from the back room. "Mr. Wilmot" he said with utter surprise. He stopped in his tracks. Samuel was the last person Harry expected to see standing in the front of his shop.

Warily, Harry said "I wasn't aware that you were planning a trip up. I'm sorry that Olive didn't mention this to me or I would have greeted you at the train station."

It had become such commonplace practice for Harry to blame Olive for every shortcoming that he spoke before thinking that doing so to her own father might not be quite the thing.

For a man so glib with his tongue, the sudden appearance of his father-in-law left Harry's mind blank. It had never occurred to him that he might one day face Olive's father and have to explain their elopement but, with the man suddenly in front of him, he felt his anger rise. He knew an ambush when he saw one.

But Samuel appeared anything but confrontational, casually moving about the shop, appearing very much just as any parent might; curious and interested.

"I gave no warning, Harry" replied Samuel. "It was only in the past month that I learned of your new venture. As I am to leave for England shortly for a year's duration, I felt compelled to see how life is for the two of you before going."

With Samuel's calm words, Harry managed to bring a measure of control to himself and came forward holding out his hand.

"As you can see," he said to Samuel, sweeping his arms proudly to take in the shop, "we plan to take advantage of the burgeoning growth in the north. I am able to supply any man's needs." Harry was intent on recognition for all that he had accomplished, wanting to impress upon the man that his daughter's faith had not been misguided.

"But I am sure you are anxious to see Olive. She is in our rooms behind the shop if you'd like to go back. I believe she's preparing our dinner. She will certainly be surprised to see you."

Samuel went into the shop's back room, through a door, arriving in a dingy room with one small window with a burlap curtain pulled up. He was somewhat surprised at the rustic appearance of the room. Despite the wood stove, the lack of furniture left it feeling cold. He could see a small bedroom with a bed and dresser but, clearly, the water closet was outside. Hooks on the wall held their outer clothes and shelves on the wall, their dishes.

Olive was preparing biscuits by candlelight since the day was dim and little light came in through the window. She looked up thinking Harry had come back for something and was astonished to see her father standing before her. The shock on her face was soon replaced by the wide smile Samuel had so missed. Her unreserved happy squeal delighted him as she came around the table, wiping her hands on her apron, to embrace Samuel warmly. He had missed out on her life of the previous year but resolved in that instant to put his anger aside.

"Whatever brought you to our doorstep, I am grateful for" said Olive. "You can't imagine how much I have missed you." As a result of the poor light in the room, Samuel didn't immediately see any changes in his girl but he thought she seemed much thinner when they embraced.

"Well, my girl" replied Samuel, "I'm here now. I will be leaving for England shortly for a year's duration and couldn't, in good conscience, make the journey without knowing all was well with you.

"Oh, Papa" Olive sighed, "you have no idea how often I have dreamt of seeing you again. I am just grateful that you are here."

Sensing his girl had more to say and feeling the restriction of Harry so close, Samuel said "It was a long train ride, Olive, and I would love to stretch my legs. Why don't we take a short stroll around the town and you can tell me all about your life?"

Chapter 31

Olive tried to hide the shake in her hands as she removed her apron, grabbed her shawl off a hook on the wall and turned to her father. She was sure her knees would give out on her as she took a step toward him but feeling his firm hand on her arm steadied her. In all of her despair over the past year, she had never imagined a scene in which her father would suddenly stand before her. The sight of him made her forget every assault.

The reality of her situation quickly replaced her absolute joy: how would she ever be able to say goodbye to him once he was satisfied with her situation? Her father brought a feeling of peace to her heart but she was too conditioned by Harry to think this was anything but short-lived. As the two set out, she was already preparing herself for the inevitable.

Even with dusk upon them, Samuel was shocked when he got a better look at Olive in natural light. They hadn't gone many steps when he stopped her. "Let me take a look at you, girl. It's been so long since I laid eyes on you."

With no warning of his visit, Olive had had no time to wash her face or brush her hair. Doing so would have little effect in any event. Her skin had a sallow colour and her hair had lost its vibrancy and natural shine. But it was the marks on Olive's face and neck that brought him to a standstill. "What has happened to you, Olive? How did you get those bruises?" he asked. "Don't try to tell me that things are well because you yourself are the evidence that they are not."

"Papa, poor Harry lives with such frustration in this new venture. Business is not what he had been led to believe it might be and he worries daily about what to do. The bruise is from Harry but I am not in the least surprised that he hit me. A man has limits to what he can handle and I picked an inopportune moment to question him about his plans. Please don't hold this against him."

Samuel took a deep breath and began walking again to gather his thoughts. He managed only just to control himself as he replied. "A man does not take out his frustrations in life on the woman he loves, Olive. I have been around enough in my lifetime to believe that this is not the first abuse Harry has shown toward you. Pray, tell me all."

Her hesitancy to reveal the truth of Harry was soon replaced by such a sense of relief that someone was finally asking her. Words tumbled out: her year of never quite pleasing Harry; of second-guessing her own behaviour and words; of looking over her shoulder and fearing how he was interpreting her actions. Now he had brought her north, where she was the only woman.

Samuel took this last statement in with true alarm. Understanding the man that Harry was made him suspicious of what his real plans for Olive were. By beating her down, he was taking away the last vestige of strength and dignity she once had. Samuel's thoughts started down an evil path before he pulled back but not before he had made up his mind.

"I will not allow you to suffer one day longer for my lapse in judgment. I'm taking you away with me; you will no longer be this man's wife" Samuel said firmly.

As much as Olive rejoiced inside to hear her father's words, terror also struck at her heart at the thought of Harry's reaction. "Oh, Papa, you have no idea what Harry's rage is like. If you were to tell him this, I can imagine how he will react" replied Olive.

"I am not afraid to confront him Olive, but I don't wish any more unpleasantness for you. We will do this in a stealthy fashion. I know what time the train leaves in the morning. Let's behave as though all is normal tonight but, with Harry in the shop tomorrow, you and I will simply walk out the back door and head over to the station with little time to spare. Once we are on the train, he is not likely to come after you. I've met men like Harry in the past. They don't have the courage to pursue. He will just live with anger over how he has been treated."

"Now, let's head back and put on our best faces when he comes through the door. If you falter, just look to me and I will give you the strength you need to get through the night."

Returning to the rooms, they found Harry putting up a cot in the main room. "I'm afraid this is the only type of bed in the shop, Mr. Wilmot" he said. "I brought these in for the lumber camps to purchase, not realizing that they have their own store." The note of resentment in his voice was clear and Samuel was disturbed that he took no blame for his own lack of research. "I know it doesn't begin to

compare to what you are used to but Olive and I have learned to make do until the business begins to do well."

"It's just fine, Harry, and more than I could have expected when you had no knowledge of my visit."

Olive busied herself with preparing the simple evening meal as Harry regaled Samuel with tales of the characters they had met since moving north. *'He always was charming when he wanted to be,'* Olive thought, listening to her husband. *'He may be able to command a room but his weak character shows loudly by his lack of apology to Papa for the secret wedding'* she thought.

Thinking similar thoughts and more, after seeing Olive, it took all of Samuel's inner strength not to punch the man in the face but he had never been a violent man. As much anger as he felt toward Harry, he felt toward himself as well. Samuel feigned interest in Harry's stories, contributing the odd comment, managing to keep Harry from suspicion that anything was amiss.

Eventually, Olive felt herself relax somewhat, as she reminded herself she just had to get through the night. After the months of fear, confusion and uncertainty, the reassurance of her father's presence and a profound relief for what was to come the next day finally took hold. So much so, that when it was time to say goodnight, her old playfulness came over her. Saying goodnight to her father, she said, loudly enough that Harry in the next room would hear, "Goodnight Papa. I wonder what adventure we will get up to tomorrow."

Chapter 32

The next day dawned and Olive slipped quietly from her bed. She started the fire in the wood stove and then stepped outside to use the outside facilities, washing at the well despite the cold. She returned to find her father sitting at the table, dressed and clearly ready for the day.

The two were eating a breakfast of oatmeal and biscuits when Harry came out from the bedroom. Olive had warned Samuel that early mornings were not Harry's best time and they should not try to engage him in conversation until he'd had some time to waken so they became quiet until he joined them at the table.

After Olive had served him, Harry turned to Samuel, asking "how long do you think you will remain with us, Mr. Wilmot?"

"I'll return on tomorrow's train, Harry. I have very little time left before my ship sails and still much to do." As Olive protested, quite convincingly, she thought, Samuel played his part. He let Harry think his purpose in the visit was to see with his own eyes how the two of them fared and, now that he had, he could undertake his journey with his mind at ease.

"It was kind of you to travel so far to do so, Sir" said Harry. "I look forward to spending more time with you this evening after I close the shop." Samuel could only marvel at Harry's nerve when he had the effrontery to add, "Perhaps we might discuss opportunities for you to invest in this enterprise."

"But for now, I must get moving to set up for the day." Putting on his coat, he stepped through the door and into the shop.

"Alright, Olive, we have a bit of time before the train departs so take a few moments to gather your wits" said Samuel. "Pack a small bag that is easily carried with just your necessities. You clearly have left most of your wardrobe in Toronto and I'll have that sent for once we are home."

Olive couldn't help the tears that came to her eyes, although she was uncertain whether they were from relief or regret at how her marriage was ending. In truth, she was a jumble of emotions; had been since confiding in her father the previous day. She'd slept little, thinking how strange it was that life could change so much in a heartbeat. From resigning herself to her fate, she had suddenly been

given permission to remove herself from it. She was going to be fine. Once they completed this bold escape, that is.

"I hear the train whistle, Olive" said Samuel as she put the last of her things in her carpetbag. "We'd best make our way over."

He took her hand, giving it a squeeze, as they closed the door and headed around the building away from the shop. Luckily the train station was situated so that they would not need to cross in front of the shop. Olive knew Harry left the outside cleaning to her so the likelihood that he would see them was slim. Even so, her heart was beating like a drum as she walked quickly beside her father.

The train was nearly empty when they boarded. Samuel said they needn't stop to buy tickets; he would get them from the Conductor once they were underway. They had only just stowed their bags and sat down when the train began to move. As Olive looked back toward the town, tears flowed freely.

"Olive, I am sorry this is how things must end but I couldn't leave you another day in that situation" said Samuel thinking her tears from sadness. "I know you will be happy to see Belmont once again."

"Oh, Papa, I really don't know why I cry except that I haven't allowed myself to in such a long time. It's true I feel regret, perhaps even shame, that I wasn't able to make my marriage work but my relief that you are here to take me from it is far stronger. I believe the Winans, too, worried about me but really had no idea how serious it was or how to help me."

"But happy? I think it will be some time before I feel that once again. I seem to have aged greatly since my marriage and I just look forward to seeing my family and feeling the love that always surrounded me at Belmont."

"Oh, my girl," cried Samuel. "I blame my pride on not seeing you after the wedding to find out how you were doing. I will never forgive myself for standing by while you were living such a life."

"I decided my fate by choosing Harry as my husband against your wishes and we were wed before God. I have spent many hours in the past year trying to understand how I could be so deceived but I must accept that, for some reason, this is God's plan for me, Papa."

"You show strong faith and character, my dear, but, in truth, you were but a seventeen-year-old girl. Your youth led you to wed in spite of my objections. My anger on hearing what you had done shut me down but that is over."

They traveled in silence for some time but as the miles passed and Olive felt truly safe, she spoke again.

"Marriage changed me Papa. I am appalled by how easily I became a puppet to Harry, carrying out his wishes and plans without speaking for myself. What became of me? I had no idea one person could wage such control over another but I felt powerless to do anything. Harry confused me with his tenderness and then seemed to pull the rug out from under my footing so that I never quite knew where I stood."

"I don't believe you should consider marriage the culprit, Olive" surmised Samuel. "Harry was the villain in this. Marriage just provided him the necessary cover to allow the worst of his character to come out. Men like Harry are few, thank God, and I believe you are wise enough, after this, to judge them as they should be."

"Maybe so, Papa" replied Olive sadly, "but I will not have to worry about doing so. I am so grateful that you had the foresight to come up and see things for yourself. From this day on, I will dedicate the remainder of my life to you and the rest of our family. What more do I need?"

At last Olive closed her eyes and fell into a troubled sleep. Samuel knew she spoke hastily; she would gain her footing in life again and move forward but he understood that, for now, she needed the peace and security he could provide.

Looking on his daughter, Samuel came to a decision; he would take her to England with him. He certainly could not leave her alone at Belmont. Despite his confident words about Harry likely not following, no one could predict what actions the man might take. He also worried about Olive's state of mind. She would be melancholy as the past months caught up with her and having no purpose at this time would be detrimental to her healing.

'*Yes, taking her to London is just the thing*,' Samuel thought. '*She will meet new and interesting people and learn about a new city. I will tell her I need a hostess for the dinner parties I will give and a secretary of sorts to keep me organized. Maybe then she won't feel that I am asking her to go out of pity for her.*'

Once they had transferred at Union Station in Toronto to their train to Newcastle, Olive's face visibly relaxed. It was clear she was eager to get to Belmont and to leave the past behind her.

Arriving home late in the evening, Samuel sent Olive upstairs immediately; telling her what she needed now was a good night's sleep. Rather than wake Minnie at that hour, he directed her to another room and slipped into his study to compose a letter to Ted and Phoebe Winans. He felt they should be aware of what had occurred as quickly as the news could get to them. He had no wish for news of this to get out without their knowledge.

It was a difficult letter to write but Samuel wrote from his heart, believing that nothing that he had to tell them would come as a surprise. He did not mention that Harry had been physically abusive. Harry's behaviour and the condition of their life in North Bay provided plenty of justification for Samuel's action without burdening the couple more than they already were.

He told the Winans of his plan to take Olive to England and suggested this to be a viable story to tell people to stop the inevitable talk. He asked that they send her trunks to the ship directly, giving details of the sailing. His heart was heavy as he sealed the envelope and left it on the hall table for the morning post.

June 1903

Newcastle, Ontario

Chapter 33

Minnie awoke to a slight tap on her door. Unable to sleep, she had read Olive's journals long into the night and was disoriented to see Lindsell enter her room holding a tray.

"I'm sorry if I disturbed you, Mrs. Galbraith" said Olive's maid. "I thought that, with so little for me to do for Miss Olive, I would at least take care of you a little. I hope you don't mind; I brought what I would for Miss Olive, not knowing your preferences."

"This is just fine" said Minnie, pulling herself upright in bed for the breakfast tray to be settled on her lap. "I do appreciate this; Lord knows I seem incapable of even simple decisions right now so this takes one off my shoulders. How is she this morning?"

After adjusting pillows to support Minnie's back, the maid replied "No change, I'm afraid. It's strange but I keep expecting her to rise and tell me of her plans for the day." A cot had been set up for Lindsell the evening before in Olive's room. No one wanted to leave her alone for a moment.

"And I've been waiting to hear her sweet laughter, Lindsell" replied Minnie. "I suppose it's natural to yearn for her to be as we remembered despite what we know."

"Shall I run a bath for you after breakfast, Mrs. Galbraith" said Lindsell, deflecting the conversation away from the pain she was feeling. She brought Minnie's robe from the closet and laid it on the bottom of the bed, placing her slippers below.

"Please, Lindsell. I'll plan on sitting with my sister all day. I'm sure you didn't get much sleep last night so nap as you need to or go out for some air. Please feel free to spend the day as you wish. The nurse is on hand if I should need anything for Olive."

Bathed and dressed, Minnie returned to Olive's room. Before settling at her bedside, she selected the next journal (1883) from the shelf. Reliving Olive's life through the journals brought their shared history, with all of its pain, to life again.

"How strange it is to sit by your side in silence, Olive" she said, "when we've shared so many marvellous conversations. Of course, I always knew they were mostly led by you. There really are few who speak as engagingly as you. I envied your mind. Did you know that?"

"Your ability to see to the heart of people so quickly was a gift. Your quickness in character assessment was one thing but I think your true strength was in understanding when to use it to best advantage. I've seen many an unsuspecting cad brought to heel by your barbed wit but I've also watched you put the vulnerable souls in the room at ease. Perhaps that was your role on this earth … building up the weak and slaying the mean, metaphorically speaking, of course." Minnie continued, believing Olive could hear her words.

"How sad it made me to see the changes in you when Papa brought you home. That man (I can't even now bring myself to say his name) had taken your spirit and your voice; there is no doubt about that.

1883

Newcastle, Ontario

Chapter 34

Waking the next morning safely back at Belmont, Olive remained in bed, nestling under the soft quilts and linens. But she was oblivious to the luxury of the bedding. She touched the many bruises Samuel had not seen; hidden by her clothing. She vowed to herself to remember these after they had healed, when doubts would creep in, as she knew they must.

Harry's slide into physical abuse had left her wrung out; fearful. Her fears of reprisal for unwittingly committing some deed that merited punishment were so strong in her that, even now, safe in bed with her father in the same house, she worried about what she might do wrong this day. Most days in the past weeks had begun thusly and it would take some time for her mind to understand that she need no longer be fearful.

Over the breakfast table, after enquiring about her sleep, Samuel said "I have written to Mr. and Mrs. Winans, Olive. As concisely as possible, I explained the circumstances I found you in and why I have taken this action. I do not think they will be much surprised but I did try to word the letter in a way that would help them not to feel responsible."

"I also told them of my decision to take you to London; as much for their own knowledge as for Harry's when he contacts them. I hope this will help Harry to realize that the marriage is over and there is no point in coming after you."

"I've asked that they have your trunk sent directly to the ship to await our departure. I'll contact the shipping agent today to book another cabin; it shouldn't be a problem. We are at the end of the season for travel to the continent."

The days passed; Olive spending most of them just with Minnie, who was overcome to have her sister at home again. Even a wounded Olive was better than the absence they had known.

Olive knew there was no one else who would understand her. Minnie would always be her kindred spirit; her greatest support; her 'Little Mama'.

Within a few days of her return, Olive needed to be free from more than just the walls around them. She suggested she and Minnie walk the fields around Belmont. With their eyes focused on the path ahead instead of each other, Olive confided all that her life had been with Harry. She held nothing back; his indecent sexual behaviours and appetites; his ability to control her through fear and then the physical abuse. Words she hadn't been able to speak with her father now tumbled out of her.

"I'm so sorry to expose you to the ugliness of my life with Harry, Minnie, and I don't do this for you to feel pity for me or to cause you to suffer from your hearing of it. But I simply can't put these years behind me without having a witness to my experiences."

"And I don't want you to think that I will be wallowing in memories but I suffered in silence for too long and need to be heard."

"Now that I have spoken" continued Olive, "I will put these years away, never to be heard from again. They were my life but now are not."

Minnie stopped her sister, put her hand on Olive's arm and looked into her eyes. "My heart aches for you, Olive" she said. "If I had only objected to the wedding in earnest or pressed to see you more while you were at the Winans, I might have detected the truth."

"Please, Minnie. I beg of you. Do not reproach yourself" replied Olive. "I certainly have never placed any responsibility on you."

"I believe God put me with Harry to learn something. Perhaps I was too trusting of others and needed to recognize the evil they are capable of. It doesn't matter why. I will never again allow another person to control me in such a fashion. It is only through distance from it that I now begin to understand the role my naiveté and absence of judgment played in this. I may be just 18 years, but this past year has made me wiser than I could have imagined."

When the day came for Samuel and Olive to leave for England, Minnie held Olive tearfully. Olive, however, remained stoic as she reassured her sister she would write often.

Boarding the ship together, Olive turned to Samuel, saying "Thank you, Papa. If I am to heal, I believe this change will help me do

so." Samuel had grave concerns about her detached attitude but he smiled and squeezed her hand.

The seas for most of the voyage were rough and gave Olive an excuse to keep to her cabin most days. She was surprisingly weary but, after breakfast was delivered each morning, she spent time organizing her trunk, arranging with the Cabin Steward to have gowns pressed and freshened. The clothes had been packed away for months and now needed her attention.

She was doing her best to deny memories any space in her thoughts. When they did creep in, she accepted that they were what they were and nothing was to be gained by reliving them. She learned to pick up a book or focus on a task to replace the offensive memory and was reassured that she could control her thoughts in this way.

So, she was surprised by the unexpectedly visceral reaction when she touched her wedding gown at the bottom of her trunk one day.

Nausea hit her in the gut and she had to sit down until it passed. She wrapped her arms around herself and rocked back and forth, moaning softly. A simple change in thoughts wasn't going to help this time. She rode the wave of pain until it subsided finally, leaving her exhausted.

Throughout the voyage, Samuel gave her the distance she seemed to desire even from him. She ventured on deck for a short stroll in fresh air each afternoon and ate dinner in the dining room with him each evening. She conversed when addressed directly but maintained an aura of aloofness which kept other passengers at a distance. Her visible bruises had healed so the other passengers assumed she was recovering from some unknown illness because of her colour and demeanour. They were more than happy to respect her evident desire to be left alone.

Samuel was struck by how changed she was from the girl he remembered; the delightful girl who had been interested in every person she met. This Olive was polite but showed no curiosity about anyone she encountered.

He understood that her emotions must be engulfing her and that she needed to experience them. He was grateful that she had spent even a little time with Minnie before they departed and, once more, regretted that Tillie was not the mother to her girls that she should be. He felt at a loss to help Olive on an emotional level. His role could

not be confidante but he would, by God, give her a sense of security and acceptance. Time would heal, he reassured himself.

Samuel had made all arrangements for their travel to London when they disembarked at Liverpool. In the carriage, he tried to engage her in chatter about his plans for the next year but, as Olive replied little, he gradually quieted. She seemed content to watch the passing landscape.

Chapter 35

I've so missed you, Dearest Journal. It seems fitting that I return to you with this new chapter in my life. These past two years have been traumatic to me and you are the one place I should have written about it; your non-judgemental presence has always calmed my soul.

But how could I write of my life while under Harry's eagle eye? I was well aware that he read all of my mail before I did and I had no doubt that, should he have seen me writing in my beloved journal, he would have done the same. It doesn't matter. Living the horror was bad enough; why would I want to write of it as well?

I vowed to Minnie never to speak of it again and I do the same here with my journal; what would be accomplished by writing about it anyway except to leave a permanent reminder of the pain? Writing of it would give Harry a weight and a power that I don't wish him to have. I endured. That's enough. By leaving him, I took back the power that his abuse and control had taken from me. The years are memories now; behind me and perhaps, with time and prayer, one day forgettable.

I am done with it. I began healing once I spoke the truth to Minnie.

I was about to correct the housemaid when she called me 'Miss'. It took a minute for me to realize that I am, indeed, a Miss again; even if in thought only. Lawyers may argue my freedom but I am determined to take back my life. I may not be a single woman, free to marry, but I am not anyone's property anymore and, if society would question an absent husband, I am quite alright with being Miss.

Oh, how wonderful to live and to write with no fear of censorship or reprisal. At the ripe old age of 18, my life begins again.

The London townhouse Samuel had leased, at 43 Brompton Square, was four stories tall. Behind its bland exterior, like every other row house on the street, it held a graciously appointed sitting room, small library and dining room large enough for a table of twelve on the main floor and four bedrooms on the next two floors. Servants' rooms were on the top floor; the kitchen and utility rooms in the basement.

They were greeted by Martha, the housekeeper, retained by the agency Samuel had dealt with for this move. They would also have the

services of a cook and housemaid during their stay. It was the housemaid who led Olive to her room, while Samuel remained downstairs to discuss household arrangements with Martha.

Olive's room was on the third floor. She had heard that England was not as advanced in-home conveniences so was relieved to see the house included indoor plumbing with a water closet and washroom on her floor as well. The months of making do with a communal outhouse and well had brought a new appreciation for what she once had taken for granted.

"Cook will put out a light dinner for you and Mr. Wilmot in two hours, Miss," said the housemaid before taking her leave of Olive.

She was too tired to correct the girl although she felt anything but a 'Miss'. She had removed her wedding rings and left them in her room at Belmont and it was easy to see why everyone would assume a young daughter traveling with her father to be unmarried.

Olive unpacked her carpet bag of toiletries and nightwear, taking in the room that would be hers for the next year. It had everything she would need; a four-poster bed, large dresser, wardrobe and vanity table. For a row house, the room had a surprising amount of natural light thanks to the afternoon sunlight streaming through two long, low windows. The window wells were deep enough to sit in and when Olive looked out the window, she saw children playing in the parkland below while nannies stood watching nearby. *'There is normal life'* she thought. *'I quite forgot what that looks like.'*

Returning downstairs to await dinner, she entered the library in search of a book to read until dinner was announced. She was pleased by the size of the library and knew she would be occupied by many hours of reading through the coming year.

She had given little thought to how she would spend her time until now but the idea of quiet hours writing letters and reading some new novels was appealing. Of all people, she was most anxious to write to Harry's grandmother, Mrs. Wells, and yet she lacked the courage. To admit to anyone, least of all Harry's grandmother that she had run away was not something she was ready to take on. She also knew it would be unwise for Harry to know where she was, even though she thought it highly unlikely he would pursue her all the way to England.

She read various titles as her finger trailed a series of books on a shelf and came across an interesting one that looked new; *Portrait of a Lady* by Henry James. *'Perhaps I'll learn where I went wrong'* she thought, pulling the book from the shelf. *'If I had been more of a lady, would Harry have had more respect for me?'*

She finished the first chapters about Isabel Archer's life as her father returned downstairs and the two were called to the dining room.

"The maid called me 'Miss', Papa, and I hadn't the heart to correct her. Was that terrible of me?"

"Actually, I gave this some thought on the voyage, my dear. I think it would be best if we not mention that you had been married. No one on this side of the Atlantic will be aware and I think it's less complicated than trying to explain why you are here and your husband, there. Don't you agree?"

"I'm sure you're right, Papa. Besides, I have no intention of making intimate friends here and have no desire to share my story. If I am just introduced as your daughter, there should be no complications; as long as no one is under the impression that I am here in search of a husband. How strange it feels, though, to pretend the past year did not happen."

As her father sat enjoying a brandy after dinner, Olive asked "What are your plans for tomorrow, Papa?"

"I had thought this first week would be for us to become accustomed to English life. We can visit some museums, familiarize ourselves with the shops and businesses around us and take in some sights. How does that sound?"

"I couldn't imagine anything nicer" replied Olive. "Once I have my bearings of the city, you will be able to go about your business and not worry about me. The last thing I want is to be a burden on you when you have so much to accomplish."

Olive leaned over Samuel to kiss him goodnight as she said, "I'll turn in now, then. I still seem to be weary and it sounds like I'll need my strength to keep up with you. Goodnight, Papa."

"Goodnight, my dear. Sleep well."

Chapter 36

"Papa felt the House of Commons drab compared to our own in Ottawa" wrote Olive, as their first week in London came to a close. *"I could not comment, never having been to Ottawa. There is so much of the world that I want to experience but, for now, I'm just grateful to be with Papa. He doesn't speak of my past, or what the two of us have endured in these past weeks; instead he takes pleasure in introducing me to the city around us and keeping my mind occupied. The sightseeing serves its purpose but I wish I could be in a spirit to enjoy it all."*

Samuel and Olive had spent their first week visiting the major sites of the city; the Tower of London; Tower Bridge; Buckingham Palace; Parliament and the House of Commons; Westminster Abbey; Madame Tussaud's Wax Museum; the British Museum and more. They were intrigued by the underground railway, finding its convenience a boon to getting around the city.

Although Olive appeared enthusiastic about each new excursion, as the week came to a close, Samuel realized that she remained unusually quiet. "I think we have had enough of history, Olive. What would you say to a thoroughly modern shopping trip?" he asked.

With Olive's agreement, they took a carriage the next day for the short drive to Harrod's. The department store was so large that it employed over 100 people and made Eatons seem like a general mercantile in comparison. Harrod's appeared to have everything a body or home might need.

Samuel led her to the women's department and watched indulgently as Olive picked out new kid gloves; evening slippers and leather boots suitable for the London winter weather. He took pleasure in seeing her delight in each item. But he had brought Olive to Harrod's with a purpose in mind.

Samuel was not a vain man but he took his position, as the Dominion's representative, very seriously. The Prince of Wales was to open the Fisheries Exhibition and Samuel knew that, as Chairman of the Canadian effort, he would be introduced to the Prince. As he had toured the city, he realized the suits he had brought might be considered a bit provincial. He left Olive in the hands of a sales lady with instructions to order herself new gowns and went on to the

Men's department to order several suits of the style he had seen around the city.

In Harrods' dining room later, Olive expressed her gratitude to her father. She was well aware that any shopping she had done that day had been meant to lift her spirits.

With their tourist week over, Olive again picked up 'Portrait of a Lady' and was soon immersed in the life of the lead character, Isobel Archer. She found parallels to the conflict Isobel had felt between her miserable marriage and social propriety.

Olive was saddened, as she came to the end of the book, to discover that Isobel chose to remain in the marriage rather than to violate the social norm in search of a happier life. Olive was crying as she closed the book; both for the sadness of Isobel's life and for the state of her own. She understood that Isabel's husband had been indifferent and unloving; while her own had been abusive, but she recognized that she and Isobel had both been led to their marriages by deceiving men. She could not be more relieved to have escaped her own and yet couldn't help but wonder what the future held for her. How would she carry off the deception of being a single woman?

Samuel's responsibilities began in earnest and he was away for the better part of most days. An office had been established near the Gardens of the Royal Horticultural Society, where the Fisheries Exhibition was to be held, and it was from here that he directed the construction of his fish hatchery. He had much to do before the opening in May.

As he worked, Olive settled into a pattern of daily walks, writing letters, needlepoint and reading. She was content with the simplicity of her days; indeed, she had little ambition to do more and preferred to remain in the community around their house.

After the natural beauty of North Bay, with its dense forests and clear lake, Olive found the congestion of London discomfiting. London's age and population growth had resulted in narrow streets lined with buildings which bordered right on the street; most were many stories tall, with no space between them. This meant the sun was blocked out and the streets felt darker than they might have. Although mostly constructed of stone and brick and built to last centuries, Olive found the buildings to be dingy. The chimney soot added to the general grime on the buildings and the smog hung over

the city most days. The cold rains of autumn didn't help to cheer things up in any way.

The city seemed to have little green space, other than small parks placed strategically within neighbourhoods. She was grateful for the view of the parkland outside her window and soon learned where other parks were located.

On pleasant days, she would wrap up warmly and take her book to sit in a local park, enjoying the solitude. Other than people she and Samuel greeted at church each Sunday, Olive had little contact with others during these weeks. She reassured Samuel, when he expressed concern for her isolation, that she was quite happy with her days and he should not feel worry on her account.

In truth, everything was as it should be on the surface only. Under the peaceful façade she managed to portray, chaos lived. She cultivated solitude, knowing only that she needed to protect herself. She told herself that time; with nature and books and a life that bore no resemblance to her life with Harry, would ease the turmoil inside her.

Olive's appetite was still not robust but she began to regain the pounds she had lost in North Bay. With each day, she looked over her shoulder less and began to feel a certain peace in life. She wanted nothing more.

Chapter 37

Over time, Samuel's social connections expanded in London and invitations arrived for he and Olive.

After a quiet Christmas spent alone, they were ready to accept the invitations. Their evenings and weekends were soon filled with dinners, theatre parties, and the occasional visit to a country estate.

As Olive's 19th birthday approached in April, Samuel was happy to see glimpses of the daughter he remembered. If asked, Olive would say she would never be the girl she had been. Her enthusiasm for people and the world around her was diminished. Why become intimate with anyone when you could be hurt?

The agent who had helped Samuel get settled in London approached him after learning of Olive's presence. She delicately let it be known that the services she offered were broad and she had had some success with introductions for young ladies from the continent whose fathers were interested in titles for them. She listed a number of matches that she had initiated as proof in point.

Had circumstances been different, Samuel would have been amused that she should think this of interest to him, or that Olive would not be able to generate the interest of gentlemen on her own merits. In fact, as the pair ventured out more and more into society, gentlemen were clearly interested.

Olive developed a pleasant manner while maintaining an air of detachment, letting no man breach her protective shield. Those of the younger set embraced the sense of fun introduced by the Prince of Wales; tired as they were of the restricted lives their parents lived by Queen Victoria's example. Men and women now openly engaged in light flirtation and the brash American women who had married into British society brought practical joking and a new openness with the previously reserved Brits.

On meeting Olive, British men made the assumption that she would be up for some fun just as the American women they knew. After a time, they soon realized she was not. The ego of a man with a title doesn't readily accept responsibility for rejection and so, while they initially found the new Canadian girl with beauty and money intriguing, they soon concluded she didn't have much to offer after all.

This left Olive just where she wanted to be; without male interest plaguing her.

Opening ceremonies for the exhibition approached and Samuel was more than a little excited as he read the Prince's schedule for opening day, knowing he was to be introduced.

Olive was interacting with people but Samuel recognized a veil of sadness underneath. She did what was expected of her but lacked enthusiasm. *'I'm going to include Olive in the reception line to meet the Prince.'* thought Samuel looking over the program. *'This will be just the ticket to excite her.'*

Young society ladies went speechless at the prospect of being presented to the future king. For many, it would be the highlight of their lives. For Olive, it was a wonder that such a thing could happen to the broken woman she believed herself to be.

She observed the overweight man as he made his way around the room and felt her knees weaken. *'How my life has changed!'* she thought as she stood by her father's side.

After an introduction to Samuel by the Chairman of the Exhibition and a word from the Prince about his love of Canada, Samuel turned to Olive and said "may I present my daughter, Olive, your Majesty".

The Prince's face lit up with his usual appreciation for attractive women. His reputation was widely known by this time but, assuming from her introduction that she was an unmarried girl, he judged her off-limits. He maintained a strict policy of only pursuing married ladies ... made life less complicated.

Propriety dictated that the Prince must speak before anyone and he surprised Olive by doing so.

"I remember my first trip to the continent, Miss Wilmot, at just about your age. Fond memories of that visit."

In fact, it was during the 1862 Canadian tour that the Prince had been introduced to the charms of married women and the course had been set for his future love life.

Gathering herself while her head was bowed and rising from her much-practiced curtsey, Olive said "My cousin, Mrs. Kate Reid, had the honour of dancing with your Majesty during your tour of Canada."

"Well, perhaps, during your stay in London, there will be opportunity for me to dance with another cousin, Miss Wilmot"

replied the Prince, clearly enjoying the diversion this attractive young woman brought to the stodgy businessmen surrounding him.

As Samuel hoped, the excitement of meeting the Prince of Wales and her tour of the Exhibition itself brought a change in Olive. For some time, she had played hostess for the dinner parties he held, mostly attended by his peers from commonwealth countries around the world and the members of the organizing committee in London. She had done so indifferently.

But with a greater understanding of her father's work, these dinners became more interesting for her. Guests were impressed by her insightful comments and intelligent questions. Samuel was more than a little proud of her.

Olive began to venture out into the world without her father. She accepted invitations to tea or for carriage rides with the wives of various men she had met through her father. Increasingly, she became Olive Wilmot again; comfortable around others. Watching what she was saying and how she behaved became a thing of the past.

Their time in England was busy but, as the year came to its end, Olive grew anxious about returning home. How would she face her community? Talk was inevitable once everyone discovered she was living permanently back home without a husband. How was she to present herself? How would she have the strength needed to face what was to come.

Chapter 38

Dear Diary,

I knew this day was coming but feel completely unprepared to face Newcastle again. I wish this ship would just keep on sailing and take me to some foreign land where no one would care about my past. I had managed to put thoughts of it behind me but, as each mile brings us closer to home, they begin to haunt my nights again.

Please God, give me the strength needed to rise above the talk around me.

Returning home in early November, Olive was anxious to see Minnie and the other members of her family. She hoped to keep the rest of Newcastle at arms length as long as possible. She was in no way ready to deal with the questions she knew she faced and certainly not without her father beside her.

But Samuel was needed immediately back in Ottawa to present to Parliament on the Exhibition. With Canada playing a leading role, Samuel's position had gained importance in setting policy for the future of the fishing industry.

After their year together, Olive was sad to know her father would be leaving her soon after they got home. Even more, though, she was more than a little frightened to deal with Newcastle on her own. She knew herself to be on the side of right in her actions and would hold her head up high if others learned the truth. But, as the product of a small town, she knew the damage talk would do. Knowing she would face this without his support was daunting.

Samuel didn't leave her out of callousness. His concern for her hadn't stopped with their return to Belmont but he was a pragmatic man and knew she would face talk for the remainder of her life. There really was no point in trying to delay the inevitable. He also had confidence in her as, over the past year, he had watched her regain the strength of character she seemed to have lost during her marriage. He knew she would face what came with grace.

Despite what either of them was thinking, neither was prepared for what they found waiting for them at home; a letter from the Winans.

Ted and Phoebe had written to say that Harry had returned from North Bay soon after Olive and Samuel left the country. They were

too dignified to mention that Ted lost all of the money invested in Harry's new venture but they did say they had made it clear to Harry that he was no longer welcome in their home. He had since left for parts unknown in the Midwest of the United States and they had not had news of him in several months.

The purpose of their letter was to let Olive know they had let it be known to everyone that Harry had deserted her. *'We were not naïve to the reputation Harry had throughout the city'* they wrote *'and we had no wish for you to be thought poorly of for your necessary action. Others also do not hold you at fault. Rest assured that you will be most welcome in any home of our friends.'*

They went on to say they hoped she would visit them anytime; indeed, they and Mrs. Wells looked forward to seeing her again. Olive was touched by the kindness of their action and words; having society at large think that he was the deserter left her to pursue her life without reprisal, albeit still married. Understanding that, in saying so, the stain of Harry's behaviour rested squarely on their shoulders brought tears to her eyes. Society looked on a 'wronged' woman with compassion. If it was known she had left, her character would be judged harshly. In the end, Ted and Phoebe had protected her reputation.

Although she would not be going to visit, she was very relieved to know that her relationship with Harry's family was left intact after her actions.

Settling back into life on the farm, Olive was aware of the chatter that quickly stopped as she approached people in the village. Although she kept close to Belmont and the surrounding countryside, she was pleased to be able to attend her beloved St. George's church every Sunday once again though it was there that she felt the most watched and there that her already straight back became even more so. Olive would steel herself before entering the church each week and walk with pride to the Wilmot pew, alongside Minnie and whichever other Wilmot might be visiting that Sunday. She had the Wilmot name to shield her and felt its strength.

Individuals sometimes had the nerve to ask her directly what had happened. A few asked from concern; the Wilmots were widely admired. But success and money also bring envy and many who

approached Olive were motivated by jealousy. To see the mighty Wilmots falter meant their lives were not perfect.

Olive developed a way to respond to each individual. With a sad smile on her face, something in her eyes made the person feel chastised for having the presumption of such inquisitiveness. "Oh, my life is such a dull story" she would say and follow with a query about someone or something in the person's life.

In this manner, she successfully deflected the story back to the inquisitive person and away from herself. The details of what had happened to her handsome young husband or why their marriage had begun in such haste and ended so quickly were not about to be shared.

The one person outside of her own family who Olive did confide in was Rev. Brent. On Samuel's recommendation, she regularly sat with the kind cleric to try to make sense of her life. For his part, he felt true remorse for not having successfully counselled her from the marriage to begin with.

They met weekly and it was through this relationship that Olive slowly came to terms with her ill-fated marriage. Rev. Brent offered a thoughtful ear and wise comments although Olive kept the details of her tortuous marriage to herself. She sought understanding on a spiritual level, not recrimination toward Harry.

Rev. Brent knew only that Samuel had felt compelled to remove Olive from the marriage. He let Olive know he did not judge Harry; this was up to God, after all; but instead relieved some of the guilt she continued to feel over the outcome.

He helped her to see that she had little recourse other than to leave a situation which was so destructive to her health and wellbeing. Of course, he reminded her that she must remain a chaste, single woman for the remainder of Harry's life, since they were still married in God's eyes.

To Olive, the idea of remaining a married woman, unable to pursue other relationships, was tolerable. She was determined never again to allow a man to have control over her life or body.

Chapter 39

1889

Five years passed within the security of Belmont. Olive's days were quiet but she was content; she read everything in her father's extensive library; spent hours walking and riding the lands around Belmont; and completed numerous needlepoint projects. Together, she and Minnie managed the household in their father's frequent absences.

Life was modulated by the seasons. During the busiest times of the year; berry and harvest time; Olive and Minnie joined the women in the kitchen to put up the extensive preserves, listening to the stories of their families, all of whom she had grown up around. The children her age were all married now with growing families.

Olive sometimes regretted that life was not to bring her the children she so desperately wanted. When the maternal feelings hit she put them aside. This was the price she had paid for marrying and leaving Harry and she accepted that. There had to be some punishment for her selfish choices, after all.

Her common sense told her that her life was extraordinary compared to many and she had no patience for self-pity. She was financially free to live as she chose and she didn't feel lonely.

Her father's frequent absences meant Belmont did not see the entertaining that it once had but she had no desire for more.

When she was in need of new garments, a book or two or just to see something outside of her own village, she and Minnie would take the train in to the city, staying with their sister, Helen. She didn't contact the Winans during these visits. She still felt great sadness after learning of the passing of Harry's grandmother, Mrs. Wells, and thought the family had experienced enough grief. She was certain that a visit from her would revive old hurts and perhaps make Ted and Phoebe feel sorry for her; something she wouldn't tolerate.

As the Wilmot family rang in the new year of 1889 together, they had something exciting to celebrate: Minnie had become engaged to Duncan Galbraith.

At 30, Minnie had accepted her life as a spinster. She was active in the community and won ribbons in local shows for her carriage driving. The previous winter, her brother Charlie had met the Galbraith brothers at the local cutter races on the ice in Newcastle's harbour.

The Galbraith's bred and trained carriage horses and Charlie was impressed. Minnie shared his love of horses and Charlie suggested she accompany him to the races to meet the brothers.

One brother, Duncan, made a strong impression on Minnie and the two were soon courting. Less than a year later, they sat toasting the engagement.

Samuel looked at Olive as they raised the glasses.

'*What will become of Olive without Minnie*' he wondered.

As wedding plans progressed, Olive became increasingly sad thinking about a life without Minnie in it daily. They promised they would see each other often but Olive understood that Minnie's priority would soon become Duncan. Without a priority of her own, she felt adrift for the first time since her return home.

Until she overheard a young woman in church telling another about her plans to go to New York City to study for a nursing program.

Olive had never heard of this but was intrigued at the idea. '*Imagine life beyond the confines of Newcastle*' she thought. '*No one would know me. I'd be free of whispers and inquisitive people. I think I might even do some good*'.

She wrote her Uncle John who lived in New York City and asked him to send contact details of the various nursing schools in the city.

It was time she made her own life happen, without a husband; a father or even an older sister behind her.

June 1903
Newcastle, Ontario

Chapter 40

Minnie dropped the journal she'd just pulled from the shelf as she heard a strange sound come from the bed. She stood over her sister, calling "Nurse". She felt the irony in doing so. Calling another woman by that title for her own dear sister who had been such a capable one just seemed wrong.

The nurse explained that patients often did this; breath would stop for a beat or two and then restart loudly; until the time when it didn't.

Tears came to Minnie's eyes as she realized her time with Olive was running out. She felt the need to know how much time and asked the nurse. With little compassion for Minnie's feelings, the nurse replied plainly that there was no way to know; each patient was different. People had been known to live as long as seven days without food or water but the nurse had never determined what it was that kept some going so long.

Minnie knew that Olive would not give up easily. She had proven herself again and again to be strong and determined. "Please don't leave us yet, Olive. I'm not ready to say goodbye."

The housekeeper knocked gently on the door to say luncheon was laid for Mrs. Galbraith in the dining room.

"Please bring it on a tray here, Mrs. Thomson" she said, unable to think of leaving Olive. "I don't know how much more time I will have with her."

She bent to pick up the journal she'd dropped. It was written the year of her marriage and as Olive began what Minnie thought of as her true life – in New York City.

Which reminded her – she'd given no thought to Olive's husband, Henry, lying down the hall.

"How is Mr. Sanford, Nurse?" she asked. "His chest remains congested" replied the competent woman, "but he is able to clear it through his coughing. I think the mustard drafts I am applying are helping but there's no doubt he gets weaker by the effort. He is sleeping a great deal, which is the best thing for him. In my

experience, a recurrence of pneumonia becomes more difficult to fight each time."

Minnie walked to Henry's room and knocked quietly. "Come in" said the feeble voice she had come to accept as Henry's.

"Henry, I'm not sure how much more time we have with Olive. Her breath is becoming erratic. Would you like to sit with her for a little while?"

The man who stared back at her bore no resemblance to the hearty, life-gulping, 'never say no to life' man she had known. Until this past year, his age had never slowed him down. Olive had often said she had trouble keeping up with him.

While the world might take Olive's marriage to a wealthy man so much older than herself at face value, Minnie knew it to be anything but the cliché it appeared to be.

"I just can't, Minnie" Henry replied, so quietly she had to lean in to hear. "I don't think my heart could take seeing Olive in any other way than I remember her. Can you forgive me?

"Of course, Henry; I do understand. Although I'd like to believe otherwise, I can say with confidence that she would not know you. She is well cared for so you just rest yourself." She left her brother-in-law, thinking *'God knows; you're going to need your strength for what is to come'*.

Minnie wearily returned to Olive's room and settled herself back in the chair, opening the journal. After reliving the heartache Olive had known through her first marriage, she almost looked forward to this next chapter in her sister's life. Almost – if only her sister didn't lie dying beside her.

1889

Newcastle, Ontario

Chapter 41

The idea of leaving home to earn a respectable living answered the prayers of many unwed young women facing a life dependent on a father or older brother. For many young women living sheltered lives, nursing offered the added excitement of life in a strange city.

The programs, led by senior nurses, had high expectations for the young women enrolled; decorum; obedience; self-discipline and initiative. And yet the rewards were far from attractive; long hours; low pay; little life outside of the hospital. A few lucky women met and married doctors; many more lived simple lives driven by their dedication to service and caring for others.

Olive put the package from her Uncle John on the desk and experienced something she hadn't felt in years; eagerness!

After reading about the New York Training School for Nurses at Bellevue Hospital, she was impatient to enrol. She'd chosen this school because it followed Florence Nightingale's nursing principles. Olive had read enough about this impressive woman to see her as an admirable role model. The pamphlet she held described Bellevue's early nursing training which involved instruction in basic cleanliness, neatness and patient comfort.

The hospital information explained that modern medicine was changing hospitals from palliative and chronic care institutions to centers with a focus on fighting disease. Where once most medical visits took place in the physician's residence or patients' homes, the new hospitals were opening clinics for patient care. This was changing nursing care from its traditional roots in childbirth and home nursing care to a much more vital role supporting physicians in a centralized setting.

To think that she might help patients regain their health or die with dignity appealed to her. Her innate care for people had been rekindled with the idea of nursing. Olive understood that the years of protecting herself with Harry had left her unable to think about the needs of others.

She completed the application in the package and sent it off.

She received a response from the Superintendent's office surprisingly quickly; her application had been accepted! She had no idea that her Uncle John was a generous benefactor of the hospital and had been influential in her acceptance.

Training would begin that September which gave her a few short months to prepare. The letter included further information about the program and what she should expect.

Superintendent Brennan explained that students lived in 'The Nurse's Home' at 426 E. 26th Street in a building dedicated to both classroom and dormitory. The school had established this since the long and irregular hours made living at home problematic even for residents of New York city.

Olive recalled her years at Bishop Strachan and the fond memories she had of sharing living arrangements with other girls. She could well imagine the camaraderie she might expect with other women sharing the trials of work in a hospital. The 'home' had a resident chaperone responsible for overseeing the daily lives of the nurses, thereby reassuring mothers nervous about sending their daughters.

Although uniforms were not yet mandatory, nursing students were identifiable by the dresses they wore made from a common fabric; a crisp blue and white stripe. The designs, however, were of their own choosing allowing a bit of individuality.

The letter explained that a bolt of this fabric would be sent shortly and advised Olive to have a minimum of two dresses made. Although they wore aprons, the nature of their daily activities often resulted in stains that were difficult to remove and a nurse was always expected to be crisply, and cleanly, turned out.

No one outside of her immediate family knew of Olive's plans. She wanted to make a complete break from her old community, without any chance of talk preceding her to her new life. The family had decided to let it be known in Newcastle that Olive was staying with her uncle in New York indefinitely.

Her departure from Belmont was not a sorrowful one; Minnie knew it was the right thing for Olive to do and she had her own exciting future ahead of her. Samuel was too relieved that there was to be more in life for her to feel sorrow.

1889

New York City

Chapter 42

Accompanied by her Uncle John, Olive was greeted at the Nurses Home by the house chaperone, Mrs. Cawthorn. Her uncle made his goodbyes and Mrs. Cawthorn took Olive to the room assigned to her, pointing out the classrooms and communal areas of the home as they passed each.

"There is little free time to enjoy the lounges, I'm afraid," she said, in a thick Yorkshire accent. "I find the girls are always surprised by the amount of study necessary after full days on the wards."

"Oh, I've had my share of leisure time in the last few years, Mrs. Cawthorn. I can't imagine anything grander than the busy days and nights ahead" replied Olive.

"Here we are, then, Miss Wilmot," the woman said, opening one of many doorways off a long hallway on the third floor. "If you pass the probation period, this will be your home away from home for as long as you are nursing. Here is your room and house key and you know which room I am in should you need me. I hope you will be comfortable."

Olive looked around the small room; equipped with a single bed with iron bedstead; small dresser; secretary desk; wardrobe; and wash stand. Although the home, like the hospital itself, was equipped with a modern washroom on each floor, the wash stand was provided to allow each girl to sponge bathe in her room between the twice-weekly bath she would be scheduled for. Olive could see a chamber pot tucked beneath the bed which would be necessary, she imagined, with so many women making use of the one washroom.

Her trunk had been shipped from Belmont, including the new dresses she had ordered in the required fabric. A pile of linens had been placed on the bed; nursing students were expected to make their own beds and keep their rooms clean at all times. Seeing two nursing caps and aprons on the bed gave her a small thrill. Mrs. Cawthorn had explained that they were required to be worn at all times when on duty or in the classroom.

The atmosphere in the dining room that evening was quieter than she would have expected in a room full of women living away from home. She and her table mates introduced themselves. Each was a little nervous about the morrow, making for limited conversation. As Olive soon learned, the tables with senior nurses were just as hushed as they were often too exhausted to carry on more than cursory discussions.

"I wasn't expecting such quiet," said the girl to her right, who had introduced herself as Lisbeth Eichmann. "This quiet will take some getting used to after my home" she said, softly.

"Are you from a large family?" asked Olive.

"Not so much large as loud" replied Lisbeth. "There is no shortage of opinions in my family and we like to share them at every meal. One would think I would enjoy a peaceful meal but I find myself missing the raucous atmosphere at home."

"My family is similar when we are all together, although these days, that rarely happens. Everyone is moving on in their own households and families and our opportunities for large family meals are limited to the holidays" said Olive. "I am from Canada. Where is your home?"

"Oh, right here in the city" replied Lisbeth. "My grandfather brought the family from Germany in the 1840s and settled in the city where tailors were needed. He opened a shop and my father and his brothers have since developed it into a successful department store."

"My brothers are now working in the business as well but there was no role for a mere girl. I find the whole business of homemaking to be tedious so I was very excited to find out about nursing."

"Does it seem strange that I should be a boarder since I live in the city" Lisbeth asked. "I was told of the long hours involved and our home is too far to make travel back and forth feasible. I don't know about you but I'm as nervous as a bride on her wedding day."

Olive thought the comparison most appropriate, amused by Lisbeth's change of topic. She might not share as much information as her table mate did but she found herself liking the chatty girl.

"Yes, I imagine we all are feeling the same tonight. They likely put the month of probation into the program to see how everyone stands up under pressure?"

Missing Minnie greatly, Olive suggested "let's make a pact, shall we, to seek each other out if we are ever feeling overwhelmed. That way, we'll always know there is someone we can share our feelings with. I'm sure that will help us get through this next month."

"You are a wise one, Miss Wilmot. I like that idea and will certainly come to see you when my nerves get the better of me" replied Lisbeth.

Olive stood proudly in her cap and apron outside Superintendent Brennan's office the next morning but she was more than a little nervous. Nothing in her life had prepared her for what she was about to take on. Pride aside, she had no idea whether she would make a good nurse.

The one-month probationary period was certain to be challenging so that only the best would carry on into the two-year program. She was determined to be one of those few who did so. After all, this meant a new life for her; one in which she would be judged based on her performance and character, rather than rumour and gossip.

"Are you settled in the 'Home', Miss Wilmot?" Superintendent Brennan asked once Olive had been introduced. "Yes, Matron. Mrs. Cawthorn was most helpful. She gave me a tour and explained the rules of the Home to me. I expect I shall be very comfortable in my new room" replied Olive.

"Good. I won't keep you long today. I like to meet all of the new girls before they become immersed in their studies and daily routines. Although probation is just one month long, the speed at which we move along can be daunting; you will be learning by doing with a senior nurse at your side until we are confident in your abilities."

"I hope you understand that the majority of our patients are the poorest of the city. Their sicknesses are the result of overwork, overcrowding, over drinking and every other excess their sad lives present. Our hope for all of our girls is that they will shine as moral examples, without judgment, to our patients."

"Many of our patients do not bathe on a regular basis and the focus when they first arrive is to clean them up and make them comfortable. Despite their initial objection to soap and water, you will be surprised by how a proper bath and attention to personal hygiene will improve a person's outlook in life."

"Patients will watch you move about your duties through the wards and want to be like you. Despite their personal agony, I have witnessed the effect our girls can have on a patient. Many speak crudely initially but, by example and rules within the wards, this is often softened during their stay in hospital."

"I want you to remember that, beyond the technical knowledge you will gain in this program, it is the impact you can have on another's life that will bring you the most reward. Of course, you are never required to tolerate rudeness. Senior nurses are never far away and will take action when necessary."

"Some of our patients are with us for extended times, as in end of life cases, and your role will become more than that of a nurse. If you have time to write a short letter for one of them, or give a small treat to bring pleasure, feel free. End of life is as important as recovery."

With that, Matron rose and came around from behind her desk. "Welcome to Bellevue, Miss Wilmot. You are one of just 39 new students on probation for the next month. Quite an honour when you consider we had over 1,800 applicants."

"After your probation period, you will either return home or continue in the program. I, myself, am a graduate of the Training School and can attest to the rewards of this chosen career. I have no doubt you will manage well but my door is always open if you have concerns during your probation."

"Thank you, Matron. I won't let you down" replied Olive.

Olive was met outside the Matron's office by a senior nurse who explained that she would be her primary instructor, outside of the classroom and lecture hall. She took Olive on a tour of the hospital, paying particular attention to the ward they would work in. Matron's words resonated with Olive, as she looked upon the many patients and watched the nurses move about their tasks. Their professionalism was evident and Olive knew this accompanied a pride in their role. She couldn't wait to get started.

The initial probation month in the nursing program consisted of direct patient care. She shadowed her senior nurse and learned the fundamental tasks required: making beds; changing soiled linens; helping patients in and out of bed while maintaining their dignity; keeping order in the ward.

It pleased her to go about her day, easing the discomfort of the patients in her charge. She became adept at taking their pulse and temperature; redressing wounds and helping the senior nurse give out medications.

Olive learned another side of life on the wards. Despite their pain, patients often found life in the hospital preferable to the life they knew at home. The regular meals, comfortable bed that didn't have to be shared, and caring touch were often missing in their own lives.

Hospitals had been established as charity centres; the wealthy continued to receive medical care in their homes. Hospital stays were generally long since individuals rarely went to hospital until they were extremely sick.

Her height and outstanding beauty meant she was noticed but it was her approachability and warmth that made her welcome at every bedside. Olive's kindness and respect for every individual made her popular with the patients. They looked forward to a few words with her each day.

When time permitted, she sat with those who missed their families or were experiencing pain. She would distract them with stories of her own family and life experiences and it didn't take long before even the most petulant patients were sharing their own stories with her. She hid her surprise at their lack of discretion but soon understood that, when you lived in crowded conditions, little was left private in life.

The elderly women on the ward received Olive's particular attention. Most were in palliative care and Olive would spend time with them, asking about their lives and families, drawing out their memories, hoping them might forget their pain for a short while.

Bellevue's senior nurses were pleased with Olive's progress in nursing skill and with her compassion. Glowing reports to Superintendent Brennan were unanimous and meant she passed probation and became a full student.

Olive received word in a note delivered to her room after a long day on the ward. The month had proved more rewarding than she could have imagined and she hadn't considered what she would do if she didn't pass probation. Even so, a large sigh of gratitude escaped her as she read the note. As tired as she was, she sat down immediately to write Minnie and share her good news.

After dropping the letter in the outbound mail tray in the front hall, Olive went in search of Lisbeth. Finding her in the downstairs lounge, she knew immediately from the girl's smile that she, too, would be continuing in the program. The girls spent a happy hour chatting together about the future before them before turning in for the night.

Chapter 43

Ministering personal hygiene to bedridden patients and laying out those who have died gave a nurse intimate knowledge of the human body. As Olive went through her days and weeks on the wards, she had no reservations about what was asked of her. Indeed, the care she displayed toward every patient was because of the reverence she felt toward her role.

Other than the years with Harry, which she never thought of on a conscious level, she began to see that her life to date had bordered on frivolous and certainly self-centred.

Here, on the wards, she saw for the first time the difference one could make in the world. Entire days went by with no thought to her own comfort, faced as she was with such human suffering.

Olive excelled at the practical side of nursing because of the respect she brought to each patient but she felt truly alive in the classroom and lecture halls.

Bellevue was innovative in offering lectures by the medical staff to nursing students and others. These lectures introduced concepts beyond the basics of human anatomy. The lecture topics and speakers were posted in the lobby of the Home and were open to any practicing or student nurse whose schedule allowed attendance.

Olive signed up for every possible lecture, listening closely, enthralled as physicians discussed germ theory or the challenges involved in administering ether. These doctors were passionate about their work; many had created ground-breaking surgical procedures for illnesses that once would have been fatal.

She understood she was involved at a unique time with medical treatments improving rapidly. Her grasp of the technical side of medicine and her obvious enthusiasm impressed each lecturer. She asked astute questions and often stayed behind to speak directly to the physicians.

These same doctors, when encountering her on the wards while making their rounds, found her demeanour a pleasure to be around. She had developed an ability to anticipate their needs.

As she rotated throughout the hospital wards, classrooms and lecture halls, Olive felt a sense of purpose she could never have imagined. Nursing brought her joy and the challenging medical

lectures stimulated her mind, reminding her how much she had always enjoyed learning.

In June of 1891, with graduation just around the corner, Olive was surprised when she returned to her room one evening to find a note from the Matron's office:

'Your attendance is requested tomorrow morning at 11:00 am'. She knew that nothing untoward had occurred in her performance so assumed the visit was a routine one to check in on her progress before the official ceremony. She wasn't aware of the many reports the Superintendent had received concerning her.

"I'm hearing encouraging things about your aptitude, Miss Wilmot" said Matron the following morning. "With graduation just weeks away, it has been suggested by some physicians that you might be a suitable candidate for operating theatre nursing."

"I will tell you this is very different from the ward care you are currently doing. There is nothing pretty about an operating theatre. All that is foul about the human body is witnessed in that room. Blood is the least of it."

"And there is little common decency involved in surgery. Physicians who are busy saving lives have no time for decorum or etiquette. Nurses in the operating theatre see and hear things that no woman should but the role they play is vital and this is an exciting time in surgery."

"Would you be interested in this, Miss Wilmot?"

Olive took no time to consider, jumping right in to respond. "Oh, my goodness, I would love nothing more. I enjoy caring for patients in the wards but I will admit that sometimes, since coming to Bellevue, I have regretted that I wasn't born a man, able to take a medical degree. It would be so much more worthwhile to be at the front end of treatment for patients rather than stepping in after the doctors have done their work."

"You voice the frustration of many nurses, Miss Wilmot. It is the limitation we are born with. I'm certain you would make a very capable physician but let's get you established as a surgical nurse, shall we?"

"I will speak with the head of surgery. It will be necessary for you to be vetted by the surgical rotation committee for final approval but I think this is likely a formality in your case. If you are accepted, the

committee will determine where you might fit in to the rotation. There is an observation period followed by an extensive training period."

"Carry on with your routine, in the meantime. I will send a note around to your room once I have heard from the committee."

Olive felt light-hearted as she headed back to her ward. She was anxious to share her news and get some insights with one or two senior nurses who did surgery rotation.

It didn't take long for word to come; physicians were always anxious to add capable nurses to their teams, especially when so many were lost through marriage.

Matron had been wrong about one thing, though. The discussion amongst the committee members had been anything but a formality. There was a heated debate about Olive's suitability though not for lack of ability.

The committee members were unanimous in their support of her qualifications and aptitude. It was her striking looks that caused the uncertainty. Without a doubt, she would be one of the nurses they would lose through marriage.

The chairman had eventually swayed the discussion by making the point that all of the surgical physicians at Bellevue were in their sixties and married.

"Let's be realistic, Gentlemen. None of us are husband material. Motion to accept Miss Wilmot as a surgical nurse is moved."

Chapter 44

"You are good to come today, Uncle John" said Olive after her graduation ceremony was over. She was pleased to have someone from her family in the audience to witness her achievement. She had been surprised to be presented with a particular award which recognized her high scores on all exams.

"You make our family proud, Olive" he told her during the reception following. "With school behind you, I hope we will see more of you." Her schedule had allowed only a few visits with her uncle during the previous two years.

"It may be some time before my life will be my own, Uncle" replied Olive. "I begin training for the operating theatre next week and I must be available for emergency surgeries beyond those scheduled.

"Well, my Dear" her uncle said. "You are to be commended for your ambition. Many women your age would be content with pouring tea for 'at homes' and sharing gossip with their peers."

Olive's prediction that her life would be just as busy following graduation proved correct but she had never felt so alive. As the months went by and her surgical experience grew, she gained a reputation as a focused, capable surgery nurse and every surgeon was soon requesting her to assist in their theatre.

She thrilled that she was playing a part in saving lives although she soon learned to deal with the opposite as well. As many inroads as physicians were making in surgical techniques, there was still much that was unknown and experimental.

She discovered a core group of nurses in the residence who were intent on their careers and these women became her social circle. Lisbeth was amongst them, although she continued as a ward nurse. Their friendship had grown and they tried to coordinate their off hours together to visit the many attractions the city offered.

Despite the passing of years, a pain lived deep inside Olive from Harry's abuse but she kept this tightly to herself. Lisbeth often wondered that Olive spoke so little about her life experience when she was clearly not an innocent woman. Nothing about nursing shocked Olive.

Lisbeth respected her friend's apparent need for privacy while still sharing much of her own life, all of which endeared her to Olive more.

When not working different shifts, the girls looked forward to dining together and speaking of their day. One day in November, Olive was busting to tell Lisbeth about a surgical case she had worked on.

"Have you met the visiting surgeon, Dr. Burchard, yet Lisbeth?" she asked, knowing that Lisbeth worked the post-surgical ward.

"I have" replied her friend. "There aren't many physicians like him. He spoke at length with an elderly man, calming his fears and listening to his concerns. Most of our doctors are perfunctory in their follow up visits to the ward. Dr. Burchard stood out to me."

"To me, as well" said Olive. "He was performing an appendectomy today and I was assigned to his surgery. He took time to explain what he was doing to those of us around him. Did you know he pioneered the appendectomy which saves so many lives?"

"I had heard that" replied Lisbeth, "although only from other nurses on my ward. From the few encounters I've had with Dr. Burchard, I believe him to be that rare beast; a humble physician."

Thomas was at Bellevue filling in for his uncle, Lewis Sayre, a Professor of Orthopedic and Clinical Surgery at Bellevue. Thomas was a frequent guest lecturer and was well known at the hospital. As was the practice of most physicians of their era and financial means, his uncle was taking a European sabbatical that winter to share his newest techniques in orthopedics with German physicians.

Olive was assigned to Dr. Burchard's surgeries throughout his tenure at Bellevue that winter and spring. She also attended each lecture he gave, sitting in the front row to minimize the distractions around her.

The doctor noted her attentiveness at his lectures. '*What a strange creature,*' he thought to himself. '*A young woman with so much going for her and yet she chooses to work long hours in such an unglamorous pursuit and then attend lectures after doing so.*'

At 6' tall, Thomas loomed over many of his peers. He was a quiet-spoken man who rarely wasted words. When he did speak, others listened, drawn to his thoughtful approach on subjects.

Thomas' wife Irene died in 1889, leaving him alone to raise two young sons. Since her death he avoided society, preferring a quiet life.

But while Irene had been alive, they had been part of the social elite of New York. Thomas was a graduate of Yale University and a

member of the Union League Club, along with fellow members Theodore Roosevelt and John Pierpont Morgan.

His brownstone at 53 W. 52nd Street was within blocks of Wm. Kissam and Alva Vanderbilt's home on 5th Avenue and he was friends with Willie Vanderbilt.

Although the Burchard's money was considerably more modest than the Vanderbilts, Thomas' early roots in New York meant that he was one of the '400'; the social elite so decided upon by Mrs. Astor when her new ballroom could only accommodate 400 people.

The social calendar for New Yorker's was tied to the seasons. As weather changed, people travelled from one locale to another.

Saratoga Springs was one such retreat and the friendship between Wm. Vanderbilt and Thomas was strengthened during their many visits to the resort community. Both were devotees of Saratoga, although for different reasons. The Vanderbilt horses were renowned amongst the horse-racing and gambling set but Thomas made regular visits to partake of the waters.

The doctor's social standing and good looks were irrelevant to Olive. She found herself attracted to his character and demeanour and began to look forward to their conversations post-surgery, as they removed their aprons and moved into the surgery anteroom.

She wouldn't deny that Thomas was handsome. His high forehead, round chin and straight nose were more than pleasant to the eye. But it was on gazing into his gentle gray eyes that one realized how attractive he was. The way he kept his eyes on her as she spoke made Olive feel special.

As weeks went by, their brief conversations became longer and personal questions were asked. He enquired about her family; she about his two young sons. She was pleased to see his face light up when he spoke of the boys. Olive had many memories of her own younger brothers at the same ages and she and Thomas often ended in laughter before parting.

Thomas also looked forward to these moments with Olive. She was the first woman to bring him laughter since Irene and he liked the feelings he had been certain he would never feel again.

Chapter 45

As Thomas' tenure at Bellevue came to an end, Olive felt sad to lose his presence from her daily life. She believed they had developed a tender friendship and this had filled a void in her life that she hadn't admitted existed, even to herself.

Because they had never been anything but proper with each other, she had no way of knowing that Thomas was feeling the same emotions. He knew he could not imagine a life that did not feature Olive.

Although Thomas had stopped socializing after Irene's death, he thought that returning now would give opportunities to see Olive. She and Thomas had told each other of their respective lack of a social life, although Olive pretended her reason to be a by product of her nursing career. Thomas felt intuitively that there was more to this than Olive let on since many nurses managed to have full lives in addition to their work in the hospital.

He was by no means a prying man but felt there must be a way to introduce Olive to society in a way that she would be comfortable with. He was confident that, once New York met her, she would be invited to every salon and dining room increasing the opportunities to see each other. New York City was a social bee-hive and one could be out every evening if it was desired.

Olive had told Thomas that her uncle was a benefactor of the hospital; had been since his own wife's illness and death some years previously. Giving his plan some thought one evening, he realized that John Wilmot's connection to the hospital provided a perfect opportunity for him.

During an evening with his newly returned uncle Lewis at their club, Thomas spoke of various subjects concerning the hospital and his tenure, although he did not mention Olive. He was aware of her position as a single woman in the city and was sensitive to her reputation.

"Uncle Lewis," he said, as they were approaching the end of their evening, "I was very impressed with the resources Bellevue has and learned from the other physicians that the hospital has many generous patrons. Has any thought ever been given to a dinner for these benefactors? Such an invitation, with their spouses or guests, would

provide an opportunity to express gratitude and keep the hospital foremost in these generous hearts and minds."

"That is a sound idea, Thomas" replied his uncle thoughtfully. "In fact, I think having these benefactors spend time with the physicians they support could be very beneficial. Every man likes to know how his generosity is serving his community and we have much to be proud of at Bellevue.

Thomas realized this entire plan was a shot in the dark. After all, there was no certainty that Olive's uncle would be free to attend the evening or that he would invite her as his guest but he believed that both were highly possible. Given her familiarity with the physicians, it made sense that her widowed uncle would want to include her.

John Wilmot, upon receiving his invitation, thought precisely that. Who better to accompany him than his gracious niece who had personal experience with these doctors? He sent a note of acceptance.

Invitations to the home of Dr. Lewis and Eliza Sayre, at 285 Fifth Avenue, were highly sought after. Guest lists were always an equal mix of people of medicine, science and those involved in the arts. This diversity led to lively discussion.

Lewis was a renowned surgeon, known the world over for his work and methods; an academic with a brilliant mind who was treated with utmost respect by his peers. But, to the world at large, he presented a humble exterior and was most approachable.

Eliza Sayre was the daughter of artists and an artist herself. Her creativity was a balm to the stresses of Lewis' scientific world. Their differences still delighted them. The love and happiness they felt in each other's company made for a home filled with warmth and generous hospitality.

Olive knew none of this as she and her Uncle John approached the home on a mild evening in early April. During her training, she had assisted in the operating theatre with Dr. Sayre many times but was at a loss to tell her uncle about his character.

While some doctors talked freely during surgeries, his manner was one of focus. He behaved toward her as a professional patron might; helpful in explanations to her during her training period but otherwise keeping to himself. She knew from Thomas that Lewis was his uncle but very little about him otherwise.

The door was opened to their knock by an elderly manservant. As he took their outer clothing, a tall, attractive, middle-aged woman approached them with hand outstretched, introducing herself as Eliza Sayre. John took her hand, saying "I am John Wilmot, Mrs. Sayre, and this is my niece, Olive. Thank you for the invitation to your lovely home. It is most kind of you and Dr. Sayre."

"We thought it was high time some gratitude was shown to our larger hospital benefactors, Mr. Wilmot. My husband's research and that of the other physicians here tonight would amount to very little without the generous support of yourself and the others we have invited. Please, come to the drawing room and allow me to introduce some of our other guests."

Olive was not surprised to see Thomas in the drawing room but certainly was by the butterflies she felt. She had missed his company at the hospital finding the other physicians soberer in their approach to the nursing staff.

It hadn't been long since Thomas had finished his tenure at Bellevue but he, too, felt a jump in his heart rate as Olive entered the room. '*What is this*?' he thought. '*Am I a love-struck school-boy once again?*'

After a suitable period of time, he made his way around the room to Olive's side and she introduced him to her uncle.

"The patients have missed you, Dr. Burchard" she said, after her uncle had excused himself to speak with a colleague he had spotted across the room. The minute the words were out, she knew it was she who missed him.

"I find myself missing them and the staff at Bellevue, also, Miss Wilmot" replied Thomas. "It seems strange to become attached to a place after a few short months but I certainly did. It's a pleasure to see you outside of the hospital and looking so lovely in something other than your usual uniform."

Olive blushed at the flattery but was inwardly touched. There was warmth in Thomas' eyes that was difficult to mistake for anything other than interest in her. Although discomfited by his attentions on the surface, she wanted nothing more than to stand by his side throughout the evening.

Eliza returned at that moment and spirited her away to meet others before everyone was called to the dining room.

They were seated too far away from each other for conversation but were on opposite sides which meant Olive could see Thomas. Her eyes returned to him whenever she could discreetly do so and, once or twice, she found his own watching her. '*What is happening here*' she asked herself. '*I am not free to become involved with anyone. Whatever this is must stop now.*'

She turned her attention to the gentlemen on either side of her, as etiquette dictated. Despite her thoughts being elsewhere, both of her table companions thought her a lovely, intelligent girl, well versed in the various medical discussions that arose.

The evening came to a close all too soon as Olive donned her coat and accessories in the front hall.

'*I likely won't see him again*', she thought with a twinge of regret, despite her earlier resolve.

But, raising her head from fastening her gloves, she found Thomas at her side. "I look forward to seeing you again, Miss Wilmot" he said, taking her hand in his own. Her voice failed her as she looked into his eyes briefly before stepping outside with her uncle.

Chapter 46

Thomas' Aunt Eliza was intrigued by the surprising young woman who was a part of her husband's world. As long as she had lived with Lewis, she had never ventured beyond a general awareness of his medical pursuits. Those discussions were shared by the men at their clubs over cigars and brandy.

Eliza knew nurses were crucial to her husband's surgical team but she had imagined them to be homely spinsters with few options in the world. Here was a gracious, intelligent and beautiful woman who threw Eliza's preconceptions out the window. What could her motives be for the career she had chosen, wondered Eliza, wanting to know more.

Eliza sent an invitation to Olive for tea with a group of her friends. Reading the invitation made Olive pause; she had certainly enjoyed herself at the dinner and, after months of keeping to herself and her nursing co-workers, realized how much she would enjoy an afternoon with women outside of the profession. She had enjoyed speaking with Eliza and was curious about the artistic life she lived.

She accepted the invitation, knowing in her heart that doing so was also keeping a connection to Thomas alive.

Olive enjoyed every bit of her afternoon at The Russian Tearoom; the ambience; the food; service and the company of the six other women Eliza had invited.

Olive told them what a treat it was to wear 'street' clothes and to hear about the daily goings on of other women. In turn, the women plied Olive with questions about her nursing career and Olive gladly shared anecdotal comments about her duties, leaving out any detail of the human devastation she witnessed so often. The women appreciated that she was exposed to much more than she spoke of and were intrigued by this beautiful girl who they believed lived on the edge by her chosen career. The fact that she was privy to the world men occupied daily, and doing so willingly, made her a curious creature; one who deserved getting to know better.

When Olive received two more invitations the decision to accept came easily and before many weeks had passed, she found herself involved in the swirl of New York activity in the spring. Concerts; the Opera; and dinners brought her, if not in close contact with, at least near the leading and powerful of the city. For proprieties sake, she

frequently asked Lisbeth to accompany her but stopped short of attending balls since she had no male escort. Despite working in a man's world, to attend a ball as a single woman was not done.

The fact that Thomas was present at most events contributed to Olive's pleasure with this new life, although she believed her ease with it was easier to explain. For the first time since her marriage to Harry, Olive was once again enjoying a life where she felt free to be herself. With Harry, she learned to be guarded in presenting herself. In London, she had been uncomfortable because she felt deceitful in presenting herself as 'Miss' Wilmot. In Newcastle she had just avoided a social life altogether to prevent further talk.

New York had given Olive an identity: she was a well-educated woman of good breeding who was also a nurse. Her uncle was well known in commerce and she was usually introduced as his niece. Beauty and grace were always welcome into this society but her wit and charm cemented her place.

Here, as she had been as a young woman, Olive was welcomed for her empathy. She was quick to learn the stories of each person she was introduced to and to remember them at the next encounter. There was something about Olive that made others confide in her. Everyone felt her to be a circumspect woman; one who would offer understanding with no fear that their issue would be fodder for gossip at the next event.

Thomas' return to society was welcomed without suspect of his motives. It had been two years since Irene had passed, a more than reasonable mourning period, and his peers had always welcomed him. Men were not threatened by Thomas and women enjoyed his warmth.

It was coincidental, everyone thought, that Thomas should have returned to society just as this beautiful, and single, woman had emerged on their scene. They were both young and unencumbered (everyone believed) and hostesses began to take the usual pleasure in presenting opportunities for the two to engage with each other. They were seated beside one another at many dinners and often found themselves in the same box at the Opera, thanks to generous hosts.

Olive hid the shivers she felt when he occasionally took her arm or put a protective arm at her back. She could no longer deny her feelings for this tall, handsome and gentle man. He was the antithesis of Harry

which made it easier for her to imagine life with him. But an imaginary life with him was all that she could ever hope for.

The law both restrained and protected her. She enjoyed her increasing interactions with Thomas but was not free to marry. Even had she been free, Olive knew that intimacy with another man was impossible. Her pain and humiliation continued to haunt her. And no man would accept a partial marriage. No, Olive was grateful for the law.

As summer turned to autumn, she had convinced herself that she could continue seeing him as a strong friend, as much as a man and a woman could be without stirring society to talk.

Thomas, though, was certain he wanted to wed this woman. Each time they met only reinforced this in his mind and heart. Although always amongst others, they enjoyed spirited conversations; something he had missed since Irene's passing. He was impressed with Olive's ability to structure sound arguments and stand by her opinions, even in the face of opposition. He thought she debated very like a man. Time spent in her company was never dull.

By the end of September, Thomas knew he must ask for her hand. Finding adequate time to put his case forward, in an appropriate place; one which would not compromise her reputation, was uppermost in his mind. In the end, he knew the only solution was to recruit the help of his Aunt Eliza. He knew her to be a hopeless romantic and that she, too, had become very fond of Olive.

"Aunt Eliza, I have rather a large favour to ask of you" said Thomas one night when his uncle had left the room. "I don't think you'll be surprised to learn that I have become very fond of Miss Wilmot. I intend to ask for her hand but believe I need some time alone with her to plead my case since I'm not entirely certain she is aware of my feelings."

"Oh, Thomas, I am so pleased" replied his Aunt. "I think the dear girl is a treasure. Of course you can count on my discretion. Why don't I invite her to call on me one afternoon and you can drop by? I can then leave the two of you alone in the parlour without interruption."

"I do believe this is not the first time you have colluded for love, Aunt," said Thomas with a twinkle in his eye, "but I couldn't be more grateful. Let's set up a date for next month, shall we. I need a bit of time to formulate my approach."

Chapter 47

Eliza feigned surprise when her manservant announced Thomas' arrival after she and Olive had been served tea.

"Well, what a lovely treat to see you in the afternoon, Thomas" she said as he entered the room. "Wilfred, please bring another cup for Dr. Burchard. Do sit down, Thomas. You have arrived just as Miss Wilmot and I were discussing the new art display at the gallery. Perhaps you have seen it and have thoughts as well?"

Thomas had not and so was quiet as the two women chattered. After he had been settled with his own cup of tea, Eliza stood, saying "I have something for the boys, Thomas. If you and Miss Wilmot do not mind, I'll go see if I can find it; I'm not exactly certain where I put it." With that, she left the room and Thomas and Olive found themselves alone together for the first time.

Although surprised by Thomas' unplanned visit to his Aunt while she happened to be visiting, Olive thought nothing amiss. She supposed he often dropped in on her unexpectedly. She was prepared to speak casually with him about this and that when Thomas suddenly moved beside her on the settee and took one of her hands.

"I can't let an opportunity like this go by, Miss Wilmot, without letting you know the extent of my feelings for you. You know that my heart was broken when I lost my wife, Irene, but working so closely with you, as I did, has led to a high regard for you. Seeing you socially over the past months has made me realize just how much I hold you dear. I understand that this is likely catching you unaware but I just had to make my feelings known."

"I will not be so rude as to ask you to marry me today and put you on the spot but I would like to know that you will consider such a proposition. Once you have had some time to digest this, I hope we may speak alone again and decide if we might have a future together. I won't speak of it anymore for now so let us carry on as friends might until my Aunt returns."

Since Thomas had, quite literally, taken Olive's breath away, she remained speechless for some minutes. She was saved from a need to respond by Eliza's re-entry to the room.

"Here it is, Thomas. I discovered this kite tucked away in a shop and immediately thought of the boys. They might still get some use out of it before the snow flies."

"Thank you, Aunt Eliza. I know they will be most touched that you thought of them. Time has gotten away from me and I must be going. Miss Wilmot" he said, nodding toward her, "a pleasure, as always. No need to see me out, Aunt. Thank you for the tea."

"Excuse me, Mrs. Sayer" said Olive, somewhat breathlessly. "I've just thought of something I should have mentioned to Dr. Burchard." With that, she almost ran from the room to catch Thomas just as the manservant was helping him into his coat.

"There can be no future for us, Dr. Burchard, but I couldn't let you leave without knowing that my feelings are the same."

With that, she stood on her toes to leave a feather-like kiss on his cheek and then returned, as sedately as she could manage, to the parlour and Mrs. Sayer.

Thomas touched his cheek with wonder and turned to exit the house, whistling a happy tune as he went.

Olive somehow managed to keep her composure after Thomas' departure but she brought the visit to a close soon after. She found the idea of idle chatter difficult now and was most anxious to head home to think her thoughts in the quiet of her room.

Chapter 48

Now I've done it, Olive wrote in her journal that evening. *What a silly chit I am to have behaved so. What on earth shall I tell him now after giving him such hope? But I simply had no choice. I would not be able to live with myself if I hadn't expressed how I feel to him.*

But, really, what schoolgirl silliness was that? If I am unable at my age to manage my emotions, what is ahead for me? Now I am left with the reality. How can I speak of such intimate things that will need to be told if he is to understand my situation? God knows, if it were possible, I would marry this man tomorrow.

This is not a discussion I ever thought I would have. To reveal the ugly truth, and to someone so gentle and kind, will be the most difficult speech I will ever give in my life. But it must be done so that he will see the impossibility of any attachment to me. Why have you put this man in my path, God? What purpose does it serve my life to fall in love now?

Olive was not surprised to receive a note the following day.

My Dearest,

I haven't slept a wink. Despite your doubts, the sooner we can meet to talk of our possible future together, the quicker life will return to normal for me.

Are you free for a walk in Central Park this Sunday afternoon? Please ask Lisbeth to join us for propriety's sake but I pray she will keep a discrete distance from us as we walk.

I will pick you both up at 1:00 in my carriage if you just confirm.

I wait anxiously for your reply.

Fondly,
Thomas

Olive sat with the note in her lap, momentarily dreaming about what might be. She could imagine greeting this man at the end of his busy day at the hospital, listening to his stories about patients and treatments, fellow doctors and nurses. She believed herself to be in a unique position; able to understand his trials and challenges. She would dedicate her life to his comfort and ease, calmly managing his household with efficiency.

But, oh, she had been so wrong about Harry. If she could be so wrong once, what would stop her from being so again? Where had her

self-protective shell gone, she wondered? It had stood her well all these years since leaving Harry and yet, here she was, dreaming of married life again.

Her thoughts were just that – dreams. There was no point in imagining any life with another man when she was still married.

She would meet with Thomas but only to say what he proposed was impossible.

After checking with Lisbeth, she sent a quick reply to Thomas agreeing to his plan and went through the motions during the remaining days until they were to meet.

Chapter 49

Olive held a secret hope that an emergency surgery would prevent their tryst but Sunday dawned with no note from the hospital to change her schedule. And, despite her prayers for inclement weather, the day was sunny and unseasonably warm for late September.

'It appears that I must face the day with courage,' she thought as she knelt in chapel that morning. *'Please, God, I ask for you guidance today. If ever I needed help in guarding my words, it will be today.'*

Lisbeth was waiting for Olive at the front entrance when she returned from freshening up after lunch. Although Olive had not said anything specific to her friend about the purpose of this outing, Lisbeth was keenly aware of how Olive's face lit up when she spoke of Dr. Burchard. This was also the first direct invitation Olive had received from him.

'It doesn't take a lug nut to gather what this means,' thought Lisbeth. *'I'm certain this excursion marks the beginning of a courtship. I'll play along with the ruse, though. I know to do otherwise would just embarrass Olive.'*

"How thoughtful of Dr. Burchard to consider two lonely nurses on such a lovely Sunday" said Lisbeth. "I'm sure he must have many others who would enjoy his company but I, for one, won't balk at his suggestion on such a beautiful day. What better way to enjoy this weather than a stroll through the park?"

Thomas pulled up in a hansom carriage and stepped out to assist both ladies up. "Good day, Miss Eichmann; Miss Wilmot" he said. "Are we not lucky to have chosen a day such as this for a stroll?"

"Indeed we are, Dr. Burchard" replied Lisbeth. "I am grateful for your kind invitation."

"The pleasure is mine" said Thomas. "A stroll through the park is vastly improved by the company of two lovely ladies."

The two chattered during the short drive to the entrance to the park, while Olive remained quiet. She was still formulating in her mind what she was to say.

After Thomas had paid the hansom driver, the three walked together through the entrance. As they passed the baseball diamonds, Lisbeth said, "I believe I would like to sit and watch this ballgame for a bit. Would you two mind terribly if I did so and left you to stroll alone?"

'How does she know we want to speak alone?' Olive wondered. *'I've said nothing to her. What a dear friend she is.'*

"Of course we don't mind, Lisbeth. Let's get you settled on the bleacher and we will know where to find you on our return" said Olive.

When Thomas and Olive had carried on along a little way, he said "I trust, under these circumstances, that I might be so bold as to call you Olive? And I would be so happy if you might call me Thomas. I've thought of little else all week but seeing you today".

"Oh, Thomas" said Olive, surprised by how easily his given name slipped from her tongue, "we have much to talk about and I struggle with where to begin. Might we sit on this bench for a while? I think it might be easier to speak."

Thomas held her arm as she settled on a bench and then sat down beside her, turning his body toward hers. "The most important thing I must tell you, Thomas, is something which will shock you. I am married."

Instead of shocked, Thomas merely looked surprised but his eyes clearly showed her he was waiting for her to continue.

"I was married at 17, against my family's wishes, but was back at my father's house before turning 20. It was my father, in fact, who took me away from my husband's house. My husband was abusive and when my father learned of it he helped me to abandon my husband and marriage vows. I am not proud of walking away from the marriage but have realized in the intervening years that I had little choice."

"Let me begin at the beginning, shall I? The abuse began almost immediately after our marriage. There was an ugly side to the abuse that I don't wish to share but time has helped me to see that everything he did to me was calculated and intended to mould me into an obedient wife; one who would not object to his profligate lifestyle. Much was subtle; imperceptible, really, by others in the household. He established a fear in me which left him free to terrorize me."

"He was involved in his family's business but within a year of our wedding, had been terminated for his behaviours which were reflecting poorly on the business. He then arranged for the two of us to move to a remote town in northern Ontario to pursue a new business venture."

"It was here, with no family around us, where the abuse escalated. It took a surprise visit from my father for me to recognize just how

out of control he had become. Fear had kept me quiet and a lack of money meant I had no resources to leave even had I had the strength to do so but my father presented opportunity and encouragement. We just walked away one day, while Harry was at work and I have tried very hard not to look back since."

"Harry's family wrote to let me know he had left for the United States soon after and no one had heard from him. There is no good social outcome for a woman who finds herself alone so soon after marriage, whether she leaves or is abandoned. I was prepared to face whatever was thrown at me as a result of my actions but his mother and father were generous enough to tell everyone in Toronto that he had deserted me so that I might appear blameless. It was a thoughtful move on their part but it did nothing to stem the curiosity of my own community."

"I lived with my father in England for a year following which helped me to recuperate and then for another five years back on our family farm before coming to New York to study nursing. I have presented myself as a single woman because it makes life easier than explaining the absence of a husband but you can see the impossibility of another marriage."

"Oh, my lovely girl" said Thomas. "It pains me to hear all of this. I want to do nothing more than bring you joy for the rest of my life to make up for those terrible years. I vow to treat you with tenderness and respect."

"But…" began Olive, before Thomas interrupted her to continue. "No. No. Say no more. I am fully aware of the legal impediment but I refuse to believe there is not some way around this situation. No woman should suffer what you have endured and then continue to suffer after escaping such a life."

"With your permission, I will consult with my brother who is a lawyer. He will know more about the marital laws in Canada and the United States and may very well have ideas. For now, Olive, please just let me know that you feel as I do and that, under different circumstances, you would have accepted my proposal without condition."

Spent by the emotions her confession had brought back to her, Olive was able only to put her hand on Thomas' and nod her assent. "That is all I need, Olive" he said. "Let us return to Lisbeth now and we three will have our tea."

Thomas wasted no time; after dropping Olive and Lisbeth back at their residence; he had the driver take him directly to his brother, Lewis' home. This was impetuous behaviour for Thomas, who had no idea if his brother was even at home.

"Wait for me, Driver" he said, as he stepped from the carriage. Climbing the stairs of Lewis' brownstone two at a time, he was out of breath by the time the housekeeper answered his knock. "Is Mr. Burchard at home, Mrs. Peters?"

Reassured that Lewis was, indeed, at home, and leaving his hat and coat with her, Thomas strode through to the study, closing the door behind him.

"To what do I owe this surprise visit, Thomas" asked Lewis, with concern, for his brother had never arrived unannounced in the past. "Would you like some tea or something stronger perhaps" he asked, with an apprehensive look at his brother's face.

"No, nothing; I've just come from tea. It's about the woman I had tea with that I've come. I scarcely know where to begin, Lewis, but am in need of your legal counsel on a highly confidential matter."

"Sit, Thomas. You are making me anxious with your pacing. Now, begin at the beginning and I'll see what advice I might have for you."

"It may surprise you to hear Lewis that I have proposed to another woman. Rest assured this is not a sudden move on my part. We have known each other for the better part of a year. She is a nurse and we worked together at Bellevue for several months and have been meeting socially for many more. Her name is Olive Wilmot."

"Oh, I recall her, Thomas. She was at the Beekmann's dinner that we both attended some weeks past. I remember a little curiosity about the beauty taking New York by storm. You certainly hid your interest well; I have no memory of you giving special attention to her through the evening."

"I've tried to be cautious Lewis. Once I was certain of my feelings, I asked Aunt Eliza to arrange a private meeting between us for me to propose. It was Olive's response to my proposal that brings me here to you" said Thomas, raising his eyes to Lewis' face with a forlorn look.

"Olive told me that she had been and, indeed, still is, married. She was married at 17 to an abusive man and, with her father's help and blessing, had left his household before the age of 20. She has lived an

exemplary life since then and is adamant that we have no right to marry, despite our feelings."

"Her husband moved to the US soon after and hasn't been heard from. His own family let it be known that he had deserted her in an effort to save her reputation so I would presume they knew something of the abuse."

"I simply can't accept that laws would prohibit a victim such as Olive from living a full life as she is certainly meant to be doing, Lewis. I am beside myself. How could God put such a perfect creature in my path and than prohibit our marriage?

There must be some way around the Canadian marital laws which will allow a remarriage. I understand that divorce is reprehensible in most situations but I don't believe it to be so in this case. I would stand proudly at Olive's side, shielding her from the stigma of being known as a 'Divorcee' if we might somehow make this happen."

"I won't say that marital law is something I am fluent in, Thomas, but I certainly know others who are. They may have suggestions for you. Do you give me permission to seek their advice, using hypotheticals, of course? I will never let your name or Olive's be known."

"Do what you must, Lewis," replied Thomas. "I know you will be discrete. Just make haste with your enquiries; I can barely function as it is. I will warn you that I won't take a negative reply well. I'm determined to marry this woman, within the law or not."

"I will pretend I didn't hear that, Thomas. Please leave this with me and go about your life until you hear back from me. I won't dally, I promise you."

The two men shook hands on parting. They were very fond of each other and Lewis felt for Thomas. He was also very aware of Thomas' weak heart and felt enormous concern for the strain this situation might put on it. '*However I manage it, I must come back with a plan that will suit him*' thought Lewis. '*I vowed to Irene that I would protect him and protect him, I shall*'.

Thomas was very pleased, just a week later, to receive Lewis' note advising he would be calling that evening. Despite a very full schedule that day, Thomas' mind was on the pending visit.

"Come in, come in" he said, as Lewis stepped through his door that night. "I have sherry set out in the library so let me pour as you tell me all."

Taking the glass from Thomas, Lewis began. "A divorce in Canada is out of the question, Thomas. The process is time-consuming, very public and damaging to all members of both families. At any rate, I suspect Olive would be unable to contact her husband, which would make obtaining a divorce impossible, since both parties must present their petitions to a judge.

"Now don't look so crestfallen. I have learned that, with her husband now a resident of the United States, a divorce in the US *is* possible, although it will not be recognized by authorities in Canada and any remarriage by Olive would also not be recognized there. "

"This divorce can be obtained on the grounds of desertion and would, at the very least, give Olive some credibility when others question a remarriage. I would hazard to say that most are naïve about marital law, anyway."

"With the divorce recognized in the US, my advice would be to then have a private wedding in New York State so that you both know you are legally married, in the US at least. Since that will be your principle residence, I think that should ease Olive's mind."

"I would then suggest you have another ceremony in Canada. I would not normally counsel you to do anything illegal but this ceremony would be for appearances only, putting rumours to rest. Everyone in Canada would assume that, if Olive were able to remarry, a divorce recognized in Canada must have been obtained."

"If you plan this ceremony in an unfamiliar church which neither of you are affiliated with, they are not likely to question foreign divorce documents, which are still rare to most ministers."

"This plan may sound simplistic, Thomas, and it is in reality but I beg you to give serious thought to the social stigma that Olive, and you by extension, will face. We both know how society will receive a divorced Olive and you both need very strong backbones to brave the disgrace many will recognize it as."

"The process in the US doesn't take a great deal of time and is far more discrete for her family, which may help them to accept this. If Olive decides to go ahead with this, I would suggest that her family be informed. When she faces the judge, it helps her case to have family members standing with her."

"Let me give you the name and address for the lawyer I consulted with. He is on alert for your contact."

"You have made me extremely happy, Lewis," said Thomas, smiling. "I am fully aware of how society will view us but I believe our inner circle will embrace Olive and time will change others. Thank you for your advice and for your brotherly concern."

Chapter 50

On Thomas' urging, Eliza Sayer sent another invitation to tea to Olive's residence. Olive sent a note of acceptance with very mixed feelings. She was certain that Thomas would have discovered the impossibility of their marriage and renewed sadness overcame her as she waited to hear it from him.

Seeing Thomas on the settee as she entered the Sayer's parlour caused Olive's heart to flutter. She wasn't surprised when Eliza excused herself once she had seen Olive comfortably settled at his side. Eliza let her servant know that the pair was not to be disturbed. Although out of the norm in society, Eliza's servants had all been with her for years and were well used to her eccentricities. Providing a private room for a young couple to be alone was the least of these.

Once Olive caught her breath, she realized Thomas looked quite happy. She had supposed that he would be as heartbroken as she when he understood their inability to wed.

"Well, my Dearest. There is really no need to look so dour. It appears that, if we follow my brother's advice, a door has opened for us. Let me explain."

Thomas spent the next twenty minutes outlining everything. In the days since his meeting with Lewis, he had contacted the lawyer his brother referred and now had a solid plan to get the divorce underway. All that was needed was Olive's agreement to go ahead. He in no way took this for granted. He knew what he was asking of her.

As Thomas spoke, Olive's face betrayed the many emotions she was experiencing.

"So, you can see that, as long as we reside in the United States, any marriage here will be legal," explained Thomas.

"I'm sorry to say I can't say the same for Canada but since our primary residence will be here, I hope that won't concern you overly much. If you and your family are able to accept this, I don't believe anything stands in the way of our being married."

"I am well aware what I am asking of you, Olive. There is no way around the impact this will have on the reputations of both you and your family. A divorcee is shunned in many societies. Although you have my complete assurance that I will protect you from all that I can, ultimately how you feel about yourself is far more important than how

society views us. I need to know that you would be able to accept yourself as a divorcee and that remarriage is what you truly desire."

"Before you reply, there is something I have not shared with you to this point, Olive. Some years ago, I was diagnosed with a weak heart which means my life is managed in such a way as to prevent any further damage. I try to live as normally as possible but am faced with increasing restrictions with each passing year. I don't expect to live to old age but, with care, should have a great many years remaining to me. Can you accept life with a man with such limitations?"

Olive replied without thinking. "My goodness, Thomas, you couldn't consider me so shallow to think that I might withhold my love for want of a vibrant life. I think I am the perfect person to be at your side in the coming years. Beyond my love, you will have my nursing knowledge and I will be glad to apply it to someone I care so deeply about."

"Oh, my; I suppose I've just answered your question about what I truly desire."

Olive lowered her eyes and continued. "My dear, sweet man, I can't tell you how grateful I am for you but you are not the only one who comes to this union less than whole. The abuse I spoke of was the least of what I suffered at my husband's hands."

"There was much more which was ugly and unspeakable and this has left me with emotional scars. I must be frank that the thought of intimacy is abhorrent to me." Looking once again into Thomas eyes, Olive said "Now the question is – can you accept life with a woman who comes with such limitations?"

Thomas was so disturbed by her words that he was unable to reply, wrapping her in an embrace instead. When he was finally able to speak, his reply surprised her. "We are a pair, Olive, but I want you in my life even if we must forego intimacy. I only pray that my love will erase all memory of that man and that life from your mind."

Feeling more secure than she had in years, Olive relished the feeling of his arms around her but it was she who eventually broke away, saying "I am simply overwhelmed, Thomas. I have worked so hard to create a world I could accept and which would accept me and now it is being overturned in an instant. It's a little difficult to grasp: that which I thought impossible is, in fact, now possible. With each moment's passing, I feel more and more like singing!"

"Tell me, what must we do?"

"I suggest we first write to your father for his blessing on all of this" replied Thomas. "Regardless of the legality, I understand we must still consider 'the eyes of God' and your family. I know that My God will bless this union but each of us must reconcile this within our own hearts. You must write to him; let him know of your feelings for me and your desire and I will write to ask his permission."

The pair stood and embraced again. Separating, Thomas gently put his hands on either side of Olive's face and leaned down for a tender kiss. "You have made me so happy, my Darling girl" he said softly in her ear.

Samuel was perplexed when he received Olive's letter; she wrote with passion about the man she had fallen in love with. How had she managed to keep such strong feelings to herself, he wondered? But it was Thomas' letter that made his decision. Clearly, this was the man Samuel had always wished for his Olive. His instincts told him Thomas was the rational, loving, compassionate man Olive deserved.

He struggled with the idea of her remarriage but, on an emotional level, he had only to look at his own separation from Tillie to see the inadequacy of living a lie. He reconciled his religious objections to the divorce on his own current marital reality, wondering if such an option had been available to him if he mightn't have considered it.

Samuel wrote back to each with his blessing, replying to Thomas that he would plan to be in New York when the case went to the Judge. He would ask his brother, John, to be there as well. Surely such family representation would sway the Judge's decision.

Chapter 51

Well, who would ever have imagined this turn of events in my life? Olive wrote in her journal just three months later. The legal divorce decree lay open in front of her. *After just ninety days, I am free to wed Thomas and have a life I wouldn't have dreamt possible. Thank you, God, for giving this your blessing. I'm certain you have done so otherwise the divorce would not have been granted.*

With a US divorce obtained by early February, plans for the wedding began in earnest.

She and Thomas had seen little of each other in the weeks since the divorce process began, believing it best that she be seen to have undertaken it without his involvement. Lewis acted as her consultant throughout and she managed short visits with Thomas at Lewis' home from time to time.

They both knew that word of Olive's divorce was now public knowledge so they did all they could to keep news of the pending wedding as quiet as possible.

The ceremony was planned for April 10, 1893 in Alexandria Bay in the 1,000 Islands region of upper New York State where Thomas had a summer home. The town's population was small pre-season which ensured the wedding would remain a quiet affair. By mail, Thomas registered with the Rector of the small church he attended in the summers, carefully giving just as much information as was needed.

They would present the divorce document at the time of the wedding to prevent any prior thoughts the Rector might have concerning the matter. As legal as they all felt the divorce might be, it was still such a rare occurrence that few in the Church would know how it fit in with their doctrine and there was always a chance that a Rector would decline to perform the wedding.

Thomas and Olive would spend two nights in Alexandria Bay before boarding a train for Toronto for the second Canadian ceremony. As Lewis had suggested, this ceremony would be for those in Newcastle and Toronto who would readily question the validity of a 'foreign' wedding. Everyone involved knew the Canadian wedding would not be legal if they were to live in Canada but the ceremony was determined to be a necessary pretence. They all understood that

few would understand the legalities and would, therefore, accept that if a Canadian ceremony had taken place, Olive must have been legally free to marry again.

To reinforce this, all announcements for the wedding would be on the Canadian ceremony.

Samuel took care of arrangements on the Canadian side for the pair; registering them for a ceremony on April 13th at St. Andrews in Toronto, a church unknown to either he or Olive. He listed Olive as Episcopalian, without reference to St. George's Church in Newcastle so that there would be no contact with Rev. Brent prior to the wedding.

Samuel was as circumspect with this Minister as Thomas had been with his church. Once again, the divorce document would be presented on the day of the wedding. Samuel and Olive's brother, George, would be the only witnesses at this ceremony. All knew that the fewer people involved the better.

With plans well underway, Olive faced a difficult step that she was not looking forward to. Married women were never allowed to continue a career. Understanding this, Thomas and Olive had decided that she would leave the residence after resigning and move to her Uncle John's home until the wedding took place. The two sat together in Lewis' study one night, discussing final arrangements.

"I think the time to resign has to be now, Olive. We must hire a lady's maid for you for the sake of propriety. It's surprising that no one has seen the two of us together so far but you shouldn't be travelling around the city alone with me. A maid will also be very necessary to accompany you on the travel to our weddings. I know you've been hesitating to meet with Matron but a lady's maid in residence would never do. It's time to move to your uncle John's."

Turning to his brother, Thomas said, "Lewis, will you take care of placing an advertisement in tomorrow's newspapers and arrange for Olive to interview the women in your office? I'm certain she won't have difficulty finding someone fairly quickly."

"My goodness, Thomas" said Olive. "I don't think I would even know what tasks to give a lady's maid. I have managed for myself my entire life."

"An experienced woman will know without being instructed, Olive," explained Thomas. "It's most important that you interview for

a woman who you relate to and trust. This position is one of confidence within our household."

As they put on their outer clothing and headed down Lewis' steps to the waiting carriage, Thomas said, "There is much to do this week but I know the least desirable task on your list will be to meet with Matron. I know how much nursing means to you and I am grateful you are making that sacrifice for our marriage."

"This is why I love you so much, Thomas" said Olive as they prepared to part to separate carriages. "I doubt there are many men who would give a thought to my feelings concerning this."

Thomas had been right; it was with sadness that Olive knocked on Matron's door later that week to hand in her resignation.

"Well, Miss Wilmot" said Matron, "you are not the first pretty nurse to be swept up by a doctor but I want you to know how much this hospital, and I, will miss you. You have carried yourself well at Bellevue and we won't forget you. Of course, I wish you and Dr. Burchard best wishes."

Lisbeth was waiting for her when she returned to the residence. The two friends chatted as Olive cleared out her belongings. "I will miss you living here, Olive" said Lisbeth, sadly. "I know we'll continue to see each other but it won't be the same without you to visit at the end of each day." The pair embraced warmly before Lisbeth helped Olive downstairs with her few bags to the waiting carriage.

Things moved rapidly once Olive was settled at her Uncle's home. She interviewed several candidates at Lewis' office and was very pleased to find one woman who stood out above any other. Amy Lindsell came with strong references and clearly understood the nature of her role. Lindsell, as she was known, had experience with previous employers through their weddings as well; a fact which sealed the deal in Olive's mind.

Lewis prepared the appropriate employment contract while the pair talked about practicalities. It was arranged that Lindsell would move to John Wilmot's house within the week and Olive let her know just how much was to be done before the wedding. Olive hadn't yet given thought as to how to explain the second ceremony so didn't mention it. There would be time, once they had a chance to get to know one another a little better.

In early April, Eliza and Lewis Sayre hosted a quiet dinner for both families to come together to celebrate the upcoming wedding. Thomas' sons, Leeds and Stewart; his brothers, Lewis and Roswell; Samuel and her uncle John all attended.

Olive was grateful to her father for engaging Thomas' young sons in spirited conversation since neither appeared very impressed by this new person in their lives. She would have to work to help them see the marriage as a good thing for their father.

Eliza was secretly thrilled with the situation. She dearly loved her nephew and to see him happy. The divorce added an element of scandal which appealed to her. She loved when social norms were upset. When Thomas quietly told her of the abuse Olive had suffered, she gave her full support behind whatever action was taken for the pair to wed.

Society be damned, she thought to herself as she looked at the happy couple. *These two deserve to be happy and I will do all I can to ensure they are.*

Chapter 52

Olive and Lindsell boarded the train for Alexandria Bay in the First-Class car Thomas had thoughtfully booked for their journey. He had preceded them by two days, wanting to check that all arrangements at his summer home were in place.

After the long days she had worked at Bellevue, Olive had enjoyed the weeks leading up to the wedding with little to do but prepare for her new life. She and Lindsell had visited the many dressmakers and stores that New York boasted, replenishing her wardrobe and choosing a suitable wedding gown.

Thomas instructed Olive to be generous to herself with her trousseau, adding that all bills were to be sent to his accountant who would see they were paid. He reminded her that they would be travelling to Europe in the not too distant future and she would need several traveling gowns as well as a ball gown for the adventures that awaited them.

Despite her initial objections, it hadn't taken Olive long to adapt to the comforts a lady's maid provided, although Olive preferred to think of Lindsell as a companion of sorts. As Thomas had predicted, the maid was forthcoming in letting Olive know how she might best serve her but the company she provided was perhaps the most valuable. Living in her Uncle's home was lonely for Olive, after the dormitory existence in the nursing residence, and she found herself chatting to Lindsell more than she might otherwise have.

Lindsell was ten years older than Olive and had an air of quiet wisdom about her. Initially circumspect in her comments, Olive's friendly overtures soon had the two women conversing at ease, although it was clear that Lindsell would never forget her position. She had always performed her role with pride and a chatty mistress didn't change her work ethic or the respect for the role she held dear.

The eight-hour train ride passed quietly; Olive read for much of it and then completed a checklist in her mind of all that she had packed. The plan was for she and Lindsell to stay at The Alexandria Arms for the night and dress in their suite. Thomas' younger brother, Roswell, had made the journey with him and he would pick Olive up at the Inn for the ceremony.

As the train pulled into the station, Thomas was waiting on the platform. Seeing him brought a wide smile to Olive's face and it took all of her restraint not to embrace him as she stepped off the train steps.

"Oh, Thomas," she said. "One short night remains before we will be together. As much as I am pleased to have Lindsell's company, I am tired of staying apart for appearance sake. Is all set at the Church? Do we need to meet with the Rector today before the ceremony? Has Roswell arrived?" The questions would have continued had Thomas not cut her off with an amused smile on his face.

"Everything is taken care of, my Dear" replied Thomas, looking at her indulgently. "Trust me; I am just as impatient as you. I will see you settled at the Inn and leave you time to rest and then Roswell and I will return for dinner this evening."

The Alexandria Arms served a surprisingly good meal for the off season. Olive, Thomas and Roswell were not the only guests in the dining room but there were few enough that the three could enjoy their meal together privately.

Olive knew she could speak freely in front of Roswell; she and Thomas had explained all to everyone in their families.

"I am sorry Lewis isn't able to join us, after all of the work and kindness he has done for us. As simple as the ceremony that awaits us tomorrow will be, it still feels earth-shattering to me. Since leaving Harry, I never entertained hope of a happy marriage again. I know it to be unconventional but I would like to make a toast to the Burchard men, one and all, who have changed my life forever."

Roswell nodded modestly and Thomas grinned. Since greeting Olive at the train, he had been struck by how giddy she was. He had never seen this side of her and her happiness pleased him greatly.

At the end of their meal, the two men rose as Olive prepared to leave the table. "I think we all could use a good night's sleep" she said, touching Thomas' face gently.

"Sleep well, my Love," replied Thomas. "I will send a carriage for you and Lindsell at 11:00 tomorrow. Don't worry about your belongings; my houseman will make a trip later in the day to the Inn to bring everything to my home."

Her wedding day dawned sunny and dry and Olive devoured all of her breakfast, saying to Lindsell, "I think I will take a walk around the

town while you're packing. I'll be back in plenty of time to get dressed."

'How my future has changed,' she thought, as she walked around Alexandria Bay, barely aware of the beautiful waterfront scenery before her. *'I don't know what I have done to deserve all of this, God, but I promise you, I will be grateful every day. It's strange that I can think of Harry again without pain; I suppose that's because of the love and security I feel with Thomas. He has helped me to see that time of my life as just the past: all of which shapes us but doesn't define us. I can almost wish poor, misguided Harry well; not quite, but almost.'*

Thomas held Olive's hands so tightly through the ceremony, she thought she might gasp. She knew he had been anxious, despite all of his reassurances, that the wedding go forward without incident. As they signed the register, the Rector had paused when faced with the divorce documents but, whatever went through his mind didn't stop him from officially declaring them Man and Wife.

For many reasons, as the day crept on, Olive found it more and more difficult to concentrate. In spite of her best efforts, memories of her first wedding day kept crowding in; her innocence forever lost. Her emotions threatened to take over the calm she was working so hard to project as she pictured living so closely with Thomas.

She managed to acknowledge the housekeeper for the wonderful luncheon she had organized and graciously said her goodbyes to Roswell, who was taking the afternoon train back to the city.

Thomas sensed her disquiet and suggested a stroll. Olive didn't tell him she had already explored the town earlier in the day; indeed, she barely remembered any of it, deep in her thoughts as she had been. Instead, she followed Thomas to the bedroom which would be her own, where Lindsell waited to help her change from the wedding gown into an afternoon dress.

Thomas kept the conversation light during their walk. They discussed their return to the city and time with his sons. Both boys were at boarding school but would be home for spring break soon after Thomas and Olive returned to New York. The pleasure she felt about spending time with the boys was tainted by an equal measure of anxiety. If the dinner Lewis and Eliza had hosted was any indication, the boys were not overly happy with their father's marriage.

The housekeeper served a simple supper, after which Thomas suggested they move to the comfort of the library for a sherry. He had no doubt Olive's nerves needed something to steady them. Olive did feel calmer after and, when the time came for them to retire, she climbed the staircase with composure.

Lindsell once again helped her from her gown and into the beautiful lace peignoir set purchased for her trousseau. After storing Olive's clothes and jewellery; turning down the bed; brushing and plaiting her hair, Lindsell excused herself to head up to the third-floor room assigned to her.

Olive had a few moments to herself before Thomas gently rapped on her door to say goodnight. She took those moments to remind herself of the depth of love she felt for Thomas and the goodness in the man. Her face, when Thomas entered, appeared serene.

Crossing the room, Thomas took her in his arms and began to kiss her with abandon. "Oh my God," he said, "It feels as though I've waited years for you." Although they had enjoyed several quick, stolen kisses throughout their courtship, Olive was surprised to find these kisses arousing. *'I had no idea kissing could be so lovely.'*

"Do you think we could just lie together a while, Thomas. I would like to be close to you before you retire."

Thomas led her toward the bed in answer. She was barely aware of lying down as they continued kissing. It greatly surprised Olive when she realized Thomas' slow and gentle caresses were awakening something new in her; things she had never felt with Harry.

"I will do only what you are comfortable with, Olive" whispered Thomas. "Please tell me at any time if you would like me to stop."

But she needed no words; her body responded for her, pushing against him of its own will.

Chapter 53

Olive woke first, nestled in Thomas' arms. She was grateful he had remained through the night rather than returning to his own bed. By doing so, he removed any embarrassment she may have felt on seeing him in the morning. And she was enjoying how she felt in his arms; secure, content, loved. She had experienced none of the fear or hurt she had known with Harry, just unhurried sweet tenderness.

'Now I know just how disturbed Harry was' she thought to herself. *'Why would he not have encouraged such beauty as this between us? What was in his heart that he preferred it to be ugly and hurtful? That's enough, Olive'*, she decided. *'I won't think of him again. Today I am Mrs. Thomas Burchard and it is nothing but lovely.'*

She must have stirred because Thomas whispered "Are you awake, my wife?"

"I am" she replied, as she turned around to look into his eyes, "and just pondering how wonderful it feels to wake as your wife."

Kissing her forehead gently, Thomas reached around to lift the bedclothes and rose from the bed. For a large man, he was surprisingly light in his movements. Putting on his robe, he said "I will go and get myself ready for the day and ask Lindsell to bring you a tray in bed. There is no need to rush the day; the train for Toronto doesn't leave until 2:00 this afternoon." He bent down to kiss her lingeringly on her lips and she was surprised anew at what a delicious sensation kissing him gave her. "I will be in the library when you are ready to come down."

Olive stretched her arms luxuriously above her head after he had left. *I am going to be very happy married to this man*, she thought, saying a quiet prayer for his health; something that would become a ritual with her morning prayers from then on.

Lindsell knocked lightly and entered with a tray. "How quickly a life can change, Lindsell" Olive said as the woman settled the bed tray on her lap. "It wasn't many months ago that I was delivering trays to patients in their beds. I feel completely pampered."

"As every bride should" replied Lindsell. "The trunks are packed and ready for the train," she said, changing the topic. "Is there anything else you would like me to do before we leave?"

"No thank you, Lindsell. The morning is your own. I know it will be a late night tonight getting settled once we arrive in Toronto."

The train ride into Toronto was uneventful for Olive who discovered that Thomas and Lindsell had taken care of all arrangements. She rather enjoyed this new life. Despite her independence over the past years, she was not averse to the comforts now provided.

She had time to think about seeing her father again and her brother, George, who would be at the wedding. Along with her father and brother, Olive and Lindsell would be staying the night at her sister, Helen's, home in Toronto while Thomas and his man were registered at the Empress Hotel on Yonge Street.

It was after 6:00 pm when the train arrived at Union Station. On the platform, Thomas behaved toward Olive as any future groom would. Olive was very aware of how frequently people from Newcastle travelled to the city and she and Thomas had discussed how important it was to keep up the pretence. She had finally confided the truth to Lindsell, who readily went along with the deception. As though she had acted her entire life, she referred to Olive as 'Miss Wilmot' when speaking to her around others.

After arranging with the porters for their luggage to be put aboard two separate carriages, Thomas and Olive parted ways for one more night.

"Here is our lovely girl" said Samuel coming to the door with Helen to greet her. He gave her a warm embrace and then followed as Helen led them all into the parlour.

"Georgie" cried Olive on seeing her brother in the room. "I'm so pleased you could be in town for the ceremony."

Dinner was announced and they moved to the dining room. "All is arranged for tomorrow, Olive" said Samuel solemnly as they tucked in to the first course.

"Thank you, Papa. It will be such a relief when all of this is behind us. We had no issues with the Reverend in Alexandria Bay so I do hope it will be the same for us here. Helen" said Olive, wanting to change the topic, "tell me all about the children. What has everyone been up to?"

Minnie had shared with Olive just how consumed Helen had become by her need for laudanum. Administered during her last

difficult birth and recovery, the drug had quickly become necessary to Helen. Only the doctor in Newcastle fed this habit so she stayed in the village whenever possible. On this evening, her sister was alert and Olive appreciated the effort she was obviously making on her behalf.

The remainder of dinner was spent happily catching up. For all of their letter writing, Olive had felt very distant from her family over the past years away from Canada. Coming back had given her a lift of spirit that she had not been aware had been low. It made her realize how important the ties to one's home country are. She hoped that she and Thomas would be able to return often.

As Helen and Olive headed upstairs to turn in, Olive quietly asked, "Have you any news of Mr. and Mrs. Winans, Helen?"

"Their health appears to be low, although I only see them at church so don't speak with authority. We are merely nodding acquaintances at this point. The talk settled down after a time and life for all of us has returned to somewhat normal but I don't go out of my way to chat with them. I'm certain it is all still hurtful for them."

"Harry will have a lot to answer for in the next life, if not this one" said Olive, as she entered the bedroom given to her. "Thank you for a lovely dinner, Helen. I'm glad to see you so well. Good night."

As they had all hoped, the wedding ceremony at St. Andrews the next day was a quiet one. Reverend Macdonnell appeared surprised when the divorce documents were presented but he believed a document notarized by a Judge to carry weight, even if it was in another country. He was an elderly cleric, looking forward to his retirement years shortly and facing a divorced woman just reminded him how out of touch he had become. He wished the younger men following in his footsteps well with all of the changes a new century seemed to be bringing to the church.

If he had any reservations about the divorce, the presence of Olive's father, a man now well known and respected in Canada, was enough to convince Rev. Macdonnell that all was above board.

The small wedding party walked back down the aisle and stepped outside. Olive and Thomas were to take the return train to New York following the ceremony and there was little time before departure. Saying goodbye to Samuel and George, they boarded a waiting carriage for Union Station where Thomas' valet and Lindsell waited with their trunks."

"Welcome to your home, Olive" Thomas said as they entered his house later that night. "Mrs. Moreton, may I present my wife, Mrs. Burchard," said Thomas to the housekeeper. "Mrs. Moreton will be able to answer all of your questions concerning the household, Olive. She has been with me for many years. Mrs. Moreton, I concede all household decisions to my wife. I have no doubt she will want to make changes."

"Lovely to meet you, Mrs. Moreton" said Olive. "I look forward to meeting the other staff and becoming familiar with the household."

"Mrs. Moreton will take you up to your room, Olive" said Thomas, turning into the study. "I will just look over the mail and see if there are any issues needing my attention. I won't be long."

Olive stepped over the threshold of the room that would be her own and looked around admiringly. A William Morris print of delicate vines and small roses was on the wallpaper and bedspread. The silk draperies were in a shade of deep pink perfectly matching the roses in the spread. In addition to the four-poster bed, a vanity table, large dresser and two comfortable chairs placed in front of a fireplace completed the look.

'I have never seen a more beautiful room' she thought. From Thomas' description of his late wife, she knew instantly that the décor had been her choice and reflected her own elegance in the selection of fabrics and décor.

Another woman might have felt awkward stepping into a bedroom her husband's previous wife had occupied but not Olive. She and Thomas had spoken often of his love for his late wife and how much his life had changed with her gone. Olive was at peace with this love, understanding that his first wife's role as mother of his sons made her distinctive.

Olive had no intention of trying to usurp the dead woman's life. She was content with the love Thomas felt for her now, understanding that this love was separate from his feelings for Irene. What she and Thomas had was unique to them.

Another woman might also have been concerned about comparison with her predecessor but not Olive. Looking at Irene's legacy imprinted in the décor of the room, Olive knew she would have liked to have known this woman. *'Do I have your blessing?'* she wondered. *'I will do all in my power to care for this lovely man and your boys.'*

Chapter 54

Settling into her new home on W. 52nd Street came easily. With the guidance of Mrs. Moreton, Olive was soon directing household activities, much as she had done at Belmont in her mother's absence.

Olive enjoyed every bit of her new life, including the sons she welcomed into her heart.

Arriving home for their spring holiday, both knew as they entered the house that something had shifted. Fresh flowers filled the rooms and a major spring cleaning had taken place. Stewart recognized the lighter and brighter carpets and draperies from summers in his childhood. The heavier, more sombre winter fabrics and textiles brought out when his mother passed had not changed since. Stewart felt lighter just seeing the summer colours again.

Even so, he was not about to let this 'prettifying' sway him. Nor was he going to be influenced by a pretty face (and his new step-mother had a very pretty one). Since his mother's passing, he thought life in the Burchard home with the three 'bachelors' just fine, thank you. At 14, he was protective of his father's health and serious in his role as elder brother and believed 'the men' were managing perfectly well.

At10, Leeds' memories of his mother were fading. The home he returned to on school breaks was silent, not like those of the friends he sometimes visited on holidays. He had decided that homes with mothers had a livelier spirit, filled with boisterous activity. He was too young to realize that the sedate atmosphere in his own home was grief, not the lack of a woman. He adored his father and older brother but secretly longed for such spirit at home. He had high hope that there would be now with a woman in the house.

Stewart's memories of his mother remained strong and he felt it was his duty to keep these alive. He was determined, at every opportunity, to make this woman understand that she would never be their mother.

Thomas summoned the boys into the morning room before they had a chance to head up to their rooms. "Boys, please come and greet your new Mother" he said, gently bringing Olive forward with a hand at the small of her back.

"Oh, I don't expect you to call me Mother since I could never replace your own dear mother. I can only imagine how much you miss her. Why don't you call me by my Christian name, Olive?"

"If neither of you mind too much, I will ask about your mother often. I believe she was a woman I would like to have known. I hope that, together, we will keep her memories alive and you can help me understand the woman who raised such fine young men."

Stewart was gob smacked. Had she read his mind? Olive had just voiced his exact thoughts on entering the room.

'Well, that's something,' he thought. *'At least I won't have to pretend to love her as a mother.'* Leeds, by his side, already worshipped her for the beauty and glamour that she had introduced into their home, which had lacked all things feminine.

That first week with the boys passed too quickly for Olive. She enjoyed her time with each; asking Stewart about his favourite books and Leeds about the sports he was so fond of at school.

Stewart determinedly tried to hold back but he had to admit he enjoyed the changes Olive brought to their home. He remembered his mother's influence in the house and had missed it greatly. Seeing his father happy again removed the weight from his shoulders that arrived unbidden as he witnessed his father's grief over the past years. The gentleness and love that passed between his father and Olive, which might have caused jealousy, instead returned peace of mind to Stewart.

The boys became Olive's shadow; content to sit with her as she read or wrote letters but usually clamouring for her stories. She told them stories about her brothers; stories of family fun and tricks played on each other. Listening, Stewart and Leeds could only wish themselves part of such a large, diverse family.

Olive was an entertaining story-teller and her lively family provided a lifetime of anecdotes to share. When she told them about her brothers' decision to bring a pony up the back staircase of their home, Stewart and Leeds were flabbergasted.

Her description of the difficulties they encountered on the way up the stairs and then the dilemma when the animal could not be coerced back down had both boys hysterical with laughter. Unfortunately, her father had not been so amused. This was one of the escapades that eventually led to her brothers' banishment to boarding school.

Maybe because of her brothers, Stewart thought Olive surprisingly aware of the challenges a young man faced. Before the week was out, he asked some delicate questions which had been troubling him about girls. Flattered and knowing how serious his issues were, Olive took her time in replying. She phrased her answers in a way that let Stewart know his interest and concerns were respected.

Thomas smiled fondly at the three of them as they sat in the drawing room on their last evening together. He was enormously pleased with how well Olive had been accepted. He would never have imagined that he could feel such contentment again after losing Irene but content he was.

"Boys, after you return to school, Olive and I will be sailing to Europe. We'll be away two months but back for your summer break and our move up to Alexandria Bay."

"You will write to me, won't you boys" said Olive looking at each one. "Oh, yes, Olive" replied Leeds. "I'll have to write to tell you how our teams fair in the year end meets."

"I have no doubt you'll place first, Leeds" replied Olive. "I've met enough excellent sportsmen in my time to recognize one when I meet him."

Both boys returned to school with lighter hearts than they had known in years.

With the boys once again settled at their schools, Olive and Thomas began to organize themselves for their European honeymoon. The trip was brought about by several invitations Thomas had received to lecture on his pioneering appendectomy procedure. The papers he had written on his new surgical technique and the statistics of lives saved had received a great deal of interest at home and on the continent.

On May 5, as plans were well underway, New York City experienced an unprecedented stock market crash. In the ensuing days, there was such a run on the banks that many closed.

Thomas trusted his brothers for their financial and legal advice and the three met to discuss what action should be taken for their various investments, many of which were held jointly. They were reassured that their primary bank was solid and investments were secure in the long term, although they had all taken a major hit on paper. The three were wise enough investors to understand the

importance of doing nothing in the short term and all three could still live well based on their own salaries.

"We will go ahead as planned, Olive" said Thomas that night. "But our trip will be far from the grand adventure I had hoped for us. Several physicians will host us in the cities that I will lecture in but our hotel stays will be far more modest than I had planned."

"You forget, Thomas," replied Olive "that I'm used to boarding house living. I would be comfortable even in a hostel with you by my side. This trip is about you and spreading your medical knowledge. Consider me a tag-along who hopes to help with your comforts along the way."

With no expectations, the two had a wonderful time exploring each city on their tour. Knowing only the dreariness of London and peaceful fields of rural England, Olive was enthusiastic in her response to the sun-filled countries they visited. She absorbed the culture, beauty and history eagerly.

Each of their host physicians introduced Thomas and Olive to the best of their city, in a manner the pair might not have done on their own. Olive loved the courtly manners and attention of the Italian, French and German men she met and was as big a hit with everyone as Thomas.

Without saying so, Thomas planned the trip to consider his weak heart. The itinerary included maximum rest time for him. The sites they visited involved a minimum of stairs and climbs but that still left more museums, galleries and historic wonders than they could hope to visit in one tour. They even managed time at the seaside in the south of Italy. Occasionally, visiting a site, Olive would be moved to climb with a tour guide to see something in greater detail, leaving Thomas in a café below smiling tenderly as she set off.

She sat through Thomas' lectures and met many of the doctors present, basking in their admiration of her husband. She had no idea this admiration extended to her as well once she shared her own knowledge of the procedure, having assisted at many. Doctors were envious of Thomas and his beautiful wife who was unexpectedly knowledgeable.

Thomas' new surgical technique was saving countless lives and doctors were eager to adopt it. In larger cities, Thomas was invited to do a surgery so that the hospital physicians could witness his approach

firsthand. During each, the operating theatres' observation tiers were standing room only.

Without Olive's knowledge, Thomas also made arrangements to be examined by the best heart specialists in each city. He refused to believe that his diagnosis was a life sentence and, just as his own surgical technique was now saving lives, trusted a new one would turn up for his own benefit. The outcome was the same with each specialist; nothing yet was on the horizon that would extend Thomas' life.

On board the ship returning to New York, Thomas relaxed completely. With his lectures and their travels behind him, he could fully enjoy the peacefulness of the crossing.

"I almost regret that the crossings are getting shorter with each faster ship built," he said one night as they enjoyed dinner in the dining room. "Could there be anything more tranquil than to be captive at sea with no patients, lectures or business concerns? I wonder why no one has thought to introduce some sort of rolling motion in our hospital beds. Except for the poor souls who suffer from nausea, I believe the motion calms one as a mother's womb must for a baby."

Olive was reassured to see Thomas so rested. His pallor and tiredness had concerned her during their tour and she had quietly cancelled plans on several occasions, feigning fatigue of her own. They both delighted in the ease of shipboard life; spending their days reading on loungers, strolling the decks, and playing the odd game of cards with other passengers.

June 1903
Newcastle, Ontario

Chapter 55

After a brief call to Duncan (just to hear his voice and news of the girls), Minnie returned to her bedside vigil, painfully aware of the increasing gaps in Olive's breaths.

It was the third day since Olive's stroke and, surprising everyone, she continued to survive. Whatever inner drive kept her body living, though, had not extended to her mind. She had not regained consciousness at any moment since her collapse.

Minnie's grief at the loss of her sister had begun to fill her heart when she lost hope of any recovery. Now she questioned what could keep her body going.

"Papa is waiting for you, Olive" she said quietly, leaning over her sister. "You don't have to hang on for any of us here. It is so like you to think of all of us, but it's time for you now. Please release yourself from this earth and go to God."

Tears streamed down Minnie's face as she clasped Olive's lifeless hand. Lindsell had joined her by the bedside, the grief on her face a mirror to Minnie's.

Almost as though hearing Minnie's words, Olive's breath stopped. The two women unconsciously leaned in, waiting for the gasp of her breath restarting as it had done each time before. Seconds went by and then minutes.

Minnie and Lindsell turned to each other with disbelief. It had finally happened; Olive was dead.

Minnie lay over her sister, wrapped her arms around her and cried quietly as the nurse approached. The woman waited for Minnie to rise and then began her routine examination to give the doctor a report when he arrived and would formally declare her death.

As though walking through water, Minnie heavily trod down the stairs to find Mrs. Thomson. There would be much to do but, first, she must contact Sayre who was Olive's Trustee and Executor. It was he who would organize the funeral.

Against all usual household practice, Minnie entered the kitchen. Finding Mrs. Thomson, she said "Mrs. Sanford has passed away. Please send a telegram to Mr. Van Duzer to return immediately."

In New York City, the telegram dropped from Sayre's hand. Although he had known to expect it, the reality of Olive's death was too much to swallow. He knew he should be gathering his files and returning home to retrieve his luggage but his thoughts turned instead to his life since Olive had entered it.

1893

New York City

Chapter 56

Olive looked forward to their first summer with the boys in Alexandria Bay. Thomas had explained that they always spent the fourth of July on the lake. The spectacle of lights and fireworks on the islands was something he couldn't wait for her to see.

He teased her about returning to the scene of their wedding night which made her blush, but just a little. They were easy with their intimacy together. Although not frequent, both took great pleasure in their lovemaking and had learned to accommodate Thomas' weak heart. Olive's reticence had evaporated with Thomas' gentle touch and respect. Olive now understood how marriages could be strengthened through this tender physical connection.

Summer life was relaxed; the boys enjoyed swimming and taking their own small boat around to explore; Thomas and Olive sailed on the lake and all enjoyed quiet hours on the porch swing and hammocks overlooking the lake.

Each summer, the town experienced an influx of people who managed to entertain themselves away from the city. The local inns hosted daily afternoon teas and weekend dances. Concerts at the band shell in the park were enjoyed by everyone in the family. Leeds found other boys his age to run through the park with; Stewart walked more sedately, aware of the eyes of girls on him; while Thomas and Olive enjoyed the music and a picnic supper on a blanket on the lawns.

They were invited to dinners and picnics and hosted a few of their own but, overall, they chose to live a quiet life that summer.

A sleek new wooden motor boat drew up at their dock not long after they arrived. The solitary passenger eagerly strode up the hill to their home.

"Trust you to have the newest speedboat" said Thomas to the fellow, extending his hand and looking admiringly at the boat. "I've been waiting for you. Olive, allow me to introduce my most favoured cousin, Sayre Van Duzer. You'll have to take us for a spin, Sayre."

Bowing slightly and removing his hat, Sayre took Olive's hand. "Mrs. Burchard, I do hope we will use Christian names with each other. There is little formality between the Van Duzers and the Burchards. Please call me Sayre as well."

"With pleasure, Sayre," replied Olive, immediately drawn to his gentle eyes. She found His slightly crooked smile to be contagious. One could easily see the family resemblance in their similar features; the high forehead, deep set eyes, straight nose and round chin. The entire face expressed warmth. "Thomas has told me much about you."

Sayre differed from Thomas in his obvious vanity about his grooming. He boasted a finely trimmed beard with a moustache that turned fashionably up at the ends. His hair, a warm chestnut colour, was shaped and pomaded in such a way that said this man cared about his appearance. The casual linen suit he wore fitted his frame like a glove and his tie was done in some sort of knot Olive hadn't seen before.

Thomas had told Olive about all of the people they would likely meet while staying in Alexandria Bay. The same families had been visiting the islands for decades and the social life they would enjoy that summer would be predictable.

But of everyone, Thomas spoke the most about Sayre. His cousin was determinedly unmarried, about ten years older than Olive and a keen athlete and lover of literature. He had a successful law practice in New York City and he and Thomas were closer than all of the cousins.

Sayre's father, one of the most prominent wholesale druggists in the US, owned four homes including Stony Crest, the 24 room mansion on a one acre island in the Thousand Islands. When not off Manhattan and Long Island Sound, his father's 132' schooner rigged steam yacht could be seen moored in the 200' sheltered deep water dockage the island provided.

In spite of his family's extreme wealth and his own success, Sayre was approachable and without airs. As a child, his summers in Alexandria Bay with his governess cemented his relationship with Thomas until they were more like brothers than second cousins.

Life was more relaxed in the Bay which suited everyone after the structure of society in the city. 'Dropping by' was unheard of in New York but the lakeside lifestyle made for relaxed social etiquette. Whenever he was in residence, Sayre joined Thomas and Olive, enjoying lemonade on the porch or dining with the family. The boys

enjoyed 'Uncle Sayre' as much as Thomas and he was always a welcome guest.

Sayre's new boat provided the three adults with peaceful afternoon excursions. They travelled the lake, with Thomas and Sayre pointing out sites of interest and telling Olive about the families in each cottage. They took the boat to Sayre's home, Stony Crest, for afternoons of tennis (for Olive and Sayre) and leisurely strolls around the property.

Olive loved to sit in the cool shade of their porch swing, listening as Sayre and Thomas played chess and debated the merits of Dickens vs Thackeray. Sayre was considered quite an expert on Thackeray and he had a renowned collection of first editions and manuscripts. Occasionally, Olive would contribute a comment of her own, especially when the topic turned to the writing of Henry James. She kept a copy of 'Portrait of a Lady' at hand and had re-read it several times since first encountering it in London.

The novel still spoke to her, although when she looked back on the paths she had taken since leaving Harry, she was grateful that she hadn't done the right thing by staying with him as James' character, Isabel Archer, had.

Thomas, Olive and Sayre spent countless enjoyable hours together that summer. There was much strife in the world around them; the economy still suffered and Thomas grew weaker, even with the slow pace of the lakeside. The three would remember the summer, together and away from the stress of the city, as idyllic.

Sayre and Olive became friends that summer; a friendship begun because of their shared love for Thomas. Before summer was out, this friendship was firmly cemented for its own reasons. They identified with each other in ways neither had with anyone in their life to that point. They were pleased to discover a common wry outlook on the world, sense of humour and gift for storytelling and mimicry.

It was a friendship with no complications. Through her work in the hospital, Olive had seen much of the world. She was enough of a beauty that, when a man did not respond to her charms, she required no explanation. Without putting the thought into words, she understood Sayre's preference was not for women. Beyond that understanding she sought no deeper knowledge. She naturally

respected all people of kind heart without judgment of their lifestyle or proclivities.

When Thomas was down at the lakeshore with the boys one day, the pair had time to speak privately. "It's a relief to have people around us who know Thomas so well, Sayre. It makes life easier when we don't have to mask his limitations but can just enjoy peaceful pursuits together" said Olive.

"I'm happy you feel so, Olive, but I hope I don't overstay my welcome this summer. Thomas is like a big brother to me and I want to spend as much time with him as possible" replied Sayre. "We have grown up together, in the city and summers here. My own heart breaks seeing the weakness in his but I will never make our time together be about that. He is too good a man to live as an invalid and we have the resources to give him ease in his life to live as normally as possible for as long as possible."

He continued, "I don't mean to diminish the feelings you have for each other but I must tell you it gives me peace of mind to know your background in nursing."

"Oh, I don't mind at all, Sayre, and do understand. I'm a realist more than a romantic but you should also know just how much this man has brought to my life. Every day I have with him is a blessing to me. Now shush; I see he's coming up the path."

"What great ages my boys are," said Thomas as he climbed the steps to the porch, winded, grateful for the glass of lemonade Olive handed him. "Do you remember the escapades we got up to here at that age, Sayre?"

"Do I? I should point out, Olive, that, while the two of us were complicit in most of our adventures; it was generally me who was disciplined when we went too far. This man doesn't just have a gentle face now. He managed to look innocent every time blame was looking for a place to land" said Sayre, grinning. "I was intimate with the switch most summers."

"You exaggerate, Sayre" laughed Thomas. "I will admit my face proved useful once or twice but, my God, this boy could run, Olive. His Governess was a dear old soul and unable to walk far, never mind run. Sayre would take off like a shot and just keep running until it was time for the next meal. By then, tempers had cooled and he would slide to his seat at the table, as though nothing had happened in the

meantime. I believe we took years off that poor woman's life, Sayre, but your audacity was admirable." The two men laughed at their memories.

Olive loved to see such joy on Thomas' face. When Sayre was around, the two enjoyed playful banter and Sayre had a comedic sense of humour, delivering punch lines with perfect timing, keeping the entire family laughing. But Olive could see that Thomas also respected Sayre's ideas during their deep discussions over a glass of port also. She decided that summer that they would both benefit if Sayre were a staple in their life in the city as well.

Her biggest challenge would be how to even the numbers at their dinners. As a 'confirmed bachelor', Olive had no intention of trying to match-make but an equal mix of the sexes was the norm when entertaining. Thomas had explained that many hostesses had made the mistake of trying, unsuccessfully, to interest Sayre in the debutants of each season. Olive thought to herself '*Surely, there must be interesting single women in the city who would add much to a dinner party and balance out the genders.*'

Their return to New York in the fall of 1893 coincided with the start of the social season. Thomas and Olive began to welcome friends into their home. The financial crash that had begun in May kept the country in a serious depression with unemployment mounting and soup kitchens growing. For the first time since Alva Vanderbilt had entered New York society and taken entertaining to ostentatious heights, entertaining was once again pared down to modest levels. For some, this was of necessity since many of the oldest New York families had lost much of their investments. For Thomas and Olive, this gave a perfect pretext for the smaller parties that would suit his health.

Thomas continued to monitor the economy as it impacted his own investments. He and Olive adjusted their lifestyle, scaling back wherever possible. Olive modeled her entertaining after that of Lewis and Eliza; inviting eclectic groups of people to their table for all to enjoy lively discussions on diverse topics. They entertained weekly; quiet, intimate dinner parties of 10 or fewer, and after theatre suppers; evenings that Thomas could enjoy without stress.

They also kept their evenings out each week to just one; far fewer than the majority of their crowd. It was considered bad form to decline too many invitations but the rules were changing rapidly in

the new realm of financial restraint and no one commented on their fewer public appearances.

Thomas didn't let on to Olive that they were receiving fewer invitations than a normal season would bring. He suspected the reason had nothing to do with the economy. Certain hostesses were choosing to exclude them because of the divorce.

But Olive had experienced snubs beyond those that Thomas recognized.

The first time she was aware of it was while shopping. She had been at the glove counter of Macy's when a pair of women walked by. Recognizing Olive, they began to whisper between them. Lindsell, in a protective move, stepped between the women and Olive trying to conceal their behaviour.

When they were outside again, Olive said "that was kind of you, Lindsell, but you don't need to worry about me. My skin is thicker than it seems and talk has never bothered me. If they were talking about me, it must have been very dull conversation indeed."

"Yes, but …" broke in Lindsell.

"No, no, let's hear no more about it. If they *are* talking about *me*, then some other poor soul's character is not being maligned."

Grateful for the many changes in her life, Olive saw much that was good and chose to ignore anything other.

Sitting down together on Sunday afternoons to plan their social life soon became a delightful ritual for the she and Thomas. They would organize their own dinner party first, choosing the guest list together. Sayre was often included. Including a single man at the table hadn't proven to be as difficult as she had imagined; there were several very interesting independent women in the city who Olive enjoyed spending time with.

Thomas also was inclined to include the widows of associates who passed away once they were out of mourning. As a widower, he had been grateful to those who extended kindness to him and vowed to do the same. Since many physicians married later in life, these widows were often of an age closer to Olive. These women were ideal guests for their dinners since they were generally not looking for a husband.

After writing out invitations, she then selected menus and wines with the cook; flowers and staffing with Mrs. Moreton; always with an eye to cost saving. Olive had a knack for creating seasonal décor with

what was at hand, another practice that set their table apart from the crowd. In fact, the simplicity of her arrangements were admired and talked about.

With their own evening sorted, Thomas would open all of the invitations received and they would decide which to accept. As he opened an elaborately embossed invitation card one Sunday, Thomas chuckled.

"Trust Mrs. Vanderbilt to host a grand event during a depression" he said. "While everyone around her behaves in a prudent way, she has planned another Ball! Sometimes her self-assurance is too much."

"Oh, Thomas, I have so wanted to meet her and to see inside their mansion. I know how you feel about crowded social events but wonder if we couldn't make an exception for that one night?"

"Of course we can" replied Thomas indulgently. "One night isn't going to hurt me. I know the Vanderbilts are heading off for a family cruise to India on their yacht so this will likely be the only event of this type for the year. I will put their invitation on the yes pile for you to respond."

Olive knew that Thomas and Willie and Alva Vanderbilt visited Saratoga Springs most summers for the horse races. However, that summer, she and Thomas had chosen not to, preferring to stay in Alexandria Bay with the boys as long as possible. This meant that Olive had yet to meet the Saratoga crowd, including their neighbours, the Vanderbilts.

Although the Vanderbilt mansion was less than a block from their home, Mrs. Vanderbilt had not called on Olive. Society required a woman of higher social standing be the first to call, but Alva Vanderbilt continually bent the rules to suit herself. Olive wasn't sure if the lack of a call from Alva was because of the divorce or some other reason but she hoped the invitation would hasten her entry to society, putting a few tongues to rest.

Stepping over the Vanderbilt threshold three weeks later, Olive was awestruck; here was entertaining at its most lavish. She had heard much of the home but nothing could have prepared her for its grandeur. The servants were many, wearing identical livery, and yet nearly invisible, taking care of each guest's needs almost before they knew them.

Leaving their outerwear with one of many footmen, Thomas and Olive made their way through the receiving line to greet their hosts. Olive whispered "I had no idea such opulence existed, Thomas. Pinch me. I can't believe what I see." Thomas obliged, grinning at the giggle from Olive.

Her expectations for Alva's reception were dimmed by the greeting she received. Alva lacked warmth and quickly passed Olive along to the person beside her. Olive hadn't known what she had expected of the infamous Mrs. Vanderbilt but it certainly wasn't behaviour bordering on rudeness.

Although forewarned about the reaction people would take toward a divorce, Olive felt more than a little surprised by Mrs. Vanderbilt. She had to assume the woman had heard the gossip about her divorce but, by her invitation, thought she was making a statement that she was not disturbed by it.

'*Perhaps her manner is so with everyone*' thought Olive, moving through the others in the receiving line. Thomas made the introduction as they approached Willie Vanderbilt. The sparkle in Willie's eye as he took Olive's hand made up for his wife's curtness and left her no doubt about the character of this man. She was reminded of the Prince of Wales and knew this man to be a lover of beautiful women.

Coming to the end of the receiving line she spied Sayre across the room and made her way to his side. "Why didn't you warn me, Sayre? This home; this party; Mrs. Vanderbilt ... it's all just tooo much."

"I could have told you what to expect but that would have taken the fun out of seeing your face, Olive" he replied, laughing. "Mrs. Vanderbilt still has the ability to shock New York, even after ten years. The house continues to amaze and we can count on at least one lavish ball each year which will be talked about for weeks after. I'm certain that is Mrs. V's goal; to be the most talked about. Shall we dance?"

The lady under discussion, with her greeting duties over, made her way to Thomas' side. Taking his arm and indicating Olive dancing with Sayre, she said "How society changes, Dr. Burchard. Receiving a divorcee in the past would have been unthinkable but I have heard much of this lady of yours."

Thomas, well acquainted with Alva's frank talk, took no offence.

"You must tell me all about this divorce. I am fascinated" she said. Alva had a specific reason for her curiosity. When she returned from India, she intended to start proceedings against Willie K. She was tired of his open philandering and saw no need to put up with it any longer.

"Oh, it was a long and unpleasant process for Olive and one we don't wish to dwell on. I have no doubt, once you have time to get to know her, you will find the whole business immaterial to the woman, Mrs. Vanderbilt."

Although she had no intention of getting to know Olive better, the woman watched Olive intently whenever she caught glimpses of her throughout the evening. *'She doesn't appear remorseful or to suffer for her actions'* thought Alva, watching the number of people who approached Olive throughout the night. *'Surely, if an unknown such as Mrs. Burchard is accepted, no one would dream of snubbing me.'*

Several men asked Olive to dance but she danced with Sayre just as much. She felt as comfortable with Sayre as she might with one of her brothers and had been delighted to discover how well he danced. As with everything he did, Sayre excelled on the dance floor. His tall, athletic body moved fluidly to the music and the pair was admired throughout the room.

"You don't mind your wife dancing with Van Duzer so often?" asked one forward gentleman of Thomas.

"Not at all" replied Thomas. "I asked him to make sure Olive had a dance partner knowing I'm held back by a touch of gout" he lied. Like Olive, Thomas had no time for people with narrow minds and was more than a little annoyed by the man's question. He had been enjoying watching Olive and Sayre on the dance floor together as he conversed with several people. The understanding that Sayre posed no threat, despite what others might think, was knowledge he kept to himself.

Olive, ever alert to Thomas, recognized when it was time for him to leave. She insisted they grab a carriage for the short ride home; exhaustion evident on his face. She kept his thoughts occupied, chattering away happily about the women she had recognized and details of the Vanderbilt home and their hostess.

Chapter 57

Life settled into a pleasant flow for Thomas and Olive. The season of 1893/1894 was a golden one. Thomas' health necessitated a cut back in his time at the hospital but this gave them more time to enjoy together.

When they went out in the city, Sayre was often with them; in their box at the Opera or at the theatre, and the three were soon seen around town as a 'set'. It was not uncommon for gay men to attach themselves to a couple; doing so provided a harmless way to enjoy society. Sayre was an amusing, intelligent man and hostesses liked to include him in their parties despite his continued lack of interest in the debutants presented to him.

On the evenings when Thomas was not up to leaving their home, he encouraged Olive and Sayre to continue without him. Any talk this might bring about didn't concern them; they had managed the gossip about Olive's divorce, after all. A woman out alone with a family member without her husband seemed so much less scandalous. Olive's affection for Sayre grew, clearly understanding Thomas' feelings for him. He in no way replaced Thomas in her mind; she thought of him as an agreeable addition to their life, enjoying his company and humour.

Winters were difficult for Thomas; the many layers of clothing were tiresome and trudging through snow packed streets was a strain. The stuffy heat caused by coal or wood fireplaces also aggravated his weak heart and he sought more moderate climes to escape it. In the winter of 1894, Bermuda offered this respite, in the guise of a vacation home of a fellow doctor.

Winter temperatures were mild on the island and the journey to get there was an easy two-day sail away, drawing many New Yorkers. The money that Americans spent each winter brought a boost to their economy and they were heartily welcomed by island residents.

Thomas and Olive quickly assimilated into island life, with visiting Americans and residents alike. The house they leased was fully staffed which meant they were able to reciprocate the invitations. Olive even managed to organize a surprise celebration of Thomas' 45th birthday on March 19th. The group she invited was convivial and conversation was light-hearted. Not one to make a fuss about a

birthday, Thomas was grateful, nonetheless, to be able to see another and enjoyed the evening more than he could have imagined. Still, he was also grateful for the proper British etiquette which meant the guests were gone soon after midnight.

It was a relaxed and healthy Thomas who returned to New York at the end of March. Olive had enjoyed their time away but the return home meant responsibilities which must be seen to. She had arranged for her sister, Minnie, her husband, Duncan and their infant daughter Marjorie to visit them for Easter and she was anxious to get the house ready and to see Stewart and Leeds on their spring break. The boys' frequent letters to Bermuda always brought a smile to Thomas' face.

Thomas returned to his hospital duties on their return, although still on a scaled down level. Olive didn't mind his absence; she set to work immediately, directing everyone's efforts in turning the house around from its heavy winter décor. The process took many days and, finishing just hours before Minnie's arrival, she was standing eagerly in the front foyer as Minnie and Duncan's carriage pulled up.

The sisters embraced warmly and Olive gave Duncan a kiss. She was very fond of her brother-in-law but her attention was quickly directed to the adorable child at his side. Although she and Thomas had not conceived the child she so desperately craved, she was delighted for Minnie. Meeting and marrying Duncan in her mid thirties had not stopped God from giving her the family she had always wanted.

Mrs. Moreton led the nanny with Marjorie upstairs to the makeshift nursery she and Olive had enjoyed putting together.

Ushering the pair into the drawing room, she could barely get her words out coherently. "Tell me everything. How is Papa? What news have you from Helen? Has Charles settled? What about Jack? Have you heard from George or Seymour?"

Laughing, Minnie settled beside Olive and the pair became engrossed by all things Wilmot. When Thomas arrived home from the hospital later, he soon had something stronger than tea in Duncan's hand and the two men shared their own news.

The US economy continued to plague them and its effect was even reaching Duncan in Newcastle. He had purchased 400 acres of Belmont land to add to his already sizeable homestead north of Newcastle. His crop yield was substantial but the US markets which

had welcomed his crops previously had dried up with the tightened economy.

Minnie, Duncan and Marjorie remained in New York for Thomas and Olive's first anniversary. Olive joyfully pushed the babe in the boys' pram which Thomas had brought out of storage and had cleaned up. The two sisters took advantage of the unseasonably mild Easter weather to parade through the streets of New York City, Olive pointing out all of the homes and businesses she frequented. Minnie was struck dumb at the sight of the Vanderbilt mansion just down the street but it was just one of many grand homes.

The couples enjoyed an evening together at Delmonico's Restaurant, where Minnie and Duncan were introduced to Lobster Newberg. They toasted Olive and Thomas with champagne. The women were tipsy when they finally left the restaurant.

The night before their departure, Thomas and Olive hosted a large dinner party for Minnie and Duncan. The guests included Uncle John and Sayre. Minnie enjoyed the banter between Olive and Sayre and said to Duncan later that she could now relax, seeing Olive in this new life with so many around her who cared for her.

Olive felt melancholy as the carriage pulled away from the curb at the end of their visit but her days soon filled and, before she knew it, it was again time for the family to head to the lake.

Summer in Alexandria Bay was a repeat of the previous; relaxing and casual, but, as August approached, Olive was concerned that Thomas had not regained his health while resting at their summer home. She proposed a visit to Saratoga Springs. She had hopes the mineral springs might revive him. He, himself, had such a strong belief in the hydrotherapy benefits to health, that he had written a well-received clinical essay on the subject in 1892.

While the springs were good for the body, Thomas also felt the annual horse races were good for the soul and he had faired well placing wagers on Willie Vanderbilt's prize horses through the years.

Thomas looked forward to seeing Willie. Since their cruise to India, Willie had remained out of the country. Alva had indeed filed for divorce and Thomas assumed Willie was making it easier by staying on the continent during the proceedings. However, he knew Willie well enough to know that he wouldn't miss the annual races in Saratoga.

Olive thoroughly enjoyed their time at the springs; re-igniting her love of horse racing. She and Thomas were invited to Willie's private box every day and she found Willie far more approachable than Alva had been. Willie was surprised to learn how well informed Olive was about horse flesh and the two spent time measuring up the merits of each horse. Olive was thrilled when Willie's horse once again took top prize and she came away with some prize money of her own.

When it was time for the Burchard's return to New York, Willie said his goodbyes. He would be returning to the continent and future stays in New York would be at his club; he was giving the house on 5th Avenue which she took such pride in to Alva. Willie and Thomas promised to reconnect during Thomas' next trip over. Willie, gallantly put Olive's hand to his lips and said "I look forward to seeing you again, Mrs. Burchard." Other women were easily overcome by the attention of this charming multi-millionaire but Olive just looked at Thomas with a knowing smile and replied, "As will Thomas and I, Mr. Vanderbilt."

June 1903

Newcastle, Ontario

Chapter 58

Minnie sat once again at Olive's desk to write out telegrams to be sent to Henry's son, Simon, at Yale and to his grandchildren; Kitty and Henry Jr. She made it clear to Simon that his father needed him as quickly as he could make the journey. She worried deeply about Henry's health once he heard the news and felt it was now up to his son to take charge.

She then wrote telegrams to each of her brothers and sisters. By the time she had completed the last one, all of the energy reserves which had sustained her through the past days suddenly left her. She very nearly collapsed as Mrs. Thomson entered to say the driver had the car out front to take her home. She found it hard to believe a mere three days had passed since he had first brought her to Olive.

There were still details to be taken care of before she could return to her own home and family. She told the housekeeper to prepare the house. There would be many mourners.

"I'll leave all of the food and beverage up to you and Cook, Mrs. Thomson" she said. "Mr. Van Duzer will likely return on today's train and he is charged with arrangements for the funeral. Bring in whatever is needed and he will ensure the merchants are paid.

Minnie left the housekeeper and climbed the stairs heavily, not looking forward to what lay ahead of her.

Henry looked up from his bed with surprise as she opened the door of his room without knocking. It seemed that courtesy had escaped her but, on seeing her face; Henry immediately understood the reason for this lapse.

"She's gone, Henry" said Minnie. "Our darling girl is gone."

Minnie stepped quietly from the room as Henry turned his face to the wall, saying "without Olive, there is no point in living."

Henry's shoulders shook silently in grief as his thoughts replayed his first night with her.

1895

New York City

Chapter 59

Returning from their third summer at Alexandria Bay, Thomas and Olive discovered they had acquired a new neighbour in their absence.

Henry Sanford, a 72 year old widower, had purchased the home at 50 W. 52nd over the summer. Henry had been President of Adams Express transportation and investment firm when the doctor had given his wife, Nancy, her diagnosis. In order to be at her side for her final weeks, he stepped down from his busy position, remaining on the Board of Directors. He had been at her side when she passed in November at their Connecticut home.

While still in mourning for Nancy, Henry discovered serious malfeasance by an executive at Adams Express. As a Board member, Henry brought criminal charges against the man, leaving the company with a void at the executive level.

While he had not intended to step back into an active role with the company again, the situation had sent the management team into a tailspin. The Board knew Henry was the one man who could take control of the company. Feeling somewhat responsible, he agreed to return in a lesser position, at least until he felt up to full responsibility once again.

This new commitment meant more time in New York City and he quickly tired of staying at his club. He maintained the home he and his wife had shared in Bridgeport, Connecticut but purchased the town home on 52nd Street for its convenience to his office.

Despite its size, New York City remained a relatively tight-knit community for those of the upper classes. Thomas and Olive knew of Henry and the circumstances of his wife's death but, other than a nodding acquaintance when their paths crossed in the neighbourhood, chose to leave the man alone during their first months back.

With Henry officially out of mourning in November, Olive suggested they include him in one of their dinner parties.

Thomas' health remained poor on their return but he reassured Olive that these dinner parties gave him something other than himself to think about. Their guest lists generally included individuals who were successful but not necessarily conventional; they had acquired a knack for attracting the interesting among New York's successful people. Experiencing exclusion themselves gave them greater resolve not to exclude anyone just for seeming outside the norms of society.

Olive was pleased to receive Henry's acceptance and looked forward to getting to know their new neighbour better.

The evening turned out to be cold and blustery which suited Henry's mood. Dressing for dinner, he regretted accepting the invitation. An evening surrounded by doctors promised to be dull.

As his valet brushed his coat and stepped aside, Henry said "Why I allow myself to be coerced into social events I really don't know, Carter."

"When did I become such a pushover?" Henry asked his image in the mirror. "I have allowed myself to be persuaded to move to the city and rejoin society when I have no desire to do either?"

Turning to his valet, he said, "It's not the same without her, is it, Carter?"

The valet had been with Henry a lifetime and knew he referred to Nancy.

"No, sir, it certainly isn't. I remember how you used to relish an evening of dinner and conversation when Mrs. Sanford was here to accompany you." Carter picked up his grooming implements and headed out the door as Henry replied, "Too true, Carter; too true."

It was also true that those who had known him in his prime could be excused for not recognizing the Henry who stepped out his door that night. He looked every one of his 72 years and more. Losing Nancy had knocked the stuffing out of him as nothing previously in his life had been able to do.

One could be forgiven, based on his appearance this night, for mistaking Henry as a 'soft' man; he was anything but. In spite of his advanced years, he still stood 6 feet tall and had wide shoulders. He cast a shadow over most men and his size had proven useful when pursuing a goal.

His features appeared stern to those who didn't know him; high forehead, prominent nose and full mouth; black eyes that missed little

and a pronounced chin. His hair might be iron gray but he still had a full head of it.

In his youth, he had tried his hand at several careers including Private Secretary to P.T. Barnum, working with this innovator of entertainment for several years. Henry cut his teeth in business under the influence of Barnum; learning to recognize opportunity; pursue it unyieldingly and then market the hell out of it. The business practices employed by Barnum would ultimately stand Henry well in the rough and tumble world of the mid 1800s.

Titans were born in the U.S. and fortunes made by those vanguards who saw opportunity with railroads and steel; anything that helped bridge the distance between settlers from east to west and north to south.

In an era of murder, stage coach and train robberies, Henry had what it took to deal with thieves and politicians alike. He understood that all success was not achieved through courtesy and diplomacy and he was not averse to 'strong arm' methods when pursuing a goal.

His career spanned over fifty years, the bulk of it spent at Adams Express, a company he helped grow and which prospered through his immense drive and perseverance. He had been there as the company developed from a stage coach line into the communication and transportation business it had become by 1895. Like the company he devoted his life to, he had developed from the rough riding days of his youth to a life of comfort and great wealth.

But he had seen adventures along the way. During the Civil War he saw opportunity and negotiated contracts with the railroads and express companies for delivery of packages and payroll to the Union troops and for shipment of war materials purchased in Europe.

He was perhaps best known for his role in saving Lincoln in February of 1861.

The President-Elect was travelling to Washington, D.C. through Baltimore, when word got to the ears of the men at Adams Express of a plot afoot to assassinate Lincoln during his journey. Lincoln's election had prompted the southern States to declare their succession from the Union causing extreme unrest in the country. Henry was a son of the North and staunch supporter of Lincoln and was appalled when he heard of this plan. His suggestion that the telegraph wires be

cut outside of Harrisburg, Pennsylvania to prevent knowledge of the President's movements ultimately saved Lincoln's life.

Adams Express gained from Henry's action through government contracts and passage of favourable legislation. In fact, the patronage of the White House helped Adams Express to become hugely successful and Henry to become an extremely wealthy man.

But the Henry who stepped out his door on that blustery December evening thought of none of that. He just resolved to excuse himself as soon after dinner as possible to return to his comfortable study for a cigar and Port before retiring to his lonely bed.

Giving his outer clothing to Mrs. Moreton, Henry stepped across the threshold of the Drawing Room. Seeing him, Olive excused herself from the conversation she had been involved in and made her way over to him.

Her movements were graceful and it appeared to Henry as though she floated across the room. He was struck by her height and beauty; he hadn't really seen much beyond the wraps she wore as he noticed her getting in and out of carriages. But it was her smile that captivated. Henry was spellbound the moment she turned the brilliance of it onto him.

"Mr. Sanford! We are so pleased you are able to join us", said Olive, taking his arm and guiding him toward the chair Thomas was sitting in. Thomas began to rise but Henry motioned him to remain seated, shaking his hand as Olive introduced him.

Henry was aware of Thomas' weak heart, having been told by a member of his club who learned he had moved near the much talked about young couple. While Thomas lacked the robustness generally seen in a man in his late 40s, one could discern his character through his intelligent eyes. Henry liked him on sight.

Thomas welcomed Henry to their home and, belatedly, to their neighbourhood and the two men enjoyed conversing until Olive appeared at their side once again. Linking her arm in Henry's, she said "There will be plenty of time for you two to chat over dinner but I would like to introduce you to our other guests, Mr. Sanford". Even had he wanted to decline, Henry knew he was powerless against her charm.

Henry was pleased to discover that his expectation about the guest list had been misguided. Rather than all doctors, the guests

were members of many professions; a Senator, a Professor of Philosophy, a Lawyer, even a Suffragette (although she wasn't introduced as such; Henry discerned this during dinner). Olive included Sayre in the evening who, it turned out, knew Henry through some legal transactions and the two spoke briefly of mutual interests.

By their choice of guests, Olive and Thomas set in motion the free-flowing, engaging conversation they so enjoyed. For the first time in months, Henry enjoyed himself.

Observing Olive's attentiveness to Thomas throughout the evening, he recognized their union as one of love, versus those of convenience so commonly seen. Contrary to most hosts who sat at opposite ends of the table, Olive chose to sit at Thomas' immediate left. Henry was surprised by such a breach of the social norm but he soon realized this was a reflection of how much they enjoyed each other. The attention she gave him throughout dinner was loving rather than cloying and Thomas clearly welcomed it.

The pair looked out for their guests' needs and frequently called on individuals for their thoughts on the various discussions around the table. With such driven, successful people, opinions could be strongly expressed and Henry marvelled as Olive, on several occasions, stepped in to diffuse the raised voices with humour and diplomacy. She managed to make each guest feel they were in the right with the argument they proposed.

'*My God, she can command a room*' thought Henry after one such incident.

The evening passed pleasantly and Henry saw it was close to midnight when he checked his watch chain. Olive had not followed the usual custom of leading the ladies away to leave the gentlemen to enjoy cigars and after dinner drinks and more explicit conversations. In this home, it seemed, women were considered equal to discussions of all types.

Olive led the way on many topics, proving herself to be a woman with life experience and a curious mind. While the antics of children and issues of running a household engaged most women, Olive held her own on such topics as politics, current medical practice and women's' rights. She appeared unthreatened by other strong women since the two unwed female guests were intelligent and lively.

Far from being an early night for Henry, it was 1:00 am when he retrieved his outer clothing and made his farewells. Thomas looked fatigued as he wished the guests a goodnight but Olive seemed just as fresh as she had at the start of the evening. Henry walked home with a spring in his step, recalling the evening's highlights.

That first dinner led to many subsequent invitations from Thomas and Olive. He enjoyed Thomas' company greatly but was becoming exceedingly fond of Olive. For her part, Olive enjoyed having Henry as an elder neighbour; he reminded her of her father; both remarkable men for their accomplishments and drive, continuing even into an advanced age.

With their increasing familiarity, Henry consulted Olive on entertaining advice and concerns about his granddaughter, Kitty, citing his loss of Nancy and need for a feminine viewpoint. Henry showed his gratitude to Olive with small, elegant gifts; a bible bound in soft, supple leather; one of the new fountain pens; engraved stationery. A married woman could not accept personal gifts from another man so he ensured the gifts were always in the best of taste and appeared as tokens of appreciation. In truth, Henry enjoyed sending her gifts.

Despite his advanced age, he was a man of extreme vigor and the move to New York proved to be exactly what he needed to get his old blood boiling once again. Reserving box seats at the Metropolitan Opera for the season soon had him on the guest list of every matron in his social sphere.

Chapter 60

Thanksgiving for Thomas and Olive was a quiet affair, with just the boys and Thomas' brothers, Lewis and Roswell, present.

While he presented a strong face to the world, Thomas' health continued to weaken. Each day began not unlike the new electricity in their home, shining brightly until too many demands were put on it and the lights would flicker and dim ever so slightly. By day's end, it was all he could do to get himself up the stairs to bed.

Together, he and Olive sought avenues of respite in warm climates and peaceful settings and just enjoyed each others' company, never knowing how much time they would have together. Immediately following Thanksgiving, they departed for Florida, where they planned to spend the month of December. The boys would join them once school had let out.

Thomas had also arranged for a return to the warmer climes of Europe. He had obtained a passport for their travels but news from Newcastle made it impossible for Olive to leave the country.

Minnie was expecting again and her age made this pregnancy a concern. Olive would never forgive herself if something happened to her beloved sister or the baby and she was so far away.

Choosing between her ailing husband and her sister was a dreadful decision for Olive to have to make but Thomas immediately put her at ease.

"I would never ask you to be so far from home when Minnie may need you quickly, Olive" he said. "This trip for me is exploratory and to rest. I have no plans to embark on any adventures. I will ask Roswell to accompany me so you needn't worry about my welfare."

She agreed with his decision and was grateful when a note arrived from his brother confirming he would join Thomas. In contrast to their first trip abroad, Thomas had been honest with Olive about the appointments he had made with specialists in each country. He was once again seeking out their opinions in hopes of extending his life. She wrote a heart-felt thank you letter to Roswell for the part he was to play in this journey, understanding that he would be a better companion than she in the physical assistance he would be able to give.

The wisdom of the decision didn't remove Olive's sadness at the thought of three months without Thomas. He was to leave as the

worst of January presented itself and had booked a return sailing on March 28th. Olive was grateful for the commitments she had in New York City which would keep her mind and body busy; commitments which Thomas had initiated.

After their first year together, with no sign of Olive conceiving a child, Thomas had referred her to a peer of his who specialized in gynaecological issues. The doctor explained the significance of her lifelong struggle with hypertension and the many 'female' issues she had experienced. Her dreams of motherhood were achingly put aside.

Olive was despondent at the diagnosis. Thomas thought her love of children could also help others. Looking for a charity that would most benefit by her help, he settled on The Babies' Hospital for the care of sick children of destitute mothers at Lexington and 51st Street. After a tour of the hospital with the Matron, Olive was soon happily dedicating hours each week as a volunteer on the wards.

The Matron knew she had gold in Olive; both for her nursing skill and her sensibilities. The hospital ran on a shoestring budget, relying solely on private contributions and the struggle to keep donations coming in was constant. Matron thought her new volunteer's knowledge and character would be helpful in raising money and requested that Olive join the fundraising committee as well. Olive gently declined.

Unlike other wealthy women, Olive had not been involved in any charity work. She justified this by her belief that caring for Thomas was her primary calling in life. But this was not entirely true.

She had learned much after leaving Henry Winans; self-protection and a new awareness of the voices of others. With Thomas, she lived in a controlled environment avoiding the members of society who publicly condemned her still for the divorce. Joining philanthropic groups meant risking exposure to these same people, something she preferred to avoid.

But, as the hospital's inadequacies and her concern for the children grew, she found it hard to deny these needs. She agreed to join the fundraising committee. She felt the overall need eclipsed her concerns about a group of New York's most standoffish matrons.

Olive put on her courageous face as she entered her first meeting. She expected the usual snubs she still very much felt. The faces on the women reflected mixed reactions to having a divorcee in their midst.

Some looked at Olive with frank curiosity. These women wondered if she was a jezebel or a victim but withheld judgement.

A few looked scornfully at Olive, turning their faces away immediately after being introduced. Their judgement had been made based on the divorce and not the woman.

But Olive was pleased to recognize three women she had met socially prior to her marriage to Thomas. Because they had known her before the scandal, their judgement was based on her character as they had come to know it. They smiled in welcome.

Olive focused on these friendly faces and charged ahead. Her commitment and work ethic and success in bringing dollars in couldn't be disputed. As new donors materialized, even the women least willing to give Olive a chance had to admit they may have been wrong. The dollar eventually trumps all.

As Matron had hoped, Olive was very successful at fundraising. When she put her mind to a cause, little could stop her. Her friends and family began to direct charitable dollars to the hospital as well. Sayre and Henry Sanford, in particular, became very generous donors.

By the time plans were underway for the hospital's one major annual event, everyone on the committee was working as one. Committee members put all of their efforts into hosting a successful event; a charity ball in April.

As Thomas' departure neared, Olive wrote notes for him to discover, plotting with his valet during the packing for appropriate places to hide them. She had no expectations for the trip; doubting it would result in any hope, but she understood her husband's need to do something rather than sit quietly waiting his fate.

In the week prior to his departure, they hosted one final intimate dinner party with just Sayre, Henry Sanford and his granddaughter, Kitty, and Olive's friend, Lisbeth. As Sayre, Kitty and Lisbeth were getting their coats at the end of the evening, Thomas pulled Henry aside.

"I know I will not be imposing on you, Henry, in asking you to watch over Olive in my absence" he said. "I don't expect her to sit idly at home waiting my return but there are still those who would disparage her in this city. I believe it would go a long way if she were seen to be under your protection."

"Of course, Thomas, it will be my pleasure," replied Henry, with a distinct feeling that Thomas' request was intended for more than this trip to Europe.

Henry was sincere in his assurances to Thomas. He would certainly watch over her, accompanying her to formal events in the city as needed. But he also valued Olive's advice about Kitty and it would be helpful to him to have Olive in the city during this time.

He was in the midst of arranging a marriage for Kitty, after a scandalous affair had threatened her future, and he was sorely missing his wife Nancy's perspective, especially in light of Kitty's lack of enthusiasm for the entire business.

He brushed these thoughts aside as he retrieved his coat. He didn't like being reminded of the scandal Kitty had brought on them all.

Chapter 61

Henry and Nancy had just one child; Simon. He was a quieter version of Nancy, with none of Henry's boisterous charm.

With Henry on the road a great deal, Simon and Nancy developed a strong bond. She recognized the gentleness in him and fostered his creative nature. A truly gifted musician, he studied under teachers in New York and Paris. He was recognized by many as a brilliant concert musician but lacked the hunger necessary for success. This was not unusual for children who lived privileged lives.

Even had he desired to be a concert performer, his father would have none of it. Henry insisted Simon attend Yale.

Simon was a young man of routine who had spent a great deal of his life alone. The life of a student suited him. His music classes were primarily independent study and practice and his lodging was in a quiet area of New Haven. The concentration he gave to school meant he finished his years at school with distinction.

After graduation, with no clear direction (and no need to work), he set out to bring world class musicians back to the university to build the reputation of the music department. The funds he bestowed on the university and the connections he had with musicians around the world ensured his place on the campus. He became a professor of music of sorts, although never accepting a penny in salary.

His father, on the other hand, was an orchestrator of lives and watching Simon 'waste' his life away did not please him. He knew that Nancy longed for grandchildren but Simon showed no inclination to facilitate this. Henry took matters into his own hands, introducing Simon to the daughter of an Adams Express executive. While Simon would not have put any effort into a courtship on his own, on meeting Kate, he was surprised to learn of her love and appreciation for music.

He and Kate married and children soon followed; Catherine (Kitty) first, followed by Henry Jr. Kate was not a strong woman and Nancy proved instrumental in arranging for suitable nannies for the children and generally overseeing their household. Kate's health continued to decline and the family was devastated when she died tragically at the age of 25, leaving Simon with two young children.

Plunged into a deep despair at the loss of his beautiful Kate, Simon was barely able to care for himself. Nancy continued to oversee their

household during her own grief, naturally taking on the responsibility for the children. She soon recognized her own limitations; overseeing two households and the care of two young children was taking a toll.

A few months after Kate's funeral, Nancy said to Henry, "What would you think of raising Kitty and Henry Jr. in our home, Henry?"

Henry replied, "By God, you always know what I'm thinking, Nancy. The very same idea has been in my mind these past weeks. These two will inherit a great deal one day and I can't help feel that Simon is not up to rearing them with the stern hand needed." Nancy was not surprised by his business view of the situation. This was, after all, what had made him a successful self-made man.

Together, Henry and Nancy shared their thoughts with Simon, broaching the idea as a temporary one until Simon would be able to take charge of the children. Of course, he loved his children but raising them alone was something he was entirely ill-equipped to do. He accepted his parent's proposal and immediately made plans for a trip to the continent to get his mind off Kate, remaining away for the following year.

Kitty and Henry Jr. remained with Nancy and Henry in Bridgeport for their childhood while Simon, when he returned to Connecticut, spent his time at his home at 52 Hillhouse Avenue in New Haven, close to his beloved Yale. As the years went by and Simon did not remarry, there seemed no reason to change the situation of Kitty and Henry Jr.

Simon spent his life promoting music. In the absence of his family, he made it his purpose to bring great music to the US. He used his wealth and the freedom that being a single man provided to pursue great music on the Continent in the realm of composers and performers, eventually convincing Edward Elgar to come to the US when many others had failed to do so.

Kitty and Henry Jr. enjoyed an indulged childhood filled with all the pleasures that money provided. Nancy was an involved grandmother, lovingly acting as the stand-in for their mother.

Kitty resembled her grandfather in character and charm, and Henry Jr., was very like Simon as a boy. He was quiet and easily led by his wilful sister. They rarely got into any mischief of note but, on the rare occasions that they did, Nancy intuitively knew that Kitty was the mastermind, steering Henry Jr. into mischief.

Even with the help of nannies and governesses, Nancy was not a young woman to be raising two children. As they reached their teenage years, she found herself increasingly unequal to the challenges Kitty, in particular, presented. When Kitty turned 18, Henry's concerns for Nancy's health prompted him to propose a season on the Continent for their granddaughter. Nancy agreed reluctantly knowing she would miss the girl a great deal. A suitable chaperone was arranged and Kitty sailed for Liverpool.

Despite the absence of Kitty and the stress she had placed on her grandmother, Nancy's health continued to decline. The highlight of her days was reading the frequent letters Kitty sent. Nancy was pleased the girl was enjoying the sights and societies of the various countries she was visiting.

Her letters from Monte Carlo were particularly light-hearted, apparently due to a young man she had met; Robert Peel, grandson of Britain's Prime Minister, Sir Robert Peel. Nancy's delight quickly turned to concern when Kitty's next letter gleefully said the young man had followed her to Paris. Mentioning this to Henry brought an explosive outburst from him.

"That scallywag has a reputation as depraved as any I've heard of" he said. "Few papers are published in England without some story or other about him with actresses. Prominent family be damned – he's a fortune hunter!"

Although Nancy preferred to think Henry's reaction was from concern for his granddaughter, she knew that he had been contemplating a courtship for Kitty with the son of a member of Bridgeport's leading legal firm. The firm did a great deal of business for Adams Express and the union would bring two business concerns together nicely.

"I'd better telegraph Simon in London and tell him to get over to Paris to put a stop to this" Henry said angrily.

Despite their haste, Simon was too late. By the time he arrived at Kitty's hotel, the damage was done; Robert had proposed and Kitty had accepted. While Henry might have dealt with the situation in a more abrupt manner, Simon, consulting with Henry by telegraph, convinced the couple to wait a year and brought Kitty back with him to Bridgeport for Nancy and Henry to distract her.

In defiance of Simon's request, Peel followed them to Connecticut. Learning of this, Henry stepped in. When Peel arrived at the house, Henry refused him access to Kitty.

Kitty was heartbroken and called her grandfather all manner of names. "My friends' families would be delighted to see their daughters marry a British Lord. Robert's breeding is evident in his charm, Grandfather. How can you deny us our happiness?"

"My darling Kitty," replied Henry, wryly. "Most American girls who snag a member of the British aristocracy soon regret the day they laid eyes on them. How many are still living with their charming British husbands, I ask? Once the Brit gets his hands on the American money all charm is forgotten leaving many an heiress heartbroken."

"I know that every girl believes their fairy tale wedding will be different and I don't dispute the beauty and charm you bring but I do hope you can see that my years of experience make me an astute judge of character. I believe Peel's primary motive to be fortune hunting and I could not live with myself to see you neglected or, worse, abandoned once the marriage had taken place."

Henry departed for New York to give her time to cool down (and remove himself from the drama taking place in the household). He believed the affair was behind him and was, therefore, outraged when young Peel had the gall to call upon him at his New York office. Although receiving him coldly, Peel was a persistent suitor, insisting on knowing the reasons for Henry's objection to the marriage.

Henry spared no words, telling the man he was a Libertine and that his affairs with actresses were well known in the US as well as in England. He was surprised when Peel didn't deny it. Instead, Peel tried to reason with Henry, responding that this behaviour was in his youth while he was sowing his wild oats and was well behind him.

Henry was not about to believe him; without a doubt, Peel was seeking a pretty face with a fortune. He gave the man the reception he deserved and sent him on his way.

As Henry would tell it later, the cad then had the nerve to report in the papers that Henry was the rudest man he had ever met, saying "he may be worth $15 million" (making Henry laugh at the inflation of his net worth) "but he doesn't know how to deal with a gentleman" referring to Henry as a Puritan.

Henry decided to impart some 'Puritan' justice to Peel for maligning his reputation on his own home turf. He brought the matter to his law firm with instructions to deal with it and to do everything possible to obtain the letters Kitty had written young Peel. The law firm set their associate, Guthrie, on the case.

One evening, Guthrie followed Peel to Delmonico's. After allowing the man to console himself with several drinks, Guthrie approached a table of newsmen always hungry for scandal. Acting as press agent for the Sanford family and pointing to the drunken Peel, he hinted that it was unlikely an American girl of Kitty's social and financial standing would consider marrying such a dissolute member of the British aristocracy.

The newsmen grabbed at the idea, printing the story the next day, adding salacious details of Peel's previous amours with Marie Tempest and Lillie Langtry to illustrate just how depraved the man was.

Peel was indignant when he read the paper. He knew he had been treated disgracefully and retaliated by contacting the press himself. His protests against the deceitful and insulting attacks were printed by another paper.

With Peel's anger now directed at the press, Guthrie followed Henry's instructions and approached the young man, requesting that, as a gentleman, he return all of Miss Sanford's letters. Peel refused.

This failure aside, Henry felt his efforts to protect Kitty had been successful. He had kept the two apart although she continued to declare her undying love for Peel. Henry never doubted the man's true motives and had no regret over his actions. He believed Kitty and even Nancy to be taken in by the romance of the situation. It fell to him to take care of his granddaughter's best interests.

Henry watched helplessly as Nancy's health suffered even more by the strain of this situation. Kitty's anguish caused Nancy heartache and took away any strength she might have had to fight her illness. She passed away in November.

Kitty's grief at losing her grandmother was profound. She was devastated by what she thought had been her part in her Grandmother's illness and resigned herself to live quietly at Bridgeport with her Grandfather and her brother throughout the year long mourning period.

Chapter 62

When mourning ended, Henry was determined to see Kitty married before she could get herself into any more undesirable relationships.

Settled in New York in his new home, he set about finding a suitable young man for her. Kitty became accustomed, on her frequent visits to the city, to meeting young men her grandfather deemed appropriate. While she might have protested, the situation with Peel had opened Kitty's eyes to the steps her grandfather would take in her 'best' interests.

"You really must be making a decision, Kitty" said Henry after yet another man left his home. "Every one of these young men has come from a solid background and has great prospects. I don't know what you are holding out for but it's time to make a choice."

Kitty might have fought her grandfather yet again but she really didn't have the strength to, even had she been so inclined. But, despite the number of men she was introduced to, no other young man stirred her emotions as Peel had. Her heart was still with him.

Emotions and reality were two very different things and Kitty was realistic. She knew if she allowed Peel back into her life after she reached the age of majority, Grandfather would cut her off. A voice in her head worried he was right about Peel's motives.

Olive came to know Kitty well during her visits to her grandfather's townhouse. The two spent many pleasant hours shopping around the city together. As Kitty continued to show no interest in suitors, Henry decided to enlist Olive's help.

Sharing the details of his granddaughter's thwarted love affair, he managed to leave out most of his role in the affair. The situation captured Olive's fragile heart. It was too close to her own impetuousness with her first marriage. Unaware of Olive's first marriage or the sharp similarities between Kitty's story and her own, Henry simply desired a strong woman to explain life's realities to his granddaughter.

Olive felt heartsick for the girl, understanding only too well how strong the pull of young love could be. She promised Henry she would do what she could, deciding to share her own story with Kitty.

While the two sat over tea one afternoon, Olive delicately broached the subject.

"Your grandfather has told me of your love affair, Kitty. I understand only too well how angry you were with him," said Olive, refilling their tea cups.

"Your grandfather is not aware of this but, by the time I was your age, I had left my first husband. I have told very few people of this marriage; for many reasons, not the least of which is the pain it brings me to recall it. If you don't mind, I would like to tell you of my experiences. Even though it may shock you, I think it may put your grandfather's actions in perspective."

"Of course, Mrs. Burchard, although, I certainly do not wish to bring you pain." Kitty was very fond of her grandfather's beautiful neighbour, often thinking how wonderful it might have been to have a mother like Olive.

"I think the situation calls for it" said Olive. "Sometimes we need to be reminded of the mistakes we've made in life and, in this case, I hope you might learn from mine."

Olive spent the next hour confiding in Kitty. She used delicate language but left out little in order to impress upon Kitty the vulnerability of young girls. Kitty was indeed shocked as she listened to the elegant woman tell a story of seduction followed by control, brutality and ultimately abuse. It might have been a tale from a novel had she not known the victim was the woman in front of her.

Coming to the end, Olive said "I think you can see why I felt compelled to share my sad story with you, Kitty. Had I only listened to what my father had learned of my husband, I would not have subjected myself to the pain and sorrow I came to know. I thought I knew myself best, believing my heart incapable of steering me wrong.

My father recognized the cruelty in this man and believed that, in forbidding the marriage, I would be saved from it. He never dreamt I could be deceitful. It was my own foolishness that led to my downfall."

"Sometimes, in our youth, we see the charming handsome man as the only one in the world for us. Life will teach you that the steady, average man makes a far better husband. As dull as it may seem when we are young, less drama and more stability is what is ultimately best for us and will make us happy in the long term" said Olive.

Kitty sat in disbelief. How could this calm, beautiful woman before her have experienced such things? Kitty had felt alone in her feelings for Peel but, hearing of the horrific events that came about after Olive acted on the same feelings, she now wondered if her grandfather had not saved her from something that may have turned out as dreadful. She would always remember Peel as her first love but now understood what her path should be.

When her grandfather produced the next young potential suitor, Victor Thorne, Kitty felt he would not be an offensive life companion. Remembering Olive's words, she wearily agreed to the match and Henry gratefully moved forward with plans for a small wedding in his Bridgeport home on June 10th.

"It falls to me to host an engagement luncheon for the pair, Olive," Henry said soon after Thomas had departed for England, "and I find myself out of my depth. I wonder if you might be in a position to help me with the necessary decisions."

"Of course, Henry" replied Olive. "I would be delighted and it will be something to fill time while Thomas is away. Let's begin with the guest list so that I have some idea of the scope of the event. I'll be in a better position to offer appropriate suggestions then."

Chapter 63

As it happened, Olive's father was in England when Thomas arrived with Roswell in January of 1896. Samuel was spending several months in discussions with his counterparts in England. The goal was for him to pave the way for a fisheries policy for the entire Commonwealth which had been drafted in Canada.

Without Thomas' knowledge, Olive had written to her father to request that he consider returning on the same ship as Thomas. She didn't go so far as to suggest he would be checking on her husband but her concern for his welfare was evident in her words. Since the March 28th sailing suited his own timing, he didn't hesitate to change his return passage.

Thomas looked up from his menu on the first evening of his return voyage to see his father-in-law entering the dining room. He stood as Samuel made his way toward their table. The two men exchanged warm greetings and Samuel acknowledged Roswell before Thomas encouraged Samuel to join them.

"How is it that we are on the same ship, Sir," asked Thomas, bewildered. He was not disappointed to see Olive's father; to the contrary, he was more than pleased. He had become very fond of the man and, after his three-month tour of various doctors and clinics, was feeling quite low. The sight of his father-in-law reminded him of Olive waiting at home.

"Olive disclosed your plans when she wrote, Thomas. Since this sailing worked well with my plans, I thought I might as well join you and Roswell for the return. I could use the genial company after the months I've spent courting politicians."

Samuel was surprised by Thomas' appearance. He had quite evidently lost weight since they had last been together and his complexion was drawn. His exhaustion was clear in both his face and how he held his body.

"Well, we're very glad our plans coincided, Sir. I'm sure Roswell is tired of seeing just my old mug after these past three months." Roswell smiled but Samuel could detect the sadness in his face. Clearly Olive had not exaggerated her concern for Thomas; Samuel doubted whether they would have the man with them a year hence.

"I hope your pleasure continues, Thomas, when you hear that I plan on stopping in your home for a week or two before returning to Canada" Samuel said.

Their sailing was surprisingly calm for March and the men enjoyed quiet conversation, reading and walking the decks together. In light of Thomas' appearance and demeanour, Samuel was grateful for the time with his son-in-law.

Although Thomas had telegraphed Olive not to meet them at the port, he was very pleased to see her smiling and waving from the dock as the group departed from the ship.

"You didn't really think I could wait for you to arrive home, did you? I've been anxious all week and just had to be here to see you" said Olive, reaching for his arm. Turning to her father, Olive said "Papa, I'm so happy we are able to enjoy a reunion at the same time."

Thomas was more than pleased to see her and, in his tiredness, allowed Olive to guide him toward the hired carriage, leaving his valet to direct the unloading and gathering of their luggage and Samuel's. The nine pieces were soon stowed on the back and under their feet and the party climbed into the vehicle for the journey to Manhattan.

The boys, home for spring break, were overjoyed to see their father, although they shared Olive's concern on seeing him. The week was spent quietly; Stewart read the newspaper to his father in the mornings and the pair discussed current events; Leeds enjoyed games of checkers after Thomas' afternoon naps. Both boys were well aware their father was dying before their eyes.

As Olive and her father walked together at the end of his visit, Samuel imparted advice and suggestions for Olive.

"I hope you won't object if I speak frankly about Thomas' condition, Olive" he said. "It's evident that your time with him is limited. I know you understood that when you agreed to marry him. All that was unknown was how much time that might be. After seeing him this week, I would suggest you put plans in place."

"It's so painful for me to consider life without him, Papa, but Thomas and I have always been open with each other about this eventuality. Thomas confided the details of his arrangements long ago so there should be no surprises. Lewis will act as Executor for him and will take guardianship of the boys. Thomas feels they need the hand of a man at this point in their lives and I agree. I will still see them often;

in fact, we've agreed that they should spend their school vacations in the house with me since it is the only home they've ever known. Lewis will make all decisions concerning their schooling and financial needs. I'm relieved really since I know little about raising young men."

"I applaud Thomas for the thought he put into everything" Samuel commented. "By putting this arrangement for the boys in place, he has ensured your relationship with them will be one of emotional support. They will not hold grudges against you as tough decisions concerning their future come up."

"Now," continued Samuel as they arrived back at the house, "let's focus on how we might help the boys through their grief." Wise Samuel knew that putting Olive's attention on the boys would occupy her mind and heart and might go some way to taking her thoughts away from her own impending loss.

Once the Babies Hospital charity ball in April was over, Olive backed away from all commitments to spend her time exclusively with Thomas. They managed short walks every day and brief visits from family but, for the most part, their life was quiet.

She did follow through with Kitty's rehearsal party arrangements. She was too fond of Henry and Kitty to leave the final details to someone else. When Kitty pulled Olive aside at the event to thank her, Olive took the opportunity to give their regrets for her June wedding.

"A trip to Bridgeport is just not possible for Dr. Burchard" Olive said sadly.

"I have to be honest, Mrs. Burchard" replied Kitty. "Grandfather and Victor's parents have blown this event way out of proportion. With over 2,000 attending my ceremony, I doubt I will know who is there and who is not. The intimate luncheon I opted for at Grandfather's home is now over 200. So, please don't give this another thought. We will have plenty of opportunity to see each other once I return from my honeymoon."

Kitty's use of "I" and "my" said much to Olive. The girl was clearly going through the motions but still had not embraced the idea of her marriage. It saddened Olive that the vibrant, beautiful girl before her was not going to know the love she and Thomas shared but she understood the ways of money. A union such as this was the lot of many young girls of privilege.

Returning home, Olive gratefully swept up the stairs to Thomas. She shared her disappointment for Kitty. She and Thomas openly talked about their brief time remaining, making every minute count. Their conversations were honest; both in pain and in pleasure.

Olive was oblivious to the world outside the life they created that summer and early fall. Other than spending time in a lounge out in the courtyard on warm days, Thomas rarely left the house. Olive read to him and wrote letters on his behalf. Sayre visited weekly, bringing laughter and cheer to the house, albeit forced on his part. His presence uplifted Olive and he always managed to bring a smile to Thomas, no matter how weak he was feeling.

Thomas' valet took care of his personal grooming and Olive was grateful to the man for his devotion as well as his strength. It wasn't necessary to hire additional nursing staff; between the two of them, they were able to take care of all of Thomas' needs.

November brought cold winds and the doctor's pronouncement that Thomas would not likely see the end of the month. Olive wired Leeds and Stewart to return home immediately and sent notes to Lewis and Roswell.

The doctor visited every morning and Olive spent every day and night with Thomas, refusing to leave his side despite the urgings of everyone in the household, including Thomas. She didn't consider it a deathbed vigil; she just wanted every last minute with him.

When he breathed his last on November 14th, it was with Olive, Leeds and Stewart at his side. The three had said their goodbyes to the man they so loved. They wearily held each other in their grief.

The shades were drawn and black bands displayed outside the house. The glum atmosphere suited Olive.

Thomas' funeral was large and overwhelming for Olive. Leeds and Stewart stood by her side throughout the many hours of greeting mourners. Sayre and Thomas' brothers were present through it all; each concerned for Olive while at the same time feeling the weight of their own loss.

It was not possible for either her father or Minnie to attend; the reason for one a glorious addition and the other, a tragic loss.

Minnie had delivered a healthy baby girl, Vivian, and was at home still in confinement.

But, as Thomas lay dying, Belmont had been destroyed by fire. Samuel was not home at the time and, thankfully, no one in the home was injured.

Samuel kept the news from Olive, sending a brief telegram saying they would be unable to attend the funeral. He followed this with a letter, trying as much as possible to soften the news, knowing the vulnerable state Olive was in. Minnie and Duncan had decided to rebuild Belmont and take the home as their own and Samuel focused on these plans to alleviate her distress at the loss of her childhood home. He reassured Olive that he was well, living with Helen in her home in Newcastle.

Reading the letter, Olive was too numb to process the news; feeling exhaustion to her very bones. She put the letter aside to think about later. She spent most days just sitting. Even conversation seemed too much for her.

As Thomas had directed, Lewis put everything in motion from the will, ensuring that Olive would be taken care of and need think of nothing in the coming months. He had requested that his body be interred beside Irene's. Olive understood.

Thomas had suggested that Sayre become Olive's lawyer to keep separation of her interests from those of the estate as a whole. She shared equally in Thomas' estate with the boys and would stay in the house as long as she wished to. None of it brought her comfort. All that she desired was to wake up and find Thomas lying beside her.

She received visits from family and friends but was content to follow society's dictate that social events were curtailed during mourning periods. Life without Thomas was colourless for her and the thought of trying to be charming in a crowd or taking pleasure in light entertainment overwhelmed her. The only outings she managed during the year were weekly church service or strolls around her neighbourhood in fine weather with the many friends who visited.

Kitty was true to her word, visiting frequently now that she and Victor were residents of the city. Lisbeth made regular visits; bringing news of the hospital and many of the people Olive and Thomas had once entertained.

Lewis, as Executor, made regular calls to take care of the bills of the household. These could have been sent to his office but he used the opportunity to watch over Olive, as he had promised Thomas to do.

She also continued to see Henry Sanford on a regular basis; both with and without Kitty. Henry made it a practice to visit weekly, sometimes escorting her to Sunday services.

In August of 1897, Sayre suggested she and the boys accompany him to Alexandria Bay. Although Thomas' summer home had been sold, Sayre's family island offered plenty of room for everyone to spread out. Olive was pleased with the suggestion, anxious to give the boys some lakefront fun again.

The visit was a turning point in everyone's grief. The boys were both mature young men and Sayre, with cautions, allowed them to take out his wooden speed boat; a pleasure to any young man. They reacquainted themselves with summertime friends, bringing stories home to Olive and Sayre each evening.

Olive enjoyed her time on the island; the seclusion amidst the beauty of nature a tonic to her soul and Sayre's company comforting. They were all in lighter spirits and looked healthier for the sunshine they had enjoyed.

The months since Thomas had passed had created a void in Olive's life larger than his absence. She awoke each morning with only herself to dictate the direction for the day. For the first time in many years, no one needed her. She lacked purpose.

After Alexandria Bay, the boys returned to school and Olive was alone in the house once again. The time away had left her with a strong desire now to renew her volunteering at the Babies' Hospital. She returned to her service one day a week and gradually began to re-integrate into life beyond her grief.

As the anniversary of Thomas' death approached, Olive sent for her seamstress and had her wardrobe altered (she had lost considerable weight during the year). She and Lindsell stored her black dresses away. Wearing widow's weeds had reflected her state of mind in grief. The colour had left her world with his passing.

The end of mourning brought changes to her life; Kitty was soon pushing Olive to accompany her on shopping expeditions. She always managed to have the day finish at the Russian Tea Room where everyone went to see or be seen. Olive went along with lively Kitty, understanding her kind motives, but her initial visit to the restaurant brought a little sadness to Olive, remembering her first visit with Eliza Sayre who had passed away following Thomas' death.

With the social season of 1897 in full swing, Sayre had plans for her. After much cajoling in his humorous manner, he was able to coax her out of the house for the occasional opera or musical concert.

But it was a quieter Olive who joined him. Although she had returned to society, her vibrant nature seemed to stay behind. She would smile at Sayre's jokes and jests but didn't return with the witty comments she once would have. She appeared to her friend to be a shadow of the woman she had been.

Henry Sanford looked for any opportunity to spend time with Olive and her return to society presented this. He let her know he was more than happy to escort her to the major social events when she was ready, even saying that it had been Thomas' wish for him to accompany her during his absence in Europe.

"I receive multiple invitations weekly, Olive, and would very much like to attend some of them. I have not been comfortable attending balls or galas alone since losing Nancy and wonder if you and I might support each other through one or two of these events?" Olive agreed and soon the elderly man accompanied by his young neighbour became a common sight to New York society.

Thus, a pattern of life arose. These friends, instrumental to Olive's gradual re-emergence to society, began to see glimmers of the woman they had known.

Chapter 64

With the arrival of spring in 1898, Olive felt restless. She oversaw the spring cleaning in the house, discarding her heavy heart along with the heavy fabrics and dirt. Unable to put her finger on the cause of her disquiet, she just felt bound by the house and her life in the city. With arrangements made for the boys to spend the coming summer break with friends in Alexandria Bay, she didn't even have their return home to look forward to. Time seemed to stretch before her.

She felt overwhelmingly homesick for Belmont and the activity spring always brought to the farm. Even knowing it wasn't possible, she yearned to wake in her old bed with a view of the orchards and the sound of birdsong through her window.

Everyone in New York would soon be moving to escape the city and she would be alone. It suddenly made perfect sense for her to return to Newcastle for the summer. Excited by her decision, Olive wrote her father and Minnie. She would stay with Duncan and Minnie on their farm but was anxious to see the reconstruction of Belmont underway.

With the letters sent, restlessness was replaced with purpose. Lindsell was surprised to hear her humming as she went about her preparations. Going through her summer wardrobe, Olive realized how long it had been since she had purchased a new gown. Her clothing was out of date and, in some cases, in poor condition, despite Lindsell's best efforts. It was time for a refresh.

She sent a note to Kitty inviting her young friend to shop. Kitty was the perfect companion for the excursion; up on the newest styles and dressmakers and possessing a real flair for fashion. The pair spent the day in search of dresses; choosing fabrics, ordering new gowns and purchasing gloves, hats, shoes and other necessities. Olive was lighthearted, excited both with her new purchases and the prospect of her visit home.

Seeing her father the next day, Kitty idly mentioned how much she was going to miss Olive. Henry had not heard of Olive's plans and instantly felt very low at the prospect of not seeing her for several months. The news made him realize that this separation was just the first of many. After all, she was a free agent. '*By God*' he thought. '*I've been an idiot to assume life could continue as it has. She's a beautiful woman and it's only a matter of time before another man makes a move.*'

He had known for some time that he was in love with her but the difference in their ages made him settle for their weekly visits and social outings. This new turn of events changed that; he wanted Olive in his life regardless of the obstacles. He came to a decision he could not have contemplated before; he would ask Olive to marry him.

He had no illusion of keeping up with a woman forty years younger than himself, or that she would want to spend all of her time with him, but he was determined to have her by his side for whatever years remained to him.

He would present it as an arrangement that would suit them both: he would gain a beautiful, vivacious wife to act as hostess and travel companion; she would get the security of marriage to protect her from other men's advances. He knew that marriage to him would also advance her considerably in society but knew this would not be an inducement to her.

He gave great thought to what he believed might persuade her. The proposal would take delicacy and just the right arguments.

First, he thought of how to approach her, quickly realizing it would be unseemly to approach her himself since it was not, in most respects, the usual proposal of marriage. Instead, he would enlist Olive's lawyer and friend, Sayre, to present his terms to her.

Henry was aware of Sayre's inclinations and his affection for Olive. He would include the reassurance that their friendship would continue and felt this would make Sayre support his stand and negotiate in good faith on his behalf. After all, Henry was of an age that attending all of the social events of society held little interest anymore. He envisioned Sayre continuing to act as a very suitable stand-in even after the marriage.

Kitty had said Olive would leaved within the month so he had no time to waste. He pulled a fresh sheet of stationery out and wrote a note requesting Sayre drop by to discuss a business matter.

"I dare say you will be shocked by the purpose of this visit" said Henry to Sayre the following day after putting a glass of brandy in the man's hand.

Above all things, Henry was a realist. He knew Olive would not accept the proposal of a man forty years older than she without sound arguments but he was satisfied that the hours he had spent crafting his points had been worthwhile. He explained them to Sayre.

There would be no talk of love; theirs would be a partnership of friendship and companionship. He would settle $100,000 to ensure her independence.

But Olive was a complex woman. She would not likely accept for money's sake. Henry also understood that she was not the type of woman to do so for social advancement. While Olive's name was published in New York's Social Register, a listing of some 2,000 entitled individuals, Henry was included in Mrs. Astor's 400, the most select social group in the city.

Unlike the other blue bloods on this list, he had achieved his position in thanks to his wealth and support of the many charitable endeavours of the Astors and others like them. In turn, his philanthropy had ensured many profitable contracts for Adams Express. Mrs. Astor might be concerned with one's lineage but it was the men of society and their money that made the world go around.

While marriage to him meant that Olive would be moving in these circles, acceptance by the doyennes of society would not come easily even though her new status as widow had removed the stain divorce had painted her with.

Olive and Thomas had been content to choose their own position in polite society, both because of Thomas' health and the stigma of her divorce. They had no aspirations to mix with blue bloods.

But Henry knew that Olive would rise to this; indeed, she would shine. He had watched as she effortlessly engaged even the most standoffish Society Matron in conversation.

Henry understood her love for Newcastle and her family there. He would propose she buy a home in the village in her own name.

As Henry finished outlining the terms of his proposal, he looked at Sayre and said, "So, was I correct in thinking you are shocked?"

Sayre was at a loss for words but gathered himself to speak. "Surprised, certainly, Sir" he said. "Not that you desire her; I think every man in her life is a little in love with her. But I had thought you felt yourself to be more of a guiding father figure toward her."

"Regardless" continued Sayre, "my views on it have no bearing. Our concern here is how Olive will feel toward the proposal."

Henry, looking relieved, continued. "Rest assured I am fully aware of the age difference. I no longer desire to attend all of the social events of each season. This is where I see your role in my plan."

"I will continue to reserve the best boxes at each theatre and, of course, cover Olive's social and travel expenses. My personal train car will be at her disposal as well. I realize you are a man of means yourself so I don't imply that I am doing something you are not able to. Indeed, your blue blood puts you in an ideal position to escort Olive throughout the season."

"By telling you this, I am letting you know I understand the relationship you two share and this will not change if she and I are wed. I think you know that, should another man come forward with intentions for Olive's hand, the same would not be the case."

Sayre recognized the truth of this. Henry said "I am aware that she loved Thomas deeply. She is not likely to find such love again so why shouldn't she, instead, enjoy a life of comfort and friendship with me, while maintaining the same friendships she has in the past."

"You present a compelling argument, Mr. Sanford" Sayre said. "However, while it seems to consider Olive's best interests as well as my own desires, as I said earlier, it will be up to Olive to decide if this is how she sees her own life unfolding."

"Of course, of course" replied Henry. "I just wanted to reassure you that I had factored your interests in to this."

Sayre took his leave. Walking from the house, he regretted that he had not thought of the idea himself. It was not uncommon for men like himself to marry. The law judged his type harshly and the security of a marriage mitigated this threat. He had certainly missed an opportunity, he realized, but Sanford had enlisted his help and his ethics prohibited him from taking advantage of that.

Besides, he was too set in his ways to suffer the disruption a woman would bring to his household.

Saying so to himself, he then put his efforts to thinking just how he would present Henry's proposal.

Chapter 65

"I read something recently, Olive, and I can't seem to get it out of my mind" said Sayre over tea the following day.

"An elderly man asked a young woman to wed, saying she could do what she wanted, spend what she wanted and he would give her a settlement of money. Ever since reading it, I haven't been able to decide how a woman might feel receiving such a proposal."

"Do you ask a riddle of me, Sayre? Surely you speak of the scene from Vanity Fair and the offer of marriage Old Sir Pitt Crawley gave to the governess, Rebecca Sharp? How often we debated this proposal in the past! But what makes you dwell on it now?" asked Olive.

Surprisingly, Sayre had failed to note this connection to his treasured author, Thackeray. *'My goodness, I am off my game'* he thought.

"Well," replied Sayre, "it so happens that I come with such a proposal in hand for you to consider.

Noting the look of surprise on her face, he continued. "Without identifying the individual, but with all assurances that the man behind the proposal is a gentleman and well thought of in polite society, the offer is a sound one. Although of advanced years, his health remains strong. The arrangement would give you a companion to fully experience life again. I know the restrictions placed on you as a widow hold you back from the life you would have. Under this man's protection, you would be protected from scandal, allowing you to live freely."

"So, on the assurance that this man would treat you with the utmost respect, how do you think you might reply" asked Sayre.

"Oh please, Sayre" said Olive crossly. "You can't really believe I would entertain such a proposal without knowledge of the person making it. Who do you speak for?"

"Oh, my" said Sayre "I'm making a muddle of this aren't I? I don't mean to be cryptic, Olive, only I was at a loss as to how to introduce the topic and thought a general overview might be the ticket. Please don't be cross with me. The gentleman in question is Henry Sanford."

Olive simply stared at Sayre as he continued. "His argument is sound in my mind, Olive, but it rests with you, of course. Let me explain."

As Sayre outlined each of Henry's points, Olive sat blank-faced. Coming to the end, he looked closely to gain some idea of her thoughts.

"Henry reassures me that our friendship would continue as is. He points out, and I agree, that the same could not be said if you were to wed another man."

Olive's thoughts were many and confused. She gave voice to some.

"I do enjoy his company and *would* enjoy the life he could give me but he's seventy-five if he's a day" she said. Her confusion was evident as she continued speaking her thoughts as they came to her.

"Even so, Henry could not be said to be set in his ways. He is often the first to purchase any new invention and is certainly comfortable and at ease amongst young people. His grandchildren adore him and they and their friends enjoy his company."

"Until this moment, I hadn't really given thought to another husband. I realize now how short-sighted that was; suitors will be knocking on the door soon, no doubt. I'm what could be called a 'catch'" she said, sarcastically. "Since I had no intention of marrying again, this proposal, by the sound of it, would give me the independence I wish with the security of a ring. I wouldn't have to worry about the advances of other men."

Looking at Sayre's hopeful face, Olive continued "Now don't presume to think I am decided, but I recognize the merits to the proposal. It goes without saying that I would not countenance such a union if I didn't have some affection for him, which I do, but, for my family's sake, I must also consider how it would look."

"I know you too well, my dear Olive, to believe your prime concern to be about the talk of others when you want something. Could it be you are just looking for someone to validate your decision? I will do so. I can think of no reason for you to say no and will support you if you decide to accept."

"It's much too soon for me to make a decision, Sayre" she replied. "I must have the night and perhaps longer before I can make sense of this. It reassures me that you give your support; I know you would not do so lightly. But, really, this is too big a decision to make without serious consideration."

In fact, Olive spent the remainder of the week doing little else. She wrote the details in her journal, hoping that reading them would bring a decision. She walked the seven blocks to and then around Central Park, with Lindsell following, hoping fresh air and exercise would bring clarity to her thinking. She wrote of her dilemma in a letter to

Minnie but didn't mail it. *'No sense in upsetting anyone until a decision, one way or another, has been made.'* Writing it helped her not a bit in coming to a decision.

Olive spent time weighing the benefits of the alliance against the obvious downside of being tied to a man her father's age, even one as vibrant as Henry. But had she not willingly tied herself to a man with debilitating heart disease?

She thought back to her experience with Henry Winans; a young, attractive man, and how much he had destroyed her soul. She had come a long way from the girl whose head could be turned by looks or charm or youth.

She knew she had been blessed by Thomas' love. The fact that it had lasted just a few short years had her wondering if that was to be the extent of romantic love in her life. She knew many women who never experienced the kind of love she had known with Thomas. Her own parents' marriage, after all, had fallen apart, despite the birth of many children. In fact, Olive was challenged to think of many marriages that had been based on romantic love. Most began from mutual admiration and benefit and had an element of respect rather than romance.

In the end, her decision was based on what she didn't want rather than what she wanted; to be pursued by other men with the intention of marriage. She had no wish to be subjected to this.

To consider any other man was unthinkable; she might find herself tied to another like her first husband. On the other hand, she would never find another love like that which she had shared with Thomas. The alternative, of living alone, was foolhardy for a woman of her time and age.

And, according to Sayre, their friendship would not alter greatly with the marriage.

The thought of entering the social sphere that Henry was part of without an advocate by her side made her grateful for this. Sayre had been born to this society and she trusted him to see her come to no harm.

'I am decided' she thought. *'How strange life is and what roads it takes us on'*.

She penned a short note to Henry Sanford, saying, "Your proposal is thoughtfully accepted."

Henry lost no time once he had Olive's response in hand.

Chapter 66

Henry wrote first to Olive's father. He had met Samuel on several occasions since becoming Olive's neighbour and respected the man greatly. He also understood the concern a man might feel on learning his daughter was to marry someone his own age.

The letter was an explanation of the security he would give Olive. Her life and reputation would be safe under his auspices and their union would bring her a life of ease. He wrote of his plans for their life, including the purchase of a home in Newcastle, which would be her own, where they would spend summers with the Wilmots.

He believed Samuel would not object to the union and was proven correct when he received Samuel's reply. It was clear to Henry that, before Thomas had entered Olive's life, Samuel had been much concerned for her. With his passing, this had resurfaced. He could now lay these concerns to rest. He gave the marriage his blessing.

Henry wrote a more intimate letter to Olive; one he hoped would introduce the tenderness he felt toward her.

Dearest Olive,

I can't tell you how happy you have made me with your acceptance.

I know you are aware how lonely my life has been since I lost Nancy. I've seen the same loneliness in you since Thomas passed. I believe this marriage will benefit us both, although I fully accept it will be a union of mutual respect rather than physical love. I am too old a man to be concerned with the same needs a younger man might have. Your presence in my bed is not required. I am content to have you at my table and in my home and will enjoy your company in our travels together.

I have known you for these three years past; as a happily married woman and as a circumspect widow. I've met and become familiar with your family during their visits here and respect them greatly. You have been a great support to me with Kitty as I try to grandparent alone and my family thinks highly of you. I believe that, despite the difference in our ages, we have become friends.

Although I may be a wealthy man, money doesn't bring me pleasure when there is no one to enjoy it with.

You are aware of my home in Connecticut as well as the home I have here. The Bridgeport house is in a more scenic setting to this city home and I know you enjoy the charms a rural home provides.

I think we could spend the spring and fall there; winter in New York and summer in Newcastle. My rail car will transport us very comfortably, making this travel more agreeable.

Beginning with a tour immediately after we are married, we will make regular trips to the continent – I would enjoy taking you to my favourite sites and restaurants in Paris and London. And I am not too old to appreciate the value a woman places on a wardrobe from Worth. A visit to his atelier will be mandatory whenever we are in Paris, beginning with our honeymoon sojourn.

I hope you will understand that the money I intend to settle on you is not meant to suggest I am buying your acceptance. It is rather to give you independence. With it, you can buy a house in your own name in Newcastle. Other than this one directed purchase, the remainder of the money is yours to use as you wish and will be managed by Sayre on your behalf. In addition to this gift, you will want for nothing as long as we are married.

But I would never want a wife to stay with me for financial reasons. The money I give you is to ensure we both know that we are together because it suits us. If, for any reason, you find the marriage no longer satisfactory, you will have the freedom to return to a single life but to do so independent of everyone.

I make none of these points as means to reinforce your decision; they simply reflect how pleased I am at the prospect of sharing life with you, however many years I have left to me.

Fondly,

Your Henry

Chapter 67

Olive felt awkward the first time Henry called on her after receiving his letter. She blushed on reading the comment about his bed. Although not romantic in nature, their very comfortable friendship had evolved into something quite different and she wasn't at all sure how to behave in this new relationship.

She thought the best thing to do was allow Henry to take the lead. Looking at her, sitting demurely with hands folded in her lap, Henry felt like a schoolboy again. Embarrassed by his emotion, he turned his thoughts to what he was comfortable with; the business side of the marriage.

"With your agreement, I will make all of the arrangements for the wedding ceremony, Olive" he said. "I see no reason to delay so we will plan a day in September after your return from Newcastle. I have taken the liberty of speaking with Rev. Morgan at the Church of the Heavenly Rest and he advises that September 12th is available for a morning ceremony."

"I think we should keep things small but there are a number of people I would include and you must give me a list of those you would like to invite. Your father has been kind enough to suggest he will host the wedding breakfast."

"Please don't feel the need for an elaborate trousseau. We will take care of whatever new gowns you may need in due course. For our wedding tour, I will book cabins on the Kaiser Wilhelm. It's said to be the fastest ship afloat and well appointed. We will begin and end in Paris and include a visit to the House of Worth in our itinerary. The gowns you order there will be ready for final fitting when we are ready to return home two months later."

"In the meantime, perhaps visit your dressmaker and arrange for whatever you might need for the ceremony and travel. These could be made up while you are in Newcastle. Please direct the dressmaker to send all invoices to me."

"I hope this doesn't all seem to be happening too quickly but I would like to know arrangements are in place so that you can enjoy your time with your family without concerns. Please let me know the date you wish to leave for Newcastle. I will make arrangements for my rail car to be available."

"You are very thoughtful, Henry" replied Olive, softly. "I admit I am still in a bit of a fog about it all but can appreciate that there is no reason to delay the wedding. It seems you have thought of everything but you can send a telegram to my sister, Minnie, if anything needs my attention before I return. I plan to remain the better part of the summer. I hope this will not cause inconvenience."

"Not at all" Henry reassured. "I'm sure you are anxious to be back with your family and all will proceed here during the interim. Enjoy the visit. I know I will sleep peacefully in your absence, Olive, knowing that soon I need never be far from you."

Standing, Henry took Olive's hands in his own. "I fully understand your position in this union, my dear. This will be a marriage of convenience; a business partnership, if you will, although I believe I am the partner with the most to gain."

At Grand Central Station the following week, a porter led Olive and Lindsell toward Henry's private rail car. Climbing aboard, they were met by his personal porter who took her outer clothing to hang in the coat closet. He explained that his sole responsibility was for her comfort and guided her on a tour.

The car included a luxurious bedroom at one end; a comfortable sitting area with filled book shelves and a desk stocked with personalized stationery; dining area complete with china cabinets and a table that could seat four comfortably; even a bathroom finished in marble. The rear of the car held a small kitchen, a staff water closet and accommodations; two separate rooms each equipped with pull down bunks, small dresser, and wash stands.

As Lindsell unpacked Olive's travel case, Olive walked the car in wonder. She had known Henry was a wealthy man but had never given thought to how this was reflected in the life he led. The reality of the path she was about to embark upon left her speechless.

Henry, meanwhile, wasted no time in reaching out to his son, asking him to come into the city. He knew Kitty was already a supporter of Olive but this news would no doubt astound her father, he was sure.

With no inclination of the purpose of the summons, Simon looked forward to a visit with his father who he hadn't seen in some time. As he and Simon sat to dinner together, Henry said "I have momentous

news, son. I will be marrying my widow neighbour, Olive Burchard, in September."

Simon's jaw literally dropped. What foolishness was this? He had met Olive, of course, on several occasions and understood the friendship between his father and her. But he also knew of the 40-year difference in their ages.

"Have you lost your mind, Dad?" he only just managed to get out. "Clearly, the woman is after your money, not content with what her poor departed husband has left her. Why else would a woman of her age want to be tied to a man of your years?" Simon said hurtfully.

"I did the asking" stated Henry through clenched teeth. He had expected push back from his son but was unprepared for Simon's vitriolic reaction. "I will have you know, son, that I bring more to a marriage than money. Mrs. Burchard's needs in life happen to align with my own and this partnership will suit both of us very well."

"Believe what you will, Dad, I don't judge her motives to be anything other than about your money. I don't know what pixie dust she has sprinkled over you but trust me: if she stands to inherit from your will, I will contest it."

Henry was shocked to hear his son threaten him but was even more hurt by the opinion his son held of him. *'If you think I am so old and decrepit that I am beyond managing my own life, you have much to learn'* he thought.

"Simon, this marriage is going ahead, with or without your agreement. I suggest you spend some time getting to know Mrs. Burchard before you write her off as an opportunist. For now, I will ignore your remarks, understanding they come from a place of shock. I expect nothing from you other than your acquiescence. This continues to be my life and I will direct its course until my last breath, which I will take with Olive."

For the first time in their memories, father and son parted acrimoniously.

Chapter 68

As Rev. Morgan said the blessing, Olive reflected on what she had agreed to with her "I do". The innocent, doe-like eyes that looked on Harry Winans during her first marriage vows were gone; life had given her lenses of clarity and wisdom.

She was comfortable with her decision. She knew Henry had turned 75 in January but thought his looks were those of a man a decade younger. He had a full head of hair, albeit gray, and his features remained handsome.

'He has the look of a statesman' she thought. *'I will never allow his age to make me feel self-conscious by his side. Why should I not feel pride that such a man wants me to share his home and life?"*

The guests who knew Henry well smiled to see the look on his face as the pair turned to face them. Those on Olive's side had been surprised by her decision but knew her to be sensible and supported her in it. She was particularly grateful for the presence of Thomas' brothers, Lewis with his wife, and Roswell. After accepting Henry's proposal, she had met with both to explain her reasons and they were quick to give their support. They both knew Olive would be actively pursued and worried for her. Their presence at the wedding reassured her that they held no ill feeling about her remarriage.

With another ceremony scheduled on the heels of theirs, the bride and groom wasted no time greeting everyone at the back of the church; instead heading directly out to the waiting carriage to go the few blocks to the Hotel Buckingham. Samuel, true to his promise, had made all arrangements for the wedding party breakfast. Other carriages pulled up to transport the guests and all were soon toasting the bride and groom.

Olive's guest list had been small; in addition to Thomas' brothers; her father; her sister, Helen; and, of course, Sayre.

Henry's guest list was somewhat larger and included Kitty and her husband, Victor; Victor's parents; Henry's grandson, Henry Jr.; and many friends and business associates. Kitty made it clear she was there as much for Olive as her grandfather. She was delighted that her grandfather had the courage to propose to this woman who she was so fond of, despite the difference in their ages.

The same could not be said of Kitty's father, Simon; the one member of Henry's family not in attendance. Henry understood his decision to wed Olive was a difficult one for Simon to accept. '*Time will soften him' he* thought, reading the note of regret Simon had sent before the wedding and letting it go.

Simon was perplexed as to how this situation differed from Robert Peel in his pursuit of Kitty. His father had been enraged by the prospect of the man, through Kitty, getting his hands on Henry's money and yet here he was; offering it to this woman on a platter.

He was angry with his father for so many reasons. Simon had never doubted that his own children would be the sole inheritors of Henry's large estate but was certain this new strumpet changed all that. Had his father entered senility, he wondered. He couldn't even begin to think about how this marriage would look to New York society!

Angered by Simon's reaction, Henry had not enlightened his son on the arrangements of the marriage. Simon didn't give his father the credit he deserved: Henry always took care of business first. This marriage was no different. Although she would live well while they were married, Henry had updated his will prior to the wedding. His gift to Olive of $100,000 was with the knowledge that, other than a small bequest and the home they shared, she would inherit little more. If she decided to walk away before Henry's death, she would receive no alimony. The agreement she had signed made certain of this. He might be a smitten old man but he was no fool.

With speeches and toasts made, Henry and Olive made their way around the room to say personal goodbyes.

"You'll have to find yourself another escort for this season, Sayre" she said, approaching her friend "at least until Thanksgiving. We'll return in time to organize a dinner so I trust you will keep your plans open. You must join us."

It felt strange to Olive to be returning to Henry's house with him, rather than her own just across the street.

"This is your home now, Olive" he said as he opened the door. "Mrs. Palmer will take you to your room. Your personal items and clothing were brought over and I believe Lindsell has been putting things in place for you. I have some work to do since we leave early tomorrow. I thought with the early departure, that we would have an early supper and night. I will be in the drawing room for 6:30."

As Henry surmised, Olive found Lindsell in her room putting things away. Olive said "Imagine moving right across the road, Lindsell. Did you ever think your mistress would live a life full of such twists and turns when you accepted this position?"

"Not a bit, Ma'am" Lindsell replied, helping Olive out of her wedding dress and tight stays and into her dressing gown. "It's been an adventure and looks to be even more of one with Mr. Sanford."

"I think you are right" muttered Olive, closing her eyes for a much-needed nap.

Chapter 69

The ship was true to its promise and the crossing a swift one. In the short time they shared aboard, Olive saw little change in her life with Henry, other than the close proximity they now shared. He remained the dear friend she had known prior to the marriage.

There had been no awkwardness in their interactions as husband and wife; Henry had seen to that. Always courteous; he knocked before entering her rooms, ensuring he never caught her less than fully dressed. At the end of each day, he saw her to her room, kissed her on the cheek and wished her a good night before heading to his own adjoining suite.

Once docked, they were soon on their way to Paris and the promised visit to the House of Worth. She was discomfited initially when Henry settled in to watch, glass of champagne in hand. "Isn't there something you would rather be doing elsewhere, Henry" she asked. She had never known a man to take such interest in a woman's attire.

"Not at all, my dear" he replied. "Other than reading newspapers several days old, I have little to do. I am most comfortable." In truth, he looked forward to seeing the pleasure he knew this experience would give her.

He wasn't disappointed. Olive felt like a princess as the house designer guided her in the choice of fabrics and styles for the gowns she would need for the coming seasons. As each new style was presented, she looked with wonder at the design. When she was uncertain about choice or obvious expense of a gown, she would look questioningly at Henry and discovered he had exquisite taste in women's fashion and clearly no concerns over expense. Each time he was consulted, his suggestions pleased the Worth employees.

When it was all over, Olive had ordered several ball gowns and enough day and evening dresses to last a lifetime, she thought. By the end of the day, she was exhausted but overjoyed by such indulgence.

Henry had enjoyed himself immensely. Leaving a substantial deposit, He thought *'a small price to bring such pleasure.'*

As they proceeded on their tour, Olive found herself enjoying their time abroad. She had known Henry to be an entertaining man but was pleased to learn what a curious mind he had. He often pulled

them in directions away from the packaged dialogue the tour guides were presenting because he was intrigued by something.

They visited his favourite sites in each country and explored several new ones although he was quick to leave if he felt targeted as a tourist. He had no time for the tourist traps which had sprung up around the continent to take advantage of the increase in travelers from the US. He had learned much in his youth from P.T. Barnum about theatrics in exhibits and knew instinctively when he was being taking advantage of.

Olive was also surprised by his vigor; he never tired from the walking required. Sometimes she had trouble keeping up and appreciated the irony of a man of his age having more energy than the much younger Thomas. She found his mind, too, to be just as active; the history or geography of every new discovery was researched extensively.

Henry proved to be equally interested in the arts, arranging tickets for the opera in Italy and the Folies Bergere in France. Olive found the latter slightly shocking but determined to hide her provincial attitude from her sophisticated husband. Thanks to his son Simon's influence and lifetime career in music, Henry's knowledge of the classic composers was vast. He made certain they attended concerts in whatever city they were in.

Throughout their trip, Henry showed an appreciation for the finer things in life. The restaurants they visited were superb in food and service; the hotels they stayed in luxurious. Olive was relieved to discover that her husband did not behave in the manner that had given travelling Americans a reputation; he was neither pushy nor loud and treated the staff everywhere with respect. As a result, the pair was looked after with great care.

Henry set a leisurely pace for their days. Knocking on her door at a pre-arranged time each morning, the two began the day with breakfast together, sometimes in the dining room and other days in her suite. She found herself enjoying this time with Henry, discussing and looking forward to the plans for the day.

Olive listened intently when Henry spoke; he was a brilliant conversationalist and had a breadth of knowledge that surpassed anyone she had ever known. With each day that passed, her admiration for her new husband grew.

It was inevitable that people they encountered along the way assumed them to be father and daughter. Olive was indignant each time they experienced this confusion. Her fondness for her husband was evident as she would state that she was Mrs. Henry Sanford. Henry had expected this reaction from the public and was not disturbed by the assumptions but found her reaction amusing.

The Olive who returned to the House of Worth was much different than the newly wed woman who had previously visited. A self-assured, elegant woman stood for her final fittings. But inside her still beat the heart of a young girl; it raced as she tried on one beautiful gown after another.

Looking in the mirror, she came to terms with the new Olive. Seeing Henry waiting for her in the salon, Olive came to a standstill. With new understanding, she knew it wasn't the elegant gowns or luxurious life she was living that had changed her. It was this extraordinary man who she never tired of listening to and spending time with.

She loved this man. Although both were content that their relationship would never be intimate, their marriage of convenience had become a true marriage of two harmonious souls.

Taking Henry's arm, Olive smiled up at him and said, "Let's go home, Husband."

Chapter 70

Sayre was bewildered by the woman who welcomed him that Thanksgiving. During the two months that had elapsed since he said goodbye to her, she had transformed into the confident, stylish vision who greeted him.

'What has happened to you, Olive' he thought. How had the sweet, irreverent friend he had known become this exquisite woman in so short a time? It wasn't until they had a moment alone that Sayre knew he hadn't lost his lovely friend; she had merely been repackaged and in such an elegant way.

Olive was anxious to tell Sayre all about life with Henry but thought this was best kept until they were alone. Besides, her duties as hostess required her to attend to all of their guests so their conversation would have to wait.

The guests for Henry and Olive's first Thanksgiving together were an intimate, lively group; all family other than Sayre. Olive was happy to see everyone; Kitty and Victor, Henry Jr. and his date, her Uncle John and niece, Eileen, visiting from Toronto. Henry's son, Simon, would have evened out the numbers but he had, once again, sent his regrets.

As the evening progressed, Kitty was surprised to see real affection between her grandfather and Olive. Like everyone, she knew this to be a marriage of convenience. She was enough of a woman of the world to understand that money must have been involved. This hadn't upset her; if it meant her good friend and her beloved grandfather sharing a life when both were clearly lonely and fond of each other. *'But, my goodness'* she thought. *'It seems the fondness was stronger than I realized.'*

Kitty hadn't seen her grandfather looking so vigorous in years. Olive laughed with him as he remembered the antics of their trip, correcting him occasionally as a wife of many years might. Watching them smile at one another lightened Kitty's heart. *'Good on you, Grandfather'* she thought. *'A beautiful, young woman is infatuated with you. I applaud you.'*

The youngest person at the dinner party, Olive's niece Eileen, was the couple's first houseguest. At Olive's wedding, her sister Helen had said that Eileen had no prospect of a match and she wondered if Olive

might consider having her for a visit sometime. Perhaps a suitable suitor might be found amongst the young men she could meet in New York (Olive understood Helen to be implying that it had worked for her, after all).

Helen's request was timely; at the wedding, Olive was still feeling unsettled about what to expect of life alone with Henry. She agreed readily, suggesting Eileen plan to visit once she and Henry returned from their trip abroad. This would give them little time alone together and Olive thought the distraction of a young person in the house would help any awkwardness she might feel. Looking at her niece on this evening, Olive couldn't imagine what had made her nervous but she was glad of the girl's company, all the same.

Eileen had arrived within a few days of their return and was meeting Henry's grandchildren for the first time that evening. Kitty was delighted with the young girl and, before dinner, the two sat together sipping champagne and getting to know one another. Eileen didn't know which impressed her more; her incredibly elegant aunt, the vivacious Kitty or drinking champagne.

"I have a grand idea" announced Kitty as her soup was replaced by the fish course. "Victor and I will host a party in Eileen's honour? We'll invite all of the young men from Victor's firm. They're so busy with their careers right now that most remain single. I have several as yet unmarried friends I could invite, too. It could be one giant match making evening. Wouldn't it be lovely, Eileen, if we found you a husband here in New York?"

Eileen blushed deeply but was secretly excited by the idea. She thought Kitty spirited and fun and was thrilled to have her attention. In the few days she had been with her sophisticated Aunt, she had decided that life in New York far exceeded the one she led in Toronto and Newcastle.

Since she had arrived as the season was getting underway, plans included the opera, theatre and musical evenings. Olive had taken one look at Eileen's clothes and called for a seamstress to alter some of her own older gowns. It wouldn't do to have her niece looking provincial when she herself was wearing the height of fashion.

Preparing for the first evening out, Olive stood back and surveyed her niece in the newly fitted gown. "Not bad but I think we can do better. Let me see what I can find here" she said, poking about in her

extensive jewellery collection. "Oh, here are just the things. These earrings beautifully set off that hair style Lindsell has given you." Putting the earrings on each of Eileen's ears, Olive smiled happily.

She loved having the company of her young niece and dressing her up felt just as good as dressing her dolls had when she was young.

Henry, at the bottom of the stairs, smiled broadly as the two descended together. "Aren't I the lucky fellow to take two such beautiful women to the opera" he said.

Eileen felt like a princess but an outfit doesn't change the inner girl. She was nervous as the trio stepped into the carriage for the short journey to the theatre. Olive, feeling her trembling beside her, said "I don't know if you know this, Eileen, but this is my first evening in Mr. Sanford's box since our wedding. I'm quite nervous about meeting everyone and knowing what to do. You will stay close to me, won't you?"

Eileen would never have imagined her vivacious aunt being nervous about anything; she always seemed so composed.

"I will, Aunt Olive" she replied, linking her arm through her aunt's. Olive's words had accomplished what she had hoped to; calming her young niece so that she might enjoy the evening.

The names of people introduced to her meant nothing to Eileen. Had she recognized them, she likely would have been beside herself with nerves. The couples she met included the Morgan's, Roosevelt's and Vanderbilt's, all of whom had been instrumental in the opening of the new Metropolitan and who hadn't missed an opening evening since 1883.

The remainder of Eileen's visit with Henry and Olive was magical to the young girl, filled as it was with shopping, theatre and after theatre suppers at elegant restaurants. The employees at Tiffany's greeted her aunt by name each time they visited the store.

Kitty's party was a hit amongst her crowd but unfortunately did little for Eileen. While not unattractive, her looks didn't stand out. She also lacked the wit and polish of the young people of New York society who were underwhelmed by her. With limited conversation skills and little life experience, she was no match for the lively conversation of New York's younger set.

It wasn't surprising that no young man appeared taken with Eileen during her month long stay. Although Eileen was disappointed,

she left New York with some lovely gowns, minor jewels and stories galore about her incredible visit and Aunt Olive's glamorous life in the city. She left no detail out, including the frequency of visits by her Aunt Olive's charming friend, Mr. Sayre Van Duzer.

Olive may have been unable to find a match for her niece, but the visit served to re-ignite her unfulfilled maternal instincts. She had enjoyed having a young girl in the house, buying her gifts and taking her around the city.

Olive's life with Henry was rich, in both experience and money. He loved to surprise her with gifts and little boxes from Tiffany's were frequently delivered. Henry did attend many of the events that season, pride over his new wife evident as he introduced her to everyone they met. Many commented on how marriage seemed to have renewed Henry. Men were overheard commenting on Olive's beauty and that they weren't surprised to see Henry looking younger.

It wasn't just Henry who was rejuvenated by marriage; Olive, too, was feeling a new zest for life. As she explained to Sayre during his first visit after their Thanksgiving dinner party, she was surprised she was able to enjoy life again after losing Thomas.

"Henry is a most fascinating man, Sayre. Every day we have engaging conversations. I know I will never know the love I had with Thomas but this life with Henry feels like more than I deserve. I'm not sure why he chose me to share his remaining years but I am ever so grateful he did. You can't imagine the fun we're having together."

Sayre knew his friend wasn't being coy; her humility really was surprising considering the beauty and grace she presented. He loved his cousin's widow deeply in his special way but knew that every man's gaze was drawn to her as she passed. Olive seemed not to notice the attention paid to her by other men, her attention all toward her husband and the life they shared. He knew she deserved such a life and was just pleased at the small part he had played in the turn of events.

Chapter 71

In January of 1899, Olive received a letter from Minnie. She and Duncan were hosting a house warming at the newly completed Belmont, rebuilt as a smaller version of the original home which had burned down. Olive was unable to get back to Newcastle to attend but ordered enough flowers to fill the main floor of Belmont.

Delivered by train from a Toronto florist, guests were awed by the quality and quantity of blossoms. Newcastle might be far away from New York City but this grand gesture kept villagers conjecturing for weeks about just how much money Olive must have spent. During her rare previous visits home, she had arrived without fanfare, stayed close to Belmont and left just as quietly, giving no small details to share about her. Villagers also got no information from the members of the family. The Wilmots were close mouthed when asked about Olive.

Writing to Olive afterward, Minnie filled her in on the party details. She had been overjoyed by the flowers which brought a truly festive air to the house in the middle of winter. She also said how distinguished their father had looked in his tails. Although he was frail, he managed to stay at the party until 3:00 am.

Unfortunately, only a few months later, as the New York season was coming to a close, Minnie wrote again to say that their father was not well. The winter had been harsh and Samuel had contracted pneumonia. Henry decided it was time for Olive to look for a house in Newcastle and a visit would give them time to spend with Samuel.

Minnie had also written that the Massey family was looking to sell their Newcastle home, 'Chestayne'. Olive was familiar with the house and thought, with modifications, it would be suitable. Discussions with the Masseys were begun by telegram and Sayre traveled to Toronto to take care of the purchase of the furnished house.

News of the transaction, in Olive's name only, was public and stirred curiosity but it was the arrival of Henry and Olive in his private railroad car that really set tongues going in the village. Olive's trip in the fancy rail car before her wedding had stunned the locals but it left immediately for the return trip to the city. Those who hadn't seen it could only hear of it second-hand.

With this trip, the train stayed on the Newcastle tracks. Hearing of it, everyone made their way to the station at some point to see with their own eyes. They now all knew how wealthy Olive's husband was. But he was also *old*!

Talk began immediately, soon making its way throughout the village, embellished with each telling. The stories had little basis in reality but fed a population starved for news to brighten their dull lives. Lack of real information did nothing to stop the gossip.

"Who is she to have a lady's maid, I ask" said the station master's wife over tea with a friend. Along with tea, this lady served up most news of the arrival to all who listened.

"Did you see the age of her husband?" asked one matriarch to another. "Yes, he's her father's age at the very least. There can be only one reason for a young woman to marry such a man and I think the railway car tells the story."

Olive was oblivious to the talk up and down the main streets and in farmhouse kitchens as she and Henry joined Minnie and Duncan at Belmont. Once the pair was settled, Duncan made his carriage available for Olive to travel the short drive to the village to her sister Helen's house where their father now lived. She was distressed to see how weak he was and remained with him for the better part of the day.

As previously agreed, Henry arrived late afternoon to pay his respects and to escort her to Chestayne, around the corner, to meet with a local contractor. The excitement she might have felt over this home was overshadowed by her concern for her father. Henry understood and made suggestions for the necessary changes for the house to suit them.

He chose a large bedroom overlooking the gardens at the front of the house for Olive. A sitting room immediately below would be hers alone and Henry suggested that the addition of a privy stairway directly from her bedroom would allow her private access to this room. He chose a suite at the back of the house for himself, away from the noise and bustle of the main street. Three other bedrooms would serve as guest rooms.

Renovations would convert smaller existing bedrooms into private washrooms attached to Olive and Henry's rooms as well as a main one for guests. An addition to the rear of the house would provide a trunk room for storage of luggage; an enlargement to the

kitchen and dining room on the main floor and additional servants' rooms above. Although the upkeep of the house would be handled by local day staff, Olive and Henry and their guests would travel with servants who would need to be accommodated.

The furniture would suffice, Henry decided, until Olive could visit furniture makers in Toronto or New York for pieces that suited her more.

The contractor agreed to draw up the plans and send a set to Sayre, who would coordinate all payments and stay on top of the scheduling. He would make regular visits to Newcastle to oversee but it was left in the contractor's hands to hire the necessary tradesmen.

Henry had given Sayre instructions to keep the contractor's hand well greased to keep work moving quickly. He and Olive wanted to return at the end of the summer to spend two months and wanted the majority of work completed by then. They had no plans to host guests during their first season in the house so renovations for guest accommodation could be continued after their stay, through the coming winter.

With all arrangements in place, Olive focused on her father, visiting him daily. As his condition worsened, Henry arranged for a doctor to come from Toronto by train to see Samuel but there was little that could be done. On May 17th, he breathed his last. Olive was doubly grieved when she received a telegram telling the family that her Uncle John had passed away in New York in the same hour as his brother Samuel in Newcastle.

"It's the end of an era with both of them gone" said Duncan as the four sat in Belmont's parlour following the funeral service. "At least they lived to a good old age and led productive lives." Minnie looked over at him sternly, knowing that Henry was near the age her father had been.

Chapter 72

"My husband is doing plaster work at Chestayne. Did you know Olive plans to have a private sitting room with her own staircase directly from her bedroom? Why would she need privacy, I ask you?"

"My son is painting at Chestayne. Can you imagine – Olive is having her bedroom painted pink! Now who would do that when plain white would do just fine?"

"My brother is a carpenter at Chestayne. Did you know she's having a room added just to hold luggage? Something called a *Trunk* room! Honestly, who does she think will visit – the Queen of England?"

"Did you hear that Olive was up here with that young man of hers again? No sign of her husband, I might add."

"I did. One can only imagine the goings on at that house."

Everything that was happening in Olive's life, after years of absence and too little actual information, made the locals question her character. No one had forgotten the young man she had once married or the fact that his whereabouts remained unknown. With that marriage, and her subsequent (questionable) divorce, still very much in everyone's minds, they asked each other 'What had she done since to be living the life she was now?'

The frequent visits of Sayre to oversee the construction added unnecessary fuel to the spreading gossip. Who he was and how he had such involvement in Olive's life were the questions everyone wanted answered.

Chapter 73

In the spring of 1900, Olive read of a new festival taking place in Alexandria Bay. Henry noted her sad expression as she put the paper aside. Olive had worn her grief for her father heavily throughout the past year and Henry couldn't bear to see her unhappiness. He continually looked for opportunities to brighten her spirits but trinkets from Tiffany's didn't seem to do much.

"What is it, my Dear?" he asked.

"Nothing really, Henry. I see that Alexandria Bay is hosting a new festival in June and it just reminded me of the happy times I spent there with Thomas and the boys. It was one place we could almost forget about his illness and just enjoy our time together."

Henry recognized just the opportunity to make her happy.

"Invite the boys to the festival, Olive" he said. "We can travel together as far as Alexandria Bay and I'll continue up to Newcastle. I'm anxious to see the progress on the house. When the festival is over, the train will return for you to join me."

"Once you've determined that the plan works with the boys' school schedule, Olive, I'll book rooms at The Thousand Island House for the three of you."

As always, Henry's generosity of thought and money overwhelmed Olive. What had she done to deserve this life with such a kind man? She kissed him warmly on the forehead as she passed him on her way to her writing desk.

She had maintained visits with Thomas' sons, Leeds and Stewart, when they visited the city during school holidays. With her marriage to Henry, she had no need of the house she had shared with Thomas and the boys. As Executor and Guardian, Lewis had sold the home and moved the boys into his own home.

True to his pre-marriage agreement, Henry ensured that Olive's social calendar in New York was full. Boxes at the opera and symphony and exclusive boxes for Olive for the charity balls every season. Sayre was always one of her guests but she also included Leeds and Stewart whenever they were in town and their schedules allowed. They looked forward to time spent with their stepmother and she was pleased to see them growing into young men she knew Thomas would be proud of.

The boys were very happy to receive her invitation to Alexandria Bay and the three enjoyed their stay at Thousand Island House, sharing happy times with old summer friends. Sayre decided to travel with the group, although he stayed at his family's island home. He would continue on to Newcastle with Olive to take care of some of the renovation details.

Sayre was now considered more family than friend by both Henry and Olive and they worried little about appearances. Enough time had passed since her divorce, and enough money spent by Henry to secure her status in the social circles Henry moved in.

Although Sayre was extremely cautious in his lifestyle, New York society accepted what seemed evident and no one raised an eyebrow seeing the two of them together, with or without Henry.

But Olive committed the sin of assuming that what New York accepted, Newcastle would also. She neglected to consider how jealousy and a thirst for news fuelled gossip.

She hadn't reckoned on the minds in Newcastle. Despite the presence of Lindsell and knowing Henry was already in Newcastle, the sight of Sayre helping Olive down from the train car had answered the questions on everyone's lips about who Sayre was: clearly, he was her lover.

The eyes that followed their movements saw only what appearances made true in their own minds; an unmarried man and woman had just travelled together on a railcar with a bedroom. Honestly, how much more evidence was required before it would be evident to all just what Olive was up to?

He was the man most often seen in town, on Olive's behalf. He was her lawyer but his knowledge of her likes and dislikes screamed that he was much more.

As ever, Olive didn't care about gossip. It had no effect on her. She always behaved as a lady should but a lifetime of being the subject of talk had ultimately made her unconcerned about what was said. She went about her business in the village without thought of it, believing that, eventually, something else would replace her as the topic du jour.

Chapter 74

Arriving at Chestayne, Olive was pleased with the progress of renovations. Henry greeted her warmly, letting her and Sayre know the cook had prepared a late dinner for the three of them after they'd had a chance to settle in.

Lindsell was emptying her trunk when Olive entered her suite. Watching her, Olive said, "Strange not to have Papa around the corner, Lindsell. I'm not sure I will ever enjoy this house as much as Henry had hoped now that he is gone. I will just have to set about creating new memories with Henry, I suppose."

At dinner that evening, Olive expressed her gratitude to Henry for the Alexandria Bay stay. She spoke fondly of the boys and how much she had enjoyed reliving some of the lakeside life she had once known with them.

But her pleasure over the memories quickly turned to sadness. "I know these times are coming to an end" she said. "The boys are growing up so quickly and college and other commitments will soon limit the time we can spend together. They are as close as I will ever come to being a mother in this lifetime."

Henry was well aware of Olive's disappointment over her lack of children. He wondered at fate leaving this woman out of the motherhood equation when she so clearly would have made an excellent one. But he knew the presence of children would cheer her and suggested they invite Kitty and her young son for a visit. They hadn't planned on guests while renovations continued on the house but Kitty wasn't a guest; she was family.

"Oh Henry, how wise you are. A visit is just what I need and the baby will certainly brighten this place up. I'll get a note off to her tomorrow. You can make arrangements for the railway car to travel back down to pick them up."

"Sayre," Olive said, turning to her friend, "we have more than enough room for Kitty and the nanny and the baby if you decide to stay longer or you could take advantage of the train returning if you need to get back to New York earlier."

Henry's relationship with his granddaughter had been strained following the breakdown of Kitty's marriage. She left Victor soon after Olive and Henry returned from their honeymoon, running away with

Victor's best man. Although it was a scandal at the time, the pair wed as soon as a divorce from Victor was granted.

Henry had been devastated by Kitty's actions at the time but Olive was eventually able to help him see that Kitty's marriage to Victor, arranged by Henry, was doomed to fail since she had still been in love with Robert Peel. Her argument, that they should all be happy that Kitty had chosen a man she loved with this marriage, finally prevailed.

Even while championing the young woman she so adored, society's attitude toward Kitty's divorce and her own, less than a decade earlier, didn't escape Olive. It may have been Kitty's status as a young heiress in New York which had made it easier for society to overlook the scandal, or perhaps the example set by Alva Vanderbilt. Olive preferred to hope that society mores were changing.

Kitty's life with her new husband, Sheffield, seemed happy. Henry was just relieved that his only grandson had been young when his parents separated and he appeared to be relatively unscathed by the trauma.

Henry listened fondly to Olive's plans. She really was easy to please and he, too, would benefit from Kitty's laughter. In spite of his disappointment in her, she was such a bright light to have around. And his boy ... although not one to admire children generally, Henry admitted the joy he felt to have a great-grandson named after him, and such a clever one, at that.

Chapter 75

Life revolved around the seasonal movement from house to house but Olive particularly enjoyed the relaxed weeks in Newcastle each summer. The days were filled with easy pursuits, family and laughter.

The following year, 1901, as they prepared to move their household from Bridgeport to Newcastle, Olive sent a telegram to Minnie: "Please meet Miss Lucy at the train and see that she is made comfortable at Chestayne until our arrival."

Minnie had no idea who Miss Lucy was but presumed she was some elderly matriarch friend of Henry's who Olive wished to impress. On the day in question, she had Duncan dress in his finest and set off in their carriage to meet the train. When Duncan returned to Belmont later, Minnie was curious to know more about Miss Lucy.

"Oh, I made sure she is comfortable," said Duncan. "She has fresh hay and water and looked none the worse for her journey although she seemed a little surprised that I was so well dressed for her arrival."

"What foolishness are you talking?" Minnie asked, thinking Duncan had lost his mind.

"Miss Lucy has four legs" replied Duncan with a grin. "Olive didn't mention that she is a milk cow?"

News of the 'Miss Lucy' incident spread quickly throughout the various Wilmot households, soon becoming family legend.

Minnie welcomed Olive's visits each summer. The sisters visited one another easily, something they had both missed through the years. Olive was godmother to Minnie's two girls and both spent time in New York City with their favourite aunt.

Henry attended fewer events in the city with each passing year. She and Henry entertained occasionally but the majority of her entertainment was outside their home. Sayre could always be counted on to accompany her.

Henry might not attend but he still loved to hear about her evenings out. He sat at Olive's bedside the following day as she enjoyed her breakfast and chattered away about the previous evening. Henry would throw in his own insights as she mentioned other attendees or the music or performers. Henry enjoyed Olive's gift for description and mimicry and would laugh as she imitated society

matrons, although she only ridiculed those small-minded women who snubbed her or tried to make her feel inferior.

Their life was contented until the winter of 1903 when Henry developed a cold which soon turned to pneumonia. Remembering her father's illness, Olive fussed over him. Henry recovered but was weakened.

They were all dismayed when he was stricken again in May. They usually spent late spring in Bridgeport but Henry's doctor suggested they move to Chestayne instead. New thinking on the treatment of pneumonia believed that clear, fresh air aided the lungs.

Sayre would join them after a few days. Henry's doctor and a nurse would travel to Newcastle with the couple. Once the doctor had seen to Henry's care, he would return to New York, leaving Henry in the nurse's care. Olive had protested this, knowing herself perfectly capable to taking care of her husband, but the doctor was adamant.

The group arrived at Newcastle station on a cool June afternoon. The temperatures were unseasonably cool for the month but the doctor felt this was better for Henry.

The stationmaster was alarmed to see Henry's valet and a man he didn't recognize helping the frail man down the train steps, followed quickly by a nurse in uniform and Olive. He would report later to his wife that he didn't think the old man had much time left on this earth, if his appearance was any indication. The shock he would eventually feel on learning that it was Mrs. Sanford who died would last some time.

With Henry settled, Olive sat in her morning room feeling alone despite the presence of Henry upstairs. Before returning to the train station for his return to the city, Henry's doctor had briefed her on his condition. Chills swept over her as the man made it clear Henry was not likely to survive through the summer, based on the state of his lungs. The nurse would see that Henry had fresh air and bed rest.

"It isn't called the Old Man's disease for nothing, Mrs. Sanford" he said, shaking his head. "We, in the medical profession, are powerless against it once it strikes. All that we can do is hope that the patient's physical strength can withstand the assault on his body".

"I know of no other man of Henry's age with his strength, stamina and will" replied Olive. "If anyone can survive this, it will be Henry".

Chapter 76

Sayre couldn't arrive soon enough for Olive. She spent the days alternately reading to Henry when he was awake and pacing the house. Even Mrs. Thomson was becoming concerned for her state of mind; she had never seen her employer so out of sorts.

Sayre's arrival calmed her somewhat but she was still in a state of anxiety. As Sayre listened to Olive relate the doctor's report, he became equally concerned; but for Olive as much as Henry.

"It sounds like Dr. Brown doesn't hold much hope that Henry will recover, Olive" Sayre said. "I agree, he has always been a vigorous man for his advanced years but very few elderly people can survive pneumonia."

"I think we should think about what you will do when Henry is gone, Olive" Sayre continued. "I'm speaking as your lawyer, now; not just your friend."

"We both know what Henry has stipulated in his will. He will provide a small annual allowance but little else because of his generous gifts when you married. You own Chestayne and will inherit the New York house but your allowance will not cover your expenses for both houses."

"I can appreciate that you want to keep this house to be near your family but this is not suitable during the winter months. I think we should put it on the market now. We should discuss whether to keep Henry here or return to Bridgeport for him to pass away close to his children and grandchildren."

Sayre looked into the fire, standing with a foot on the mantle. He reached for the fire poker to stoke the flame. It was a cool June and because the house lacked insulation, he was questioning the wisdom of bringing Henry to Chestayne under these conditions, unaware of the doctor's orders for fresh, cool air.

"This fire shows how badly insulated this home is, Olive." said Sayre, stirring the flames as he spoke. "We've had expressions of interest in the property from several business owners in the area and I think we should take advantage of this interest to get you set up to be comfortable without Henry. You have a full life in the city."

With his back to Olive, Sayre hadn't seen her reaction to his words and was surprised when she suddenly appeared at his side.

"I will not have you speak so, Sayre" said Olive heatedly. "Henry will recover; I have no doubt. He is the strongest man of his age that I know and I will not have you bringing bad luck to us with your words."

"Be reasonable, Olive" Sayre said louder than he intended.

"Stop" shouted Olive. "I'm not going to stand here and listen to you foretell Henry's death."

As she finished speaking, Sayre felt Olive start to collapse beside him. He turned to her, attempting to put out a protective hand to break her fall but was stunned as she seemed to fold in on herself. Slipping from his grip, she landed on the marble fireplace surround.

June 1903

Newcastle, Ontario

Chapter 77

The news of Olive's death brought Henry low to a point of grave concern to everyone. The nurse and doctor (who continued visiting every day but for his care now) were doing all they could but Sayre was relieved when Henry's son, Simon, arrived.

Simon had received Sayre's telegram on the day of a scheduled dedication ceremony for a new music building at Yale. The building had largely been funded by Simon but the Newcastle news necessitated sending last minute regrets to the university's administration. He arrived in Newcastle on the 21st, in time to support his father through Olive's funeral the following day.

Sayre thought it ironic that Simon had finally made the trip to Newcastle, after many invitations from Olive through the years; ironic because Olive was not alive to see it.

While Henry thought he had sheltered Olive from his son's disapproval, she had cleverly deduced that she was the reason Henry rarely saw his son.

Only Sayre was aware of the pain Simon had caused Olive since her marriage to his father. His distrust of her had demeaned the love she felt for Henry and made her feel like a gold digger. It took all of Sayre's self control to be civil to Simon but he was saved from spending too much time with Henry's son by the responsibilities he now faced.

Sayre carried out Olive's various requests and followed Henry's instructions for the funeral arrangements but there was no doubt that his grief made this more difficult. He was a good lawyer and, when drawing up Olive's will, made sure that she was explicit with her property and money. She left Chestayne to Minnie and Duncan and various financial bequests to each of her brothers and sisters and to Henry's grandchildren. She also left an endowment for improvements at St. George's Church.

But, by far, the most difficult dispersal for Sayre to deal with was to Lindsell. While it was relatively easy for him to distribute Olive's requests to her family, he understood that, for Lindsell, it was the end of a position and a friendship. Olive had left $2,000 to her 'faithful companion, Amy Lindsell'; a sum that would certainly bring some comfort to Lindsell but would in no way replace the woman she cared deeply for. Sayre also made arrangements for the woman's transportation after the funeral back to New York City, providing her with a commendable letter of reference.

In planning the funeral, Henry made it clear to Sayre that it should be like none that Newcastle had ever seen. A Bishop was brought from Toronto to lead the service, along with a Men's and Boy's Choir to sing the hymns. A special train was arranged to transport those arriving from New York City and elsewhere. Every inn and hotel in the area was booked. Every carriage known within a twenty-mile radius was hired and filled. As the service ended at her beloved St. George's church, the first carriages made their way north to the cemetery until the mile-long road was thick with them.

Sayre had arranged for Olive's favourite flower, roses, to be delivered in masses from Dunlop Flowers in Toronto and a blanket of them covered her coffin as it was lowered into the ground. A crypt, etched with roses, had been arranged by Henry to mark her grave in a grand manner. Anticipating that he would predecease her, he had previously taken care of many details so that she, or her family, would not need to. He wept as he looked on the grave and it took all of Simon and Sayre's strength to hold the ill man upright.

Simon wasted no time in getting Henry back to Bridgeport after the funeral, hopefully to rest and recover. But the illness that had gripped him for so long and Olive's death left Henry with few resources to draw on at that point. On Sept. 7th, he was pronounced dead. Newspapers alluded to the belief that his death had been hastened by the sudden death of his wife.

His estate, valued between $6,000,000 and $7,000,000 was left in trust to Simon, his grandchildren Henry Jr. and Kitty, and his great grandson, Henry Sanford Thorne. Until his own death in 1910, Simon maintained the New York City home that Henry and Olive had enjoyed.

The loss of her grandfather and his beautiful wife, who she had considered a friend, was great to Kitty. It was left up to her to carry out a request her grandfather had made prior to his death; that the great artist Tiffany create a stained-glass window in Olive's memory for St. George's church in Newcastle. This, along with further endowments she and her brother made to the church made it a grand church for such a small village.

Back in New York City, Sayre went through his days in sadness for his beloved friend but he knew she would appreciate his final gesture.

Well aware of the gossip they had created in the village, his last gift was arranged with this in mind.

He endowed St. George's with funds stipulating that a plaque be engraved and hung in the church which would say:

> "A fund was *affectionately* given as a partial endowment for the maintenance of the church property by her *friend*, Henry S. Van Duzer".

I can't think of a better legacy for you than to keep them talking. This should do it, my dearest girl!

Epilogue

Based on what happened following her death, the divorce Olive might have obtained was questionable even in the U.S. One month after Olive's death, her first husband, Harry Winans, married his long-time partner.

Minnie and Duncan moved into Chestayne but spent winters in a hotel in Toronto because the house was too cold for the winter weather. Minnie eventually sold the house back to the Massey family.

Henry's granddaughter, Kitty, went on to marry four times.

The talk about Olive and her lover continues in the village of Newcastle to the present day.